We appear to have lost the time

Judi Woodnutt

Published in 2019 by FeedARead.com Publishing

A CIP catalogue record for this title is available from the British
Library.

This work is based on a true story. Some names of people
and places have been changed.

In memory of my parents

Contents

Prologue
Chapter 1   Twenty-five years earlier
Chapter 2   After the flight left for Amsterdam
Chapter 3   Cabin Drill
Chapter 4   Men's Trouser World
Chapter 5   The Phone Call
Chapter 6   Tipping Point
Chapter 7   Nighthawks
Chapter 8   Round the Bend
Chapter 9   Chocks Away
Chapter 10   A Whiter Shade of Pale
Chapter 11   We're looking for a Piano
Chapter 12   The wrong thing done for the right reasons
Chapter 13   The Saints Go Marching in
Chapter 14   The way the river ran
Chapter 15   The way the river froze
Chapter 16   Smoke on the Water
Chapter 17   The way the water flowed away
Chapter 18   The Magic Carpet Ride
Chapter 19   Rites of Passage
Chapter 20   Double or Drop
Chapter 21   The Wanderer
Chapter 22   The Safe Option
Chapter 23   The Whip Hand
Chapter 24   Home on the Grange
Chapter 25   Back at the Hotel Phoenicia
Chapter 26   It's on the cards
Chapter 27   The important thing to remember
Chapter 28   Black Mass
Chapter 29   The Letter
Chapter 30   Monosyllables
Chapter 31   Open the Box!

Chapter 32   Lost on the Fens
Chapter 33   A chair is just a chair
Chapter 34   Puzzle Pieces
Chapter 35   Danger Money
Chapter 36   Absurdity over Gravity equals the square root of Guilt
Chapter 37   The Bonnie Banks
Chapter 38   The shifting of the tectonic plates
Chapter 39   Let's press on
Chapter 40   Wantacupoftea!
Chapter 41   The elephant in the room
Chapter 42   A testing time
Chapter 43   If you've got the moves, I've got the motion
Chapter 44   Just Like That!
Chapter 45   The Present of Time Past
Epilogue   No time to lose

Acknowledgements

Prologue

"We appear to have lost the time."

So said my father one Sunday afternoon after lunch, after two cups of tea and after the flight had arrived from Amsterdam.

His phone call over the hundred or so miles did not make sense. "But it's ten to three, Dad."

"Ten to three. But what does that mean, Julie?"

That was the beginning, really. The time when my parents lost the time, they lost it all. Slowly, by degrees 'it' would leave them, never to return. But for now it seemed that the time could be found as if it was a missing gold signet ring that could have rolled under the settee to be found along with Alan Bennett's cream cracker, dusty but still real. Maybe a Sunday search could locate it. Maybe a prayer to St Anthony would draw it from its hiding place so that it could be captured again to synchronise two lives that were slowly but surely unravelling, to wind them up as definitely and securely as the little brass key sticking out of the mock warming pan clock that hung in the hallway.

But meanwhile my parents had a mission: the next flight would be getting prepared for take-off and the Radio Officer's uniform must be found and pressed and the flight bag packed. Mother began her search for the uniform, the beige one, the colour of the pale chocolate stripe on a block of Neapolitan ice cream, the uniform that had not been worn for forty years and that had been handed back to the airline in 1963. She found a white shirt that had something familiar about it. It must have been the epaulettes. She took it to her husband who was standing in his dressing gown in the hall, ready to go. Like two toddlers in a dressing up game, they studied the shirt; something about it was not quite right and Father began to get agitated. "How can I fly in this? It's all creased. Where's the rest of it?"

Mother looked at him. She had been married at a time when a wife pulled rabbits out of hats every day. When silk purses were made from sow's ears at least twice a week. Finding a uniform that was not actually there, defeated her. At least she did not think they had it, or did they? Everything had become so confusing. She had made a pot of tea and was enjoying a little doze when George started to get agitated and demanded that as the Amsterdam flight had landed, it would be his turn to be part of the changeover crew. All this seemed to make sense but something was not quite right. It must be her. She must have missed something when she had that little doze.

My brother Tom arrived. He rang the doorbell of the comfortable suburban bungalow. "That will be the taxi", George said, pulling open the door to reveal his son. Tom took in the scene. There was the old green suitcase, dusty from lack of use, yawning in the corner with one black sock and an old leather belt in it. His father, looking anxious and irritated, held a white shirt by the scruff of the neck while his mother, in one swift moment, took her thumb nail from her mouth and beamed the smile of the liberated. Her greeting gushed forth like a pent up waterfall at Windsor Great Park, all long vowels and regal tone belying her upbringing in the East Midlands. Never did a *m'duck* or an *ay up yow* ever pass her lips. She was pure *Mrs Slocombe*: "Oh Tom how wonderful to see you! George and I seem to be having a few problems."

Chapter 1
Twenty-five years earlier

Scene 1 *Inside the Doctor's Surgery; an elderly male doctor is sitting behind a desk.*
Enter: George Ellis, a middle-aged man, smartly dressed in a business suit and tie.

Doctor: Hello Mr Ellis, take a seat. What can I do for you today?

George: Well Doctor, after that last business with my heart I want to guard against anything like that happening again.

Doctor: Yes, Mr Ellis that was a nasty turn you had but the tests that were carried out in hospital didn't give us conclusive evidence that you had experienced a heart attack. Clearly you were very unwell when you were admitted. How are you feeling now?

George: Much better, thank you but I am anxious to avoid ever feeling that ropey again.

Doctor: Do you smoke? How often do you drink alcohol?

George: I used to be a heavy smoker but I gave up smoking around sixteen years ago, Doctor. And drinking – well at Christmas of course but otherwise on rare occasions, I'll have half a pint of beer.

Doctor: To be frank you are at increased risk of heart attack or stroke if we take into account your age, sedentary life-style and weight. The best news you have told me is that you are a non- smoker.

George: I would like to lose some weight, Doctor. Could you suggest any reducing diets that I could try?

Doctor: Well sir, that's good; to lose weight you need to be determined just as you must have been when you gave up smoking. The best thing you can do is cut down on dairy fats, even the hidden fats in pastries, biscuits and cake, eat more fruit and vegetables and eat fish and chicken rather than red meat. Try not to eat between meals.

George: Thank you, Doctor. I will do my best to follow your instructions.

Doctor: Come and see me again in a month's time and we'll see how things are going.

Scene 2 *The living room of George and Joan's bungalow later that day. The couple are sitting in arm chairs both facing the television.*

George: Joanie, the doctor has given me all the gen about losing some weight, he says we should cut down on dairy fats, apparently there are the hidden fats in pastries, biscuits and cake, and we're to eat more fruit and vegetables and eat fish and chicken rather than red meat.

Joan: Right-O, Darling, we'll make a list and when I go to the supermarket, I'll buy only the things the doctor recommended, then. So I won't buy cheese or bacon but I'll buy some nice vegetables and delicious apples and plums. We can have some lovely meals with chicken and fish.

George: Well that's good. Except you'd better not get the plums, they go straight through me.

Joan: Oh yes, I forgot, they do rather, don't they?

George: Now with the vegetables, remember I don't like green vegetables as they give me wind. Except peas, I like peas.

Joan: Yes Darling, I'll remember.

George: And remember I don't like fish, no matter what is done to it - fish always tastes the same - unless we have fish and chips from the chip shop, of course.

Joan: Will we still be allowed to have fish and chips on the diet?

George: Once in a while, we could have it, as a special treat. Life's too short to give up everything.

Joan: Yes, once in a while we could go mad. I saw a recipe the other day that showed you could make custard with only half milk and the other half water and only using half the usual amount of sugar.

George: And what would you be pouring this custard on?

Joan: *looks nonplussed. Pause. Then in a small voice:* Bananas?

Chapter 2
After the flight left for Amsterdam

Dear Dr Vale,

I am the daughter of patients in your care: George and Joan Ellis of 25 Caldron Close. With my older brother Tom and my younger sister Janine, I share some serious concerns regarding the mental health of Mum and Dad. We are aware that in order to protect patient confidentiality, you will not be able to discuss our parents' health with us but we hope that you will understand from the following report , the reasons why we have felt moved to contact you in this way, without the knowledge of our parents.

We know that our parents present as a perfectly normal couple in their seventies. To the outside world, they appear to comprise an efficient interdependent unit with Mother's poor hearing, she is the 'eyes' and with father's poor eyesight, he is the 'ears'. In social situations, they seem to be able to say appropriate things at the right time. However, for some weeks now, we have become increasingly aware that both Mum and Dad have been encountering problems with memory and are regularly confused.

Out of the three of us, I live the furthest away in Hampshire, and therefore I am the one who may not see Mum and Dad the most often, but I do stay for weekends regularly and have the opportunity to study what is a deteriorating situation, at close hand. At first sight the bungalow is well run but when one looks closer, the fridge is full of out of date food, items that require refrigeration are stored in cupboards, plates are put away without being washed and meals seem haphazard and irregular. My mother's handbag is full of Mars bars and these seem a regular stand by meal replacement. In the past Dad was put on a weight reducing diet by his previous doctor; Mum joined him in this project and together they have closely monitored their weight. I believe that the diet was intended to be followed for a restricted period of time, not twenty-five years. Furthermore, they

11

followed their own version of the diet limiting themselves to a range of very few foods, seeming to live chiefly on chicken and boiled potatoes. They removed almost all fat from their diet; they rarely eat green vegetables and hardly ever eat fish. We are beginning to wonder if their poor diet is having a negative impact on their mental health.

Recently, I washed and set my Mum's hair and whilst I was styling it, she engaged me in conversation asking me how long I had been a hairdresser. At first I thought she was being playful but during the following half hour I came to realise that she was not recognising me as her daughter but truly believed I was a visiting hairdresser.

During the same weekend, I decided to take Mother to Leicester on the train as she rarely goes shopping – Dad becoming increasingly unwilling to leave the house. Dad gave Mum and me some money for us to spend in the shops. During the journey, Mum constantly asked me who I was and where we were going. At one time she thought we were going to Windsor (where we lived in the 1950's and 60's). There followed a highly eventful shopping trip where I felt I was wrangling a very confused elderly lady through what was clearly to her, an alien environment.

On returning to the bungalow, we showed our purchases to my dad. He started to get very agitated, saying that the money was meant for the poor orphans and that I should not have spent it. He began shouting at us both and required much soothing before he calmed down.

We have tried to persuade Mum and Dad to consult you but so far they seem unaware that anything is wrong and do not feel the need to make an appointment at the surgery. We will continue to try to get them to come along and we felt that in preparation, we should give you some insight as to the true situation that prevails at Caldron Close.

Yours sincerely
Julie Wood

Chapter 3
Cabin Drill

George

"Fancy a barley sugar, George?"

"I don't mind if I do, thanks. Just in case we get any turbulence, I cannot bear the ear popping." He tucked the cellophane wrapped sweet into his already bulging trouser pocket filled with his portable resource of 'come-in-handys'. These included a steel tape measure, a piece of string, safety pins, a set of small screwdrivers, a few plug fuses, a comb, a large handkerchief carefully folded into a square, a plastic tub of breath fresheners, a bottle of Olbas oil and a blackcurrant fruit gum – his favourite flavour – covered in pocket fluff. Gravity was the victor of the shirt- trouser war as it slowly forced the waistband to slide down the nylon of his tucked in shirt, leading to constant adjustment and irritation. *Braces, now that's what I could do with. I used to have a pair.*

"Oh, we're bound to have some turbulence with the new chap in the cockpit." said the man in the suit winking at George, conspiratorially. George studied the man's tie. *RAF. But with a blob of egg on it. 'x for breakfast', that's what we used to say, now how did it go? A for apple, B for honey, C for sailors…*

"Here's your flight plan for today," the man said, with a chuckle and another conspiratorial wink. "You can take a seat here," gesturing with his arms out straight ahead like a *Woodentops* puppet, "or here," pointing both arms away from his body like the *Angel of the North.*

The dainty air hostess in a bright yellow tailored suit took George's arm with her white gloved hand. George looked at her with admiration as she led him to an aisle seat. Although smartly dressed, he walked with the gait of Charlie Chaplin owing to the ongoing shirt-trouser conflict and when he finally came in to land, the sound of his loaded pockets making contact with the seat drew the interested attention of others sitting around him. The air hostess sat down beside

13

him. "Are you feeling alright, George? I thought we'd sit here so that you will be ready for action when the time comes."

A man dressed in black walked up the aisle and stopped when he saw George. He had kind eyes that crinkled at the corners and a puffy chin covered in white stubble making it look like a sugared doughnut. "Hello George and Joan. How are you both this beautiful evening?"

The couple smiled back and Joan said, "How lovely to see you. We are fine aren't we, George?" George looked up at the man in black and thought to himself, *standards have dropped. Fancy coming on service without having had a shave. Poor Show. Bad form.*

Suddenly the organ burst forth with the first hymn at this the Evensong Service at St Catherine's. Joan shuffled the pages of the hymn books to find the right place and the congregation staggered to their feet in the formation of a slightly drunken Mexican wave with Joan popping up between the pews like an Easter chick.

George, helped to the right page by Joan, began to sing in a clear and tuneful voice. The years fell away and he was a boy again in the choir in another church, at Ibstock.

*

Evensong was his favourite service with the light changing from white and yellow to rose and purple as it filtered through the stained glass of the ancient windows. He knew the window inscriptions and those on the memorials adorning the walls, by heart. The Church provided him with a true enrichment to his education. The education that the local school had served up was bread and butter whilst the Church delivered the intellectual equivalent of rich fruit cake. The vicar had been the cleverest person in George's world whose sermons challenged intellectually, the whole congregation. When most seated in the pews fell to thinking about their Sunday high tea, George would hang on to every word that issued forth from the rector and try to make sense of it, revelling in the cadence of the phrases, the mere sound of elaborate language. With the enthusiasm of a zealot, he committed unfamiliar words to memory with the intention of looking them up in his father's dictionary when he got home.

It was the Church's Magic Lantern shows that took the young George into another world, a brighter and more colourful world full of scenes of other lands far away. There before his eyes was the Sahara desert filling the wall of peeling paint at the end of the church hall, the pyramids rising from the dusty skirting board, the hanging gardens of Babylon suspended from the ceiling cobwebs. This potent medium had the power to ignite George's already fertile imagination; to imbibe him with dream material. He would fantasise on the prospect of leaving the grey village with its permanently wet black slate roofs and damp wooden doors painted dog dirt brown or poison green, to venture abroad to the exotic locations viewed through the coloured glass plates. He hated the life with his step mother who was like the archetypal wicked woman of fairy tales who meted out punishments as easily as some gave out smiles. Her cruelty was legendary and became the stuff of family lore.

George's mother had died of Consumption when he was two years old, leaving his father, Samuel, with three children under ten to tend and raise. George's grandmother stepped into the breach for a brief period and all his life he was to come to associate love with the kindness of this matriarch. He loved the hugs from her ample figure dressed in a soft woollen dress, covered by a spotless white apron. If he was good, he was allowed to search her apron pocket for peppermint sweets in rustling paper wrappers.

His father Samuel was doomed to work down the coal mine, but when above ground, he loved cycling and even competed in races. These competitions took him far afield and on one famous occasion won him a set of silver egg cups complete with spoons on a silver salver and, of far greater portent, the attention of one Daisy Smith. Daisy was a plain woman, thin and of small stature, whose facial complexion suffered enlarged pores, giving it the appearance of fashioned cork. There is little doubt that she must have had a hard knock life, being 'brunged up', as she described it, in various children's homes in Essex and later 'Birnigum'. Her later actions bore the mark of one who had never been offered much affection in their young life and did not know how to love others in a selfless way. What life had taught her was to snatch anything when opportunity presented itself and cling on to it doggedly. This she did on meeting Samuel. He offered her an opportunity to escape the drudgery of factory life in Birmingham by marrying him, keeping house, and taking care of his young family. She grabbed the chance with both hands and *Smaug* -like she held on to the power invested in her, the dragon power that came with the long nosed key that fitted the keyhole in the old brown wooden door to the 'entry', the dark tunnel that separated the miners' cottages.

In the 1920's and 30's, children from poor backgrounds may not have been given the luxury of a carefree childhood but Daisy, jealous of any affection that her husband may have held for the children of his first marriage, made sure that George and his two sisters Grace and Elsie were at the very least, neglected and at most, regularly punished. Following the evil step mother formula, she gave them chores that had to be completed to her exacting standards before they were allowed out to play in the yard or the street. There were windows to clean and floors to scrub, laundry to wash in the copper and push through the mangle that frequently caught small fingers between its unforgiving rollers. There were mats to wallop on the washing line with the woven cane carpet beater that hung on a peg on the kitchen wall beside the leather belt used to wallop tender flesh if all of the above tasks were not completed. Daisy kept strict control of the household in this way and ensured compliance by half starving the children under the nose of her husband. Samuel would return late from a shift down the pit to be greeted with a full plate of roast meat and vegetables. Believing that his children had been fed similarly before being sent to bed, he would attack the meal with relish. Little did he know that his son and daughters had been served a meagre meal of Yorkshire pudding to fill them up first, then a few sparse vegetables and a dribble of gravy. The nearest they got to the roast meat was the dripping: the congealed fat left in the pan from the roast, spread on bread. To the young George, the taste of bread and dripping was almost the best thing in his deprived life, second only to the taste of Heaven: bread and jam…

There is a happy land far, far away.
Where the kids eat bread and jam nine times a day
You should see them laugh and sing when the bread and jam comes in
There is a happy land, far, far away.

*

….There is a green hill far away….. The key changed from major to minor and George was back in the church again. Joan nudged him and in the loud stage whisper of a deaf person, alerted him with three words, "Time for action." George, initially startled, was slow to

16

respond to this unwelcome intrusion into his thoughts. With much rubbing of his tired brown eyes and smoothing of his thinning grey hair into a tidy arrangement across the crown of his head, he prepared for the task ahead. Mentally he addressed his arthritic knees, telling them to lever his body into an upright position whilst Joan passed him the small deep velvet bag suspended from its wooden handles. He composed the even features of his still handsome face into a sombre expression as befitted an honoured sidesman. His role was to start at the back of the church and pass the bag along each pew, collecting from the sparse congregation their offerings of small clinking change or manila tithe envelopes the size of wage packets. There was something about the envelopes that evoked a memory but the thread was broken when the vicar took the bag from George and, placing it onto a silver plate, held it aloft as he faced the altar.

George navigated his way back to his place guided by the small yellow homing beacon of Joan's outfit. Gratefully, he deposited his overstuffed trouser pockets onto the hard wood of the pew and looked around. *I think it's time for that sucky sweet.* Ignoring Joan's frown at the rustling noises, he rooted around his apparently bottomless pockets until he snagged the barley sugar. *Ah Bisto!* The vicar's incantations continued until they became a blur of white noise in George's head and he tried to trail that thought again, the one that the envelopes had evoked. *That was it, the letter.*

*

The house of his boyhood did not receive letters; most households in the village did not receive letters. Letters were for posh folk, not for the likes of miners and their wives. Who would write to them? What could this mysterious item in a manila envelope contain? His step mother placed it behind the brass candlestick on the high mantelpiece above the black leaded range to be opened "When yer father gets 'ome." George eyed it curiously as he ate his meagre supper, impatient for his father to return from his shift. Whose hand had addressed the envelope in copper plate script with such a flourish? He was to be made to wait a long time for the answer as Daisy signalled him up to bed. She did this without troubling herself to speak, just stood by the staircase and pulled back the brown chenille curtain, briskly rattling the curtain rings together.

17

Raised voices were heard coming from downstairs that night, disturbing the children's sleep and causing them to further speculate as to what the letter was all about. George was none the wiser the following morning when his questions were met with a mute response from the horizontal line of sealed lips on his stepmother's face. It reminded him of the sewn up mouth on the shrunken head that heathens had used to work their powerful magic, or so had said the vicar in one of his magic lantern shows. With Grace and Elsie, he emptied the chamber pots into the night soil, tipped the ashes onto the growing cinder path and laid the fire. Summarily dismissed once his chores were completed, he was allowed to go to school. And so he transferred from one brutal regime to another.

School was another harsh environment where George had learnt to survive by keeping his head down. The worst challenge was meted out in the playground where he suffered daily humiliation at the hands of other children. Malnutrition had made him small for his age and with his poor clothing, this compounded to make him a target for any bully. Mocked for not having a mother and constantly teased for being a 'clever dick' and still being of 'half pint' stature, George gave the bullies plenty of material. He hated most having to line up with the rest of his form when the bell rang at the end of playtime, as this gave those behind him a chance to count the many patches on the seat of his short trousers.

School did have one saving grace for George, arguably its intention: the delivery of knowledge. Learning gave George an escape from the drudgery of his humdrum existence. And he was good at it. He was at the top of the class, literally. The desks were arranged in order with the brightest pupil at the front and to the right of the teacher's blackboard and the least able child positioned in the far back left hand corner of the classroom. George excelled at reading and arithmetic but most of all, he loved writing. The smell of the ink from its tiny ceramic vessel slotted into the carved well of the desk, combined with the feel of the paper under his hand as he moved smoothly from one word to another using the regulation loops and curlicues, constituted a quiet joy to him. With handwriting neat and clear, he did not risk the whack of the teacher's ruler across his palm, rarely a blot did he make. This won him the unsought attention of his teachers and cringingly for him, his work was held up as exemplary to the rest of the class, thus creating even more ammunition for the bullies.

When he got home that afternoon, Samuel and Daisy were sitting in the front room. This behaviour was unheard of on a week day. Daisy sat on a hard wooden upright chair, looking glum. She wore her habitual paisley overall adorned with the ubiquitous brooch figuring a blue glass spider on a wrought copper web. Samuel sat in the tall wooden carver with its red seat cushion, placed facing the fire. He had his pipe in his mouth and he was drawing on it thoughtfully. There was another person in the room and astonishingly, it was Mr Hargreaves, the school headmaster. He was seated across the fireplace from Samuel, in Daisy's usual chair.

"Now George, yer Stepmum and I ave got summut we ave to say te yer," began Samuel. "Yer know this 'ere gentleman is yor 'eadmaster and he reckons as like yor good at yer studies and he has said that yor clever enough to go to the grammar school. He wrote me a letter and told me so, but…" he paused and turned to look at his wife who in turn, fixed George with scowl on her pasty face. " But, " Samuel stammered , " the plan is for you to go out to work as soon as you've finished your schoolin' at fourteen, like."

George tried to take in the import of what his father had just said. In a few sentences, his father had raised his hopes and then dashed them. Being shown a glimpse of a glittering possibility, it was now harder for him to accept the fate that hitherto he had believed was his destiny. They say that the human spirit learns to cope with despair, but hope can be painfully destructive.

Mr Hargreaves looked at George who had been struck dumb by the enormity of what he had heard. Clearing his throat, he appealed to George's parents with a line of argument that they had heard before but to which they had remained impervious. "Please reconsider your decision. These days many more pupils are staying on at school. This is likely to improve their chances of better jobs in the future. George got the highest mark of all the pupils in Leicestershire who sat this year's tests. It would be a travesty for him to waste his talent for learning, by sending him to work down the mine."

" That's as maybe,"said Samuel. " I'm proud of the lad, can't say I'm not. But he will do well whatever he does and he don't need yer fancy grammar school. Some folks might be able to afford it but it ain't for the likes of us. Even if as you say all we need to provide is the uniform. We need our lad to go out and earn his keep as soon as he can."

Nobody asked George what he thought. *Little children should be seen and not heard.* And so the meeting ended; George's future was sealed with a handshake whilst Mr Hargreaves looked across at his pupil with an expression of resignation and regret.

The blue glass of the spider brooch glinted in the firelight.

*

A blue lozenge of light appeared on the ancient paving of the church floor. George stared at it from his place in the pew, fascinated by its clarity and beauty. Looking up, he tried to work out which pane of the window was reflecting the dying rays of the sun. Broken once again from his reverie by the organ's loud introduction to the final hymn, George went through the standing procedure. And then it was over and he could shuffle out of the building with Joan on his arm. The friendly man in the suit stood at the bookcase to collect the hymnals from them. "Have a pleasant landing and a safe onward journey," he said with a wink.

Chapter 4
Men's Trouser World

Julie

Train journeys are useful for thinking and we had a long journey before us and a lot of thinking to do.

Now that I come to really think about it, we should have seen it coming. Like the gold bullion bricks cemented and whitewashed in an East End wide boy's lockup wall, the facts were hidden in plain sight.

As I look back, there were many scenes on the cutting room floor of my parents' lives that if spliced together they would make a prophetic movie, foretelling the trials ahead. It would forecast the onset of their loss of a firm grip on the structure of everyday life, the gradual failing of keeping daily systems running, of being able to function effectively inside the home or to operate in the world outside the home.

Scenes that in themselves seemed innocuous formed over time into a pattern that was not recognised until it was too late. Like the time when the permanent black ink pen was washed in the top pocket of my father's white shirt causing the whole wash to become a livid mauve. Ordinarily, this would seem an unfortunate mistake, but to my parents at the time it was an event of catastrophic proportions. Then there was the episode of the gypsies. My usually cautious father who normally never trusted strangers, allowed a group of travellers to walk all over the roof having walked all over the drive – both on the pretext that they could repave and retile at a bargain price, for cash in hand. This had prompted a phone call to me at the height of the drama. There was Dad's voice full of alarm like that of a hostage while the heavy thud of hob nailed boots on roof tiles could be heard even down the telephone line. Then there were the several car collisions with stationary objects like road signs and street furniture. Then it became usual to lose the car. Indeed the car was lost quite frequently, not just in international airports, motorway services carparks and multi-storey car parks, but in the local town carparks. Then there was the posting

21

of letters, not into red mail boxes, but into the red plastic bins meant for dog waste.

All incidents could be explained away as resulting from the vulnerability of old age with a good pinch of some eccentricity. 'All perfectly normal Darlings,' as my mother would say.

Each raindrop slid its own slow and irregular passage down the carriage window then as the train left the station and picked up speed these trails seemed to gain energy and took to zigzagging and drawing horizontal lines on the glass. So the ride north was viewed through the moisture of condensation on the inside and rain on the outside. This was fitting for our journey, as we were both miserable, harbouring tears that threatened to spill at any innocuous trigger and trickle down faces. Humour of the blackest sort would be our best tool or weapon with which to arm ourselves over the next two days. Two days they call a weekend, "And we are certainly at our weak end," my daughter Lizzy quipped, "remind me why we are going to Gibbet Roundabout in term time?" The corners of my mouth began to turn upwards unbidden; the name of the roundabout near my parents' home in Burnage had never failed to delight my imaginative kids with its connotations of historical horror.

"Because the jumper is unravelling so quickly, we can't wait until the school holidays," was the best I could come up with in my state of anxiety driven fatigue. Thank goodness she understood. She had already heard a blow by blow account of the latest family meeting and with our mother - daughter relationship that was so close, she had reached the age of majority and was considered responsible enough to share my remaining five brain cells, so further explanation was unnecessary. "Good job we both know how to knit," she said.

*

Back at *Tree Tops House* it had all seemed so much simpler. It was as if the situation could be brought back under control with a few straight forward measures just like a programme of behaviour modification for the naughty child in the classroom. But Mum and Dad would not respond to star charts. Nevertheless, being capable optimistic teachers (all of us – yes all; George and Joan's three offspring, comprising a son and two daughters, were teachers - married to teachers), we thought we could come up with a plan that could contain the situation and keep our parents safe.

The Saturday afternoon meeting involved all six of us and was hosted by my sister Janine and her husband Nick who both taught at a boys' boarding school. The couple lived at *Tree Tops* on the school campus where they were also conscientious house parents to several young charges. Our meeting, held around the large pine kitchen table, was frequently punctuated by interruptions from the boarders. Regularly a Tarquin, a Shulto or a Hugo would cough politely for attention from the threshold of the wide kitchen doorway that marked the boundary between the boys' dorm and houseparents' accommodation. The reason for the boys' appearance was to request signed permission slips which would allow them to go into the local town during their Saturday afternoon free periods. Unwittingly they were presenting a scene from an archaic world to the rest of us who did not work at a public boarding school. Their quaint courtesy and polite requests seemed from a bygone age, delivered in a particular boarding school vernacular unintelligible to most of us. It was as if we had strayed onto the set of '*Goodbye Mr Chips*'.

Seated at one long side of the huge table, which was possibly from the last century and used by Mr Chips' cook to knead bread and roll pastry, sat our sociable hosts: Janine and Nick. At the head of the table sat Tom, the eldest of the offspring, and his wife Barbara. Then on the other side of the aircraft carrier sized table, sat my husband James and I.

Well used to meetings, we knew how to run things properly and even had one of our number taking the minutes and of course, we all made our own notes in the plain pages at the back of our *Pirongs* academic diaries. We were all well equipped with stationery items; the perk of the teacher: lots of paper and pens, *red pens*. As we had some prickly issues listed on our agenda, it was good to avoid them for a time and enjoy the rare occasion of sharing each other's company once again. As the strains of a Julian Slade musical found their way from the CD player in the sitting room, they prompted a quick rendering of songs from '*Salad Days*', initiated by Tom who began using the table top as an imaginary piano. Both Janine and I could not resist joining in with the singing, despite the looks of long suffering evident on the faces of our partners. We encouraged them to sing along, we knew they knew the words too – after all it had been a necessary requirement to memorise the lyrics before marrying into the Ellis family. (A practice considered '*perfectly normal, Darlings*', as Mother would say*). The WI may have their '*Jerusalem*' but we have our '*We're *looking for a P-I-A-N-O!'* Eventually, Tom put the 'piano' away and picked up his pen but before proceedings could continue, someone asked about the health of great Aunt Lulu who was approaching her century. Tom gave us all an update and teased us with the possibility of re-telling *'The Plank Story'*, an Ellis family tale; but having seen the whites of several pairs of eyes around the table, he resisted the urge.

Then it came to facing it. Facing the fact that in Mum and Dad's rusty submarine of a situation, the rivets were about to pop. The worrying signs could no longer be ignored; indeed they were starting to become veritable elephants in several different hall ways. But no one apart from the six of us had any real insight into what was unfolding at Caldron Close. Certainly Mum and Dad were not fully aware of what was happening and the implications involved. It was up to us to do something and we needed help from other parties; to whom should we approach? In the meantime, it was all about containment and it was decided that Mum and Dad should be visited more frequently and regularly checked on. Action points were drawn up – and first and foremost was the letter to the GP.

*

"When do you expect to hear back from Dr Vale?" asked Lizzy, as she rested her head on my shoulder. She had had a very busy week and the warm, stuffy carriage was highly soporific.

"He may not feel that he can answer my letter owing to the need to protect his patients' confidentiality. But I'm glad we did it. He now has the facts and if he doesn't believe us, he will soon find his own evidence to support what I have told him." It was getting late and it would be dark by the time we arrived at Burnage. When I had phoned to tell my parents that we were about to set off, Mum had insisted on meeting us in the station carpark even though I had suggested that we take a taxi to their bungalow.

"Are we there yet and will Aslan be waiting for us?" Lizzy asked playfully, echoing her childhood bleating and reminding me that James and I, somewhat jaundiced, would describe the Midlands as Narnia in permanent winter without the magical lion, when the children were small. It may seem negative, but at least this way the coal mining spoil heaps became mystical mountains.

Lizzy looked out of the carriage window and studied the backyards of terraced houses that she could make out in the twilight. It was as if every home had its back to us, refusing to turn round. We did not feel welcome and as the train drew closer to the main Midland station where we had to change to a suburban service, it seemed to slow down, prompting her to chant a list of the scenes outside just like the items on the alternative conveyor belt to that used in '*The Generation Game*' ... *graffiti on a bridge, broken window, bike on a roof, old woman emptying out her dog, burnt out car.* There was no cuddly toy – just a *dead cat.*

So it was with some trepidation that we alighted and with desperation, ran to the platform that would take us out to a more salubrious suburb where my folks lived. Our journey had already taken us almost three hours and the district line did not seem to be getting us any closer to our destination, as the minutes ticked by. It snailed along, stopping at every tiny outpost in this area proudly termed, 'the Heart of the Shires' and 'Shakespeare country'. When eventually, the Burnage sign filled the frame of our train window, we were emotionally drained and yet we knew the real challenge was only just about to begin.

There was no sign of Mum and Dad on the platform and so we made our way through the dimly lit subway that brought us under the railway line and out into the carpark that was lit up by spotlights of the kind that would not look out of place in the recreation yard of Stalag 17. The only car parked there was Mum's Vauxhall Corsa and the windows were steamed up. As we approached, the driver's door opened and Mum stepped out. In the light of the harsh street lamps, her Duchess of Kent updo was gently unravelling, giving her a bright silver halo. She greeted us with the extravagance that would seem over the top to a polar explorer who had recently returned from a series of death defying adventures including fighting a polar bear on a fast melting ice floe. But we loved it and lapped up every endearment and revelled in every warm embrace. We were home. Well, almost.

Dad gave us his own warm and loving greeting in a more measured way from the front seat of the car and began his urging that we should all "get out of the cold and into the warm." His Tony Hancock homburg met his woollen scarf at mid ear level. I could not help thinking that he was only a bandage away from being *The Invisible Man.*

"I hope that you haven't had to wait too long for us. The last leg on the district line seemed to take forever," I said from the back seat.

25

"It's been fine Darlings," replied my mother. "We set off when you phoned so that we wouldn't be late."

"But that was over three hours ago." I was beginning to get stressed already and we had only just arrived. Their bungalow was a mere two minute drive away.

"Well, we were not sure about when you were coming and Daddy said we should get a parking spot in good time. We've had the radio on and the Mint Imperials haven't we Georgie?"

Mother wiggled in her seat as she gained top gear - a little habit of hers - and within a couple of minutes we had skirted the renowned Gibbet Roundabout, and were pulling into the drive of their bungalow in Caldron Close.

Inside the bungalow, the predictable homely smell of polish, chicken and boiled potatoes welcomed us. We had eaten on the hoof and only desired mugs of tea which we all enjoyed in the cosy lounge, talking until it was well beyond everyone's bed time. Lizzy and I were to sleep in the spare room on the double bed fitted with an electric blanket that had been on for several hours - since my phone call, I expect. As we stretched out on the mattress, our whispered giggles were based on the supposition that scrambled egg must feel like we did, lying on hot toast. One could be lulled into thinking that Mum and Dad's little world was in a state of order and that our fears had been imagined; that we were worrying unnecessarily. The toast mattress was warm and the quilt comfortingly heavy. It was then that the ghostly moaning began.

It woke both of us. Although the cry seemed to be muffled, it was a clear sign of distress akin to that of a wounded animal. Then joining the moan we heard another sound reminiscent of a saw cutting logs. "That's got to be Grandma's snoring, but what's the other noise? Grace Poole?" said Lizzy in an anxious voice, all giggles forgotten. Before we could speculate, my parents' bedroom door grazed the thick carpet and footsteps could be heard in the hallway. The moaning commenced again, louder this time with the plea repeated over and over, "Help me, the pain, oh the pain." I got out of bed and found my father outside our room. He was dressed in pyjamas and his hair, that he kept quite long to please Mum (*I like him to look like a clever musical conductor, Darlings, no more short back and sides for him, oh no*) , was sticking out wildly from his scalp. His eyes were shut and he was in danger of colliding with the cabinet of stuffed birds that graced the hall. I reached out to stop him but was intercepted by Mum who

26

had appeared suddenly as if she had passed through the wall. Swiftly, she took control of the situation saying that *Daddy was having one of his funny little turns and that I was not to worry, but should go back to bed.*

The next morning, Lizzy woke first and asked me for the time. "A quarter to dog," I mumbled, sleepily aware that our usual alarm, the neighbour's collie, would start barking in around fifteen minutes. Whilst we waited, we deliberated as to whether we should brave the kitchen and make the first drink of the day or remain in our peaceful haven of the spare bedroom. We dreaded looking in the fridge. We knew there would be milk turning to yoghurt (*yoe -ghurt* in Mumspeak) and yoghurt turning to cheese and cheese turning to Stilton.

As the baying of the local *Hound of the Baskervilles* commenced I decided to bite the bullet and get up. Stumbling around with stiff legs I managed to stub my toe on an old computer keyboard. It looked as though I had not been the first to collide with it; indeed the cracked and depressed keys already seemed to bear the shape of someone's footprint. Drawing back the curtains revealed our room, the contents of which had escaped our notice through the fatigue of the previous night. Old Amstrad computer equipment was stacked dustily alongside shoe boxes stuffed to overflowing with small cards and bits of paper of irregular size – mostly receipts. Several cheque books were lying gutted and filleted on the dressing table cum desk. Beside them lay a pack of bank cards, enough to play a decent game of Rummy, tied tightly together across both their width and their length with numerous rubber bands. On close inspection, these had all met their expiry date and must have been awaiting execution in the vast shredder that sat like an oil tanker, casting a giant shadow in the corner of the room. Behind the door was a strong metal box squatting like a sumo wrestler. Its front label advertised with pride that it was the local DIY superstore's '2000 Model Combination Safe'. The dial looked intriguing and I wondered what could possibly be placed in the safe, given that cheque books and cheque cards were strewn about the room like bankers' confetti.

The swish of door grazing carpet, followed by a light scratching on wood heralded my mother's appearance. Dressed in a flimsy night dress and her Duchess of Kent hairstyle decidedly now a 'down do', she greeted us, "Good morning, Darlings, did you sleep well?"

27

"We did, once we settled again. Is Dad alright? He seemed to be in a lot of pain in the night."

"Oh don't worry about that, Darlings. He often has a little wander in the night but once I get him back into bed, he's fine. " She sat on the edge of the bed to adjust her hearing aid that had been releasing a high pitched whistle since she entered the room. "That's better. Now what were we talking about? I know, now Lizzy, I do like your new hair style." And so my mother continued, admiring Lizzy's long chestnut coloured hair and taking a brush to its thick waves. Then she turned her attention to Lizzy's nails, keeping hold of her hand in the process. We talked about Lizzy's recent conquests with one boy in particular who had made a serious impression. Grandma Joan wanted to hear all about him. Such moments are golden.

"Joanie are you there?" The call issuing forth from the depths of the master bedroom prompted a change of mood; briskly Mum left us and so Lizzy and I set about getting washed and dressed. Then together – just holding back from holding hands – we ventured into the kitchen, in fear and trepidation as to what we might find.

The work surfaces gave away no clues. The tea pot was sitting in its usual place and the mugs from last night were standing in the sink. At first sight, the room looked clean and ordered. When we began opening cupboards, we found dirty glasses and plates which we placed into the empty dishwasher. Then, stealing ourselves to the task, we opened the fridge. A waft of cold stale air met our noses. "Phasers on stun setting," I whispered to Lizzy as we braved an inspection of the blue-white plastic interior. The first creatures to be rescued were the organisms in the Bio Yoghurt pot. Their numbers had clearly multiplied over the past few weeks so that they had now succeeded in building a fortress with surrounding miniature earthworks and hedge. "Get the rocket bin, Mr Spock. This civilisation can be sling shot round the moon and then boldly go to start a new life on another planet."

"Aye Aye, Captain," Lizzy replied and fetched the stainless steel pedal bin so that the large yoghurt pot could be unceremoniously thrown in. Next to meet the same fate was the jar of raspberry jam with the bonsai tree of green mould growing inside it, looking really quite pretty. Then there was an object at the back of the shelf that was organic but we could not identify exactly what it might once have been. We thought it looked most like an ear. "Could this be one of yours, Mr Spock?" I said, turning to Lizzy. Shuddering, we decided it must have been fungus. In any case, it was not for human consumption. Damien Hirst had designed the next item we found: out of date chicken breasts suspended in a viscous pink liquid. These joined the other assorted items in the rocket to the stars.

"Did you find what you needed, Darlings? Let's have some breakfast," Mum said as she entered the kitchen and casually took a bottle of *once upon a time it was fresh* milk from the dark cupboard under the sink. Lizzy and I exchanged lifted eyebrow glances. We had not thought to look there.

"Why don't Lizzy and I pop and get some croissants for a treat, Mum?" Neither of us relished what Mum had on offer.

"That would be lovely, Darlings. Daddy would love that. We could have some jam with them, I think there is a jar somewhere."

Lizzy and I bustled out of the front door, desperate for fresh air and a chance to speak at a natural volume. So far we had overused the two extreme levels of our range: whispering to avoid being overheard and speaking loudly to be heard. As we walked through the smart housing estate with its well- kept gardens and block paved drives, we reviewed the weekend so far. My father's night time behaviour was clearly a concern but my mother seemed to be able to pacify him. The food hygiene was a big issue and we discussed alerting Mum to the 'use by' dates on foods by checking with the calendar; simple, or so we thought.

Eventually, we came to the local parade of shops comprising a hairdressing salon, a newsagent, a fish and chip shop and finally, a small supermarket. We purchased items to replace those we had jettisoned to outer space plus the longed- for croissants, and returned with a more hopeful tread. The situation was not half as bad as we had thought.

Re- entering the bungalow, we found Mum and Dad fully dressed and sitting at the dining room table. To this cosy family tableau, we served the warmed croissants a few minutes later. We all enjoyed these whilst we caught up with news of the neighbourhood gossip – Vera. She lived opposite; her house could be viewed with ease from the dining table. She found ways to enter every house in the close and spread tittle-tattle and to talk mostly about her favourite subject: Vera.

"Do you know she has a bathroom with wallpaper decorated with pale blue, pink and white flowers and so she has a pale blue toilet roll, a pink toilet roll and a white one on display? And do you know she got forty thousand pounds from her son the other day, that's after winning two hundred at Bingo? And she is going to buy some more rings with the money, she loves big flashy rings," said Mother who loved big flashy rings.

"I will not have that woman in this house, Joanie, ever again. The last time she came round she talked endlessly in the hallway and I was in the toilet. I was trapped. I wasn't going to come out while she was there and you two were nattering away for hours," said Father.

"Yes, Georgie, that was rather unfortunate," Mother said with a smile in our direction. "Daddy had to sit and read his paper from cover to cover. I wasn't aware he was there. I thought he was in the bedroom and I was desperate not to invite Vera in so we talked at the front door but she just would not go! Well not until she had boasted all about her latest windfalls."

It was good to hear my father enter into conversation albeit in delivering a complaint; I was even more delighted when he expressed the wish to show me something important in the lounge. This turned out to be a cutting taken from a local newspaper. In prime position on the page was an advertisement claiming to 'STOP THAT HERNIA PAIN NOW!' Featured within the bold black frame of the advert was a line drawing in the style of Victorian engraving of a pair of men's underpants. The diagram included circles describing sources of potential pain and arrows pointing to the areas of special support offered by these sturdy garments. Not well versed in the health problems of the older male, I could only blush and fluster when he asked me what I thought of these extraordinary constructions.

"Do you feel that you need a pair of these, Dad?" was all that came out of my dry mouth.

"Yes, I do. I have been getting lots of pain in that area there," he said pointing to that embarrassing area there circled on the Victorian gentleman's private parts.

"Have you talked to Dr Vale about this?" Before he could answer, my mother interrupted us with, "Oh we don't need to worry the doctor with that, do we Georgie? I am sure we could get some pants like this at Marks and Spencer. Why don't I take the girls to Pit Head Park and we can have a look for some?"

And so it was that the three of us headed off to Pit Head Park Shopping Centre with a mission. It was taken for granted that Father would not be joining us; he rarely left the bungalow. Once again, I was given hope. It must have been a hernia causing him pain and that had led to Dad's night time wanderings. All we had to do was get the right upholstery to the nether regions and, voila! Problem solved.

Mum drove on the route that was very familiar to her and positioned the car in the vast parking lot outside the popular shopping mall in Section Orange, Bay 160. Fearing the regular lost car scenario, we played memory games, trying to imagine an orange with 160 segments. For insurance, I made Mum write the car's location on a piece of paper to put in her purse.

The equation: three women plus large shopping centre plus access to cash minus restraining male guidance equals three hours. Lizzy was in her element of course, enjoying the many different outlets devoted to female fashion and its accoutrements. For a time, Mum and I left her to enjoy this while we sought our quarry in the store of the biggest retailer of under garments in the West. There was a special section for men, a kind of retail fortress encompassed by a circular white wall at shoulder height defended by angry looking trunk and torso mannequins placed at intervals along its length. Like the severed heads on Traitor's Gate, the following message was conveyed loud and clear: those who stray into men's trouser world with evil intent can expect to be dismembered. I felt as comfortable in its environs as a Roman Catholic priest might feel in a Ladies' Lingerie department. I did not know where to look; I was back to blushing and flustering as I tried to avoid looking directly at the male mannequins who seemed immensely pleased to see me – or anybody for that matter.

Mother had no such shyness or hesitation. She took to the task with the zeal of a missionary, walking from one stand to the next, studying labels and diagrams and looking up intensely at the army of models on the battlements. On the third circuit of the fortress, with me trailing in her wake, Mother stopped and began reaching for a particular trunk mannequin. Her struggles were rewarded eventually when the model dislodged itself from the wall and ended up in her arms. She proceeded to examine what it was wearing by pulling at the elastic at the legs and waist and then, most embarrassing of all, she placed her hand into the pants at the crotch area and started to pull and push the fabric so that it was even further extended. It was with her words, "Nice gusset here, aren't men strange creatures? Yes that would fit nicely over that crucial fullness," that I almost died of shame as from the corner of my eye I saw not one, but two assistants approach. To my dismay they were male.

When we met up with Lizzy much later, I was relieved to inform her that we did not get arrested but that I for one would never be returning to that store again. The assistants were very pleasant and helpful in the end but naturally, they had taken exception to our disturbing their displays. What they thought of my mother's fondling of the models is anyone's guess. At least we had succeeded in our mission; we had purchased for my father a pack of reinforced underpants and a pair of black socks.

Back at the bungalow, we were enjoying a cup of tea in the lounge when Dad decided to leave the room to try on the new underwear. He called for Joanie to come and see him in them and much discussion of a positive nature filtered through to us from the master bedroom. Lizzy and I exchanged glances; signs were that our expedition had been a success. Better and better. Now all we had to do was get Dad to see the doctor to confirm the self-diagnosis, sort out the food sell-by dates and we could begin to reconsider our over-reaction to recent events.

Mum came back into the lounge with a smile on her face and her right thumb up in the air. Dad called my name from the bedroom and I glanced enquiringly at Mum who reassured me that Dad was now fully dressed. I had never seen my father without clothes, ever. I went into the bedroom and he was sitting on the bed with the new socks.

"Julie, thank you for getting the socks but you didn't get enough. It's no good only having two socks, what do I put on my third foot?"

Chapter 5
The Phone Call

Julie

"Hello is that Mrs Wood? It's Doctor Vale here. You wrote to me about your parents George and Joan Ellis. I hope you don't mind me ringing but I felt it was easier just to talk to you rather than reply by letter."

His voice was reassuring with its soft, Leicestershire accent. I received the call on my mobile phone during the lunch break at the sixth form college where I worked. I braced myself, finding a corner in the corridor between some tall grey lockers. I put my finger in my left ear and shut my eyes in an effort to block out the cacophony of different noises around me. All the sounds associated with the tense teenage life that was playing out around me could not be escaped. There were three girls sitting on the floor of the corridor, constantly having to wind in their legs every time someone walked past; they were sharing crisps and discussing their next Psychology assignment that had to be handed in by the end of the week. Their shrill voices seemed to get louder and higher as their panic set in. There were two boys treating a vending machine to something just a little shy of GBH in their efforts to get cans of some caffeine rich sugary drink with a noble savage sounding name. No wonder they were hooked, the package offered it all. There were even sounds emitting from the normally silent Chess Club where I had just accompanied the disabled student in my charge. I could see Matt through the window in the classroom door, giving his opponent the famous hard stare. It was necessary for me to maintain a discreet presence within hailing distance of Matt should he require a toilet break, but I needed to get somewhere quiet enough to be able to concentrate on what the doctor had to say to me. It was no good; this space between the lockers would have to do and I must get a grip.

Would the doctor believe me? Would he question my motives in writing to him? Since the *black sock weekend*, I knew that there was no fooling ourselves, this really was happening. Somehow I had to put my emotions on hold and maintain a professional demeanour firstly so that I could respond sensibly to Dr Vale and secondly because I was at my place of work. I took a deep breath, particularly conscious that on no account must I be seen with tears in my eyes by Chess Master, the ever observant Matt.

"Thank you so much for making contact, Doctor. I hope you didn't mind me writing to you but, well, my brother, sister and I, we didn't know what to do and who else to turn to," I began.

"I think if I had been in your situation, I would have done the same. It is as you said in your letter, your mum and dad both come to surgery presenting as a loving and happy couple who no doubt rely on each other greatly, but I wouldn't have suspected that anything was happening that would raise any alarm. I do note what you said in your letter and I definitely think it bears further investigation. As they haven't been to see me for a bit, I could invite them in to our surgery for a general health check and we could run a few tests."

"That's so good of you, Doctor. We are getting increasingly worried about them. When I stayed with them recently, Mum seemed on reasonably good form apart from the food issues I mentioned in my letter and occasional bouts of confusion, but my dad was very withdrawn and I am beginning to think that he is losing a sense of reality. Mum is very good at calming him and filling in gaps, papering over the cracks that seem to be getting wider and wider. "

"Well, let's get them in and we'll see what shows up from the screens, then. Try not to worry," he added kindly.

The corridor began to fill with students signalling the end of the lunch period and so our conversation had to be brought to a close. Taking out my hand bag mirror, I assessed the damage. *Well, all looks fine, a bit flushed but no mascara runs. I think I've got away with it. Deep breath. Onward and upward,* I said to myself.

Matt steered his powered wheelchair through the chess club doorway with his usual swagger thereby broadcasting that he had once again thrashed the opposition – probably several times over. We set off to the lift together.

"What's the matter with you Julie? Have you been crying?" he asked.

Chapter 6
Tipping Point

Joan

Joan was having a little doze by the coal-effect gas fire which gave off the tropical heat punishingly endured, nay expected, by the elderly. Suddenly, she began to cough – her usual prelude to waking up. She was annoyed with that tickle in her throat, wishing to climb back into the delicious cocoon of sleep that she had woven about herself during the hour since lunch time. She heard the clock tick. This was a new sensation as her hearing had diminished over the years and she could not remember hearing such a thing for a very long time. The clock was one of those 'digital' devices, just showing numbers on a face the size of a television screen. Tom had bought it for them. *Such a wonderful son; he thinks of everything. George can see the numbers on the clock, no trouble, and I can hear the tick. George says it's loud but I like to hear it.*

Promising herself a cup of tea in compensation for reluctantly ending her doze, she slowly opened her eyes. George was in the room but not in his usual armchair. He was standing upright beside the arm of the settee, looking as if he was a soldier standing to attention. '*Songs of Praise*' was showing on the television.

"George, would you like a nice cup of tea?"

"Not now, Joanie. I'm on parade. Sidesman duties call. I'll be needed in a moment to collect the tithe envelopes."

At this, Joanie was a little nonplussed. George did do some strange things sometimes but she usually put it down to malaria. *There was that time when he was definitely delirious with the malaria or something like it; otherwise how could you explain why he wrapped all the bedclothes round himself, even over his head, saying he was in his wigwam? Then there was that other time when we went to stay with Julie and James and he told the grandchildren to look for the biscuits in the curtains. All perfectly normal for people with malaria, I expect. All those years ago in the desert, you'd have thought the malaria would have gone by now.*

Joan went off to the kitchen to make a cup of tea anyway. She decided that she would persuade George that he needed to sit down and rest, not stand up all afternoon. She placed her favourite mugs on the floral tray and poured into them a drop of skimmed milk that was almost blue, followed by a weak brew from the brown teapot. By the time she returned to the lounge, George had left his post and was nowhere to be seen. Placing the tray on a small table, she called out: "A nice cup of tea is awaiting you in the lounge, Darling." She settled in her favourite armchair once again and casually watched the television, registering that 'Songs of Praise' had now come to an end. Her attention was drawn to the outsized digital clock as it issued forth a loud, even to her ears, clunking sound as the numbers changed to announce a new hour.

Suddenly, as if on cue, George rushed into the room. He moved so quickly, it was as if he was being chased by somebody. He was clearly alarmed or perhaps excited about something. Whatever the cause, to Joan's bewildered eyes, he appeared like a small boy wearing the costume of an old man. Before Joan could deliver the question that was slowly forming in her mind, George did something most extraordinary. Her husband whom she had known practically all her adult life, whom she knew to be quiet and reserved to the point of being shy, dignified and proper, jumped upon the seat of the settee as if it was a circus trampoline. Jumping from this springy platform, he caused scatter cushions to do as their name suggests – ejecting feather filled squares across the room in all directions. Amongst them he landed upright with a grace and agility that belied his age before launching himself onto his armchair to bounce on its seat pad dangerously, the scattered heap of cushions, his only safety net.

Adopting the same shocked stance as the china cats on the mantelpiece, Joan was agog as she witnessed the bizarre scene before her, played out within the homely lounge - hitherto, her literal comfort zone. Now in her world with the circular Persian rug at its centre, and with her secure borders marked by the chintz shaded standard lamp to the west and the watercolour of Swithland bluebell woods to the east, some kind of chaos was occurring.

This is beyond anything he has done before. This cannot be malaria. This cannot be depression.

Before she could say anything aloud, it was all over; George had left the room. She began to think she may have imagined it all. *I know that I get muddled sometimes, like I said to that nice Dr Vale the other day. Did I just dream it?*

"George, are you there? Are you alright, Darling? You shook me rigid just then. Where are you?"

Receiving no response to her questions, she decided to set off on a search of the bungalow. However, before she had even left the lounge, she concluded where George would be. Indeed she was right; the smallest room in the house was occupied and he had locked himself in.

Joan went to sit on the low wooden chair in the hallway outside the toilet, not knowing what to do next other than to wait for George to emerge. The embroidered seat cushion with its bouquet of spring flowers skilfully worked in Persian wool still looked bright in spite of its age. It seemed to have fared better than the wooden chair frame on which it sat which was showing distinct signs of wear. Joan studied the cushion as she lowered herself onto the original woven seagrass seat which, in contrast to the cushion, was in a very poor state of repair. She ran her small hand with its dainty fingers across the fabric, enjoying the texture of the crewel work. The cushion spoke of a different era, of a time when, in spite of dark houses and poor lighting, a woman would spend hundreds of hours decorating a functional item such as this. *Great Aunty Violet embroidered this cushion all those years ago. She and Granny B. taught me so much. They insisted that I must not eat in the street, even so much as an ice cream and they instructed me on table manners, how to speak the King's English properly and without that dreadful Leicestershire dialect, now how did it go? 'Soft soap and something similar' – they made me practise it over and over again until I could say it perfectly. Oh yes, they taught me how to present myself with elegance and style, in their words, 'put on a top show'. Perhaps if I put on my red skirt with its matching jacket, it will cheer George up and bring him out of his mood.*

This tended to be the solution Joan found for many problems involving her husband. If he was depressed, anxious or angry she believed it must be owing to some fault on her part and so felt she must rectify the situation by changing something of herself like her clothing, or changing her plans to accommodate George's wishes. Most of their lives, George would be at the helm and in control but if he did ask her to make a decision affecting them both at any given moment, she was wired up to stifle her own needs and to try to second guess what he would like and supply that as her wish. The Victorians, who had been deeply involved in her upbringing, would be proud of their protégé: she was a self- sacrificing, *men know best, Darlings- I'll fetch your pipe and slippers*, shape shifter. And everyone loved her.

And she loved George. *The day we married was the best day of my life. George rescued me from a life of misery in the village, he took me far away to the South where everything was easy and no one knew me and I could be free to be myself. When I married George, my life properly began.*

*

Joan and George were both brought up in the village of Ibstock in Leicestershire. At that time, the village held the proud claim of being the largest in England. This may have been one of the reasons why George and Joan did not meet until they were teenagers. In parallel, they may have shared the same gritty coal smoke laden air, played in the same sooty streets and rambled in the same drab fields, but were not aware of each other's existence until George was seventeen and Joan was fourteen. However, there was another reason why the paths of the two had not converged until that pivotal concert at the church hall: they were both from very different social backgrounds.

Joan's father and his two brothers ran the local bakery which served the inhabitants of the village and its surrounding countryside. This made Joan, in the eyes of the locals, a member of the social elite. During her teens, she became noticed and talked about in the community when she began serving in the large shop attached to the *Bake House*. The sharp eyes of the gossips detected her good and even white teeth regularly displayed and framed by smiling lips (*a smiling face is never ugly, Darlings*). They remarked on her trim figure which confounded them; surely ready access to bread and cakes would not be conducive in creating such a sylph- like form? Most of the locals warmed to her. They were charmed by her kind, friendly manner and wanted ownership of this exotic flower but 'Our Joan' was a veritable bouquet of anomalies that kept her beyond their grasp.

It was her speech that set her apart from others more than any other feature, giving customers the impression that she held herself aloof. Her pronunciation, delivered in the style of a bygone age, seemed to underscore her place on the village's top social shelf. As a consequence, the customers were slightly in awe of her, knowing that she would answer their strangled "Ay up ocha any cobs?" with a "Good Morning Mrs So and So. If you please, now what would you care to have today? Round crusty rolls?"

But to the delight of the gossips, Joan's highly polished *top show* veneer was part of an attempt to hide a secret shame. Some locals went along with the charade, admiring her efforts to rise above the dark truth, but for those less kindly disposed, the discussion in the bread queue always came to the same conclusion: *"poor girl needn't try so 'ard, we all know 'er dad's an alc'olic."*

Joan's father, Ernie, operated the mobile part of the bakery business. While his sober brothers ran the bakery and shop, Ernie delivered the bread and cakes to the customers within the broad catchment, from the back of a horse drawn cart. His horse may have looked tired and ill groomed, his vehicle may have appeared shabby but Ernie's personality was as fresh and appealing as the new bread he carried. For a salesman in a bakery business, this was an important asset. He could charm the birds from the trees in spring (*more about that later, Darlings*) and the customers from their cosy kitchens on a winter's day. With his ready wit and dazzling smile, he maintained a roaring trade. Customers came for the banter, the flirting and the news. He carried snippets of gossip from village to hamlet to farm to tiny settlement insufficient to support a one-eyed cat; delivering all with the lustre of creative embellishment, to eager ears. In the early years of the war, when the horse and cart were replaced by an equally tired and shabby motor vehicle, he chalked news on the side of his van. As time went on, the news became far more important to him than loaves and scones and he developed his alter ego - one of swaggering newspaper hack.

The newspaper editor of the *Leicester Mercury* was taken in by this charismatic self- modelled reporter and began to pay him for his regular offerings on life in rural Leicestershire. Ernie knew how to tell a story and could take the germ of an idea and develop it into an article that would delight and entertain as well as inform. Occasionally, like much that is committed to newsprint, it was not strictly true.

There was the famous occasion when, at a dearth of anything newsworthy, he decided to write a piece about the countryside on the brink of spring. A first sign of the long awaited season was the call of the cuckoo which he described hearing in great detail. This was sheer poetic licence. He had not heard the bird sing at all that year; indeed it was far too early for the cuckoo to make its usual appearance. As the piece was well written and appealing, it was passed to other editors in the newspaper group enabling it to reach the attention of folk across the country. Before long, *The Mercury* was contacted by ornithologists asking serious questions about where precisely the bird's call had been witnessed. When experts made the long journey up from London, asking to be taken to the location where such a ground- breaking event had taken place, Ernie knew his number was up. His powerful charm was the only weapon he had against such scrutiny and the local pub, the only place to go, and the phrase "Let me buy you a drink," was the answer to everything.

Drink was part of the hack persona and his already expansive and generous personality was more at home in a pub (*public house, Darlings*) than in the terraced house on Chapel Street. In the Whimsey Inn, he was everybody's pal where he could enjoy a welcome and where there was a platform for his performance. He was a show man, a larger than life personality with a charisma that drew like a magnet. He professed to speak in several languages and tried them out on the local crowd:

" 'Ichy pal a say. Ichy bon voy.' Now, Gentlemen that means: ' do you live near here? I come from afar.' And now contrast this with ' Eny yotcha?' which is pure Leicestershire for 'do you have a light on you, my fine fellow?' "

A born entertainer, he could play the piano (*always with his white gloves on, Darlings*) and the saxophone; he became the leading light in the 'Ibstock Syncopated Band' which played at pubs and working men's clubs in the locality. While he was well known and appreciated by those in the village's convivial drinking establishments, he did not meet with similar approval at home.

After the pub bell chimed for last orders, a transformation took place. The yoke of responsibility did not sit easily on Ernie's shoulders and with the reality of empty pockets, having spent his earnings on drinking chums, he could not look forward to a warm welcome from his wife, Maudie. There were five children at home: Joan the eldest child, with four younger brothers. Maudie ensured that the youngest children were in bed when their father, often the worse for drink (*He was such a lovely father when he had not had a liquid lunch, Darlings*), rolled up the dark entry. Only Joan and the eldest of her brothers, Walter, would be on guard when their dad stumbled through the kitchen door. Their job was to protect their mother from their father.

*

Yes, Darling George rescued me. He took me away from all that.

"George, are you alright? Do you need anything? You've been in there an awfully long time." There was a resounding snap as the small bolt was drawn back and the toilet door slowly opened and George emerged wearing just his underpants. Before Joan could voice her concern, he had lifted the car keys from their hook and proceeded with haste in the direction of the garage.

"Where are you going, Darling? Aren't you feeling a little cold?" As this did not cause a break in his stride, Joan tried another tack; after all she could not have him *driving about in this weather with no clothes on. What would the neighbours say?* "Georgie dear, you know that we agreed that I should always do the driving ever since you had your cataracts. Now let me make you a lovely cup of tea while you put your clothes back on."

George looked at her anxious face. He was confused. The person before him was an enemy, despite their benign looks, who was trying to find out the secrets he carried and with which he had been entrusted, on pain of death. *Careless talk costs lives. Perhaps if I pretend to play along, I'll find another escape route,* he thought. The enemy appeared to be backing him into a corner at the far end of the bungalow. Before he could get his bearings, he had been lured into the bedroom and told firmly to stay there. *I'll do as you say,* he thought, *but you'll get nothing out of me. I've left no clues. I was thorough, oh yes, very thorough. You will not find so much as a bus ticket or a cinema ticket stub on me. Nothing, not even a crumb can you find that would connect me with my airbase.* He heard the small catch click on the door and knew he had been locked in.

It was several hours later, as the day had turned to evening, that Janine arrived. Janine lived over seventy miles away and had taken the Fosse Way in an already fraught state having had to extricate herself from a raft of duties at the boys' boarding school. When her mother's anxious call had come through to *Tree Tops House*, Janine knew she had to get into the car and go to her aid without delay. She did not have any idea what would be awaiting her at the end of the journey. Tom, who lived locally, was the usual first responder to any crisis at Caldron Close. However, he and his wife Barbara had gone to Scotland for the weekend, and so the task had fallen to Janine.

George woke from the sleep that he had been enjoying, tucked up in the duvet on his twin bed next to the warm radiator. The electric blanket had been left switched on for a considerable time and his cheeks were flushed with the cosiness of his personal haven. There had been lots of voices raised earlier he seemed to recall, but he thought that one of them might have been his. He certainly had a sore throat and the skin of his right hand was very bruised and tender to the touch. Voices outside his room had awoken him, first high pitched women's sounds and then the lower, more authoritative tones of a male. He pushed himself up onto unsteady legs and groped his way to the door, dragging the duvet cover with him. He tried the handle and after some whispering outside the door, it was eventually opened to reveal Dr Vale and another man he did not recognise. Then behind them, was the lovely surprise. There, if his old cataract eyes did not deceive him, was his own little Janine. *What could she be doing? She has got all her students to look after.*

She was the first one to speak, gazing warmly at him with that smile of hers that had the power to light up any room.

"Daddy, are you feeling better now? You have been giving us all a fright with your banging and shouting. You've had us all worried so we asked the doctor to come to see you. "

Then it was Joan's turn to attempt to take control of a situation which was completely baffling her. Like Dickens' character *Mr Dick*, she resorted to the wisdom of meeting an incomprehensible problem with a simple practical solution, saying to her husband, "Georgie, shall we go and put some nice warm clothes on?"

George, equally bemused by the day's turn of events, succumbed to his wife's ministrations and allowed himself to be persuaded into clothing. Eventually, the couple emerged from the sanctuary of their bedroom, latterly the place of George's temporary incarceration, to join the professionals in the lounge. By this time, there was no fire in George's belly and nothing to fight for and no one to fight with, he was simply confused and very, very tired. The doctor and his colleague explained to George that a stay in hospital would be the right course of action for him.

George's immediate future was once again being decided by other people. Nevertheless, he accepted the decision with an air of resignation. He knew he had come to the end of the line; life had caught up with him. Time to give himself up and apologise for all the trouble he had caused.

The pathos of the situation had a deep impact on Janine. She had been talking with the doctor and was beginning to understand the alarming extent of her father's psychiatric problems. She knew that all his life her dad had *dodged the depression bullet*, calling it 'nervous trouble,' refusing to accept that there was anything wrong. As a child she had asked him what the word 'depression' meant and he had responded adamantly: "You don't want to know what it means- you are too young to even *think* of such a thing." Like many members of his generation, he would not readily admit to any such weakness. Acknowledging 'depression' or 'nervous trouble' led to the inevitable transfer of power to those in authority; his boss would have the upper hand - *Bad show, old boy*. Better to keep it hidden, to let it become another chip of shame to carry discreetly on his shoulder, along with all the others.

It was beginning to dawn on Joan that this was not the effect of malaria or simple 'nervous trouble'. It was more than depression. It was not something she could explain away. This was something else entirely and it was taking her wonderful husband away from her.

It was beginning to dawn on George that his long struggle to avoid being caught out was over. There was some relief in that realisation. So it was with nobility and dignity that he climbed into the secure hospital vehicle.

Chapter 7
Nighthawks

Julie

"Mum, did you go on HRT when you went through the Menopause?"

"HRT Darling? No Darling… What's HRT?" Mother paused in her stride and came to a standstill causing Lizzy and I to do the same, jolting into each other, attached as we were with arms linked like three women who had just failed to pass the audition to join the Tiller Girls.

"It's Hormone Replacement Therapy," I said.

"Oh that HRT. No, Darling. Is that when you drink your own urine?"

Laughing out loud with shock, Lizzy and I told her that we did not think that was what the therapy involved. It transpired that Mum just "sailed through the change of life, Darlings. I don't know what all the fuss is about."

I was not aboard any such trusty ship; I had gone to sea on a raft.

Irrespective of our true hormonal stages, we were behaving like three teenagers on a night out clubbing. Lizzy and I walked with Mother in the middle, arms akimbo, as we took the road down the hill and into town. We giggled as if we had pre-drunk an oversized handbag full of vodka - the necessary ingredient for a wild evening. In reality, we had all enjoyed a nice mug of Rington's tea before we put on warm coats and set off; but to Mum, our actions were nonetheless wild. This was the first occasion in many years, other than to attend Evensong at St Catherine's, that she had gone out of her home after dark. To walk into the town on a Saturday evening after supper had been hitherto unthinkable. She was lit up with the excitement of a child on the last day of the Christmas term and nothing and nobody was going to dampen her enthusiasm.

This state of euphoria, brittle and short lived though it might be, had been achieved on the rebound from the dark shock of my father's departure. It was as if my mother's mind could not cope with facing the reality of what had happened. Everything, that my mother had been trying to keep together over recent weeks and months, had been torn apart. After all her effort, her husband was now in another place and it seemed that as he walked out of the bungalow, her sense of purpose went with him.

When Lizzy and I had arrived for another Gibbet Roundabout weekend, it was clear that Mother was struggling to come to terms with the new situation, deeply missing having her husband by her side. She had not been to see him in the hospital; it was considered too soon to do so by the professionals. George, we had all been advised, must settle in the ward. Lizzy and I tried to reassure Mother stating platitudes like, "You know that he is in the best place for the time being. He will be looked after there and you'll soon be able to see him again." She was impervious to our attempts to comfort her, roaming around the bungalow picking up cushions and putting them down again, twitching a curtain here and re-aligning a picture there. She seemed to have been cast adrift from her moorings, like a proud but weather-beaten ship. It was a pathetic sight to see such an elegant woman lose her gloss; hair a tumbled mess and dressing gown stained. *Not Mum. Not Grandma.*

Then with the aim of distracting her, we told her about our little family, how well Lizzy was doing on her course, how my husband James was working very long hours and going into school at weekends to catch up on his all-consuming job as head teacher of our local primary school. How Simon was enjoying university life combined with his job at a coffee shop. "He tells us he's a qualified barista, Mum."

"Well Darling, that's very good. And he's done that so quickly. Will he have to go into court every day?"

"No Grandma. A *barista* is someone who can blend and prepare coffee," Lizzy gently corrected.

"Well I am sure judges and all the court people enjoy their hot drinks," her Grandma replied with authority.

Lizzy looked at me, rolling her eyes with mute appeal. I returned her glance with a facial expression that I hoped conveyed, *"Moving swiftly on."*

I dredged up some news of various friends of mine that Mum had met in the past and she listened with apparent interest before slipping back into wishing George was there to hear it all.

It was then that Lizzy and I had hit on the plan to take her out for this little jaunt. Mother's reaction was astounding and child-like; she seemed to undergo a transformation in front of us with her eyes lighting up and all manner of questions asked: "What shall I wear? Where are we going? What shall we do there? " It became clear that such a modest outing was a great novelty; that she was experiencing a sense of freedom and elation after many years of being cloistered. A sociable person by nature, in recent years she had had to limit her contact with friends especially the office girls with whom she once worked at County Hall. George had become increasingly reclusive and unwilling to leave the bungalow unless it was to do the supermarket shopping with Joan or to attend church. As Joan did not like to leave George on his own for long periods, her few opportunities for social contact were often gracefully declined.

We huddled together and walked briskly as the October evening temperatures began to fall, our faces taking the full force of the chill wind. We had only two scarves between us so Lizzy and Mother shared one, binding them together ever closer so they giggled all the more as the lights of the High Street twinkled ahead. We were drawn to them as we smartened our pace and took great gulps of fresh air. Although a woman in her seventies, Mother was free from any mobility problems and was able to keep up with my daughter and me. Indeed she seemed to cast the years aside as, with a little burst of tap dancing, she told us of her days on the stage in the village hall at Ibstock. It had been on the occasion of her solo tap dance to the song 'Little- Mister- Baggy- Britches- I - love-you,' that George had first noticed her. "But it was not the first time that I had noticed George," she said with a twinkle in her eye which slowly began to turn into a tear.

Lizzy was quick to create a distraction and seeing a large sign in the distance marking our destination, she said, "There it is, Grandma, the golden arches. That's where we're going."

"It looks like a big M to me, Darlings. That one on the pole? "

"That's it Grandma. It's called McDonalds."

"Oh yes. Scottish. I have heard of this place, Darlings, it's where all you young people go."

"I have an idea," I said, "I think that whilst we are going through the Menopause, we women should wear a tiara with a big M made of diamante. It would be a kind of badge of honour and would

46

alert other people that we may bite their heads off at any given moment."

"Or that you had worked for twenty years at McDonalds," quipped Lizzy.

"Priceless, Darling. I don't think it will catch on," Mum laughed gently.

We looked through the windows of the café; the clientele in freeze-frame like an Edward Hopper painting. But these nighthawks were dressed in fleeces and knitted hats and sat hunched at low tables bolted to the floor. As we entered, the figures in our painting came to life, Lizzy and my mother sought out a table with a cosy corner banquette while I queued for the hot chocolate drinks. Returning a few minutes later, I saw them in the depths of conspiratorial whispers watching the comings and goings of people on the steep flight of stairs leading to the toilets. These were mostly young girls although the young lads seemed more inclined to station themselves at the foot of the staircase.

I placed the plastic tray on the table and waited for the reaction. I was not to be disappointed. There in front of us were three tubs of ice cream with pointed swirling peaks sprinkled with nuts and impaled with chocolate flakes. Mother was full of childlike glee as she studied the foamy confection. "Well Darlings what do we say? There's a little rhyme we used to say, but I've forgotten how it goes."

"I scream, you scream, we all scream for ice cream!" chorused Lizzy and I.

"That's it. Wonderful, Darlings. And a hot chocolate too, I am being spoilt. I did not know you could go out and have ice cream in the evening, in the winter."

"Yes Mum, you can have it any time and you are eating at a table and not out in the street."

"Precisely. We were never allowed to eat in the street, it was considered common. Though I don't know what Aunt Violet or Granny B would make of all this. And I don't know how these girls can go around with next to nothing on and not catch their death of cold. Lizzy and I have been watching them go up and down those steps. They don't seem to be eating here, just using the toilets. And they have skimpy tops on when on a night like this they need vests. But the most shocking of all is that they've got no knickers on!"

So this had been the reason for the giggling in the corner. It transpired that Grandma Nighthawk had not missed the flash of nubile buttocks as they ascended the stairs under the shortest of short skirts; neither had the boys who had strategically placed themselves at ground level. However, in all fairness to the girls, it was time for us to explain to Mum what a thong was. It took considerable debate, visual demonstration and mime to exonerate the girls in Mum's eyes – and even a picture drawn on the back of an envelope to convince her.

Intrigued, Mum decided she needed to access the *Stairway to Enlightenment* and visit the facilities. Clutching her handbag which made her look as if she had a fat and contented hen under her arm, she made her way to the stairs followed by her trusty attendant, Lizzy. Once inside the Ladies' toilet, she was able to study the girls at close quarters and listen to their noisy interaction. Even her impaired hearing had no trouble registering the shrieks and squeals of the girls as they adjusted their hair and make-up at the tiny vanity unit. In their excitement, there was no deference to old age; no inhibition to their language or exuberance. Mum absorbed it all with the awed wonder of a tomb raider. She manoeuvred to a corner where she could see her reflection under a girl's thin raised arm but realised that her fat hen handbag, the size of a mothership, did not contain a single lipstick. Lizzy came to the rescue, offering her own lip gloss and watched her grandmother applying it to her mouth with skill, pressing her lips together to smooth the result in time honoured fashion. There are some things you never forget.

The next day dawned in the bungalow at Burnage. If last night's scene was straight from the '*Moulin Rouge*', the curtains that came up the following morning were to reveal a scene more likely to have come from '*Waiting for Godot*' or '*Great Expectations*'. Mother was speaking in a depressed monotone and wandering the house in Miss Havisham style dishabille, twitching curtains and turning over cushions like so many pebbles on a beach. With a promise of tea and toast, we persuaded her to sit down on the settee. Lizzy sat with her and tried to hold her attention with snippets of news from her world, encouraging her grandma to talk about her own youth. Meanwhile, I went into the kitchen to begin food preparations.

On the kitchen counter, I noticed the dosette box. I remembered that Tom had organised this to make life easier for Mum. The white box was composed of separate units containing daily doses of medication, so that Mum would not get into a muddle with her tablets. With guilt and horror, I noted that Mum had not taken her medication the previous evening. Realising that this might account for her morning lethargy, I took the dosette box into the lounge.

"I'm sorry, Mum. I think in all our excitement of last night, I distracted you away from your routine and you did not take your night time tablets."

"Oh, don't worry Darlings. I often forget to take them. I don't like taking them anyway. I'm sure I don't need them. Especially those little brown jobs, I don't like what they do to me at all. Tom has got me this little box thing. Isn't it pretty? It's got little doors just like that game show programme George and I used to watch years ago, now what was it called? You could *Take the Money or Open the Box*! We always wanted them to *Open the Box*!"

"What was in the box, Grandma?" asked Lizzy.

"Well it could be even more money or a big prize like a holiday- or sometimes it was a booby prize like an old sock!"

"Well, Mum, let's *Open the Box* and see what you have won this morning," I said, trying to capitalise on the positive enthusiasm of the moment. Engaging Lizzy's eye, she touched the tiny door catch and with a theatrical flourish worthy of a magician's plumed assistant, opened the door to the tiny unit marked 'Sunday morning'. Revealed lay four small tablets which Mum tipped into her palm. On a roll, I fetched a glass of water from the kitchen and stood above her, waiting for her to take it after she had downed the medicine. No such luck. The tablets remained on her palm, being examined as she watched the light pass glitteringly through one and bounce densely off another, allowing one to roll along her life-line and another to squat smugly in the crease of her heart line. It took all of Lizzy's and my combined powers of persuasion, considerable cajoling, promises of a wonderful breakfast afterwards , culminating in a sophisticated good cop/bad cop routine before she was to consume the full dose.

Later in the kitchen, Lizzy and I were back to sotto voce. "I was beginning to think we would have to use the old sugar cube trick like we used to use on the dog. Do you remember? Take a sugar cube and stick the tablet on one side with a blob of jam. Offer to the pup, with tablet facing away from him. Bob's your uncle! Or should I say Bob Martin?"

"That would never have worked with Grandma. She's too canny and stubborn! Bless her. But we got her to take them this time! High Five!"

The glow from our 'high fives' in the kitchen did not have any long lasting effect as it dawned on us that Mum was already having difficulty with the time and even ascertaining which day of the week it was. How could she possibly keep track of her doses accurately, even with the dinky dosette box? Not long ago, Mother was strong, able to guide my father through the maze of their microcosmic world. Almost overnight, that drive had diminished and she was reduced to needing help herself, looking to us to lead her. The Family Committee would need to have a total re-think. With the central pivot of her life removed, the daily challenges of getting up, washing and dressing, eating and taking medication were increasingly difficult for her to meet. A structure needed to be put in place where Mum was regularly checked on and prompted to take her medication at the right times. I had much to discuss with my brother and sister.

With these thoughts in my mind, I looked up to see her enter the kitchen. With a childlike trust and without a word, she put her right arm through mine and then motioned to Lizzy to link with her left in the tiller girl line up, before starting her dance routine on the tappy tiles of the kitchen floor. She began to sing in a little girl voice as she took us through the steps of the measure, her eyes turning to me every so often to gain a reassuring nod. Slowly and gracefully, a shift in dynamics was taking place; all it took was a chorus of '*Little Mister Baggy Britches*' to effect a role reversal that was set to become permanent.

Chapter 8
Round the bend

Julie and Janine

"We'll stop at a nice little farm shop I know off the Fosse Way. They serve some good lunches there – and we'll need our strength for the next few hours," suggested my sister Janine. She was driving her little red car, taking me with her (*Thelma and Louise*, we called ourselves) to the psychiatric hospital to visit Dad there for the first time. We were not in any hurry.

The farm shop café delivered hearty jacket potatoes and we both cleared our plates of all except the red onion garnish which we carefully extracted in strands and placed on the side. So alike in so many ways, it was uncanny. Sometimes mistaken for twins, we both had brown hair and brown eyes. However, Janine took after our mother in her fine build and dainty feet whereas I had inherited my father's more stocky physique and wore shoes two sizes bigger than my younger sister. Although we lived far apart and met infrequently, we found we had more and more things in common. For example, when freshening up in the Ladies' toilets after our café lunch, we unzipped our cosmetic bags to reveal the identical make and shade of foundation, mascara and eye shadow. We discussed these and other entertaining coincidences at length; still not in any hurry.

After a further foray into the delights on offer in the farm's retail hall, all at a dawdling pace, we could not put off the second stage of our journey any longer. So with regret and an increasing sense of dread, we loaded the guilt souvenirs of frilly bonneted jars of chilli mustard relish and apple chutney into the car's boot and headed off.

"Dad will be so pleased that we came via the Fosse Way," I said, once we had re-joined the main route. "He always asks James and me which road we used and always says there is no better way; I wonder if he will ask us today?"

"It will be interesting to see how much he does respond to us. He certainly recognised me on that dreadful day when we had to call for the men in white coats. I feel so bad about all that but at the time it seemed the only way forward," said Janine, changing gear frequently as the criss-cross of road junctions demanded.

"Don't beat yourself up. The whole situation was a powder keg waiting to go off bang. We should have seen it coming – all the signs were there but we didn't want to see them. None of us did. Very sadly, now the explosion has well and truly detonated but I think that although Dad is a casualty, it does mean that he will get the professional help he needs - has needed for a long time."

We tried to comfort each other, to reassure ourselves that we had done the right thing. But guilt is something that is ever-present. In facing the truth we had to lift up a corner of that thick and heavy blanket of guilt. What followed was the urge to try to smooth it out again as quickly as possible to avoid the pain that knowledge brings. However hard we tried, there was always a corner left untucked.

We talked of our mother's decline since Dad's departure to hospital; we planned to take her to visit him once we had been there ourselves. We needed to prepare her. We did not know how to prepare ourselves. I had talked to our brother Tom on the phone recently as he had visited Dad several times already. On each occasion, Dad had recognised him but seemed confused as to where he was. What would we find when we got there?

"Tom talked about the design of the ward, how separate lounges are linked with circulating corridors. This means that a patient can take a walk around without coming up against a dead end. Apparently, coming to a blank wall can disorientate the more vulnerable patients but with this design, they can just keep walking round the bend into the next big sitting room. Oh dear, did I really just say that?"

"Yes you did," said Janine with a wry smile, "maybe that's where the phrase comes from."

We went on to talk about the plans that had been put in place to keep Mum well fed, cared for and safe in the bungalow. There had been further family meetings at *Treetops* and frequent communication between the three of us so that in a relatively short time, we had become well versed in the role of social workers, the relevant benefits system and the care packages available. However, it was proving to take much longer to realise our plans. A full assessment of Mum's needs had to be made, the team of care givers had to be found and engaged, frozen meals had to be ordered and delivered; that was just the beginning. In the interim Tom and Barbara, who lived the closest to Mum, had been checking on her daily, with Janine and I making regular visits also.

"But aren't we forgetting the main fly in this neat ointment? Mum may not see the point of the care package; she may not even let the Home Helps into the house," I ventured.

"We'll have to sell the idea to her, somehow," said Janine. "One day at a time."

The sprawling hospital with its variety of architectural styles representing every decade since its first foundation stone was laid in Queen Victoria's reign, was surprisingly well served with car parks. We followed the signs to Branscombe psychiatric wing and found a space, delaying the inevitable for a few more minutes in the car before gritting, then baring our teeth according to family tradition(*a smiling face is never ugly, Darlings*), and making our way to the entrance.

Once in this modern building which was a tribute to elegant architecture at the turn of the millennium, our senses were assaulted. The most effective of our senses seemed to be that of smell; indeed our olfactory organs were working overtime as they took in the heady mix of antiseptic, floor cleaning fluid and *Attar of Roses*. "Ah! A new perfume blend. I shall name this fragrance *Mask*," I whispered to my sister.

"Don't you mean *Musk*?" said Janine.

"No. I mean *Mask*. Think what smells it might be covering up."

In the foyer, we saw several signs directing visitors to report to the nurses' station. Once there, wc waited to speak to the well upholstered charge nurse who was studying her computer screen. She smiled in greeting when she saw us standing in front of her desk and asked us who we were visiting, and then with an attitude both brisk and motherly, she took us through the entry and exit procedure.

"Now ducks, in a minute I'll open the door for yer and you can check in to the nurse's office inside. Someone will show you where yer dad is. Now when yer wanting to come out you have to punch in this code like. It's today's date with a zero on the end. Please to mek sure that none of the patients follow yer out. They're very crafty you see and they nip out quick like then we have all hell to pay trying to catch 'em again."

She opened the security door and there waiting on the other side was a tiny lady in a lilac skirt and cream frilly blouse. She had dainty features which spread into a wide smile, exposing bright white dentures. Swift on her feet, she came towards us, holding out her hands and grasping ours in a friendly handshake. "How wonderful of you to visit me. It's been such a long time since I've seen you both. How are you? Now what's your name? I'm afraid I forget names these days but I never forget a face."

Our mother would be proud as we started to *do the pretty* with this dear old lady and introduced ourselves properly. Then we tried to explain that we did not think that we had had the pleasure of meeting her before and in fact we had travelled a long way to see our father. We took leave of her gently, taking the circular corridor whose charms we had heard all about. We thought that our *Meet and Greet* lady would return to her watch but with surprising speed for one of advanced years, she continued to follow us. We turned to face her and she looked up at us with the eyes of a trusting puppy and began her loop again. "How wonderful of you to visit me. It's been such a long time since I've seen you both. How are you? Now what's your name? I'm afraid I forget names these days but I never forget a face."

"Just let's keep walking. Don't look her in the eye. Don't engage. Or we'll never find Dad," said Janine, with the surprising skill of a ventriloquist: under her breath and without moving her lips.

"It's like one of those computer games or Greek hero tasks. *Don't look the woman with the wild snakey hairdo in the eye or she'll turn you to stone.* Just now we seem to be in the labyrinth," I said as we increased our pace and looked back to see the tiny woman become even tinier in our wake.

"And look, there's the Minotaur," replied Janine. The apparently never ending corridor had at last opened out to reveal a spacious lounge furnished with many high backed armchairs in calming shades of blue and green. Elderly male and female patients were sitting around the room, in the process of being served cups of tea from a large urn squatting on a giant trolley. Behind the giant trolley was an even larger male nurse, the afore-mentioned Minotaur who had tufts of horny hair growing out of his scalp and decorating both sides of his face like mutton chops. Belying his appearance which featured a tense muscle bound physique that tested every seam of his uniform, he surprised us with the nimble dexterity and measured care with which he gently ensured every patient received their drink and Rich Tea biscuit.

My sister and I stood nervously behind the trolley with its proficient attendant feeling as if we were in the wings waiting for our moment to go on the stage. In truth, we did not know what we should do. This was beyond our experience. There seemed no one to ask where our father was, the nurses' office appeared empty and we did not like to interrupt our Minotaur cum gentle giant in his ministrations. The latter was contributing to the atmosphere in more ways than the visual as his aftershave began to assail our nostrils, activated by the heat of the tea urn. "What was that you said about fragrance? I think that's a *Musk*, don't you think?" said Janine, sotto voce and again without moving her lips. She really had missed her vocation.

"Well, I do have to agree and through knowledge gleaned from many years of being married to a countryman, I'd say it was *territory marking scent recently sprayed, and registers on the British Stench Scale a measure equal to the power of ten foxes,"* I replied with some authority. Janine's singular expression told me she agreed with this hypothesis and was disgusted at the same time.

"Can you see Dad anywhere?" I whispered to my sister. She shook her head. We both continued to study the scene before us with increasing alarm. In so many respects, order prevailed in the room. Patients were being served their drinks in turn; most were seated although some chose to form a queue near the trolley. Some patients were more mobile than others and were walking around the room, seemingly unaware of proceedings or perhaps they were not interested in taking a drink. One elderly gentleman was walking slowly, looking at each foot as he picked it up and placed it on the floor. One old lady was walking quite smartly with her stick, her slipper bootees grazing the low pile carpet tiles as she headed down the corridor, seemingly on a vital mission. Some patients were dozing with their heads on their chests, a few were sound asleep with their heads lolling and mouths open. There were some patients fully dressed in daytime clothing but a few were in their night clothes and dressing gowns. Many had their feet stretched out before them, on display. At first sight, this could be just a geriatric ward, but after a few moments of observation, we saw the reality. It was all in the faces. In some you could see that blank look as if nothing of interest registered sufficient to respond with a facial expression. In others there could be seen the bewildered look like that of a frightened child. Then on other faces was etched the falsely happy confidence of the confused. What look would Dad be displaying when we found him?

"How did this happen? How did our wonderful father with all his talents and qualities come to need the care offered within these four walls?" I whispered to myself, although Janine heard me and gave my arm a comforting squeeze.

Then, amidst a sea of chairs, a nurse emerged from her place where she had been crouching to assist a patient with their tea, and came towards us. "Welcome. Who are you visiting today?"

"Thank you, Nurse. We were hoping to see our father, George Ellis," we said, almost in chorus.

"Well I can see you are sisters! Like two peas in a pod. And you've got your dad's big brown eyes. Now George has settled in fine. He's very quiet but your brother said that's normal for your dad- he prefers to keep himself to himself. I'll take you to him and if you've got any questions after you've seen him, don't hesitate to ask. I'll be in my office if I'm not in here." She led us through the lounge and back into another stretch of the circular corridor which once again opened out into another lounge, this time much smaller. There were large picture windows to one side, overlooking a pleasant garden with a combination of formal flower beds with plants in regimented rows alongside patches of wild flowers in riot. Sitting on the window seat enjoying the garden view was a stooped, grey haired elderly gentleman: our father.

The nurse, whose badge declared that she was Senior Charge Nurse Carter, went up to Dad and walked her fingers up his left arm just as I used to do to my children when we played *Incy Wincy Spider*. This gentle action made my father turn round without alarm and look up at the Nurse. Immediately he took her hand and held it fast, looking into her eyes while she told him that he had some visitors. We could see him in profile and his facial expression changed from blank to bewilderment. The nurse smiled at Dad in a reassuring way and directed him to look at us. Moving his hand up to his collar to adjust a non- existent tie, he stood up and came towards us, using his elbow to hitch up the loose waistband of his trousers.

"Hello Dad!" we said and took turns to kiss him on the cheek and give his little limp body a hug. We were children once again; he was our 'Daddy' and we were his little girls.

With vain attempts at controlling our emotion, we turned to Nurse Carter and thanked her. As busy as she was, she offered to arrange for us all to have a pot of tea to share with our father and at the mention of 'biscuits included', Dad smiled for the first time. Nurse Carter proposed that we could have our tea in one of the therapy rooms. At this suggestion, Dad came to life.

"Come into my office," he said, his spine visibly stiffening, his shoulders squaring into military formation before our eyes. He started to march behind Nurse Carter and we meekly followed him until we came to Green Room 3 where we were all invited to make ourselves comfortable while Nurse Carter went off to order the tea. The room contained an armchair and a therapy plinth set at waist height. We insisted that Dad should take the armchair and we sat side by side on the plinth. After the tension of the previous hour, such unconventional seating caused us to break into giggles as the combination of the height of the backless couch and our shortness of stature meant that our legs swung free. We both had some trouble gaining a purchase on the slippery leatherette and further mirth erupted when the cover made rude noises that such vinyl covers are wont to do when one shifts position.

This barely seemed to register with Dad. He was pensive and with his head cocked to one side, said, "Shush. Listen. Careless talk costs lives. I don't tell them anything. But that doesn't stop me getting the messages. Listen. It's Morse. *Dah dit dit dit, dit, dit dah dit,dit dah dit dit.* That's B E R L. Listen can you hear it?" And indeed we could hear it: the tinny sounds tapped out on metal with irregular pauses between. The sounds of wartime apparently transmitted on radio waves to be decoded by this elderly former RAF Wireless Operator.

"Oh, I've lost it now," he said in frustration. "It could have been BERLIN. Just a minute, I'm picking up again and it's getting louder." He continued to translate, "C A L ..."

The urgent message was interrupted when the door opened and the tea and biscuits arrived on a large tray carried by our trusty Minotaur. He placed the china crockery and large stainless steel tea pot on a low table, keeping the door ajar with an enormous foot shod in a white clog like a hoof. Through the doorway, Janine and I watched the Morse code operator pass by in the corridor in her silent slipper bootees, tapping the central heating pipework with her walking stick.

Janine and I looked at each other, saying wordlessly: *Mystery solved.*

We poured the tea and Dad, taking his cup and saucer into his hands, proceeded to dunk his biscuit with relish. Then at a loss as to how to start, I said the first thing that came into my head that I thought would please him, "We came via the Fosse Way, Dad."

This seemed to unlock the flood gates and Dad began a monologue that began:

"Well I got to work early today as the traffic on the Fosse Way wasn't too bad. There's no better way, you know. I am pleased Tom and I did the oil change at the weekend and she's running well now. She was sounding like a bag of hammers before we got her sorted. Anyhow, Vanessa was in the office. She's a nice little girl –will go to the print room whenever you need her to, without complaint. Les said to me that she must have a new bra on because he said she was walking about like a trussed up chicken. I said I didn't think he should say such things as she's a nice little girl. But you know what that Les is like. Then I had a phone call from my mate Jaffa at the consulting engineers based in London. He said tie a knot in your old man and make sure you don't forget the meeting next month. I shall have to go down to their offices but it'll be well worth it. And he said Well George you should make sure you have all the facts before you start to work on the Guyana project. He said that most of the relay boxes will be in jungle, in remote locations. There won't be towns anywhere near so they will have to make sure that the units can withstand the humidity and the temperatures let alone the jungle vegetation. They will have to be sealed, unmanned buildings that can run with little or no maintenance. Then Brian and I had lunch in the canteen. I had my sandwiches and my two apples but he had a big cottage pie and chips followed by apple crumble and custard. After that he sat using his business card like a tooth pick, cleaning food out from between his teeth. Revolting to watch. Then he puts the card back in his wallet to use again. Then in the afternoon we all had to go down to the planning room for a big meeting which went on for ages. But at the end of it they said that the telecommunication project co-ordinator for Guyana was me."

…and the monologue was to continue for well over an hour. We hung onto every word initially, as he told us about the day he had just had. Of course, he had not just had that particular day. The day he described happened at least thirty years ago but must have been one of his best days in the office during the time when he held the post of senior engineer at a large telecommunications company. Every evening our mother had always insisted that our father told us all about his day as we gathered at the round table for supper in the kitchen. Often his nightly report continued long after we had finished eating our meal. As awkward teenagers, we found this a trial. But our parents believed that we should hear how their days had unfolded and they wanted us to tell them about our day also. We rarely shared our experiences. Well, we were teenagers. Prevented from leaving the table, we would create our own amusements using the debris left on the table cloth. We would roll crumbs of bread into balls, cut giant sets of comedy teeth from orange peel and wedge them between our lips in a ghastly Halloween grimace or play with Leviathan, our fondly named gluggle water jug in the shape of a large fish that made loud gurgling noises whenever you poured a drink. Occasionally, we resorted to pretending to nod off with the boredom of hearing about personalities we would never meet and of places we would never visit. It was grown up stuff and we were missing '*Top of the Pops*' that would be showing in black and white on the television in the living room.

Now we were the grown-ups and I'm very ashamed to report that just as all those years ago around the supper table, I was to nod off, this time for real. To my shame, my eye lids grew heavy and I dozed, then tipping sideways, I slid off the end of the plinth to land ungainly on the floor; once again an awkward adolescent. I awoke to Janine's barely suppressed giggle which turned into a beautifully executed silent laugh and with her shoulders moving up and down, I regained my perch with an inelegant squeak of leatherette.

Dad had not even paused for breath.

We heard a shrill bell ring in the corridor outside, the signal for the end of visiting time. We stood up noisily, thanks to the unforgiving plinth, and told Dad that it was time for us to make our way home. He seemed to accept this without question and left the therapy room with us and walked alongside as we negotiated the now busy corridor. It became clear that the bell was also the signal for supper time and those patients who were mobile and aware of the routine, were intent on getting to the dining hall without delay. Indeed there was a barely concealed sense of a race taking place as the air hummed with the steady beat of walking stick ferrules and the grip of spinning wheelchair tyres on low pile carpet.

At the doors to the dining room, we took leave of our father. As we parted, the words that passed between us held a hollow ring with the stilted language of strangers. Dad's goodbye was a formal dismissal, lacking all the usual warm endearments. Would we ever hear loving words from him again?

*

I had some visitors to my office today, my two girls. I am glad that they saw where I work now. They keep me very busy here with all the secrets I have to keep but I think I'm doing a good job. The girls would have seen that. They know their old dad does his best.

George entered the dining room. This was a large area filled with rectangular tables covered with paper table coverings, laid with knives and forks. Some patients were able to queue at the serving hatch with their trays, expectantly, while those less mobile were seated and staff brought their meals to them. George had a piece of battered fish put on his plate along with a serving of chips and a small salad. Alongside this on his black plastic tray was a slice of fruit flan which had his favourite jelly glaze. *Joanie knows how much I love jelly. Jelly takes a long time to set. She used to make me jelly often but she always tried too hard. She used to make it set quicker by putting it in an ice cube tray in the freezer.* His gums winced with the memory of the ice crystals that always lay at the bottom. *If you scraped the top layer off, you had jelly, but below that was raspberry permafrost.*

He began eating the flan; it was delicious with a sponge crust reminiscent of a bicycle tyre. Looking at the pattern, touching it with the edge of his spoon, his mind returned to the time when he experienced the most amazing event in his childhood when he received the birthday bicycle; the special bicycle that had been given to him after grammar school had been taken away.

He had never been given a gift on this scale ever before. Birthdays were largely ignored. At Christmas, like many children of his working class background, he received an orange and a small wooden toy or a bag of marbles plus a part share of the new oil cloth that was laid on the living room floor. They were presents as he had hitherto understood the concept. Yet here was a lovingly restored and conditioned bicycle with a smooth black leather saddle and a bell on the sleek handlebars – and it was all for him. He could not sleep that night in June, in anticipation of the next day when his father had promised him that he would teach him how to ride the new machine which he had immediately named '*The Flying Fish*'. He imagined all the lanes he would ride, the fords and puddles he could splash through, the hills he would speed down, freewheeling. Once his dad had taught him how to ride, he could try riding without holding the handlebars like the baker boy.

The next day dawned and George and his father, Samuel, went into the back yard to collect their bikes. There was his father's trusty boneshaker but next to it rested George's bicycle, no longer in its glory - its tyres had been viciously slashed. Looking back at the house, through hot tears threatening to spill, George saw the net curtain twitch in the dark kitchen.

A sad assessment carried out by his father determined that the tyres were beyond repair and that nothing could be done to rectify the situation especially since the day was a Sunday. Money had to be saved for replacements and it would be several weeks before he was to know the joy of riding his bicycle. Back in the house, the balance of power had been restored; the Master's attention had been reverted once more to his wife, the Mistress, to her satisfaction. Samuel had been placated by Daisy's offered supposition that someone must have come over the back wall and done the deed. But George knew differently, he had seen the empty space by the green metal water pump where the scullery knife usually lay.

That Daisy thought she could manipulate my dad. And she was right. But he did get his way in the end over the pit. He never let me go down there.

"George, aren't you going to eat your lovely fish and chips?" said Nurse Carter, breaking through his thoughts.

"I have to eat my pudding first then I'm allowed to eat my dinner," he answered, pointing to his dinner plate and removing the red onion garnish absent-mindedly.

Chapter 9
Chocks away

George

All those years ago, sitting at Daisy's table, George was passed a cracked plate. Sitting on the blue willow pattern design had been slopped a portion of suet pudding speckled sparsely with currants and liberally with fat globules. As unappetising as it looked, he ate without reserve; he had cycled ten miles, done a full day's work with very little to eat during the day, just a fold-over of stale bread smeared with dripping. The pudding was eventually consumed, heartily assuaging the pangs of hunger that had assailed him all day and leaving him with a satisfying sense of fullness. He ate alone, the last member of the family to return home from work; his meal had been kept warm on a covered plate over a pan of hot water. He took his pudding plate to the kitchen and returned to the table with his equally unappetising dinner. This consisted of two boiled potatoes, some limp pale green cabbage leaves and one thin slice of meat. This was how the old trick worked: you filled up on the cheap, stodgy pudding so you ate less of the expensive protein.

In spite of the poor quality of the meal, to George it was a vast improvement on the meals he had endured when he was a school boy. Now that he had gained the status of wage earner in the household, the family dynamics had begun to change radically. Suddenly he was an important asset who was to be kept fed and kept healthy to keep the wage packet coming into the household or more precisely, into Daisy's hands.

George's first job was at H. Seal and Company in Whitwick, a firm that made knitted elastic and rigid webbing material for various civilian and military purposes. He did not work on the factory floor as he had anticipated, but in the office. He was to be a white collar worker, an elevated position earned through the recommendation of his headmaster who, disappointed that George had not gone to grammar school, did his best to help him up the career ladder. George, grateful that he had been spared the horror of working down the pit, enjoyed the work that began as general office boy, doing errands, making tea and sharpening pencils but later developed to general clerical duties and then to book keeping and managing customer accounts. His neat handwriting, his love of order and his ability to develop new systems were all qualities well matched to the demands of the job. His manager made it plain that he was more than satisfied with his promising young employee and gave him increasingly challenging tasks to perform. This was underscored when George was given a position of trust within six months of joining the firm, as he was sent to assist the Head of Finance organise the wages on pay day. This duty was carried out in the confines of the inner sanctum of the Counting House where the company's black metal safe was located.

In hushed tones, the Finance Manager would read from the large and heavy employee ledger with its thick cover and page edges decorated with marbled ink, the wage earned by every individual who worked for the Company. George would then set up the amounts due to each employee in stacks of coins and pound notes, ready to be checked by the Finance Manager before they were placed into small brown wage packets. George's own pay packet was light in comparison to that of some workers but heavier when balanced against a few. Fair, he thought. What was not fair was that the bulk of whatever he earned went into his stepmother's purse, even his bonuses. He had to hand over his wage packet sealed and his stepmother would tear it open and extract a tiny sum that she would give him as a weekly allowance. To redress this unfair balance, he came up with a plan.

His job gave him access to wage envelopes so he would leave work on a Friday with a spare one in his pocket. Then, on his cycle ride home, he would stop by the side of the road and open up his wage packet, remove any extra pay he had received and put the bulk of his wage in the new envelope which he would then seal and deliver, as usual, to his stepmother. The sense of achievement that this crafty plan gave him far outweighed the value of the pennies jangling in his pocket. For George now aged almost fifteen, these were moments of victory on the path to freedom.

Over time, these victory coins accumulated and on one special Saturday in May, George spent them on something that was to take him further along that freedom path. It was Empire Air Day and to celebrate the work of the RAF there was to be a demonstration of aircraft at the airfield formerly used during the First World War at Desford, a village within cycling distance of Ibstock. He had always been fascinated by the idea of man-powered flight and when, on rare occasions, he saw an aircraft overhead he became transfixed by the sight, straining his eyes to follow its path until it vanished in the clouds. His interest was further fuelled by his love of reading adventure books like his favourite blue cloth bound edition of '*Flying to Fortune*' in which cunning spies and dastardly crooks fought it out in flying machines over the pyramids. So it was with great excitement that he cycled the lanes on a spring day blessed with the brightest sunshine that made the grass, jewelled with drops of dew, look unreal-the colour of paint box viridian. As he neared the airfield he heard a sound reminiscent of bees, large angry bees; then, looking up, he saw a biplane. He stopped his bicycle to watch it swoop like a bird of prey towards the ground then abruptly change direction and soar upwards until it was a tiny speck in the intense blue sky.

Following the noise of machinery, he soon found the airfield and leaned his trusty bicycle against the hedge, unable to take his eyes off the spectacle before him. Here were the machines of his imagination; these were the magical devices that could take you up to the clouds to a place where the birds flew.

George joined an increasing crowd of spectators as they sauntered around the aircraft that included biplanes like the one he had just observed, and the more modern monoplanes. The air was pungent with the exciting smell of hot oil and the heady dope mixture used to finish the skin of some of the wings, making them watertight. There were two machines lined up next to each other that, thanks to his collection of cigarette cards, George could name. He had never seen the real things before, but without a doubt these were: the *Miles Majester* known by the crews as '*Maggie*' and the *Avro Anson.* Groups of enthusiasts, mostly youths like him, stood around in awe studying these apparently flimsy craft and asking questions of the pilots who with their sheepskin flying jackets and leather helmets, took on the stature of heroes.

There was a red and white striped canvas booth nearby where a queue had formed and George went to investigate. With his heart beating fit to burst, he discovered that not only was there the chance to go up in an aeroplane on offer, but that he had enough money to accomplish such a wish. Without further thought, he bought his ticket and waited impatiently for his turn; sitting on a bench outside the booth and watching the machines trace lazy circles above him.

At last, he was walking towards the aircraft with legs that suddenly had trouble supporting him. He was to fly in one of the aeroplanes he had identified earlier, a *Majester*, a monoplane with an open cockpit. He was handed a warm jacket, headgear and thick uncomfortable goggles and once he had donned these, he was roughly hoisted up into his seat and given brief and simple instructions delivered in a no nonsense manner. Basically, he was to strap himself in, stay put and do nothing. Being small and lithe in build, George had little trouble getting himself secure in the tiny space allotted to him in front of the pilot's seat. Then it was time for the ground crew to crank the propeller releasing more intense fumes suggestive of hot latent power from the ear splitting engine, as it burst into life. Wooden chocks were pulled away and the machine lurched forward and began bumping ungainly over the field. As the pilot swung the fragile craft round to gain access to the runway, it seemed to list to one side but quickly righting itself, progressed along the weed strewn track at an increasingly impressive speed. George, his senses overloaded with the experience, was sorely tempted to shut his eyes but his spirit of adventure denied him this retreat and taking a deep breath, forced his eyes to open wide. In the machine, he was now travelling faster than he had ever done before: faster than free-wheeling down a steep hill, faster than falling. Then his stomach lurched, his heart skipped a beat and he knew they were airborne.

What had been ungainly on land became serene in the air. The machine flew. It really flew. At first he could not believe that he was detached from the ground until he dared to look down from the cockpit to see below him the tiny buildings on the airfield, the green cotton wool balls of trees lining the grey ribbon of country lane that he had cycled along earlier. Landmarks that loomed large when he had passed them on his way to the show now seemed to have been miniaturised and scattered on green cloth like a child's game of five stones.

In spite of the noise roaring in the cockpit and the wind tugging at his leather helmet, he felt strangely detached as if his ears were stopped and he had entered a silent world, *the domain of eagles,* he thought fancifully. The exhilaration he felt was like swinging on the best swing in the playground, the old wooden swing that you could stand on and push with your knees until you swung so high you could rise over the top of the metal frame. George could not say how long the flight had lasted. Time had stood still for him during this adventure -his adventure; he was *flying to fortune*.

When at last the pilot took the machine into its descent, George was not afraid when the ground seemed to come up and meet the tiny, disproportionate undercarriage. The aeroplane came to land with a jolt that shook the whole craft, and then taxied on the uneven surface of the field to come to rest in its original starting position. His senses overwhelmed, George was robbed of speech. As he was helped out of his seat, all he could utter was, "That was wizard!"

Chapter 10
A whiter shade of pale

Julie

"I'll get the door, Mum. You stay in the bathroom."

I had been in the process of dyeing Mum's hair a fetching brighter shade of grey, or as the colorant box proudly proclaimed, 'Nordic Silver'. I could not help but smile at this name, imagining svelte, fur clad Viking women, rowing their long boats. Maybe not an appropriate look for a lady in her seventies, or then again, maybe it is. There is no doubt that Mum was beginning to exhibit a great deal of steely determination; once she was focused on an idea, or had embarked on a mission there was no stopping her. She could quickly slip into long boat ramming speed if the mood took her.

I had been humming the tune to '*A whiter shade of pale*' as I finished applying the colour treatment when the door bell had issued its summons. It was as I had feared, on opening the door there was Vera dressed in a jaunty navy and white striped top and white cropped trousers. Her hair and nails were immaculate but it was her face that I was drawn to. Her eyes were as big as my brother's best marbles and moved just as swiftly, taking in every detail of her surroundings. Her mouth was equally on the move all the time; even when she was not speaking, it was constantly altering its expression. Since my father's move into hospital, Vera had regained her toehold of an entry into the bungalow and used it regularly to collect and spread as much gossip as possible. Despite my initially irritated response to her appearance at the door, I had to concede that she did appear to care about Mum, was an excellent human alarm system cum watchdog and as far as today was concerned, caused a distraction which both Mum and I needed.

"Ooh it's you, Julie. Let me in. It's blowing a hooligan out there! What a surprise to see you. Are you staying with your mam?" she smiled inquiringly as if she had not been on intense police style surveillance for the past however many hours and had not recorded my arrival and all my movements since as part of her stake out. She may not have had a pair of binoculars trained on the bungalow but the periscope of a mirror arrangement in her front room gave her a constant stream of reflected information. Such a good actress, she had missed her vocation. I could see her as a Midlands version of Maggie Smith playing *Mrs Malaprop*; she delivered all the best lines.

"Yes, I'm staying for the weekend, Vera. If you'll excuse me, I am in the middle of colouring Mum's hair; hence my unusual outfit."

"Oh yes, Duck. That must be one of yer dad's old pyjama jackets. Very stylish; paisley is it? Well I 'ope yer dad has got plenty of sets of pyjamas in horse-pital. When my friend Marjorie went in to have her Mary-Ellen seen to, if you know what I mean Duck, her down belows – well I never did see her in her own nice nighties. I reckon all yer clothes get spread to the four winds in a place like that. Them care 'omes are even worse. I wouldn't touch 'em with a bath troll if I could help it. Silly me, what am I saying? I mean bath pole. And yer mam, she's in the bathroom is she? I'll just nip along."

Round the corner she went to find Mum sitting patiently on the low white wooden bathroom chair with, fortunately, nary a bath troll or bath pole in sight. She wore another of Dad's old pyjama jackets, her hair plastered down with dye, making her head look smaller than ever. Like a little peg doll, her whole scalp appeared black at this point in the chemical reaction, with drip lines advancing steadily down her forehead. I gave them a gentle dab with a cotton wool ball, trying to rub the stains away. I could tell that she did not like her privacy invaded by her neighbour but she still kept her polite loop of welcome running with a: "Hello. How nice of you to call. How are you today?"

"Ooh Joan. As I said to our Julie, it's blowing a hooligan out there! My washing got dry in no time. I saw you hadn't put yours out. Maybe you are expecting rain. Although that Joy over the road, she said it should be dry for the rest of the day. What are you having done, Duck? Oh I see you're giving yer hair a fresh up."

"Yes. I can recommend this hairdresser but she tells me she doesn't live round here. She came here on the train, just to do my hair."

"It's me, Mum, Julie. I'm not a hairdresser." *Oh God, she's lost the plot again.*

Mum looked at me with a puzzled expression, shrugged her shoulders and did her artificial three note laugh. This tinkly bell 'ha-huh-ha' device was one that suited a vast range of situations and Mum used it when she did not hear what somebody said and did not like to ask them to repeat themselves, or when she was confused, or when she did not want to answer a question, or when she was lost for words, or when she wanted to fill a silence or a gap in a conversation.

"Well, m' Duck I'll go and put the kettle on, even though it doesn't suit me. Ha ha," Vera said with a mime artist's action of pretending to wiggle a kettle over her wiry body. "I expect you'll want a nice cuppatea once our Julie's rinsed that stuff off yer 'ead."

Once 'our Julie' had rinsed the dye out of Mum's hair and towelled it dry, we went into the kitchen to catch Vera looking through the Home Help log book. She had the grace to look guilty but with a twinge of smugness; now she had some more juicy gossip material to take away with her. I sighed with resignation, considering this a trade-off for the distracting entertainment Vera offered. But I made a mental note to put the log in a zippy bag away from probing, prying eyes in future. *Anyhow on with the Vera show.*

"Ooh Joan, do you like my sandals? I got them up the Co-op. A nice little wedge heel but not as high as I used to wear them. Do you remember, Joan, how we gals used ta wear our high heels and them seamed stockings? Cause in them days, our Julie, we couldn't always afford nylons cos they was so expensive. So we used to draw the line in up the back of our bare legs like with brown eye brow pencil. One day I couldn't find me pencil so I made the line with gravy browning mixed with a bit of water and me brother painted the lines on for me with his paintbrush. Trouble was, I got followed by all the dogs sniffin' me legs and lickin' me lines off! Oh it were a scream!

I'll put the mugs on this tray like and I see you've got some of them Hobnob biscuits in the cupboard. We'll ave some of them, they're lovely. But no dunkin' 'em mind cos they crumble something terrible. You end up with a load of sludge in the bottom of yer tea. Can't read yer tea leaves then. Ha ha. We'll take the tray into the lounge and I'll tell you all about the jig-saw puzzle I'm doin' at the minute. It's got five thousand pieces and it's a scene of a beach in Hackabilko or some such place. All them little boats on the sea and all them sunbathers in bikinis. It'll keep me quiet for a day or so."

Whilst Vera rambled, I found myself linking the two ideas idly together in my mind. Two major interests of those attaining senior years are biscuits and jig-saw puzzles. Maybe there is a market for biscuits in the shape of jig-saw pieces? I can see the packets now in pleasant shades of beige with red labels calling the twice baked products catchy names like: 'edgy bits' or 'biscuts' or 'jig bicks'? I continued to ruminate on this half-baked idea that at its conception had seemed vital to patent, when I realised Vera had asked me a question.

"Have you lost some weight, our Julie? Now you don't want to lose too much cos it'll show in yer face. A bit o' fat always helps you look young. Now our Joan, she's got very thin these days, haven't yer Duck? You need a few more chip butties like that one I brought you over the other day."

"Yes that was ver ver nice," said Mum in her best lady voice, with "Ha-huh-ha," the artificial three note laugh again, meaning totally the reverse of what she had just said. I knew the code.

"Anyway, that Joy were telling me her daughter Trixie, you know the one who got so huge she couldn't get into her car, well she couldn't lose weight through dieting like. She just ate too much so in the end, she went into horse-pital and the doctors gave her one of them plastic gastric elastic bands and a stapler in her stomach. They told her like that she was not to eat more than like a tea cup full of food for meals. Not very much I suppose but they know what they are doing these doctors. And apparently there are some foods that you are told not to eat at all, like, not ever again. Well this Trixie, she got fed up with soup and healthy vegetable poo-ray and the like and she fancied one of them pitzzas one night and it came to the house in a big box and them pitzzas is one of the things she ain't supposed to eat. Well she ate it like and now it's all gone pear shaped. Well she has anyway, poor duck!"

By this time, we had arrived at the coffee table in the lounge and Vera was serving us tea. But before she had started to drink hers, she stood up and took centre stage on the round Persian rug. She showed us her sandals again and made Mum try one of them on. "Ooh I remember when our Bill and I were courting, I had a really high pair of 'eels on and we went out dancing. I had lovely legs then, well they're not so bad now are they Ducks? Anyhow, on the way home from the Pallay it were rainin' and we was rushin' to get the last bus like. And then it 'appened. I tripped and me 'eel snapped off. Well then one foot were up here on the good 'eel and one foot were down there. Down at 'eel ha ha! Any road up, I 'ad to walk with the 'eeled foot in the gutter like and the broken shoe with no 'eel on the edge of the kerb. That kind o' balanced me up like. Ooh it were a laugh!"

She entertained us further by walking about the lounge with her one shoe on, limping and swaying her body from side to side to re-enact the rainy-night-lost-heel saga. Mum began to laugh naturally, not her usual artificial three tone cadence. She moved her upper body to match the swing of Vera's shoulders as she sat watching her from her position on the sofa. This entertainment was doing her good and I began to realise how rarely she laughed these days.

Vera returned to her seat, tears of mirth streaming from her eyes, and began to dunk her biscuit dangerously into her mug of tea. "Life is all about taking risks," she said as she skilfully avoided losing the Hobnob in her brew.

The doorbell sounded once again. "That will be the Home Help," I said.

"Oh, one of the nice ladies? They come and see me all the time, Vera. We have little chats and I make them a cup of tea and sometimes a meal, in the microwave," said Mum. As I walked to the front door, I could not stop the wry smile creeping across my lips, aware that aside from the chats, the reality was almost the complete reverse. The carer came to encourage Mum to look after herself, to prompt her to make her own drink and meals. In another way I was heartened, Mum was keeping her dignity and probably did believe that she was attending to her hostess duties, a role she had enjoyed so much in the past.

The carer was called Liz, or so I learnt from the identity card swinging from her blue cord lanyard. She had the friendly open face of one used to working with the elderly. Her engaging smile, cheerful loud voice and brisk manner offered reassurance and comfort. She was certainly having a positive effect on me, and I was not the official recipient. It felt liberating being able to hand over responsibility for a short time. I introduced myself and said that although I was staying with Mum for the week-end and would be doing the cooking, I did not want to cancel the carers' calls aware that routine should be maintained.

"You're right," said Liz. "With your Mum having just started having a Home Help, it's good to keep things going so that she'll get used to us. Ok then I'll just do her medication and write up the log if you're ok to do her lunch? There'll be someone calling in this evening again. That's to make sure she gets herself her tea, take her meds and prompt her to get ready for bed. But I guess it'll be just a short call tonight as you'll be sorting your Mum."

Liz made her way into the kitchen and prepared Mum's doses of medication from the white gameshow style '*Take Your Pick: Take the Money or Open the Box!*' dosette box. I went into the lounge to

71

collect Mum and bring her to meet Liz. It was Vera's turn to watch and she did so with great interest, her marble eyes agog, as she followed us into the kitchen where the action was to take place; the action of a type usually found in pantomime. I was determined that this time there should not be an audience as many times before I had been involved in this thankless task myself and wanted to support the carer by allowing her space to carry out her job. Mum, like a young skittish foal was shy of taking her medication, inclined to buck at every turn. She usually began with child-like extensive and repetitive questioning as to why she had to take every tablet, in what ways was it meant to help her and what effect might it have on her. Then while answers to her questions were attempted, she would roll the tablets around the palm of her hand, and back away to the furthest corner of the room as if playing for time. She was too polite to refuse to take them outright, but she stalled and prevaricated and passively resisted as long as she could until, in the end when you least expected it, she would eventually take her tablets. By this time, the person administering the medication would be considerably mentally challenged, nigh exhausted and probably tempted to take the pills themselves.

So keenly aware of the likely scenario that was about to unfold, I towed Vera out of the kitchen and took her to a holding bay, also known as the dining room.

"Let's give them some space, shall we Vera?"

Vera appeared to go along with my suggestion but throughout the conversation that followed, I knew that she was operating her considerable skill of listening to two things at once. She was ear wigging the kitchen drama as well as having the appearance of engaging with me. How she did it I do not know, but there must be a future for her in MI5 if the acting career does not take off.

For my part I decided to employ a skill I had honed while working with children. With growing confidence I gained eye contact with her and attempted to hold it. This proved impossible as her eyes moved left and right as if she was a cartoon *Captain Pugwash* reading a book- *or perhaps a treasure map in Captain Pugwash's case*, I found myself reflecting. Then I brought myself up short. *She's done it again, she's put me off my stride and as a result I have digressed into Children's Hour circa 1960. How does she do it?*

It was all part of her effective multi-tasking talent that she continued to display as she appeared to take in what I said by nodding and smiling. Ironically, it was me that was taken in. However soldiering or swashbuckling on, I thanked her for coming over to see Mum and gave her the briefest update on Dad on a need to know basis, working on the theory that she did not need to know very much at all.

Eventually, the curtain must have come down on the kitchen pantomime as a very red faced Liz emerged briskly from the wings of the hall, her handbag slung untidily over her shoulder and her car keys rattling in an impatient hand. *Nordic Silver Woman had struck again!*

She let herself out with a brief nod and an expression of hollow victory. I knew that look; it is the same one I wear when I have succeeded in winning a small battle of wills with Mighty Mum but know that I can never win the war.

Mum joined Vera and me in the hall where we had gravitated, thanks to Vera's lodestone instinct for following any action. She looked calm and collected and greeted us with, "Hello, how very nice to see you. Shall we have a cup of tea?"

"Actually, Mum I think it's time for us to have our lunch. Please excuse us, Vera, I think Mum and I need to decide what we shall eat."

"Yes of course, Duck. Well Joan, I'll see you again tomorrow, I'spect. Tar-ra!" Vera trumpeted as she let herself out.

Back in the kitchen, Mum became the all-singing-all-dancing version of herself again as she began her little tap dance on the tiles, singing a chorus of '*Little Mister Baggy Britches.*' I found myself singing along and tapping out the rhythm with a wooden spoon on a saucepan.

We enjoyed a meal of cottage pie with vegetables and ginger pudding with custard, all courtesy of Shire Farm Foods. The excellent firm had thought of everything to delight the jaded palate that had for many years endured the limited variety that chicken and boiled potatoes have to offer. Mum, who usually ate like a linnet, was inclined to devour these Shire prepared meals albeit at the painfully slow pace of one still following her long dead Granny's instructions to the letter; chewing every mouthful at least eight times. Eventually, I was able to clear the plates away and suggest that she sit in the lounge while I washed up. This task took only a few minutes and I was soon entering the lounge with our postprandial cup of tea. However, Mum was not there. A brief search of the bungalow found her in the spare bedroom cum office where she was looking through some of the papers stacked on the table.

"Your Daddy has left all these important things and I don't know what to do with them. He gets very worried about his papers. When he comes home he will want to have them all organised. Could you do it for him?"

"I don't feel I should look at things that are private to you and Dad," I replied.

"You would be helping him. You would be helping me," she said in a sudden moment of clarity and trust.

"Well, let's get our cups of tea and sit down together and make a start. We'll spend an hour reading a few of these papers and sort them into piles. You can be the secretary."

"Yes Boss," she said, giving me a salute, "That will be fun! Ha- Huh-ha," she laughed.

And so we began to go through the paperwork that had been kept so meticulously and sometimes oh so unnecessarily, by Dad. Everything had been saved from the essential household bills to the Readers' Digest's- *you have won a million pounds* letters. For just over an hour, we consigned paper to its appropriate destination: utility bills to the ring binders we found languishing dustily under the table and share certificates to a *size 6 Rita sling back (black patent)* shoe box re- labelled 'shares, important' underlined, in Mum's stylish copperplate handwriting from a bygone age.

Chapter 11
We're looking for a piano

Julie

"Tom? We're looking for the piano, " I said, the receiver cradled in my right hand as I watched Mum wander from room to room, shaking her head and with both arms upraised like a priest at the altar during the Holy Communion service.

Tom, fast as lightning, was right on cue: "*A Piano? Yes, a piano. Not any old pia-no, the one that makes us dance…*" He sang the chorus line down the phone with all the lilting cadence of the Coalville Amateur Operatic Society's production of '*Salad Days*'. Julian Slade would have been so impressed.

"No, no, no Tom. Listen. I mean we've lost the piano. It's disappeared."

*

I was eleven and my sister Janine was nine years old when the piano came into our lives. It was second hand, and had been in the possession of an elderly lady, the one previous careful owner, who had kept the French polished surface at a very high gloss.

My sister, who is very musical, had shown early promise with the recorder and when she expressed the desire to learn to play the pianoforte, our parents - who wanted us to have all the things that they had been denied in their own childhood - arranged for her to have lessons with a local teacher. As the elder sister, it was my role to escort Janine to her weekly piano lesson taken by Miss Silcott in her prefab home at the outskirts of our village. Miss Silcott was the embodiment of the concept eccentric; in fact the word must have been invented purely to describe her. She was a single lady in her sixties who talked of her Victorian parents as if they were still alive and to perpetuate their memory, she sometimes wore their clothing. This extended to her father's tweed golfing plus fours which she found immensely

75

comfortable when astride her motorbike. With her ancient crash helmet and goggles she cut an absurd figure with her grey plaits flying in the wind at speed; and speedy she was.

The prefab reflected its owner; like her it was full of things ranging from the unusual to the bizarre. On the occasion of the first lesson, I had chance to study the interior in detail while Janine was introduced to the instrument and taught the initial notes and scales. Shower curtains hung at the front door and were drawn across the windows; these were in a pale blue plastic printed with goldfish swimming inanely over every pane of cracked glass. There was a homemade rag rug laid before the two bar electric fire and an ancient wooden framed armchair. Against a wall stood a small square dining table and one upright chair on which I had been directed to sit and wait. The only other furniture in the room was the upright piano, which despite sounding out of tune to the point of honky- tonk, was sophisticated in style with elaborate candle sconces formed of filigree brass work that emerged like metal foliage either side of the wooden music ledge. For me, these were its most interesting and elegant features and it would be forever my wish – still to date unfulfilled - to see real candles alight in those magnificent holders on a dark evening.

Abruptly the elegance ended when one's attention was drawn to the top of the piano. Stationed beside a wineglass full of water, there stood a novelty plastic duck on legs wide apart supporting a heavy bulbous yellow bottom. At regular intervals, the vibration from the piano caused the duck to nod its head slowly until its long beak supped from the wineglass before the counter weight in its bottom suddenly jolted it into rocking back upright once again. This appeared to cause Miss Silcott endless amusement and she would chuckle happily to herself calling the duck *'a silly chump'* whilst providing a swanee slide whistle sound effect to the bird's antics. Behind the novelty bird there were, inexplicably, two cuckoo clocks on the wall side by side. Like a 'spot the difference' puzzle in a comic, the two were identical in all but one feature: one was painted in bright colours whilst the other was simply carved wood. They were set for different hours thereby interrupting constantly with their cuckooing, but neither of them, according to my prized Ingersoll wristwatch, kept the actual time.

As the lesson drew to a close, Miss Silcott informed Janine that even though she did not have a piano of her own, she would still be able to practise at home. All she had to do was *pretend* that she had an instrument and tap her fingers on a table, or a desk, or a book – this would be her *imaginary piano*. Then Miss Silcott did something rather extraordinary, she touched a latch on the boxy arm chair so that its whole side swung open like a door, revealing a set of three shelves set into the wooden frame. Contained within were dainty glasses and bottles of glinting liquid. She poured us both glasses of an amber substance from a bottle and encouraged us to drink. Ever the polite girls, biddable and eager to please, we obeyed.

"Mmm. My father's apricot brandy," she said, as if that explained everything. Meanwhile, Janine and I were coughing until our eyes watered. It was to take several lessons before we were to get used to this alcoholic hit at eleven o'clock on a Saturday morning, but only one lesson to learn to enjoy it. For children who told their parents most things, we somehow failed to report this elicit imbibing. The walk home was always a warm, happy and giggly business.

It was time to leave the first lesson and I handed over the ten shilling note for Janine's class. Miss Silcott told me that the following week I would be starting my lessons and that would be a further ten shillings per week and to tell my parents so. My parents were entirely supportive of Miss Silcott and so the following Saturday, I was introduced to the piano and its wonders whilst the plastic bird, cuckoos and my sister looked on. Then at home, like *'The Music Man's'* conned hopefuls of that River City Band, two foolish girls tapped their imaginary pianos to death on every hard surface they could find. Eventually, our parents kindly obliged by procuring our high maintenance elegant wooden, ivory toothed 'lady' who was to grace the wall of the tiny cottage bedroom that we sisters shared. In tone, she was in a different class to the honky tonk from the prefab but even so, she was vetted by Miss Silcott who anointed her ivories with lily of the valley talcum powder and pronounced her a fine instrument.

Janine took to the instrument like a duck to water in a wineglass and was very soon playing Beethoven's *'Für Elise'*. Meanwhile, it soon became clear that I was not similarly talented. Indeed, my imaginary piano made wonderful music in my head but sadly this was not to be replicated on the real thing. Despite the delights of the apricot brandy, I decided that it was time for me to cease having lessons and mentioned my intention to my parents. However, they felt that I should persevere, that 'practice makes perfect,' and that I would regret giving up the chance 'of learning to play our wonderful piano properly.' I was not happy and Miss Silcott was no fool. She had got my drift, picking up on the beginnings of my mini rebellion that was expressing itself in my dog-eared music books particularly the one named *'Gentle Slopes'* that I had defaced by changing its title to *'Gentle Slops'* along with providing an edifying illustration in blue biro. Clearly disinclined to forego the money she earned from teaching me, Miss Silcott resolved to encourage and inspire me with what she described as 'more modern music pieces'. One such was *'I wonder why you keep me waiting, Charmaine?'* a love song from the 1920's. This fell wide of my mark; after all this was 1964 and we were living through Beatlemania at the time.

I plucked up the courage one day, while Janine was flying along the wonky keyboard with Elise and her friends, to face Miss Silcott directly with my final decision to leave. She looked at me with an intensity that almost made me weaken my resolve and replied bizarrely, "Can you swim?" Stunned, with my mouth open like one of the goldfish on her curtains, I shook my head. "Right. Well, next week I'll teach you to swim. Bring a swimming cap and a towel."

I did tell my parents but I think they did not believe me and after all, *I* did not believe me. I knew there was no swimming pool at Miss Silcott's prefab and I did not imagine that even she would plan to transport me to the City Baths on her motorbike. Janine and I arrived full of apprehension to Miss Silcott's door the following Saturday morning.

"Here you are then," she said, tapping out her father's pipe on the jamb of the front door's frame where she had been enjoying a smoke. "In you come. Now Janine, you start your scales. That's it, my girl. Look how straight her spine is, just like my father's poker." She reached for said poker and shoved it up the back of Janine's jumper to illustrate the point. Laughing to herself, she turned to me, "Now Julie, you come out to the back yard with me."

Outside on the slabs underneath the washing line adorned with massive bloomers and Victorian night dresses, stood a wooden stool on which had been placed a red plastic washing up bowl full of water. My new styled swimming teacher directed me to tuck all my long hair into my excruciatingly tight, blue plastic swimming hat and fasten the sensible, but choking, chin strap in place around my puppy fat.

"Now. Swimming is all about moving the water out of the way with your arms, making a space that your body moves into like so." She stood still and exercised the breast stroke with her arms and then took a little jump forward, literally filling the imagined 'space' with her lumpy body encased in Fair Isle. I was told to copy this action and then repeat it whilst she returned to teach Janine. I 'swam' round and round the yard, weaving between the sturdy items of drying laundry. Indoors, the regular scales turned into lilting melodies under Janine's nimble fingers while my dry 'swimming' progressed unhindered by any water. After fifteen minutes, Miss Silcott returned for the second part of the lesson.

"Good. Now take a breath, place you face in the water in this bowl and then turn your head and blow bubbles. That's it. Lots and lots of bubbles."

What Miss Silcott found in the yard at the end of Janine's lesson was a gasping fool looking indeed like a fish out of water. I was told to take off my swimming cap, dry any damp hair with the towel I had brought with me and come inside for a drink. Never had the apricot brandy tasted so good.

To this day, I still cannot swim but I am proud to boast that I can still play '*Charmaine*' on my imaginary piano.

*

"What? The piano in the lounge? When did you last see it?" said Tom.

"Well now I come to think about it, it wasn't here when I arrived on Friday night. I have only just realised as I've been involved with stuff with Mum, you know how it is, and I went to draw the curtains in the lounge this morning and noticed there's a space where the piano used to be."

"I can't think when I last saw it," Tom said. "Like you say, when I visit there are higher priorities like making sure Mum is ok. Is anything else missing?"

"Not as far as I can see…. Well, yet another mystery to solve. Mum said she didn't notice it was missing. Janine is going to be so upset as after all, it is her piano and all her music was stored in the piano stool."

"God, yes. I wonder if Vera knows anything about it? She rarely misses a trick and she would notice if something that large was taken out of the house."

"Good thinking, Tom. I'll have a word. Also, just to let you know that Mum asked me to help sort out Dad's papers. I'll do what I can while I'm here and try and put stuff into logical categories. I guess every payment for every bill will have to go through the Court of Protection?"

"It's such a long winded process, Julie, such a shame that Mum and Dad did not make arrangements for Enduring Power of Attorney when they were in a clear state of mind. It would have made organising the finances so much simpler. As you know, I did try to persuade Dad quite a while ago but he wasn't keen to follow it up without speaking to his solicitor and I was on the point of getting an appointment set up for him at Messrs Bustle & Bustle when everything kicked off. Sadly things have developed very quickly, well in terms of their mental health, and it is now too late. Neither Mum nor Dad would be considered able to make the decision to hand over power to someone else to manage their affairs. So everything will have to go through the Court of Protection," he said with resignation.

"I think I'm gradually getting my head round the process. Well, Tom, I'd better go now as now Mum herself seems to have disappeared and I can hear some ominous rustling coming from the office."

We signed off leaving me feeling guilty that my brother had all our parents' complex financial dealings to take on. As the eldest child, the responsibility had fallen to him, reinforced by the fact that he was the one living the closest to our parents.

I wandered into the office bedroom to identify the source and cause of the rustling; just in time for another shock. The rest of Dad's papers were being gathered up haphazardly and in cavalier fashion, shoved into plastic carrier bags. Then the handles of said bags had been tied up into the tightest of tight knots. Mum had been very busy; at her feet were ten such bulging bags and, with their ties neatly tweaked up in the air, they resembled fat white rabbits. *When did my mother become a bag lady?* On the table, ready to hand, was a pile of supermarket carrier bags neatly folded concertina style into tiny rectangles resembling those plastic rain bonnets that old ladies use to keep their perms dry.

"What are you doing, Mum? I thought you wanted me to sort out Dad's paperwork? You remember we started to do some filing together yesterday."

"Did we Darling? I thought it would be best if I put them in bags then it's easier for the rubbish men."

"Mum, these papers are important. Some of them mean you can get money. Some of them are bills that are waiting to be paid.

Please don't throw them away." I took the bunny bags and stowed them neatly under the table and then squared up the remaining papers as best I could. "Now, that looks tidier. Let's go and have some breakfast."

My mother eventually agreed to follow me to the kitchen but her mood was withdrawn and almost sullen; very different from her presentation of the previous day. I reflected that Mum, who was suffering the absence of her husband of a lifetime, was bound to struggle coping with daily life on her own. Even with the Home Help team in place, it was a challenge for her and brought home the fact of just how vulnerable she had become. If this morning's episode of confusion was anything to go by, Mum's memory was failing and her hold on reality was becoming fragile.

As if to illustrate the point, Mum sat on the chair in the kitchen, the one she used when retreating from her medication at dosette box time, and said:

"I think I may have thrown the piano away."

"How did you do that, Mum? The dustbin men wouldn't have taken it and you wouldn't have been able to get it in the car and take it to the dump." I sensed that I was sounding like a barrister and Mum was in the witness box for a crime that she had forgotten she had committed and so I decided to back-pedal. "Mum, I really don't think you threw it away, maybe someone collected it in a van? Can you remember anything like that happening?"

Mum sat with her thumb nail between her teeth, looking increasingly nervous. I was trying not to show my exasperation as I wondered how on earth we were going to break the news to Janine, when the phone rang. It was Tom.

"Hi Julie, well I have solved the mystery. It transpires that Mum offered the piano to Uncle Jack for our cousin Henry, the one with the pop group. I happened to phone Uncle Jack to give him an update on Mum and Dad and I told him about some of the fun and games we were having like disappearing pianos, and it all came out. He said that Mum had told him it was in her way and nobody in the family wanted it. He then went on to say that he had had to spend a tidy sum on restoring it as the main wooden board that holds the piano wires had warped."

"When did this all happen, Tom, did he say?"

"He said it all happened before Christmas."

"Gosh, that's months ago. It's amazing that we didn't notice before. What are we like? Did he say anything about the sheet music in the stool?"

"I didn't ask him, I was still getting over the shock that he had the piano."

"Well at least I can put Mum out of her misery now and reassure her that the piano has been found. I feel bad as I have been rather cross-examining her."

I put down the phone and went to reassure and cheer up Mum, as best I could. I could tell her that the piano had a new start with the restoration work that had been carried out and that it was being played and appreciated once again.

I found her in the dining room, looking out of the front window onto the driveway. She had put her arms up in the air again, priest-like and was shrugging her shoulders and shaking her head. She turned to me and with a trembling lip said,

"I think I may have thrown away the car."

Chapter 12
The wrong thing done for the right reasons

Julie

I looked at Mum and did not know how to begin. What I saw before me was a person whom I did not recognise as the person I knew as my mother. Certainly the outer shell of my mother was present and there had been times recently when she was a whole person who could communicate with us and be 'Mum' albeit a slightly confused version of 'Mum'. Now her facial expressions were of bewilderment and fear, in a form that had rarely held her features before.

And in this instance, we had been the cause of that bewilderment.

The plan of removing the car from the property had seemed the right course and one that we all considered was absolutely the safe thing to do. We had tortured ourselves with possible likely scenarios if Mum, previously a highly competent and confident driver, got behind the wheel again. The risk factors had increased ten-fold from the minor slips of mislaying the car in carparks. Now we had new fears that in her increasingly confused state, she might cause an accident. She might drive somewhere, become disorientated and not be able to get home. She could become muddled and might drive the wrong way down a one-way street or drive on the wrong side of the road. There had been tales reported in the press of elderly folk in a confused state, driving on motorways in the wrong direction; these stories stoked our fears. Not only did we want to keep our mother safe, but we were anxious to protect other road users.

We had talked to her as tactfully as we could, suggesting that it might be best to keep the car in the garage as we would take her to the places she needed and wanted to go. Her response had been along the lines of: "You think so Darlings, do you? Ha-huh-ha," which meant that she did not think that might be best at all. Like many drivers, her car was her right arm and she could not imagine life without it. Further to this we knew of our mother's strong will forged in Nordic silver, especially evident when about to embark on one of her missions; it would not be easy to deter her from driving anywhere she chose. Therefore drastic action was necessary. The car had to disappear.

Back in the dining room, I sat Mum down and told her that she had not thrown the car away but that it was being stored 'in a nice dry garage'. *Why did I sound as if I was talking to a child?* I spared her the details of the covert operation that took place the week before when her offspring, turned car rustlers for the night, had executed a mission of their own. No doubt our efforts did not escape the crosshairs of the field glasses belonging to someone on permanent alert not a million miles away.

"But it's my little car," she whined with justification that made my every fleeting thought guilt edged.

Just then the doorbell rang. I was never so pleased to hear its chime and I rushed to the door to welcome, I did not care who. It was Vera.

"Ooh me Duck, it's raining stair rods out there. Sorry if I drip on the rug. I've just come to see if yer Mam wants any shoppin' done seein' as how she's got no car now and you don't drive do yer Duck? My end-of-the-world cupboard needs a top up like so I thought I'd go down to the supermarket and get some tins o' peaches, and tins o' red salmon and one of them tri- hangular tins of Danish ham- you know the tins with the little key in – oh yes and some Fred Bento's corned beef. I like to have a stock of them cos you never know do you Duck?"

"Do you know something that I don't then, Vera? Is it nearing the end of the world?" I thought it a safer topic than picking up the car thread in her conversational knitting.

Vera looked at me as if I was daft. "You've not lived through a war, have you Duck? Well those of us what have, always like to keep a cupboard going with stuff just in case it's needed in an emergency. When we were all snowed in after Christmas, I were alright cos I had me supplies put by. I have to check the dates regular like to check if stuff needs eating. Mustn't go over its sell by date – not like me, I'm well past mine! Ha ha. Where's yer mam, Duck?"

Mum appeared at the dining room doorway and greeted Vera with her loop of welcome phrases followed by her three tone laugh. *I think I might have got away with it, for now anyway, just as long as she keeps distracted,* I thought.

"Joan, will yer be wantin' anything from the shop, Duck? I were just tellin' our Julie that I've got ta stock up on me end-of-the-world cupboard."

"Nuts," said Mum with a winsome smile.

"Nuts to you too, Duck! Ha ha! What kind, Duck?"

"Those long jobs about an inch long they look like teeth," sketched Mum in the air.

"I think you mean Brazil nuts, Mum," I offered with the confidence of knowing these were her favourites. "Did you want them plain or chocolate coated, Mum?"

"Oh, plain chocolate coated would be lovely."

"Right oh, Duck. I'll get you some in a nice little paper bag from the sweetie counter." *It must be catching; now Vera's talking to Mum as if she's a child.* It was time for me to step in and be a grown-up.

"Vera, thanks so much. I'm sure Mum would love that," I trilled.

"Don't she want no other food, our Julie?"

"The Shire Farm Foods provide for most of Mum's meals, Vera, and she's well stocked with those, thanks."

I was at the dismissing bay, with my fingers in position to turn the door handle when she dropped the bomb that she had bounced when she walked in. "I see yer car's been took away, Joan. First yer piano and now yer car."

Catching the piano reference grenade she threw, I held on to it for dear life.   "Yes, the piano seems to have disappeared and Tom and I thought you might have seen what happened?" I asked her.

Mum had wandered into the kitchen at this point and so, in sotto voce and with the miming and silent mouthing of a mill girl, Vera began: "Yes, Duck I seen what happened. A van drew up, one of them rentovans with nowt written on the side. Then a man gets out o' it and he kisses, yes he kisses yer Mam on the cheek like. Then out comes the piana a good half hour later with the man and a younger fella – ooh they were struggling with it. Anyhow they got the tail end down and the piana, she goes on, and up it goes. Then on goes the piana stool and they got like a blanket put over it all so it'll not get scratched I s'pose. Then off it goes and yer Mam she waves it off like. Who do you reckon it were then Duck?"

"We've discovered that Mum's brother has the piano as Mum did not want it anymore. Anyway, look there's a gap in the showers,

Vera. I won't hold you up as you'll be wanting to do your shopping. Thanks for calling in." I held open the door and she stood on the threshold looking to right and left like a seasoned commando before making a dash to her own little car.

Chapter 13
The Saints go marching in

Julie and Joan

"Off for another Gibbet Roundabout weekend, Julie? You look a bit white round the gills."

I was having lunch with my Line Manager, Sarah, in her office. We both picked disinterestedly at the healthy contents of our respective plastic boxes that had started life holding unhealthy takeaways. In the busy Student Support Department of a college, we usually worked through lunch but occasionally we grabbed ten minutes on Fridays to meet and catch up with news. Sarah, ever perceptive, had come to know me very well and could read all the signs no matter how I tried to hide them.

"You bet - and it's an important one- I'm taking Mum to visit Dad in hospital on Saturday."

"Rather you than me," she said, pushing her long blonde hair away from her face and giving me an earnest look full of empathy. *No wonder the students feel they can share all their worries with her,* I thought. She continued, "that long journey on the train with all the emotion at the end of it to deal with - and after all the stress we've had this week!"

"It has been particularly frenzied, hasn't it?" I agreed.

"We just met the deadline for applications by the skin of our teeth – up to the wire we've been. At least we've done the best we possibly could to obtain all those special exam arrangements that our disabled students need so much to make it fair for them. Mind you, there's bound to be last minute requests from some of our able bodied students. Why *must* they go skiing during the holidays? I bet it'll be like last year when two students with broken arms walked in on the day of their exam and we had to get on the blower to the Exam Board to get them special arrangements at the last second. Do you remember we needed two extra scribes pronto? "

"Fingers crossed that if that does happen, those with broken arms are sitting exams in something easy for our scribes like English or History and not Further Maths –or a foreign language!" I hoped.

" Yes indeedy. Well we'd best get on. Call in when you're ready to go at the end of the day."

Friday afternoon flew by with the same energy and speed as Matt passing my office window in his power chair. He was in the vanguard of the students leaving on the dot of four thirty. For me there was no such urgency to get on my way. That would require leaving my cosy office - the small room with the bright orange pin board adorned with a photograph of my intrepid hero, Ernest Shackleton. To emulate him, to go forth to explore (not the South Pole but the East Midlands) did not float my boat at that particular moment. *I guess dear old Ernest had similar problems with his boat,* I thought with a stupid wry smile on my face. I lingered in the department foyer checking that computers were switched off and the batteries for the hoist and spare wheelchair were put on charge and all the windows were closed. It really was time to go. I looked through the arrow slit window in Sarah's door and saw that she was in the middle of a phone call, so I entered the room quietly. She waved and mouthed, 'Good Luck' and as I could find no reason to drag a delay out any further, I set off on the ten minute walk to the railway station.

*

Meanwhile up in Leicestershire, Joan was having a good day. She had just eaten ginger pudding from the Shire Farm range and it was taking her back down a delicious memory lane. Growing up at the bake house meant that the comforting smell of warm yeast and sugar was always in the air. This had been almost replicated by the waft from the microwave when she opened its white plastic door.

She had been just a teenager when she had made that little felt pill box hat, working on it during the rare slack moments in the baker's shop. *Then when Granny B gave me that little scrap of fur, I attached it all around the crown so that I had quite the stylish creation like the one featured in Women's Realm. Then came the very best moment when I had my photograph taken with my hat, that profile photo looking up to the sky like the film stars did. Then I gave the photograph to George and it was as tiny as a postage stamp and he placed it in his wallet.*

I will never forget how he looked in that air force blue uniform. During that dreadful time of war we often saw troops on leave walking about the village but the distinctive soft blue flying uniform was a rare and exotic sight. Already a handsome man with thick black curly hair and deep brown eyes, the uniform made him something very special. We were in awe of what he could do; he could fly aeroplanes. An RAF volunteer, he had not waited for his call up papers and this further gained our respect. He'd courted other girls before me and I wanted him to remember me when he was away on service and I hoped the picture would play its part. It must have done because he wrote such lovely letters and sent a post card which had printed on it, 'to my sweetheart' with a picture of a flower garden and a girl in a big straw hat – that made me so embarrassed and proud all at the same time. I did miss him so much while he was away but life was busy with helping Mum with my younger brothers and serving in the baker's shop.

I wanted to do my bit for the war effort too and so one day, without telling my mother, I went into Leicester on the bus and put in an application to be trained as an auxiliary nurse. I was so excited that I was going to do something really useful rather than just sell bread and look after my brothers. But then, when proudly I told my parents what I had done, they announced that yet another baby was on its way and that as the eldest child and Mother's helper, I was needed at home. I was told to forget any high flown dreams of going away to join a service. I was heart-broken.

Then that young man from the church choir invited me to go to a dance with him and my mother said that I should go out and have some fun for once, so in the end I agreed. Then George came home unexpectedly for forty eight hours' leave and when he found out about Harold, that was the choir boy's name, he said that he didn't want me going out with anyone else. It was then that he asked me to marry him. It was so romantic.

We had to wait until I was twenty-one before we could get married. By that time, he was twenty-four and the war was over. It was 1947.

*

Ding dong! I had pressed the doorbell maintaining the pretence that I did not have my own set of keys to the bungalow and that Mum was still mistress of her own home. It took several ding dongs and some firm raps on the front door with a clenched fist before she heard me and opened the heavy plastic double glazed portal. She had the blinking eyes and creased rosy cheek of one who had just dozed with her face resting on her hand. I was surprised to find that her hair looked tidy. Just lately, she had stopped caring about her appearance. Today she had made an attempt to put on some make-up although the effect was old fashioned, definitely not her usual look. She had applied an orangey coloured face powder thickly and her lips were painted a very bright shade.

"What a lovely surprise. How nice it is to see you." The welcome came from her stock of phrases that were becoming predictable, reminding me of the treasured doll that belonged to my childhood friend, Molly-Anne. The doll had a ring attached to a cord that emerged through a hole in its plastic back. Every time you pulled out the cord, the dolly uttered a set of phrases in sequence: *Mam-ma I want a drink... Mam-ma I love you...Can I play with you?... I'm very tired... Please put me to bed.* Molly-Anne and I played with the doll for the whole of one sunny afternoon, following its every request: getting it drinks, playing with it and putting it to bed. To us little girls, she was real. Then the ring came away from the cord which in turn disappeared irretrievably into the plastic body cavity and the doll talked no more.

"Hello, Mum. I've come to stay for the weekend. I'll just put my bags in the spare bedroom." Mum followed me around the bungalow; I do not think she was completely certain of who I was or entirely convinced that my presence was benign. I let her look through my bag; she was especially drawn to my cosmetic purse which she rifled through with interest. "If you like, Mum, tomorrow we can go to the shops and look at the make-up. I don't expect you have bought any for a while." I remember how frugal she was with cosmetics, never throwing even a tiny stub of a lipstick away until she had scoured the plastic tube of its last dregs of fatty colour with a hair grip. Tomorrow I was determined to treat her to a new set of make-up; that would cheer her up.

Eventually, via the kitchen and after the tea making ceremony, I made it to the lounge with Mother in tow. She asked me how the family was and I was delighted to give her the latest news of James' plans for his school, of Simon's latest girlfriend and of Lizzy's latest boyfriend. "That's lovely, Darling. How is your mother?"

The next morning, I tried to be like Shackleton, to shore up my flagging spirits by drawing on my dwindling bank of optimism. The previous night I had been fooled; I had really believed that within an hour of my arrival, Mum knew who I was. Maybe she did in flashes, when connections and patterns suddenly emerge like the ones you see in a child's kaleidoscope. She certainly could not sustain a memory of me as me; it was tragically disconcerting. But onward and upward, *must keep going, think of Shackleton,* we were about to embark on our own perilous journey and who would know what might happen at our destination?

We walked to the railway station at the bottom of the hill and took the train to Leicester. Although I had done this journey with her before, it seemed a novel experience to Mum and she looked around the carriage with wide eyed interest. She asked questions about where we were going and what we were doing, adopting the form of address she would use to a polite stranger. I checked that I was not wearing the navy blue of a carer's uniform – Janine had made that mistake once with disastrous consequences – no, I was safe wearing black trousers and a maroon top. Once we had left the train and made our way to the station concourse, Mother seemed to get her bearings and look more confident.

Our first port of call was the shopping mall close to the popular local landmark, the Clock Tower. I wanted Mum to look her best before she met Dad and there was a little shopping to do to help that along. En route to the department store, we both noticed an ice cream parlour. Mum was excited by the appearance of this and I suggested that we should have an ice cream when we had done our shopping. Her reaction was childlike in its anticipation for such a treat on a cloudy day, further highlighting the role reversal that now seemed irrevocable. She put her arm through mine and seemed to grasp a connection between us and I dearly hoped that it was not fleeting.

At the make-up counter, a young assistant with a burnished golden face promoted the latest products in the cosmetic range. Mum began sampling the testers from *Vamp Red* to *Naughty Nude* with the enthusiasm of a child playing with a new box of crayons. Meanwhile like Vera, I was now practised in the mill girl art of talking soundlessly with mouth, eyes and eye brows and I was able to convey to the assistant that a good moisturiser and natural shade of foundation were what we were interested in purchasing. The bronze beauty quickly caught on and offered the rich moisturiser for Mum to try. Mum smoothed it into the thin, translucent skin on the back of her hand and then on her forehead, pronouncing that it was, "lovely, Darlings." In similar fashion, the liquid foundation was experimented with until Mum's face was transformed from a vision of papery dehydration to moisturised healthy shine - much more like the Mum I remembered.

With renewed spirit, we took the escalator to Ladies' Fashions. Then came a sparkling reminiscence from Mother that had a similar effect to that of opening a dull, dusty window to let in daylight. "Do you remember the first escalator you rode on when you were a little girl? It was at London Airport. We used to go and meet your daddy when he came off service. We would go up the escalator – except you would call it the *essle-clator*- to the waving bay and see his plane land and then after all the passengers had left, he would walk down those aircraft steps- the ones that were moved from plane to plane on wheels- and then across the tarmac and you children would wave to him and then he would look up and see us."

"I remember," I murmured, my throat thick with emotion.

The Ladies' Fashion Department was having a sale and so I encouraged Mother to pick out some items that she liked and then, gathering them in my arms, sought the changing rooms with her following in my wake. We were able to procure the largest cubicle at the end of the small corridor and hang the clothes on the pegs provided. Mum was now slight of build and a standard size and so I knew that most of the items would fit her and she would enjoy selecting the ones that suited her best. Whilst she removed her dress, I got a navy and white flowered two-piece ready and turned to help her step into the skirt. It was then that I noticed she had neglected to wear any knickers.

"Mum, I'll be back in a moment," I said as I left the cubicle swiftly in search of a pair. I was in considerable shock; usually even the chickens wore knickers in Mother's world. Quickly purchasing a pack of waist high briefs in assorted colours from the lingerie stand, I returned to the changing room fully armed. The scene that greeted me resembled a mini jumble sale with Mum working her way through the garments, rejecting some and selecting others for a second viewing in the large looking glass. I opened up the lingerie pack and she studied the briefs with a bemused look on her face. "I thought you might catch cold walking around without your knickers, Mum."

"Really, Darling? Don't I have any on?" she chuckled her highly adaptable three tone cadence. I was able to persuade her into a white pair eventually; she rejected the black and navy briefs telling me that they were men's underpants and certainly not meant for ladies. Apparently, in Mother's world, proper women only wore pastel coloured underwear; *I guess that applies to spring chickens as well.*

After nearly an hour, we emerged from the store with full shopping bags; Mother in the make-over splendour of her navy flowered outfit and new knickers. We celebrated with the promised ice cream and then we were ready for the main purpose of the excursion: to visit Dad.

My plan was for us to travel to the hospital by taxi. I remembered that there was a taxi rank in Granby Street so we set off to walk there, amongst the throng of Saturday shoppers. The city seemed particularly busy that day and we had to walk arm in arm for fear of getting separated. Such a prospect could prove disastrous: losing a confused mother in a crowd; a fragile, deaf and bewildered old lady who did not carry, or indeed know how to use, a mobile phone. So with arms closely linked we found ourselves being swept up Granby Street by the sheer force of the shopping multitude. I have never been to a rock festival but this experience of being physically moved by the crowd must be similar to being in a mosh pit at Glastonbury. My foolish mind, light headed with stress, toyed with the thought of Mum and I doing a spot of crowd surfing - after all we were fully equipped now that Mum was wearing underwear. It seemed we had no will of our own; we had to go where the shoppers were heading and fortunately that seemed to coincide with our planned route along Granby Street. However, it was at the point when we were literally cheek by jowl with the populace of Leicester city and a strand of my hair had become caught around the jacket button of a handsome man three people away from me, that Mother decided to say in the loud stage whisper of one who is hard of hearing: "There are so many black people round here. Look. Everywhere you look. Everyone is black."

Anger, frustration and shame overcame me and in nought to sixty seconds I began delivering a heart-felt discourse on racial equality. I looked deep into my mother's eyes and told her in no uncertain terms that she must embrace the rich multicultural society in which we lived. I hoped that I had created a metaphorical fire blanket with which to smother the worst effects of her remark and that the people currently sharing the same limited air space with us, would be forgiving.

Mother gave me a look of pure innocence. "But," she said, "I was just saying everyone around us is black. That's all."

It was then that I looked around me and saw what she saw. We were no longer on the pavement, but in the middle of the road and were surrounded by hundreds of young black men. As the thought began to dawn on me that they had not come to do a little shopping, a drum started to beat loudly in the rhythm of a march. Simultaneously, placards were brought out from behind marching legs to be held aloft, blooming and swaying above our heads. Then the chanting began, much of it directed towards the cordon of police officers who had materialised on either side of what was clearly a column of protesters plus two bemused females who had unwittingly joined the fray.

"O-oh we're kettled and I don't know how we are going to get out," I thought out loud.

"Yes, I would like a cup of tea, if only we could get out of this crowd," said Mum, valiantly misunderstanding.

I thought to myself that my son would know what to do. He had crowd-surfed in at least one mosh pit. Mother was beginning to look scared and I realised that I had to be the grown up. I could see the elegant frontage of the Grand Hotel emerging to our right and decided to make my move. Taking a firm hold of Mum's arm with the determination of a salmon on its upstream journey of a lifetime, I began negotiating my way diagonally across the throng towards the pavement with, " Er, please excuse us. Thank you. Please let us through. Thanks very much. Oh dear was that your foot? I'm so sorry. If I could just ask you to move to one side so that we can come through? Thank you. So kind." Whether it was the (by now almost feral) look on my salmon blushed face or whether it was out of sheer pity, the young men gently allowed us passage so that we cut a swathe through their number until we, like the proverbial chickens, had crossed the road. There before us was a female police officer who guided us to the refuge of the hotel entrance.

"Shall we put that kettle on now?" said Mum.

Placating her with the promise of a drink once we got to the hospital, I approached a taxi parked in a side road. The driver told me that he would have to make a lengthy detour to avoid the march's route to Victoria Park and I replied that I would be happy to take a sling shot detour round the dark side of the moon rather than repeat the experience we had just endured. I sat in the back with Mother, sinking gratefully into the well sprung seats, rubbing the sore patch on my scalp where once there had been a strand of hair and forgot to be anxious about our destination.

All too soon the hospital loomed large in the taxi's windscreen and our golden hiatus was over; on with the action.

"Where are we and why are we here?" asked Mother. I explained that we were going to see George and we would have that cup of tea I had promised. She came with me willingly and stood with her perfect posture and regal bearing while I spoke to the now familiar well upholstered nurse on duty at her desk in the entrance foyer. She remembered me from my previous visit and equally warmly welcomed Mum, saying that she was sure Mr Ellis would be pleased to see us both. Mother smiled in her own bewildered way and then nodded elegantly whilst simultaneously discharging her three tone laugh. *Off we go into Alice's Wonderland,* I thought, *and there through the security glass is the white rabbit in a pink and white outfit.*

Once the security procedure was followed and the door opened, we came face to face with the tiny lady in a pink skirt and frilly white top; our Meeter and Greeter was there again and as soon as she saw us, she started her loop of repetitive phrases. "How wonderful of you to visit me! It's been such a long time since I've seen you both. How are you? Now what's your name? I'm afraid I forget names these days but I never forget a face," she pattered.

To Mother this was an open invitation to do what she does best and she engaged immediately. "Well how wonderful to see you. It's such a long time since I've seen you. How's your mother?"

"Mum, do you know this lady?" I said.

"Well, I'm afraid I forget names these days but I never forget a face," Mum echoed.

"So you know this lady's face, then?" I asked Mum.

"Ha-huh-ha," emitted Mum, uncomfortably.

I found that looking from one confused lady to another equally confused lady was causing a crick in my neck akin to the effects of Wimbledon whiplash. It was time to be assertive and I thanked the Meet and Greet lady and assured her we would know her next time but that we could not talk any longer as we were on our way to visit someone. This did not seem to make any impression on her and she opened her mouth to start another loopy loop of doll phrases. So working on the theory that actions speak louder than words, I took Mum's arm and set off purposefully down the never ending corridor. Mother gave a royal wave with her free hand in her new friend's direction. With a swift backward glance I saw our fluffy pink and white sentinel reluctantly resume her position at the secure entrance, poised to loiter.

This time, I knew what was down this particular rabbit hole and drew Mother along with me at a smart pace until we arrived at the main patient lounge where once again, tea was being served. Our friendly Minotaur was about his business, gently passing drinks and biscuits to his charges who received them with varying degrees of interest. With barely suppressed delight, I spotted Dad just leaving the far side of the lounge on his way to the connecting corridor, no doubt planning to take his drink to enjoy in his favourite side ward. I took Mum's arm and we set off to follow him.

"Where are we going? I thought we were going to have a cup of tea?" said Mum, clearly agitated.

"We're going to find George and then I'll get you a cuppa to enjoy with him. *Don't worry.*" The latter phrase I said to myself, those few words had become a mantra.

We were soon able to catch up with Dad who was slowed down by the fragile burden of his cup of tea, like a competitor in an egg and spoon race. I gave him a hug but before I could say anything, Nurse Carter appeared and gently taking charge of Dad's cup and saucer ushered us all into Green Room One. Here she settled Dad into one of the three armchairs and placed his cup of tea on the low table in front of him. Then she turned to greet Mum, offering her the chair beside him.

Mum looked at Dad. Dad looked at Mum.

I could not bear to watch. *What if they did not know each other?* Just in case an introduction was needed, I laid some clues: "I'll go and get some more tea so that Mum and I can join you in a drink Dad," I said, simultaneously pointing to Mum when I said 'Mum' and pointing to Dad when I said 'Dad'. I hoped that did the trick; *light the blue touch paper and then retire to a safe distance.* Nurse Carter and I left the room and walked together towards the main lounge.

"That'll be interesting," said the nurse. "It's good to give them some space to let them have some time together. This must be the first time they have seen each other since your father's admission to hospital."

"That's right. Mum is in a fragile and confused state herself. As a result we have not rushed to bring her to see Dad in hospital, fearing that the shock of seeing him so confused may set her back even further. When we saw that he seemed more settled in himself, we felt it appropriate to give it a try. I feel bad about being in control of my parents' lives."

"Well I don't think you should see it that way. I would see it as you helping to manage your parents' situation that is both complex and emotional. There are no easy answers or solutions where mental health is concerned."

I asked about Father's medication and discovered that he was taking fewer tablets than before he came into hospital. Apparently he no longer required his heart medication as the symptoms he suffered were now thought to have stemmed from anxiety rather than angina. *All those tiny tri-nitrate tablets taken unnecessarily, placed under the tongue… all that TNT - well- gun powder,* I thought, finding this all bewildering. It was as if I really had gone through Alice's looking glass to find everything topsy-turvy; what I had hitherto accepted and believed as fact and truth had now turned out to be false.

Nurse Carter left me by the tea trolley having instructed our friendly Minotaur to arrange for two more cups of tea. I took them from him gratefully and set off back to Green Room One. On the way I had to run the gauntlet of various patients reaching out for the cups in my hand. It was then that I realised that I was wearing a maroon coloured top, the very same colour as the tabard sported by the Minotaur and the other nurses in the ward. I made a mental note to wear skybluepink with orange spots for my next visit.

I entered the Green Room gingerly to find Mum cradling Dad's empty cup.

"I'm afraid I drank the tea," said Mum who was sporting a pair of large lensed men's aviator spectacles. *Where had they come from?*

"She took it before I had the chance to drink it," said Dad.

"Never mind," I said to him. "Here's a cup you can have." I passed him the tea and Mother lifted her dainty hand to take the second cup. *I'll do without a drink,* I thought, *anything, as long as it makes Mum happy.*

I perched on the third armchair and tried to get this party started. It was not clear whether they had spoken to each other whilst

Nurse Carter and I had been out of the room. With no conversational topics currently being aired, I went to my default setting by mentioning the weather. They both agreed that it was cloudy and that the recent rain would have benefitted the plants. Dad told us that his garden was looking good and that he would show us round it later. I assumed that he meant the flower beds that could be viewed through the window of his favourite side ward.

"So how have you been keeping, Georgie Darling?" asked Mother. *This is a good sign, one of normality,* I thought. Dad reported that he was feeling "more the thing" and began to talk about the other people in the building, how they could not be trusted and he was not prepared to talk to some of them. He said that he was polite to most of the others "on the project" but he had decided that it was best not to let them get close as "you did not know what they might do with any information they learnt from you." To defuse the intensity of what was likely to become a monologue detailing his extra suspiciousness, I told Dad about my children and my husband, with little snippets of news that might amuse or entertain. He smiled to himself but did not react naturally to my chatter. Mum looked on passively, punctuating the conversation, which in itself was in danger of becoming my own intense monologue, with her three tone laugh. I felt like that nervous Dutch boy with his hand in the dyke wall, necessary to plug the gap, but incapable of holding back the water for ever.

And then the dyke was breached and out the water gushed as Mum, from her well- worn loop of phrases selected, "What have you been up to today, George?" And Dad commenced his report, telling us both about the new project that he was working on. In a few seconds it seemed to me that we were transported back to the seventies again, sitting at the round pine table in the kitchen diner, our faces bright in the corona of the orange glass lamp suspended low over the salt and pepper pot and the carved wooden fruit bowl. All those years of therapeutic confession, nightly over family supper, were being re-run. And as if Mum was literally transported, she listened and nodded and encouraged Dad to continue just as if the narrative was fresh and new and she had just returned from her day in the Treasury department at County Hall. This was heady stuff, so very tempting to pretend that this was reality; this replay of that shared cosy existence when life seemed so much simpler. So for a time I went with the flow, joining Mum nodding away like some television interviewer, while Dad spun his tale of a day in the life of the long lost office. A kind of peace settled on us all and my mind recaptured the thoughts of my teenage self and wondered what had become of her - that person I once was before college, teaching job, marriage, children...

The bell rang to mark the end of visiting time and to transport the mental time machine back to the present.

"Time for us to go now, Dad. Would you show us the garden on our way out?" I felt we should take our leave gently and in stages.

Father led us out of the Green Room, Mother tripping over the coffee table on the way and stumbling along the corridor behind him. *Poor thing, all this is taking its toll on her emotions.* I linked arms with her and supported her to the door that opened out into the courtyard garden. Blinking in the bright light, I turned to Mum to see if she was similarly affected and then realised that she still wore men's aviator spectacles on her pert little nose.

"I think you might find it easier to see where you are going without those glasses, Mum." I removed them from her face gently, making a mental note to hand them in to the duty nurse on the way out. Dad indicated with a wave of his hand, the patches of flowers and shrubs saying that sometimes he had the job of watering them. There was another old man in the corner of the courtyard with his back turned who was clearly doing the job himself although without the need of a watering can or hose.

"Oh dear," said Mum. "I think that gentleman has forgotten how to use a toilet. Ha-huh-Ha."

"The things you see when you haven't got your gun," said Dad.

Chapter 14
The way the river ran

Julie

Tom met me at Coventry's railway station carpark in his luxurious vehicle. After standing for two hours in the crowded chilly corridor outside the toilet on the cross-country service, I was more than grateful to sink into the embracing comfort of the low leather seats of Tom's top of the range car. In the sporty interior that felt like a snug cockpit, the cold could no longer reach me; indeed it was veritably banished once the heating feature embedded in the front passenger seat was deployed with the flick of a subtly concealed switch. In this cosy, rosy cocoon the journey that I had once predicted to be yet another hollow trip where little was likely to be achieved, gradually took on the optimistic character of becoming worthwhile. I had the company of my big brother and as Mother would say, *what could you wish for better than that?* This must be the archaic version of today's phrase: *What's not to like?*

Travelling comfortably through the outskirts of the city, we talked with ease, catching up on news and trivia of each other's lives. Then as we left the congested city streets behind us and gained the open road into the surrounding countryside, it was time to focus our thoughts on the latest developments in Mum and Dad's situation. We both agreed that Mum seemed to be surviving at home on her own and adjusting to the regular visits from members of the care team, although we could not say she was totally coping or that she was happy. Dad seemed to be calmer in hospital, although still very confused. My plan that weekend was to spend Friday night with Tom and Barbara at their home, then Saturday with Mum at home in Caldron Close, then on Sunday I was to visit Dad in hospital before making my way back down south once again on the cross-country service.

"Do you remember the first time Dad went into hospital?" Tom asked.

"You mean years ago when we were kids? Yes I do. I know we were only young at the time but I do remember that he was admitted because he had kidney stones through not drinking enough water. I guess in his job as member of air crew, he wouldn't get many opportunities to drink a lot of fresh water in those days."

"That's right, Julie. He used to say he was lucky if he got a thimbleful of orange juice during a flight and when he was staying in some places between flights - like Malta or Bagdad, the water was not safe to drink – he used to say he even brushed his teeth with whisky."

"I've heard of some excuses to imbibe early in the morning - that seems a valid one, especially with Dad." We both laughed, safe in the knowledge that Dad would never have over indulged; indeed he rarely drank alcohol.

"But what broke his heart was that the kidney problem led to a failed medical - he always used to be so proud of being 'A1 fit'. Mind you it wasn't long before all the radio officers were made redundant when their role got taken over by new technology in the cockpit. It must have been tough leaving the active side of civil aviation - to have to walk away from the excitement and kudos of the flight deck to work in an office on the ground at Heathrow. It must have been a very bitter blow for all the R.O.'s - to be literally 'grounded'. I think it all affected Dad more than any of us realised at the time," said Tom with tones of regret, his kind brown eyes echoing this sad awareness in the quick glance he gave me before returning his focus to the road ahead.

"And with Mum and three youngsters to feed, his hand was forced and he had to get on with it. I guess he felt lucky to still have a job but it must have been hard to see all those wonderful silver aircraft taking off to exotic places with his mates at the controls while he remained in a stuffy office at the airport," I said, never having thought about the implications before. We had always enjoyed such a happy family life in those *Riversway* days.

*

After all, the childhood that was rolled out for us was charmed and magical despite its eccentricity; free from the bonds of today's Health and Safety rules. We lived in the bungalow, so appropriately named *Riversway*, as the river was always hurrying on its way towards us. Built alongside the Thames in the village of Wraysbury, this rented house was thoughtfully constructed to be raised on a series of brick pillars. These offered the house some defence against the effects of flooding as the river regularly over spilled its banks in the days before the large embankment was created. The village itself was popular with civil aviation employees owing to its proximity to Heathrow airport, which was called rather grandly 'London Airport' then. Wraysbury's location on the banks of the Thames made it a popular resort for weekenders and holiday homes were common in Ouseley Road where we lived. In those days, there was a bohemian atmosphere in the community which supported actors, comedians and others from the world of the Arts. There was a joke my Dad heard on the radio one day, *'Are you married or do you live in Wraysbury?'* It was years before I understood what that meant. Meanwhile, in spite of its reputation for a place where secret and illicit liaisons may have been formed, we were just a simple family of five living there all the time, not just weekends.

We had an actor living next door, whom we called 'Uncle Woody'. With his large girth, ruddy complexion and West Country accent, he was famous for character parts ranging from 'jovial innkeeper' to 'cut-throat pirate' on stage and even on the silver screen in all types of drama from comedy to horror. On television, he played parts in costume dramas and early soap operas. Then towards the end of his career he had his own weekly children's programme where he drew a young audience in his role of master puppet maker. To my brother, sister and I, he played the real life role of avuncular neighbour and, in my case, attentive godfather. He often entertained us by playing tunes on his banjo, its white stretched resonator belly decorated with a painting of a lively trout, resting on his checked shirt which in turn stretched over his own rotund belly. Ever the showman, he would sit on the steps of his bungalow's side entrance framed by a fragrant climbing rose, and pick out a jaunty melody. Meanwhile we jigged and hopped around on the other side of the distressed chicken wire fence that had been buckled by much inter-neighbour-hurdling when on the hunt for a loan of a cup of sugar or jug of milk. Uncle Woody's wife Mary, a tall and elegant lady, would stand alongside him and clap to the rhythm as we squealed for more. Uncle Woody was kind and seemed to know what children liked and enjoyed, giving us discarded film scripts so that we could write and draw on the blank reverse of the neatly typed pages. One particular script that was excellent scribbling fodder for us and lasted a whole school summer holiday, was ominously titled *'The Crimson Blade'*.

Uncle Woody and his wife were good neighbours, providing company and support for Mum while Dad was away on flight duties. In their darkly furnished green interior, with curtains drawn to augment the weak glow emanating from the tiny television screen in its large walnut cabinet, Mum could always be assured of a welcome. With the backdrop of the day's racing at Ascot running its course for an excited, temporarily out of work actor on the edge of his seat, Mother would enjoy the luxury of a cup of Typhoo tea served in a bone china cup and saucer. For this Leicestershire lass formerly of Ibstock Bake House, here was the quality of life to which she had aspired and within those green walls was the affirmation that she had truly arrived.

After all, here she was living amongst interesting people in a place close to the hub of London. Her husband had a good job with prospects and together they had achieved more than they could have possibly hoped for, after the deprivations of the war years.

They had married in 1947 in Ibstock, the village of their childhood; Dad immaculate in his radio officer uniform and Mum resplendent in a pale blue suit after the style of Wallis Simpson. They made plans to set up home in the south of England in order for Dad to continue his post war appointment at BOAC, the airline formed from the merger of Imperial Airways and British Airways Ltd. To begin their new life together they travelled by train to their honeymoon destination: the hoped for seclusion of Cardigan Bay in Wales. Sadly their sense of isolation was to be rudely interrupted when they spied a fellow guest at the boarding house reading The Leicester Mercury at the breakfast table. The long arm of the provincial press had shattered their dream of an exotic retreat far away from their humdrum and humble beginnings.

However, the second part of their escape plan did come to fruition when they made their first home together in rented rooms in Reading. They were living there when Tom was born in a private nursing home the following year, two months before the National Health Service came into being. Shortly afterwards they moved to another rented property, their first home in Wraysbury, a house in Welley Road named *Colborn* to which they always referred wistfully throughout their married life. However, it was a life style fraught with problems.

Tom survived what could only be described by modern standards, as a babyhood at high risk. In those days when personal transport was rare and wartime attitudes of 'needs must' still prevailed, chances were taken. As Dad was based at London Airport, his service rota demanded that he travelled to and from Heathrow at irregular hours, day and night. Occasionally, he was able to synchronise his journey with the timetable of the local Greenline bus service but when this was not possible, he had to use his humble bicycle. This meant that he would cycle to a spot close to the airport environs, park his bike in a carefully pre-selected and discreet spot and then proceed by airport transport to crew check-in. My mother would be tasked to retrieve the bicycle since this highly valued asset could not be left tucked into a suburban hedge for long. Years later she would admit to me, at the time when I was a young and inexperienced mother myself, that she would place baby Tom *"into his pram with the hood up Darling, check he was asleep on his back, his little head resting on his soft pillow, his little body dressed in a tiny gown made of parachute silk, Darling, and wheel him into the garden. I used to stretch the net over the pram to keep off the cats. As there was no one to look after him, I had to be as quick as I could be. I would dash to the bus stop and get the Greenline bus to London Airport which was about five miles away. When I got off the bus, I would find the bicycle where Georgie had told me he was planning to leave it and ride it home, hoping that Tom would still be asleep in his pram when I got back."*

By 1952 the couple had moved to *Riversway*, the bungalow on stilts, where their family increased with my arrival and a little less than two years later, that of my sister, Janine. Meanwhile Tom, who like most infants of the time had never attended a nursery or playgroup, was of the age to start school. My parents chose to enrol him in a private day school in Slough. As a rising five year old, he was dressed in a miniscule blazer and grey flannel shorts and sent off to this prestigious establishment in the next town. Like *'Careful Hans'* of the fairy tale, he left the house on his own and bravely marched the three quarters of a mile to the bus stop where he waited for the Greenline bus that would take him to Slough. He had pennies in his pocket for his bus ticket and fortunately an innate sense of direction that helped him to find his way to school once he had arrived at the town. However, Tom did not enjoy these early days at school where the regime was strict and his left handedness was neither condoned nor encouraged. He became more and more unhappy and unwilling to go to school and his little feet dragged all the way to the top of the road where the bus stop gallows-like, stood. Initially, our parents who had

104

not received a privileged education themselves, wanted the very best for their son and so they encouraged him to get over his negative feelings, saying that everyone had to go to school and that *school days are the best days of your life and that Daddy and Mummy would be sent to prison if they did not send him to school.* He had no option but to put on his hated uniform and set out to the dreaded bus stop to wait for the horrid bus that would take him to the even more dreaded school. This he endured for the best part of a year. Until one day Tom, who has been a brilliant problem solver all his life, came up with his first major solution. Initially, he may not have planned his 'escape' from this unpleasant situation, but a train of events was to give him an opportunity that he clasped with both his little hands.

On one particular morning, he became so nervous about the prospect of school that by the time he had arrived at the bus stop he felt sick enough to vomit spectacularly into the gutter. With sick stains on his little school tie, he returned home and Mother, seeing the clear evidence of illness, kept him home for the rest of the day. When Tom appeared to have recovered by the following morning, he was sent off to the bus stop again. Here, from anxiety or by design, he was sick again and triumphantly returned home. This pattern continued for many days until eventually my parents acknowledged that a change had to be made. Tom was withdrawn from the despised school in Slough and introduced to a cosy establishment based in a large house in the village. Ironically, his new school was situated right by the infamous bus stop which overnight became the harbinger of doom, no longer. This school was more like home with its mini playing field consisting of a walled garden complete with apple trees. The latter tended to get in the way of ball games but were wonderful when it came to playing Hide and Seek or Cowboys and Indians. The teachers were all female and with their motherly approach and tolerance towards his left–handed writing, Tom began to prosper at last.

*

During my Friday night stopover, Tom and I had spent many hours reminiscing, comparing memories of childhood. Born four years apart and with entirely different perceptions and experiences, we had cause to wonder about many aspects of our shared past.

"It's still true that the eldest child certainly has to cope with a lot!" I said to Tom as we drove into Caldron Close on that Saturday morning. "Parents try out all their ideas on the first born and the ones that come later get a safer ride!"

"Well, I am pleased to say that I did survive, Julie. I think all sorts of things were very different then. Maybe Mum and Dad felt they were taking acceptable risks. Maybe life was just simpler then and maybe in some other ways, safer?"

"Well now it's our turn to keep Mum and Dad safe," I replied seeing the pale, bewildered face of our elderly mother looking at us through her front room window as we pulled into the drive. With both her palms on the glass, she had the desperate expression reminiscent of a Heathcliff cat toy, its paws stuck on a car window with suction pads. *Locked in. Can't get out. Is this the only way to keep Mum safe?*

Tom and I waved to Mum and she smiled in return and moved away from her position behind the parapet of Maltese glassware displayed in the front window. Anticipating some kind of ley line symmetry, my hunch was confirmed when on looking directly behind me to the other side of the close, there was Vera in position at her own look out post. Between them, given wartime opportunity, they could have successfully monitored the total of all shipping movements in the Straits of Gibraltar.

Tom showed me the key safe attached unobtrusively in a corner of the bungalow's porch, whilst telling me in a whisper that the code was Mum's date of birth. This key was used by the Care Team; we had our own sets of keys to the bungalow. Mum no longer had a key of her own. Gradually, piece by piece and bit by bit, Mum's power over her own life was being put into the hands of others.

However, to keep up appearances, to continue to preserve the pretence that Mum was Queen of all she surveyed, we rang the doorbell before putting one of our keys into the lock and opening the door swiftly. In the short term, it appeared to work as she greeted us in the entrance hall with a wide smile and gave us both a hug and a kiss. "How wonderful it is to see you! It's simply gorgeous, Darlings. Where have you come from?" she said, negotiating her well-worn loop of phrases.

"I came up on the train from Winchester, Mum. Tom picked me up at Coventry station yesterday and then took me back to his house where I stayed last night. Then he has driven me to you today," I replied, realising too late that I had given Mum far too much information for her to handle. I should learn to filter.

"To you today. To me to you. Shall we have a cup of tea? Tea for two! Or is it three?" she laughed her ever acceptable, suits all situations, three tone giggle. We followed her light footsteps as she tripped into the kitchen; a room that had undergone some subtle changes since the Home Help Team visited more frequently and on whom Mum had become increasingly more reliant. The room had lost its cosy country kitchen feeling as it now doubled as a work station to include the carers' manual, schedule and diary. There on the unit where the bread bin once stood, was the carers' large sheaf of paperwork. However, beside the kettle, on the scorched work surface, the fat bellied teapot was roundly ensconced exactly where it had always been, along with the Rington's tea bags in their Rington's Christmas edition tea caddy. Somehow these small items evoked a warm and cosy permanence. At least some things in my mother's life had stayed the same.

I thought that Mum was going to make the tea but after studying the tea pot, then stroking it lovingly, she paused to stare at the tea making equipment as if she was unaware what she should do next. I prompted her gently by turning on the cold tap, expecting her to fill the kettle but she offered up the cosseted teapot to the jet of water. To cover any embarrassment I said, "Well that's given the pot a good clean, now let's get a brew going." I then proceeded to fill the electric kettle and switch it on. This action caused Mum to break out of her indecision and place tea bags into the tea pot and take some cups from the mug tree. Two of the cups were heavily tea stained as if the last third of their contents had been left to congeal and partially evaporate. I swiftly rinsed them with some of the boiling water until the brown sludgy deposits were swilled away, trying not to grimace or retch like a cat with a fur ball, as I did so.

"I make tea for all the ladies that come, you know. They are all very nice. And I make their meals too," Mum told us once again, awaiting our approval, unaware of her delusion. The carers' note book had told a different story.

"That's good of you, Mum," I answered, exchanging glances with Tom. Mum had always adored being a hostess: *a hostess with the most-est, Darlings,* she used to say.

We went into the lounge and sat down to enjoy the tea that she had in fact made, albeit under supervision. Tom took his leave soon afterwards and Mum fell asleep in her fireside chair, her head resting on the pink velvet cover that she had constructed so skilfully, using her highly prized Bernina sewing machine, years before. The gas fire had been turned up to pig iron smelting level, definitely hot enough to dry out one's eyeballs. I turned the gas jets down, preventing them from licking the lumps of pretend coal quite so viciously. In spite of this action, the whole atmosphere remained soporific and to stop myself succumbing to a doze, I began to focus on objects in the room.

Some say that goods and chattels are simply that, but as I looked about me, it seemed that every item was imbued with a spirit of its own, triggering a thousand memories. I was having a 'Through the Keyhole' experience as I saw the Spitfire bursting out of the clouds from the print on the wall above the place where the piano once stood, and then glanced at the Viscount aeroplane circling over Heathrow Airport in the oil painting proudly displayed on the opposite wall. *All that energy; they could be colliding under the faux candle chandelier suspended from the centre of the ceiling any time now*, I thought, in a surreal haze as a sneaky doze tried to claim me.

My feet rested on a scuffed leather footrest that I knew had been brought back from Egypt many years ago by Dad. All the furniture and treasured possessions in that room illustrated the lives of its inhabitants and told their history.

One person was still here at home, taking her rest; the other was away in another place as he had been so often, all those years ago.

*

In the early years of his career in civil aviation, Dad's wanderlust found fulfilment in the excitement and glamour of the long distance flights to far flung locations. He would have many hours, sometimes days, of 'turnaround' time, part of which he could spend soaking up the atmosphere of the places he had learned about from the Magic Lantern shows of his boyhood. He explored the souks in Cairo and brought home strange items like that bright viridian green leather camel saddle which immediately came into service as footrest or child's stool. This outlandish object was never to lose its sickly pungent aroma even though its colour faded over time to a dull dark grey. We would play on the saddle pretending we were riding a camel and Dad would laugh and say: *"Come with me to the kazbar and we'll have a kitty cola."* For his own amusement and to cause us to shriek with laughter, he would deliver this nonsense in the deep voice of the

Egyptian traffic control officer with whom he had to make radio contact on the approach to Cairo International.

From Baghdad, he brought home baskets for Mum which, unbeknown to him, contained insect stowaways concealed in the intricate weave. These were to hatch out in some noxious splendour several days after arrival in England, causing my mother considerable alarm and fright at their appearance in her new basket amongst the sausages during her mid-week shopping trip to Budgens.

Not only did Dad bring home exotic items, but he brought home novel ideas and experiences which opened our eyes to the world outside the British Isles.

In those pioneering days of civil aviation, air crew night-stopped in the best hotels which also provided the in-flight meals for their return journeys. In this way, Dad was introduced to exotic dishes like prawn cocktail which he would try to replicate at home using a mixture of Heinz salad cream and tomato ketchup. He would wax lyrically on the merits of foreign dishes that at that time hardly anyone this side of the English Channel had even heard of, let alone tried, except perhaps Elizabeth David. At our tiny Formica surfaced kitchen table with the two heavily and deadly hinged extension flaps, he would describe meals that seemed meant for inhabitants of another world. Such dishes had strange sounding names like moussaka, paella, pizza (which he pronounced with some authority, 'pitza'), Russian salad and stroganoff. After one of his trips abroad, he brought home an electric waffle iron and he and Mum experimented with this machine, mixing batter to produce warm doughy bases that we all enjoyed with melting butter and jam. This inspired him to bake bread which he would prepare lovingly and attend to patiently throughout the course of a whole day only to watch his hungry children consume a complete batch of rolls in the short space of a few minutes.

*

A sharp cough woke me from my reverie and I looked across at Mum who punctuated her coughing bout with the words, "Don't worry …Darlings…absolutely gorgeous… keep talking… I can hear you and I am not asleep… so keep the television on. I'll hear all about your day at school… in one moment." Before I could respond, I heard a key being inserted into the lock of the front door.

"Hello Joan. Are you there? It's Gladys the 'ome 'elp. I've come to get you a bite to eat." Into the lounge marched the substantial Gladys who may have arrived without her aitches, but was otherwise complete with all guns blazing and ready for a swift turnaround on this, her tenth lunch sortie that day. She stopped dead at the sight of me and began to back up her virtual truck laden with household artillery.

"Hi Gladys. I'm Julie, Joan's daughter," I intercepted, proffering my hand. She shook it with a firm grasp, whilst I explained that there would be no need for her to prepare lunch today as I would be doing so. She looked relieved as this would mean that the visit would be greatly curtailed. "Could you just help administer the medication though please before you leave?" I added, like the coward I was.

"Sure, Duck." She then turned to Mum who was rising up through the waters of sleep and just breaking the surface, fluttering her eyelids and taking a deep breath trying not to cough. She looked mystified.

"Joan," Gladys amplified her loud haler of a mouth to maximum volume, "shall us give you yer meds now?"

"Hello. How nice to see you. Where have you been?" said Mum from her script; on such occasions there was no ad libbing.

Gladys drew up the curtain on the day's medication pantomime in the lounge, whilst I began lunch preparation in the kitchen. By the time the final ping of the microwave programme had resounded, Gladys was square bashing her way across the hall and out of the house. On her way she fixed me with a look, her eyes firmly right, in order to direct me a self-satisfied arch of an eyebrow which said it all. *She was the best; with a quick downward pull of an imaginary steam whistle handle. Oh Yes! She could get these old biddies to take their meds. No sweat!*

With Gladys' triumphant retreat marked by the rattling roar of a loose exhaust pipe, quiet descended on the bungalow once more. All I could hear were the slippered footsteps of Mum as she roamed about the bedrooms. I told her that we would be having lunch in the dining room very soon. I began to lay the table – an increasingly difficult task as there seemed to be less items of cutlery every time I did this. It was then that I heard a strange gurgling noise coming from the kitchen. I dropped the mismatched knives and forks and ran to find the source of the sound, thinking the worst. There was Mum drinking the cold

110

stewed tea from the teapot spout, looking just like the picture of the *'Tiger that Came to Tea'* from Lizzy's favourite children's story.

"Mum, what are you doing? That tea could have been hot. Why didn't you just run the tap and have a drink of water?"

"I was so thirsty. I could not wait for the tap," she said enigmatically.

Chapter 15
The way the river froze

Julie

With a Gladys type of smugness, I settled down into the warm quilt on the trusty sofa bed in the dining room, later that night. The hurdles that had had to be surmounted before I gained this delicious nest of warmth were not inconsiderable and the torture to my nerves, debilitating. Mum had chased the food around the plate at lunch and at tea time then I had chased her around the bungalow full of fear that she may harm herself on something hitherto deemed innocuous, like the friendly tea pot spout. Dangers lurked everywhere: in the razor sharp leaves of the mother-in-law's tongue plant in the hall, in the flames of the gas fire cum blast furnace in the lounge, in the flesh piercing tine of one of the many forks that kept disappearing but that may at any moment reappear sinisterly on a soft chair cushion ready for impact with an unsuspecting elderly bottom. I was getting paranoid.

Eventually, fatigue slowed us both down and the *Tom and Jerry* cartoon chase around the bungalow slackened to a dodder. I was able to ambush Mum on one of her circuits whilst brandishing a sponge and toothbrush. Then having paid lip service to some brief ablutions, she allowed herself to be changed into her night clothes and tucked into bed. When I leaned over her to kiss her goodnight she said, "Sleep tight. Dream about the fairies at the bottom of the garden."

I did think about the fairies at the bottom of the garden as I lay on the sofa bed. My thoughts were back in Wraysbury once again, during that golden, happy period of our childhood.

*

The bungalow named *Riversway* was modest, yet its few small rooms became a treasure chest of childhood memories. With my mind's eye I took a virtual tour, walking up the front path that cut across the lawn of the small hedged garden. I dwelt on a memory of my sister and me holding tightly our tortoiseshell kitten called 'Frisky'- much later to be accurately re-named, 'Fatcat'. There we are in our navy blue school uniforms: Janine with blonde hair tied back severely in a pony-tail and I with my brown short fringed mop sheared by Mum's over-enthusiastic sewing scissors.

There were three steep steps up to the front door and it was from these that one day in the severe winter of 1963, we watched our cat float by. The flood waters that year had frozen over, yet we could still see blades of bright green grass waving beneath the surface of the icy crust. The beginnings of a thaw had allowed a sheet of ice to detach itself and on this floe travelled the rare sight of an embarrassed cat, completing a domestic version of our very own polar landscape.

For Dad, the joys of roving abroad had begun to lose their appeal as his growing family became the main focus of his interest. Gradually, the time spent away travelling began to pall for him and on long haul flights especially, he found himself impatient to return home. As a consequence, he changed airlines and started a new job with British European Airways which promised shorter flights. In his later years he was to tell us that he used to spend hours looking at amazing sights in fascinating countries whilst in his heart he just wanted to be in his own home with his family. *Who needs the pyramids when you are missing your children's smiles?"*

He certainly received welcoming smiles whenever he came home. It was the most exciting of sounds to hear him enter the front door, to know that we had our Dad back with us again. We also knew that in his hand he would carry his blue flight bag that we hoped held a present for everyone. There might be hair ribbons or little silver necklaces, tin soldiers, cricket bats, games or packets of foreign stamps, dolls in national costume, skipping ropes or balls and on one occasion a miniature speed boat for bath time. Out of his bulging pockets he would produce little chocolates, samples saved from in-flight luxury; our favourite was the coffee crème in its own tiny beribboned case.

Dad certainly made the most of his time on leave, using every opportunity to take us out in his new acquisition: the shiny black Standard motor car. It was many years later that I was to hear of the personal anguish that my father suffered over that car. The day he took his driving test, he went off with confidence and optimism; after all he knew how to pilot an aeroplane *so driving a car could not be that dissimilar, could it?* As he was leaving, he promised to take us all to the seaside on his return. To his intense chagrin, he failed the test and Mother said that he actually wept when he came home, a singular occurrence; *men did not cry in those days, Darling, not considered the thing to do. He felt he had disappointed you children by not being able to fulfil the promise he had made.* Dad did pass at his second attempt and the promised trip to the coast at West Wittering did take place and was to herald many such excursions that we all adored. Loaded with sharp metal spades and colourful tin buckets, we would set off, invariably singing *'We're off to see the wizard, the wonderful wizard of Oz.'* The car had features that we could enjoy throughout the journey. The back seats were excellent for bouncing and the blind in the back window could be pulled up and down while the car was in motion. This dangerous amusement caused our father extreme stress and annoyance but we were reluctant to cease our antics until distracted by the right/left indicators. These, in the shape of little pointing fists would emerge suddenly and, it seemed to us, comically from slots at either side of the car. With any change in direction prompting a new bout of giggles, the car seemed the best game on wheels.

At the side of the house, adjacent to Uncle Woody's bungalow, a 'lean- to' car port had been built. As its name suggests, this was a relatively flimsy structure of corrugated iron, supported on one side with wooden posts and the bungalow wall on other. When the old black solid Standard had gone to the great carpark in the sky, it was replaced by a saucily named Hillman Minx model in two tone colours. Sadly, it was when this new object of pride and joy was parked lovingly under the aforesaid lean- to, that disaster struck. The *lean–to* suddenly slumped sideways to *lean-on* the car roof with considerable force, creasing and denting the metal like a parting in a smart boy's Brylcreemed hair. My father and mother wrestled the offending iron sheets of the lean-to roof from the vehicle, which by now resembled something very much less than a saucy minx. My father gritted his teeth and drove the car out from the shelter and slammed the car door with the combined total of all his pent up energy and frustration. We children, who had witnessed this extraordinary turn of events, stood around like statues in shock. Then before anyone spoke a coherent sentence or a giggle escaped, the air was ripped asunder with a resounding 'ping' and as if by magic, the metal car roof sprang back to regain its former shape with no noticeable marks to show for its mishap.

At the back of the house was a large square lawn with a small shed to one side. My father often retreated to the shed to tinker with things. Here he kept a wide range of tools that were too big to carry around in his capacious pockets, ready to embark on a range of projects and repairs for which he had a never ending source of energy and enthusiasm. For example when we were young children, we were never taken to the dentist. My father would simply explore our mouths with the dental mirror that was one of the special tools in his armoury, and then pronounce that all was well. He did all his own car maintenance and used his radio skills, gained in the RAF and as civil airline radio officer, to try his hand at mending and maintaining a range of electrical products. This included wirelesses and the early television sets of the 1950's. To get some extra cash, he took on free-lance repair jobs for a local electrical business in the village. We did not own a television at that time; only the wealthy could possess such a luxury item. However, Dad managed to organise his television repairs to co-ordinate with family entertainment, contriving to ensure that there was always a working model in the lounge, sometimes two, side by side. We may have had to suffer the odd interruption to 'Muffin the Mule', 'The Wooden Tops' and 'Andy Pandy' as Dad worked on a set, but to have access to such a modern device was beyond exciting. We became used to seeing the large mirror propped on the armchair, set up at an angle so that he could check his repair progress from his position behind the set. Reflected in the looking glass, he observed the stripes of the flashing and rolling grey screen while he worked on replacing huge and fragile valves in the back of televisions' highly finished wooden cabinets. Such beautiful items of furniture were recycled when a television was discarded; with Dad's ingenuity, they became the super smooth and fast runners for our winter sledges.

Ever resourceful, Dad could turn his hand to almost every job around the house. In the infamous winter of 1963, the water in the attic tank froze. By the time we left for school early one morning, Dad was already well into the task of melting the ice in the loft pipes, using his trusty blow torch. This became such a lengthy process that when we came home from school later that day, he was only just emerging from the loft hatch white and shivering like Scott of the Antarctic – just as the evening temperature began to drop and the ice crystals started to form again.

The film, 'Mary Poppins' had just been released when our chimney needed sweeping. Rather than engage the services of a professional sweep, Dad bought his own brush kit with a set of long bamboo canes that connected together with a series of screw-in joints to achieve the desired length. While we were at school he managed, somewhat inadvertently, to redecorate the lounge in varying tones of grey and black with the resulting sooty deposits. It was to take the rest of the day to clean up but Dad was not deterred; he had an idea up his sleeve. His plan was to place the brush back up the chimney so that when we returned from school, we would have the surprise of looking up to see its black bristles poking out of the chimney pot, just like on Mary Poppins' rooftops of London. Unfortunately, the plan backfired when at the crucial moment, the brush took its own dog leg shaped turn in its progress upwards and emerged between the bricks at the side of the chimney instead. To us children waiting below, the spectacle was not only just as great a delight as the classic brush popping out of the chimney pot scenario, it was even funnier. *Chim-chiminy-chim-chiminy- chim-chim-cher-oo.*

Owing to the vast quantities of tools kept in the shed along with bicycles and old furniture, it was only possible to stand upright in the entrance of the little wooden structure. Beside the shed was a bag of cement that had solidified when it had been left out in the rain accidentally and had formed a useful, if hard and uncomfortable, perch. It was on this unyielding sack that Dad sat plucking the Christmas turkey one year. He had decided that this idea would save the household money and so he had bought a huge and magnificently plumed bird, ripe for preparation. The whole process proved to be at the very least, messy. The fine feathers spread through his hair and stuck to his facial stubble, floated into his eyes and dried out his mouth. White feathers and fluff spread to the paving slabs in a wide arc around him and littered a vast section of the winter lawn to be trodden into the house for many days on the scuffed shoes of excited children. Once plucked, the bird shrank disappointingly to a third of its former be-feathered self. The exercise was never to be repeated.

For one particular job however, Dad did require the services of the specialists, the undisputed experts in their field, known simply as Fred and Harry.

On the path that skirted the edge of the lawn at the back of *Riversway*, there was a drain cover which was the mysterious portal to the cess pit; there being no mains drainage in Ouseley road. This pit had to be emptied regularly by the estimable Fred and Harry, the providers of this specialised sanitary service. To Mum and Dad who grew up with chamber pots under the bed, primitive outside lavatories with night soil collections and Elsan chemical toilets, the underground cess pit was a positive luxury. This relatively modern arrangement could be completely forgotten in the general routine of family life until it was time for the regular visit from the malodorous, but ever sanguine gentlemen. Like a military operation, they would park their dark green unmarked tanker lorry in the road outside the house and then proceed to unravel a long, wide diameter concertina-sided hose joined at intervals with metal coupling rings. While they were *doing their business Darlings, no need to look,* Mum would shut the windows and prepare a hot drink and biscuits for them at the kitchen table. I was allowed to help by mixing the Camp coffee liquid with the sugar in their special cups – those not used by anyone else. Then they would appear at the door, cheerful and forgivably rank, to remove their foul smelling gauntlets and partake of a dish of coffee with Mother. *All very civilised, Darlings.* However, should we entertain a sudden influx of visitors to our home; the neat and ordered sewage system became overloaded to dramatic effect. The first sign would be the pretty pink toilet paper curiously decorating the garden path- *don't walk where the pink tissue roses bloom, Darlings.* If this sign was missed, the stench that followed would soon have my parents picking up the heavy Bakelite telephone receiver and making that urgent call.

For us children, there may not have been any real fairies at the bottom of the garden, but it was no less magical. The back garden lawn was our main play area for bicycles, tricycles and scooters. For paddling pools, French cricket, football, rounders, bubble blowing and skittles (using firewood logs) and most important of all, with space to build our summer boats. During the long school holidays when the sun always seemed as bright as the one on the Sun Pat raisins packet, my brother Tom would announce that we would be 'constructing tomorrow' and the three of us would plan and create our own vessel with bow, stern and mast. Our mother allowed us the freedom to build our complicated constructions using furniture and soft furnishings from the bungalow. Most of this was second hand or post war utility quality but even so, her indulgence to our creative play was staggering. There on the lawn would be the full blown roses patterned seat cushions from the three piece suite piled on top of upended fireside chairs and draped in colourful blankets. Kitchen stools turned upside down supported broom handle masts whilst cricket bat oars completed the landlocked ship in which we played, happily occupied until tea time. Perhaps that was the real reason for Mother's tolerance over the upheaval wrought during the boat building days.

Beyond the back lawn was a wild area of overgrown shrubs and tall grasses where we rarely set foot. That was until my brother took us all on a jungle trek to the interior with the lure that he believed there was something mysterious buried in the undergrowth. He took the lead with his cricket bat machete, beating down the grass and clearing the way for his younger sisters to follow. His serpentine path led us that hot and pollen filled day to the rusty crock of a forgotten tractor. Clearing the weeds from the decomposing tyres and taking turns to climb up to the high metal driving seat, bright orange with corrosion, we felt as if we had conquered the world.

*

The next morning was Sunday, the day I had planned to visit Dad in hospital. I felt the need to telephone Tom and report on my paranoia, my fears that Mum may not be safe. Tom said that he would call in and check on Mum during the course of the day and have a word with the carers to see if they, with their experience, shared any of our concerns. This placated me and reminded me that I was not alone; this load was a shared load.

Anyhow, it was time for me to focus on Dad.

Chapter 16
Smoke on the water

Julie

Leaving Mum in the Burnage bungalow, my weekend holdall in hand, I set off on foot to the railway station. All the way there, I practised convincing myself that Mum would be alright, that she would be checked several times that day by Gladys and her army, as well as being visited by Tom. I was feeling wrung out by worry and a poor night's sleep; the fairies had not come to my aid during the night. If anything, they had reminded me of a carefree childhood that was no more. However, as I plodded down the hill, I took myself to task: *I cannot be like Peter Pan. I must be a grown up and get on with this 'awfully big adventure'.*

Breakfast had been a mini riot, not helped by the fact that I had a train to catch. The added time pressure had made me try to rush Mum and Mum could not be rushed. Earlier that morning, she had appeared at my door looking like *Miss Havisham* with her grey hair in a wild halo and her silky nightdress slipping off one shoulder. Her eyes had looked startled and her upper body had shuddered on discovering me when she was on her way to execute her mission: to draw back the dining room curtains. She asked me who I was before going through her false, yet friendly and ever convincing, loop of greetings. After my own loop of reassurances and reminders, Mum partially regained her trust in me. Indeed we were doing well until she noticed my flat black patent ankle boots. These, she coyly tried on and walked about the room like a guilty toddler trying on her mother's best shoes. Then, she studied the absence of a raised heel and after a moment's inward turmoil appeared to decide that they were men's shoes and therefore with my cropped hair, the only possible conclusion she could draw was that I was indeed, a man.

Convincing her that I was female took longer than it should, a fact that did little for my flagging feminine ego. So feeling like a lumbering *Miss Trunchbull*, I escorted her gently to the bathroom to begin the slow process of getting her washed and dressed. After many a slip twixt bra cup and satin slip, Mum was finally dressed and I could concentrate on getting myself ready. Then with care, I packed away my things; experience had taught me to hide my holdall under the sofa bed. I was not going to get caught out arriving home without half of my belongings again.

That morning the word 'breakfast' was, as always, pronounced by Mum slowly and as it is spelt 'break-fast' just like the mediaeval monks before her. For her, there were no shortened versions of the word, no 'breckfst' or 'brekkie'; all e's were long and carefully enunciated. That morning she was being particularly graceful; a factor that I could not fully appreciate as by now, I was running late. That morning the tea making ceremony had taken on geisha proportions, its intensity and attention to detail directly correlating with an increase in my blood pressure. That morning, Mother not only remembered how to make tea, but made it with skill and finesse that would make the Duchess of Kent shout "Lapsang Souchong" with her little finger pointing skywards (a ducal equivalent to a high five). That morning, the toast was well toasted and not 'ghost' as my father had often commented when presented with pale hard bread masquerading as the real thing with butter and marmalade affixed.

Event-u-all-y, with the washing up done and pots put away, I prepared to take my leave. This was done in the same way I used to exit playgroup when I was leaving my four year old for their session of rough and tumble with playdough and potato printing. I got Mum involved in something, in this case a riveting cookery programme on the television, kissed her on the forehead and quietly slipped out through the front door.

By the time I had reached the station, I was ready for a stiff drink but at ten o'clock on a Sunday morning, even I knew that would not be wise. That glass of wine awaiting me at home that evening would be nectar from the gods. Meanwhile I had hurdles to cross.

Catching the suburban service with only seconds to spare, I was relieved to arrive at the city at last. Outside the busy terminal with its ornate Victorian façade, I joined the taxi queue and began watching the fleet of black cabs sail past with fear curling in my stomach. It was as if I was waiting for a scary ride at Chessington World of Adventure even though I was too short to reach the height bar. Eventually, it was my turn to board and with some surprise I began to relax immediately, settling into the cushioned cocoon of the leather upholstery, almost forgetting to reveal to the driver, my destination. All too soon I was deposited outside the now familiar hospital building and turned to watch the cab disappear into the distance before squaring my shoulders and facing those hurdles.

Like a re-run of the old '*Jeux Sans Frontieres*' game show, I sprang from the starting blocks of yellow painted kerb stones and first negotiated the friendly charms of the well upholstered receptionist, mastered the secure door decoding procedure, bypassed politely the frilly white Meeter and Greeter, quickly checked I was not wearing the colours of the care team's uniform (no, that day I was dressed in commanding red and black like the book jacket colours of a vampire novel) until after a sprint finish, I conquered the tea urn and locked horns with its benign, bovine attendant. My Minotaur pointed his hoof to the back of the room and there was Dad in the process of leaving, no doubt on his way to his favoured spot. I thanked my new friend for the proffered drinks and set off in pursuit, shakily balancing the cups and saucers as if it was my turn to join Dad's egg and spoon race. I caught him up at the bend in the corridor, just as he was about to sit down. As no one else was around, I sat next to him, putting our drinks on the windowsill. *Take a breath.*

"Hello there. I've just been to see Mum. I know she sends her love."

"That's nice," he said.

I gave his arm a little hug and smoothed a stray wisp of grey hair from his face. Before I could think of what to say next, he came up with: "My toe hurts, Betty." *Oh dear, he doesn't know me. Should I humour him or take a stand? Would it upset him, if I challenged this?* I decided to do what I thought a grown up would do.

"I'm not Betty, Dad. I'm Julie, your daughter Julie. Tell me what is wrong with your toe. Which one hurts? Have you told the nurse?"

He looked at me and smiled. Then he took my hand gently into his comfortingly warm paw. "I know you are Julie and there is nothing wrong with my toe." I was defeated. I did not know what to say next. This conversation was taking a bizarre turn.

"That's what the birds are saying: *my toe hurts Betty.* Can't you hear them?" he asked.

It was then that I listened and there it was: the calls of some kind of wood pigeon from the tall trees in the grounds. Oo-*Ooo-Ooo-O-Oo*. It really did sound as if they were feathered Frank Spencers

121

cooing to their long suffering wives. Dad chuckled to himself and I found myself joining in. Once I had started to laugh, it was difficult to stop as I sensed the tension of the past few hours ebbing away at last.

"Now apart from keeping your eyes and ears on the birds, how have you been?" I asked, my confidence returning.

"Not so bad. I sleep a lot. I keep myself to myself. I don't like to tell them anything. You never know what they'll do with the information. Did you say you had already spoken to Mum? She's only over there."

He pointed to an old lady all bundled up in hand-knitted garments who had her bare, swollen legs on parade, her feet in felt slippers with the sides cut away to accommodate painful looking bunions. My mother never wore cardigans or slippers; *only jackets or little coats and for indoors, light shoes, Darlings.*

In order to avoid potential disappointment on everyone's part, I endeavoured to distract him by talking about life in Wraysbury. I hoped that the past was more secure in his mind and a safer topic than the present.

"I've been thinking a great deal about *Riversway* and all the fun we used to have when Mum's brothers came to stay," I prompted.

"Yes, they were good times. Tough on Mum though wasn't it?" He called across to Mrs Woolly Bundle who looked up briefly with a bemused expression on her sweet little wrinkled face.

*

Visitors to *Riversway* were many; these were usually Mum's relations. With Dad away on his travels, Mum was left to care for her young family on her own for several days at a time. To help her feel less isolated and to give themselves a holiday, Mum's brothers would come and stay, travelling the one hundred miles from the Midlands in coaches, trains, cars and once, brother Walter arrived saddle-sore on his bicycle. Mum's father, the baker cum gentleman of the Press often the worse for drink, would bring his drinking companions to visit. Unfortunately, on one historic occasion having driven all the way from Leicestershire, he lost control of his car on arrival and drove round in a large circle on the front lawn. This misadventure scored deep and muddy tracks which could not be erased before Dad returned home from service, much to Mum's mortification.

On one particular weekend, as many as ten relatives came to stay. With few beds available, the visitors had to sleep closely together in rows on the small lounge floor; this led to the room being fondly named 'the snake pit' forever afterwards. My brother, sister and I loved times when our uncles came to stay. They were younger than our parents and were full of what my mother would call, *'horseplay and mischief, Darlings'*. They did exciting and daring things that sometimes amazed and sometimes frightened us. Their trick cycling feats had us lining up eagerly for future multiple bruising; before witnessing their stunts, we would never have dreamt of riding without a death grip on the handle bars or without our feet firmly affixed to the pedals. The dangerous uncles opened up a whole new world of risk taking and we adored them.

When Mother was not looking, they showed us how to snuff out a match flame using just their fingers. Also they demonstrated the fine art of sewing your fingers together by passing a needle and thread through the rough skin of their knuckle callouses.

When Mother was not listening, they taught us rhymes that seemed meaningless, but which sent them into paroxysms of juvenile laughter when we repeated *'I chased a bug around a tree'* and *'Polish it behind the door'*. Our childish voices were encouraged to chant faster and faster and we were altogether thrilled with ourselves that we were entertaining what were fast becoming our idols.

When the dangerous uncles, joined later by girlfriends - who in time became their wives, visited *Riversway,* they were taken on tours of local beauty spots. These included Virginia Waters, the town of Windsor and its castle. It was in the remote lanes of Windsor Great Park that on two unforgettable occasions they saw glimpses of Her Majesty the Queen and the Queen Mother as the royal personages passed by in their shining vehicles. The Midlanders, lined up on the grass verge, were delighted when the royal cars slowed down especially for them and royal waves were bestowed.

Used to rural life in the Midlands, the whole Middlesex area held a fascination for the relatives and they would remark on the excessive number of motor vehicles on the roads saying this must be 'what folks mean by the *rat race'*. If an aeroplane passed low overhead, as familiar to us as a passing bus, the visitors surprised us by doing something quite extraordinary. They would go outside the house to plane spot and were even known to stop their cars in the middle of the road in order to watch an aircraft fly over.

I am sure that my mother enjoyed the company, but the extra labour the visitors caused must have been exhausting for her. Overall, my father was tolerant of this unofficial *Riversway Holiday Camp* although he could not resist making a point by painting a commercially styled sign that he pinned up in the kitchen: ' *Why not try Joan's home-made cakes?*'

*

Back in the ward, Dad and I continued to reminisce on that happy chapter of our lives. When talking of the past like this, Dad was coherent and we were able to hold a meaningful conversation albeit with the occasional lapse - when he might become suddenly silent and apparently distracted. When, through the window, we both observed a nurse taking a smoke furtively behind a large bush in the courtyard garden, Dad was prompted to remark: "All that smoking. We all did it, you know in those days. Thought it was good for you. Dried up a cough if you had a cold. Calmed the nerves, by Jingo."

*

During the fifties and early sixties, in common with most people and before it was considered harmful, Mum and Dad smoked cigarettes. I have an unlikely vision stored in my memory of Mum, usually such an upright and proper person, pegging out the washing whilst balancing a fag (*cigarette, Darlings)* on the right side of her lower lip, her right eye consequently half shut to minimise the effect of the rising smoke. Meanwhile Dad would be washing the car energetically, whilst dressed in his blue overalls over his shirt *always* complete with a collar and tie (*he had standards, Darlings)*, with a fag smouldering in the corner of his mouth. Smoking was living and breathing to them.

This stimulating activity presented a variety of apparently pleasurable options to try like the new 'king sized' cigarette, pastel cocktail coloured papers, menthol flavours and filter ends. To make the hobby even more interesting, and to prevent unsightly tobacco stained fingers, the cigarette could be extended with movie star-style ebony cigarette holders; long cigarette holders for Mum and short for Dad. Hand in hand, they progressed from Woodbines and Park Drives

– the brand that were still enjoyed by the men (and the women) of the Midlands, to Player's (Navy cut) - with the dashing sailor cameo on the carton, to finally Benson and Hedges. This latter product may have been at the high end of the market but was the brand that Dad could procure cheaply, duty free. Generous as ever, he would share his tins of Benson and Hedges with visiting relatives. Eventually, this was to result in the Great Train Smoking Competition of 1957.

One weekend my mother's four brothers came to visit and as there was a large commodity of cigarettes in the house - indeed there were enough cigarette tins for Tom to build a substantial castle out of them in his bedroom - the brothers, along with Dad, decided to hold a contest to see who could smoke the most cigarettes over two days. A tally was kept and the thin white sticks left their gold card and cellophane wrapped packets to turn to smoke and ashes in rapid succession, producing a steadily expanding acrid fug throughout the bungalow. Amidst a scene reminiscent of a Great War gas attack with individuals regularly convulsed with wracking coughs and blinded with streaming eyes, Tom moved on from castle construction and turned his hand to railway building. His uncles wiped their eyes and joined him enthusiastically along with my father, and together they laid a model track from the lounge at the front of the house, through the corridor to the kitchen at the back. As the competition reached its final stage, the uncles had heroically split up into two groups, one led by Walter camped in the Kitchen railway station with Mum, and the other team led by Jack had dug in around the rail buffers in the lounge with Dad. So it was that by the end of Sunday evening, the smoking contest was neck and neck between the two leaders: eldest brother Walter and the youngest brother Jack - whose smoking prowess was legendary; he was even known to chain smoke illegally down the coal mine where he worked as pit electrician. He was practised at escaping discovery by placing his fag between thumb and forefinger with the lit end inside his curled hand; a habit he was unable to alter even when above ground.

Then was heard my father's announcement that there was only one cigarette left. It was decided that everyone in the competition should take a drag of the final fag and the last person to have the stub in his hand when the tobacco in the cigarette was finished, would score the point. This is where the train and the contest came together. The cigarette was lit, smoked briefly by each team member in the lounge then my father placed it securely in the model train chimney and set off the motor. The train travelled into the kitchen via the corridor, delighting an excited Tom who ran alongside this miniature, but apparently real, steam train as it chugged across the carpet. In the kitchen, the cigarette was captured, smoked quickly by the rest of the contestants before being replaced in the tiny chimney for its return journey. So went the little model train back and forth until it started to lose cigarette steam. Then the final snatch and drag was made by the coughing and spluttering, yet highly acclaimed winner: Jack, of course.

As the family grew, so did Mum and Dad's responsibilities and a new incentive for smoking was to present itself in the form of the Kensitas brand. These cigarettes carried vouchers in each pack which once collected and accumulated, could be exchanged for household goods. Now Mum and Dad began smoking up for a toaster or a pedal bin, a lamp shade or a garden hose. Trips to London were always accompanied by the unwieldy Lisbon basket - a large rectangular woven straw bag of the type that Portuguese housewives used to take to market and that Dad had brought back as another gift for Mum (this time insect free). On our trips to town however, this generous hamper would be filled with watermarked coupons, banded together in hundreds like so many bank notes in a blackmailer's cache ready to be exchanged for practical and desired items seen in the glossy catalogue and available only at the Kensitas shop.

With the advent of new knowledge of the health dangers associated with tobacco, Dad and Mum did give up smoking eventually. Dad was the first to commence the painful and extended process of living without his forty a day. He replaced cigarettes with peppermints and when these began to cause tooth decay but failed to prevent his cravings, a friend told him to try sucking cloves. These seemed to help him get through cold turkey whilst providing the added benefit of infusing him with a fragrance- that many a scented candle company would envy -combining Christmas pomander with apple pie.

*

"Aren't you going to spend some time with Mum before you go," said my father, pointing to a snoozing Mrs Woolly Bundle.

Feeling my powers of maintaining the status of 'grown up' failing, I decided to humour him. "I don't like to wake her as she seems to be having a nice nap."

126

"Right oh, then. I'll probably have one m'self, when you've gone."

"Bye then, Dad. I'll be seeing you again soon," I said, kissing his dry, slack cheek.

"Bye, Betty love," he replied.

Chapter 17
The way the water flowed away

George

George settled down in the squeaky leatherette high backed armchair next to 'Joan'.

"You are looking very cosy, Joanie," he remarked affectionately.

The lady in the double knit ensemble opened a bewildered chameleon eye briefly, before closing it firmly to resume the sanctity of her slobbery doze. This did not deter George who continued to address his thoughts openly to her.

"*And they said we shouldn't look back,*" he sang in a small frail voice, yet still in tune. This gentle rendering of a lyric from his beloved '*Salad Days*' carried a poignancy that was completely lost on his dozing companion.

"Julie took me right back to those days in Wraysbury, at *Riversway*. Those were happy days, weren't they love? I feel like she has opened a box, like that Swiss chalet musical box I brought back for you from one of my trips. You know the one, you opened the lid that was the roof and inside the wooden house there was a place for cigarettes and below that, under a small wooden cover, you could see the workings of the music box and it played … now what was it … oh I know, the theme from that film, '*The Third Man*'. You know how it went…*da di da di da- di da.* Now where was I?" He trailed the happy thought and was delighted when he caught it up again. "Yes well, it's like the lid has come off and I can't stop thinking about it all. We had some fun didn't we love? Our best years. We had some wonderful times and some grand adventures like that holiday we all had in Rome. Do you remember? It was November the fifth when we flew out, the children could look out of the plane windows and see bonfires down below. That kind of helped to make up for them missing Firework night. You were lovely in your stylish hat with the wide brim and long silk gloves, just like Audrey Hepburn in that '*Roman Holiday*' film.

128

The kids were in their best outfits – it was a shame Julie was sick all down the front of hers when the plane had to circle Fiumicino airport, queueing up to land. Then, from Arrivals we were picked up by that pal of Timber Wood what was he called? I know-it was Oscar-that was his name. He picked us up and it was just getting dark so he said those immortal words in what you said was a charming Italian accent: *and now is the time for a leettle bit of the light.* So then every time we put the car headlights on even when we were back in England, for years and years we used to say … *and now is the time for a leettle bit of the light* with our best Italian twang. That Oscar, he drove us out to our rented villa on the coast. It was pitch black by the time we arrived, and cold and windy and a storm was brewing up. We tried to light a fire but the chimney was all blocked up and smoke filled the room. Then you saw that rat in the bedroom. You were that upset and disappointed. You cried and we didn't want the kids to know. Italy had not quite come up to expectation- at the start at any rate. That first night we went out to that lighthouse café bar place that had red and white plastic strip curtains instead of a door and they kept playing, '*You better come home, Speedy Gonzales*' over and over again on the juke box. It was all bright strip lights, cheap and noisy. But after that the holiday did get better and you loved St Peter's, the fountains and the squares, the Wedding Cake, the Spanish Steps and all the markets and shops. And I used to get so jealous when the Italian men used to follow you all the time or walk past you, overtake and then turn round and walk backwards saying how beautiful you are."

He turned to Mrs Woolly Bundle expectantly, but the only reply came in the form of a snoring snort, followed by a smacking of dribbly lips.

"I know you loved our life in the South and you never liked it when we came back up to the Midlands. You never let me forget," he said, his voice loaded with remorse.

When still no response came from the sleeping form beside him, George eventually became silent but his brain was far from idle. He began reliving.

In his mind he saw the bungalow bathed in late afternoon sunlight as he returned home from another Amsterdam- Gibraltar-Rome- Malta round trip. There were the girls and Tom at the door to welcome him, pulling at his flight bag to try and catch a glimpse of any treats he might have brought them, rushing to show him their latest drawings, stories, bits of holey knitting and model aeroplanes that had been created in his absence. Fighting for individual attention, they called out their own little pieces of news: "I've lost my tooth"… "I had a headache in my bottom"… "Janine's tooken my toffee and won't give it back"… "Julie knocked over all the nuts *again* and they've went all over the floor!"

Having spent the past hours navigating around and between mountains, he now had an even more complex task of negotiating the obstacles in the crowded hallway. Along the full length of the corridor was a carefully aligned row of open books, their spines upward forming an irregular triangular tunnel system. When asked, the children's excited account featured a reluctant Frisky the cat who, it was reported, had been gently encouraged to pass through this literary tunnel. However, it transpired that the wise cat had not obliged the children and so the game had been changed and the cat substituted with a range of different sized balls and marbles. It being Friday, the entrance to the lounge was blocked with an enormous cardboard egg carton box in which the weekly Budgen's order had been delivered. This was currently serving as a cart with twine clumsily threaded through two roughly hewn holes at one end, the children taking it in turns to show him its various specifications while the strains of '*Life with the Lyons*' filtered through the thirties style high- waisted lounge door.

Like the Pied Piper, he led his excited entourage through the house, on the way passing the girls' bedroom. Here he had, against his wife's wishes, allowed his daughters the freedom to choose their own wallpaper. Their taste had run to two walls of grey paper and two walls of dark red paper, all rolls decorated with Japanese figures, oriental bridges and weeping willows. This décor, more in keeping with a Chinese restaurant, composed a bizarre backdrop to their teddy bear and doll collection arranged atop the two bunk beds.

The conga style procession continued past Tom's small bedroom which was bedecked with a vast selection of model aeroplanes hanging from the ceiling with fishing line. Tom completed much of his construction of trains, boats and planes from kits in his bedroom until one day when he became overcome with fumes from the special model aeroplane dope. This all happened before the days of glue sniffing; the smell of dope and glue in a boy's bedroom was *absolutely normal, Darlings*.

After family tea in the kitchen full of chatter and the exchange of tales, he and Joanie would relax in front of the fire in the lounge –

which was also their bedroom; they slept on a small divan bed in the corner of the room. Here they would watch television on a tiny screen or listen to the wireless, play records or tapes. The bulky apparatus for the audio devices was set into a vast 'radiogram' built from a kit, by George himself. This combined radio, record player and tape deck cabinet was of a size akin to a modern commercial chest freezer. From this early music centre was to emanate an eclectic collection of audio recordings that included poetry readings by Robert Donat, Bible readings from Charlton Heston, the musical works of Bizet (pronounced Bizette by the children, he remembered with a smile), Vaughan Williams, Gilbert and Sullivan. Also in the pile of tapes and records could be found the more modern renderings of Frank Sinatra (for Joan), Dean Martin and Jack Teagarden along with film and musical soundtracks like *'South Pacific'*, *'My Fair Lady'*, *'Seven Brides for Seven Brothers'* and of course, who could ever forget *'Salad Days?'* Christmas would not be Christmas without Bernard Miles' reading of *'A Christmas Carol'* and the treasured recording of the light opera *'Amahl and the Night Visitors'* heralded every festive season.

The matching speakers, like giant shoe boxes were to demonstrate the newly invented stereo sound and he would move his armchair around the room to enjoy the best effect whilst listening to the various sound samples of trains going through tunnels, the changing of the guard and tap dancing tiller girls all featured on his state of the art record: *'A Journey into Stereo Sound'*. The speakers also served to detract the eye from the mistake in the wallpaper where he had pasted a strip upside down – potentially all the more noticeable as its design featured Spanish galleons in full sail.

Once the children were in bed Joan and he, ever industrious, would often get on with various projects. The sideboard in the bay window supported a type-writer as Joan taught herself shorthand and typing, and to the side of the room was a sewing machine. A gifted needle woman, Joan made all her own clothes, soft furnishing items and most of the children's outfits. Not just a dress maker, she could tailor garments, make hats and work exquisite embroidery. George had bought her a knitting machine and he joined her in making sweaters, hats and scarves for the family. Happy evenings were spent around the television with the constant whir and swish of the knitting machine as background accompaniment.

"Then it all stopped," he said out loud to his semi-comatose companion in homespun. "That rosy golden time, it all went. Our

131

hopes drained away, all flowed away. I got that kidney problem and then I got made redundant. I hated that time working on the ground at London airport, you know I did. And I know you didn't understand that I wanted to have some time off to paint and write and have the freedom to do all the things I had always wanted to do. Those six months were so precious to me. I never had any time I could call my own before. I loved the amateur photography and cine film making, those Art correspondence courses with the drawing lessons where I had to sketch on fine paper and then send my work off to America. I learnt a lot from that. I enjoyed oil painting even the 'painting by numbers' – it was all the rage then. Do you remember my version of *'The Laughing Cavalier'?* I wonder what happened to that? I wonder where he's laughing now and what he's laughing at? Then there was the Journalism Correspondence course and all those short stories I wrote. They were all about flying. Do you remember ? One was called *'Keep it under your hat,'* then there was *' The Final approach'* and *'My Mummy's in Cairo'* but you always said your favourite was *'Nothing to Declare.'"*

***

Nothing to Declare

We walked slowly towards the Aircrew Customs Examination Room together, and Mac said, very low: "Musical box inside the navigation bag – usual drill!"
Before I could reply he had disappeared into the office marked 'Incoming Captains' to sign the landing documents.
A burly loader dumped our personal baggage plus navigation equipment on the wooden bench which separated me from the two-ringer of a Customs Officer.
"What have you obtained abroad this trip?" his monotonous voice enquired as I nervously fumbled with the zip fastener of my hold-all.
"Just forty cigarettes and half a bottle," I frankly confessed in a small voice.
Before I had finished, his nimble fingers were expertly burying themselves between the layers of civilian clothing so hurriedly packed in my room at the Hotel Quirinale in Rome earlier that day. He stared at me owlishly for a space before he asked, "Nothing else?" I felt the

132

blood rushing to my face as I nodded and tried to force out a negative reply.

The blue chalk appeared magically from the grubby palm of his right hand, and in a moment the Clearance Squiggle was firmly on my personal kit.

Now for the navigation bag....

"Yours?" he asked curtly, his hairy hand already on the flimsy clip which guarded its secret contents. I nodded. He hesitated. In the same flat, unfriendly voice he said, "Take 'em away."

I lifted both bags down to the floor and had scarcely lit a cigarette before Mac bounced into the room to plant himself before his Inquisitor.

My lighted cigarette was our pre-arranged signal that the navigation bag had escaped search. A wry smile lit up Mac's over-confident face as he jerked out his legal quota of cigarettes and his voice carried a tint of pleasure.

The blue chalk re-appeared from nowhere, and with a flourish and a begrudged "All clear, Cap'n" the Customs Officer moved slowly away to his next victim.

The burly loader moved towards our baggage. We watched as he piled the bags onto the already over-filled trolley.

"Careful!" snapped Mac as the truck was carelessly thrown into a rate-one turn.

His order came too late – the green navigation bag hit the ground at our feet. Her Majesty's Inspector of Customs and Excise turned to see the reason for the commotion. There was a brief moment of silence before the Aircrew Examination was resounding to the defiant, tinkling strains from an expensive Italian musical box – brimming with cigarettes- and the tune-

"WHO'S AFRAID OF THE BIG, BAD WOLF?"

***

"In the end I did listen to you as you got more and more anxious and I did look for another way to earn a living. Then we had the idea of running our own business. Not as glamorous or exciting as flying, I know. Mind you, I still think we did the best thing we could do in the circumstances. Buying *Riversway* from that landlord with the BEA payoff then selling it quickly afterwards at a healthy profit was a damn good move. It meant we had capital and we could set off for a new life in the Midlands. Get back to the family. Your poor old dad was dying; we needed to be on hand to help your mother. It was the right thing to do. Mind you, I hated telling the children. All the friends they had to leave behind. And their schooling was affected - Julie was about to take her eleven plus exam and Tom, he was about to take his O levels. But it had to be done. And we found that business not far from your folks - *The Tuck Shop* on the village green - it seemed a little gold mine. It was the main store in the village and it sold just about everything. You could serve the customers like you used to do so well in the old days at the Bake House - it's in your blood. I know you wanted to do secretarial or some sort of office work but you can see the sense of us running our own business. We had the money and this was our chance to be our own boss.

How was I to know that it would turn out the way it did? That we were at the beck and call of the customers, that everyone else thought they were our boss. How could I have predicted that instead of you running the shop on your own and me getting a job, we both had to pitch in and work like slaves? We never had any time off, worked from seven in the morning till seven at night, seven days a week except Sundays when we were lucky to be closed by five. Then we had to add up the takings and clean the shop. We hardly saw the children. Just the occasional half day off when we could take them to the theatre or the cinema. Our summer holiday was three days only and we had to shut up shop then and didn't the customers moan? Where would they get their bread and their cigarettes? People pilfered from us, that woman who looked after the shop when we went to the *Cash & Carry* - she used to have all her relatives in to fill up their shopping bags when we weren't around. Then that old Harry bloke who used to brush the yard and look after the stock in the outhouse, we were thinking we were kind to give him a job, and he used to fill his snap-bag with Vim and Fairy liquid.

That first year we made a big loss, didn't we? We had to try even harder. The supermarkets were just taking off and customers came in and wound us up by telling us how much cheaper stuff was at Sainsbury's or some such. But the second year we did make a profit and the third year as well. Then you remember that confectionary commercial traveller who took me to one side one day and said: *George, you and Joan have aged ten years in the three years you've been here. Get out while you still can.*

I wonder what life would have been like if we had stayed at *Riversway*? I guess we'll never know."

"What I do know is that it's fish and chips for supper, George," said the kindly nurse, breaking into his monologue. She turned to Mrs Woolly Bundle and spoke in a loud, clear voice, " Ethel, wakey wakey, fish and chips for supper!"

With surprising alacrity, Ethel opened both chameleon eyes, came to full consciousness, rose from her chair and began to make her way to the dining room without saying a word. Taking her arm was the ever attentive, George. Ethel accepted his help with barely a nod. The two shuffled off together; close companions who did not even know each other's real names.

Chapter 18
The Magic Carpet ride

Joan and Tom

"Ooh me duck, I bet you're enjoying that chip buttie. That'll put some fat on yer bones, yer far too thin these days. Them carers, they ain't givin' you what yer need. I said to me 'usband when we come back from the chippie, I'll just tek a plate o' chips' over to our Joan to cheer 'er up."

"Thank you dear Vera," said Joan. "It is a very long time since I had fried chipped potatoes and I've never had some in a sandwich before."

"Well then duck, you've never lived. Now dip yer buttie into some of that there tom-harto sauce. It's de-lish."

"No thank you. This is fine as it is and very filling."

Vera and Joan sat on the sofa in the lounge, partaking of this treat. The coffee table in front of them shyly displayed an array of condiments that lived permanently at the back of Joan's cupboard; most had rarely seen the light of day, let alone exposure to the beam from the chintz shaded standard lamp in the lounge. Joan looked at the fatty morsel on her plate and the vinegar and ketchup bottles et al on the table with a troubled expression. *All too much.*

"Well me duck, I'd best be off else me 'usband'll think I've run away with them gypsies. Did yer see them by the way, they was callin' round again tryin' to get us to have the front yard paved. Me 'usband he were that angry he went off like one of them damp squids he did. He told 'em to sling their 'ook."

Vera slipped through the back door casually in her red sling backs. Joan left the lounge and from her sentry position in the Mdina glass edged dug out in the front room's bay window, she watched Vera return to her own bungalow opposite. Then she took the dishes from the lounge to the kitchen and put the remains of any food plus a table knife and two teaspoons into the waste bin. The rest of the crockery and cutlery, she put into the sink. It was then that she noticed that the back door was ajar. It was never ajar. Yet here she was pulling the door towards her, away from its frame. This had to be investigated. Like a mime artist she looked to each corner of the aperture and with her palms facing outwards she felt the empty space; the door was indeed open and fresh air was meeting her face in a gentle breeze. As Vera had done before her, she slipped through the opening and then through the wrought iron garden gate to gain the open driveway that had been built by the team of gypsies of whom Vera had spoken so disparagingly.

Drunk with the feeling of freedom, a mission formed in Joan's mind. She was off. Off down the road to town without a coat, a hat or a pair of gloves and without shutting the door behind her. For the first time in her adult life she did not care about such things, but she did care about where she was going. Her legs may be aching and her feet may be sore but she kept going doggedly on. After twenty minutes she found her target, a large building with smoked glass windows; it looked like a bank. She opened the heavy door, the third she had managed to negotiate successfully that day, and entered the paved marble vestibule. She approached the counter with her confidence suddenly renewed and a twinkle in her eye.

"Hello there. I'm Mrs Joan Ellis and I'd like two thousand pounds please."

The bank clerk blinked in the style of a pantomime actress and then said, "Do you have an account with us Mrs Ellis? If so, do you have any proof, any ID?"

"Eye Dee? Now what is that? I just asked for two thousand pounds and I believe that I must have more money than that because I haven't been shopping for such a very long time."

"I would like to help you but we will need your cheque book or your bank card or some other form of identification." When Joan's face fell as her newly gained confidence evaporated, the clerk looked at her with sympathy and turning to the desk behind her said, "Madam, let me look you up on our system, just a moment, please." When she left her desk to investigate, Joan took a little wander around the vestibule, pretending to read the posters on the wall and the pamphlets in the cardboard display pockets.

"Mrs Ellis? Would you come back to the counter please?" This phrase was repeated several times before Joan heard the clerk's gentle entreaties and approached the counter once again. "Mrs Ellis, Mrs Joan

Ellis? We don't appear to have any accounts in that name on our system. Are you certain that you bank with us? With Lloyds?"

"Um Lords? No, that does not sound quite right. I do not think so. I think I may have made a mistake. I am so very sorry to have troubled you. I shall go to my bank now. Thank you very much. Goodbye." Before the clerk could offer her any further assistance or ask any questions, Joan had successfully negotiated door number four and was outside on the pavement. *Where to now? Try again.*

Joan squared her shoulders and with a decisive step continued along the road that led further into town. After five minutes' walking, she entered another marble faced monolith that looked to her like a bank. She was correct in her assumption, this was indeed a bank and this time, there was a queue of people waiting to be served. She joined them patiently in line until it was her turn to ask for: "Two thousand pounds please. In cash," with the studied politeness of a bank robber from a Pinewood film studio production circa 1935. She was met with a similar set of raised eye brows, requests and questions that had assailed her at the previous establishment culminating in a similar result; she found herself once more standing on the pavement empty handed. Undeterred, she progressed through all the bank looking structures throughout the High street with the same scenario being played out again and again and with her leaving disappointed until... until finally she walked into a bank that somehow seemed familiar.

This time, when she went through her little speech, the young, well-groomed male bank teller smiled at her and after consulting his computerised banking system, agreed that Mrs Joan Ellis did indeed have an account at the bank. At this, Joan broke down in tears. The young man signalled, subtly but somewhat energetically, to his colleague for assistance while he stepped down from his work station in his pointed and highly polished leather shoes. He then opened the steel door at the side of the counter in order to escort this fragile customer to a small side office. Once she was seated, he offered her a glass of water which she accepted gratefully.

"It was all too much you see. Too rich and I don't feel well. Then I could get out and I thought I could get some money and go shopping. But now I feel unwell and I'm not sure what to do," Joan explained to the young man as she sat on the overstuffed office chair, feeling small and overwhelmed by the excitement of the afternoon's impulsive adventure. The young man listened patiently but was clearly out of his depth, unused to having to calm elderly, confused

138

ladies. Relief was writ large on his shiny, rehydrated and deeply moisturised face when Shirley, his middle aged colleague entered the small interview room. Shirley, all soft cashmere twin set and pink pearls, introduced herself to Joan and then took over, allowing young Brian to return to his safe, comfort zone of numbers and spreadsheets.

"Mrs Ellis," Shirley began, "I'm so sorry that you aren't feeling very well. Is there anyone at home whom we can call to let them know you are here? A member of your family perhaps? Do you know who we could contact? Who we could phone?"

"George isn't at home and I don't know telephone numbers."

"Perhaps if you gave us the name of your doctor?" persisted Shirley, gently.

"That's easy. It's Dr Vale. You'll find him on Twizzle or Poodle whatever it's called I'm sure," announced Joan with stunned delight; she had remembered the GP's name and this achievement made her smile for the first time. Shirley could not help but smile too.

"Dr Vale? Are you sure, Mrs Ellis? Just one moment, please. I shall make a few enquiries and I will return. Will you be alright here for a little while?"

Joan nodded; indeed it looked as if she might nod off completely and so Shirley left her to rest, putting a 'do not disturb' sign on the milky glass office door. As she made her way back to her own desk in the large open office behind the imposing marble counter, she met her line manager who asked her for a detailed update on the "confused Miss Marple situation". The boy Brian had evidently been creative in his description on his way back to his haven of numbers. "It's that Mrs Ellis," reported Shirley. "She's very confused. She shouldn't be out on her own. Did you see her? She's got no coat on and looks very cold. She said her doctor was Dr Vale that's how I know for sure she must be confused because there was that radio show Mrs Vale's Diary or some such about a country doctor when I was growing up. You know old people go back through their memories and remember stuff from long ago and think it's now. That's how I know she must be very confused, poor old dear."

So it was with a certain irony that when Shirley consulted the search engine on the internet looking at the local surgeries in the area, she found the name of Dr Vale. He did exist and was not a figment of an old lady's warped memory or a radio programme from the 1950's. Duly chastened, Shirley made a call to the surgery and as a result, received some sensible advice. A doctor would call on Mrs Ellis at her home later that day but in the meantime, it was suggested that arrangements should be made for the patient to be taken back to her bungalow in Caldron Close. The surgery passed on the emergency contact details of Mrs Ellis' son Tom, who lived locally. In due course, whilst Mrs Ellis took a well- earned nap, Tom was alerted and told of the situation. Shocked to hear of his mother's exploits after having left the house on her own, he stopped the office meeting he was chairing and set off for the bank immediately.

*

Back in the bungalow later that day, Tom and his mother sat on their habitually favoured chairs in the lounge. Joan had not wanted her usual cup of tea and was, to Tom's eyes, looking decidedly green about the gills. "Maybe you should try to eat something, Mother," he said at a loss as to what else to suggest.

"I think I want to have a lie down now. It's been such an afternoon." Tom watched her get up and make her way to the bedroom. She was still clutching the envelope containing her treasured haul in used notes; her demand having been modified to the more modest sum of two hundred pounds, paid to her by the bank cashier once Tom had been able to supply the necessary documentation.

Tom felt equally drained by the events of the previous few hours. His mother had been wandering the streets in a vulnerable state, who knows what might have happened to her? What if the bank staff had not alerted him? It would soon be dark and she would become even more disorientated. The carefully constructed system designed to keep his mother safe was dangerously flawed. In fact it was falling apart. The carers were good but they were not there all the time. The outer doors were armed with alarms but that system had failed to alert anyone or anything to the fact that his mother had silently wandered out. Julie, Janine and he were all visiting Mum regularly as well as keeping up visits to Dad in hospital. Everyone had a busy life of their own and lived varying distances away. What more should they do? What more can they do?

And then there was the imminent trip to Australia. He and Barbara had planned their holiday of a lifetime; they had saved for the best part of two years and it was all booked and paid for. The Mum and Dad situation had been steadily escalating over the past few months. Each month had presented its challenges but now the

140

problems were becoming more and more difficult to solve as their needs became more and more difficult to meet. How could he leave the country at such a time as this?

But Mum would want them to go to Australia, his internal argument continued. They would be carrying out a duty with which she had charged them, at a time when she was less confused. They were taking something special with them as her gift for the Australian relatives. To celebrate the Millennium, Mum had completed a huge embroidery depicting hands linked across the ocean uniting the Australian branch of the family with the main genealogy tree in England. There were scores of beautifully worked symbols representing both nations including animals and flags. Mum had spent hours making sure the work was finished in readiness for Tom and Barbara's visit Down Under. The embroidery had been rolled up and placed in a cardboard tube several months before. The way Mum had been lately, he guessed that she could have forgotten all about it. She no longer did any of her wonderful sewing or any of her other creative hobbies.

They were supposed to be flying off to Australia next week.

Julie and Janine knew all about it and had encouraged him to go, saying they would handle things whilst he was away, and that he had already done so much holding the family fort, on duty at first line of defence in the big parental crisis. They had said that he needed to get away and recharge his batteries.

But could he really go and walk away from this ever evolving situation that seemed to throw up unexpected challenges on a daily basis? Dad was in a sheltered hospital environment so the risk to his safety was vastly reduced. But Mum on the other hand, she was on her own in the bungalow —how would he feel if anything happened to her while he was away? Nobody could watch her every minute; was it reasonable to leave her in the care of the visiting helpers and his sisters who lived miles away? He felt trapped in a cage of guilt.

Sitting, physically inert in the confines of the old arm chair, his head in his hands, he wrestled with the inner turmoil this new dilemma evoked. It was then that he heard the cat being sick.

A few seconds later her realised he was not at home but was at Mum and Dad's bungalow. They did not have a cat.

*

Joan had arrived at her bedroom a few minutes before and had planned to have *a little lie down - what Georgie called 'some Egyptian P.T.',* she had thought with a smile. She sat on the side of her bed but her head began to spin as she tried to focus on the detail of the circular Persian rug that she loved so much. *I'm glad I moved it here from the lounge. Just mine, just here.* Increasingly feeling dizzy and nauseous, she failed to reach the bathroom before nature took over and she vomited on her favourite exotic carpeting. *Such a shame! How could I do such a thing? I am never ill like that. How terrible!*

Tom walked in on her *state of shame*, and persuaded her back to her position sitting on her bed while he went to get her a glass of water. While she sipped this slowly, he cleared up the mess. All she could say was that she was *terribly sorry Darling* and that she would clean everything up *in a minute*. That was *women's work* and he was not to do it himself. Tom ignored her treatise on the roles of men and women and continued to wash the delicate pile with the carpet foam he had found under the kitchen sink. By the time he had finished, Mother had slumped into a semi prone position so he gently encouraged her to lie down so he could cover her with a light blanket. He left the bedroom door open so that he could keep her under close observation from his watch post on the small wooden chair in the hallway. In a few moments, his head was back in his hands.

*

The doorbell heralding Dr Vale's arrival was a welcome cavalry bugle blast of relief. The harassed and overworked GP was first taken into the lounge for an update on the events of Mum's day. Tom was so grateful to be able to share his concerns with the good doctor who listened attentively. Dr Vale had concerns of his own; how could he convey to Tom that he knew that the behaviours that Mrs Ellis was exhibiting were likely to be part of a downwards spiral? That despite the hope in Tom's eyes, things were not going to get any better. The die was cast.

They both heard a weak cry from the back of the bungalow and Tom responded immediately by entering the bedroom and putting on the small bedside light. Mother was by then fully awake but seemed unaware as to what had happened to her earlier. Tom thought it best not to elucidate but did report that the dear Doctor Vale had called to see how she was, and that he was in the hallway at that moment waiting to check how she was feeling. Initially, Mother became agitated but Dr Vale was able to reassure her as he entered the room in his brisk, but friendly professional manner reminiscent of her beloved *Dr Finlay* of TV '*Casebook*' fame.

Tom heard his soothing words from the hallway where he waited anxiously. The examination seemed to take a long time and during the wait, he returned to his dilemma which now seemed to have decided itself: he and Barbara could forget Uluru and the Barrier Reef, the Aborigines and the Sidney harbour bridge and the Opera House– they would not be taking any air trips anywhere anytime soon.

Dr Vale emerged eventually and his expression was inscrutable as he requested that he had a few words with Tom before he left. Tom led him back to the lounge, his heart heavy.

"I think your mother is physically stable at the moment but I think she may need to have some gastric tests. I am not sure what happened to her today to induce the vomiting. She may have a bug or it may have been something she ate. In any case she is dehydrated so a few days in hospital for these gastric tests and to fix her up on a drip, help her get rehydrated is what I suggest. She also spoke about a pain in her head that travelled across her brow. She is definitely quite confused and she may be finding it difficult coping with the shock of having George in hospital. I know what a close couple they are and how dependent they are on each other. It must be very difficult for her, mustn't it?"

Tom heartily agreed, grateful that Dr Vale had such insight, such a full grasp of the family dynamics and the crisis that was inexorably playing out. It was agreed that admission to hospital was the most appropriate action to take.

When the doctor finally left, having made several telephone calls to his surgery and to the local hospital to make the necessary arrangements for Joan's admission later that evening, Tom looked in on his mother. Joan had slipped back into a peaceful slumber, curled up with the comforting feel of the fat envelope tucked beneath her. Tom rubbed his forehead. He too had many calls to make: to his wife, to his sisters and to the Care agency. A carer was due to be visiting shortly. He made a mental list of things he had to do to help prepare his mother for her hospital stay. This was not going to be easy. She was not going to like the idea one bit.

Chapter 19
Rites of Passage

Julie and Janine

"I came as soon as I could. When Tom called at the weekend, we were in the middle of moving Simon out of his uni digs. You know the drill; you've heard me describe it before: first we sort out the *floordrobe* – why don't they ever hang anything up? Then we take the dirty laundry to the laundrette round the corner from his digs to turn it all to that charming shade, *Hint of Putty*. In fact, did I tell you that the '*Welcome Wash-it-here-ia*' was where I spent my last birthday? At least music was playing so Lizzy and I were able to celebrate by dancing in our own mini disco when all the while the machines were churning away. Got some strange looks from the other customers waiting for their wash cycle to finish. Anyhow I digress. Then we help him pack his plastic folding crates with his books and stuff, fill in the holes in the wall where they missed the dart board, touch up the paintwork with *Hint of Magnolia* where the takeaway exploded, burn the bedding. All the usual stuff. In spite of all that, you just know that measly landlord will not cough up the full three hundred quid deposit. Simon said the last lot of students got charged for a broken window in the bathroom that was damaged when they moved in. And guess what? It's still broken so I bet Simon and his mates will also be stung for it. Nice little extra earner for Mr F. Bustard. At least I think that's what Simon said the landlord's name was." I unburdened freely to my sister when I arrived at *Treetops*. We had planned to travel north together the following day in order to visit Mum in hospital. Janine empathised; living in a boys' boarding school meant she knew all about the detail and the smell; the fragrance of a young man's room that could only be described as *Hint of Warm Shut-in Hamster*.

"Rites of passage; worth it I guess," said Janine sympathetically, leading me through the well- appointed schoolhouse to its spacious kitchen.

"For him or for me?" I said, knowing full well what she meant.

"For Simon. Wonderful that you are putting him through uni. A big financial commitment for you and James though. But it'll be worth it in the end, you'll see. And he's doing a decent subject not like some of the Mickey Mouse courses that lead to second class honours in Cut and Paste."

"Indeed," I replied, "just so long as he doesn't follow his father and me – and all his aunts and uncles for that matter, into a career in teaching. The profession is so very different now to when we all started."

"How did all that happen? We are all doing it, aren't we? I suppose there was no such thing as Career Advice when we were at school, was there?" said Janine. "You were expected to be a teacher, a nurse or a secretary."

"Teaching was what Mum and Dad wanted us to do. What they persuaded us to do. As Mum used to say: *In teaching, you will always have a secure job, Darlings, and be paid the same as a man and if you leave work to have a family, you will be able to return to work easily.* She was right in so many ways but there is so much more to the job than Mum and Dad could ever have realised."

"Too right," said Janine, "especially nowadays with all the constant changes and the testing programmes. Not a profession I would choose if I had my time again."

"I must try to give Lizzy and Simon as much choice as possible. There is a whole world of jobs out there. Mind you, if I really mean what I say about giving them a choice, then I mustn't stand in their way if they do choose teaching. At least, if they do decide to go for it, they won't be going in blind."

Later, over garlic dough balls and a very fine rioja, around the aircraft carrier deck cum pine table in *Treetops* kitchen, discussion turned to the imminent hospital visit.

"Tom said that Mum was not happy about going into the Infirmary. She told him that she was absolutely fine and that she did not need to bother the doctor and nurses with her *minor ailment, Darlings,*" I reported. "I don't know how he convinced her to go into hospital in the end. From what the doctor said, it must be absolutely the right thing to screen her and check she has not got any gastric problems. Equally, I think it will give the staff a chance to observe and monitor her mental faculties. The plate spinning act we have been trying to manage is truly going into wobble mode. And poor Tom, he must be feeling so stressed what with the Oz trip and all."

"I told him, he just *must* go! He cannot miss out on this chance. We can step up to the mark, can't we? We are sisters. *Sisters are doing it for themselves,*" Janine began singing. I found myself joining in and doing one of those punch in the air salutes. "We can manage the situation – somehow!" she said with infectious optimism; it was clear that she had managed to convince herself at any rate and this was having its positive effect on me.

The following morning saw us not quite so buoyant as we climbed into Janine's little red car. However, with our favourite music selection vibrating the vehicle's vinyl clad interior, our hope gradually started to return. The Mutual Adoration Society was once again up and running, in business and cooking on gas. Thelma and Louise were hitting the road.

"What do you think started this latest health problem with Mum?" I asked Janine, as she took the country route, avoiding the motorway. Would Louise have done that? I think not.

"Well I think she may have had a tummy upset from rich food. She's not used to having much fat. Think of the diet that Mum and Dad have got used to over the years –just chicken and boiled potatoes. Not *French fried potatoes between two slices of bread and butter Darlings!*" Janine mimicked Mumspeak expertly.

"When did it all start? They were always trying to lose weight but I do remember coming home from college and discovered no Edam in the fridge. They had stopped using butter and cheese altogether, stopped eating red meat and had started to eat stuff like muesli – 'dust and rat droppings' I called it at the time- although I have since learned to loathe it."

Janine smiled. "It did seem to be an overnight decision. One minute they were eating a simple low fat healthy diet, the next they were dining '*Les Miserables*' style."

"Do you remember when the new milk started to appear in their fridge?" I continued. "That milk skimmed of everything nice so it was thin and watery and almost blue. I know that it was supposed to be healthy but they had such a paltry diet it's no wonder they got so thin."

"A poultry diet?" said Janine. "They certainly never ate anything other than chicken."

"Apart from the Mars bars. What did the advert say? Mum used to sing the jingle: *A Mars a day helps you work rest and play.* Mum always had some in her handbag and used to say that eating one was the equivalent of having a meal."

"And there was that corn oil that suddenly appeared in the cupboard – Mazola – that was it," added Janine.

"Oh yes, and do you remember that guy we met in Abbey Park who invited us to a Mazola party?" I could not help digressing.

Janine laughed in a Louise style way and adopting the accent of a debauched Elvis lookalike deadbeat of the 1970's replied, "*U huh. Would you girls like to come to a Mazola Party?*"

"What's a Mazola Party?" I replied in a high pitched school girl lisp.

"Well gals it's where you take all the furniture out of a room and cover the floor with plastic sheets. Then you pour on a couple of them there bottles of Mazola oil. Then everyone takes off their clothes and you just squirm. U huh, Yes sir-ee. I mean SQUIRM."

"Oh that sounds disgusting!" said I in best shocked schoolgirl.

*

The fact was, in reality, we were absolutely shocked schoolgirls. During the journey, we reflected on our upbringing which would have prepared us for taking the veil more that adequately, and I do not mean the wedding sort.

Our teenage years were spent in Copcaston, the sleepy village we had moved to following Mum and Dad's selling of *The Tuck Shop*. Our schooling took place in the nearby town of Quorn, in a grammar school for girls. The combination of single sex education and living in a cul de sac meant that we rarely encountered, let alone spoke with, anyone of the male persuasion. That is apart from our father and brother, a few ancient and chalk dusty school teachers, an over friendly and vastly ugly postman, antique Daddy Greasly who lived next door and the dustbin men.

We were super-conscientious school goody-goodies who travelled straight home on the designated service coach after a day at school, wearing our round domed felt school hats fixed firmly in place by garrotting black elastic under our chins and our coats done all the way up to the top button. Our satchels bulged with Latin verbs and declensions, with the Corn Laws and the Reformation, with glaciation and volcanoes and with precis and clauses. Our house, at the end of a close in a small housing estate, would be empty on our return with both parents at work and our brother at college. So after putting the key in the Yale lock, comforting the highly strung ball of black poodle

147

curls that passed for a canine lying in wait for us across the threshold, we changed out of our stiff scratchy uniforms and into crimplene.

The journey home had been our rest break; homework tasks began in earnest almost immediately. We would sit on our bunk beds with our *Princess* or *Diana* comic annuals balanced on our knees. These were the improvised study desks that supported our many exercise books that we filled meticulously with carefully inscribed handwriting in washable Quink from the well worked nibs of our treasured fountain pens. Janine was always aiming for the *top girl in the class* prize and she was to win it over and over again. I won something too, a sort of consolation prize awarded for: *the neatest kept set of exercise books.* I am mortified to admit that I was immensely proud.

While we were ruining our eyes with study and indulging in self-denial, some of our school chums were hanging out at bus stations, ice cream soda parlours and frothy coffee bars, talking to boys and meeting them at the fair. The only male I can ever remember meeting at the fair had bulging eyes, golden scaly skin and was swimming in a leaky plastic bag.

But then Malta happened to us.

The family holiday on this little island in the Mediterranean opened the Ellis nunnery doors to romance and adventure. This was not the idea my parents had in mind when they let the apartment in Winter Street, Bugibba for a fortnight. My father had spent many hours in Malta during his flying days; in fact he was a member of the first civilian aircrew to land on the island after the end of the Second World War. The barren, rocky group of isles with its Biblical scenery, ancient history and friendly people had gained a special place in his heart. He wished to share its marvels with his wife and family, knowing that they would appreciate all that Malta had to offer. And in this he was absolutely right, but not quite in the way he had anticipated.

After a couple of days under the rays of the molten metal sun and in contact with the sea salt, Janine's and my long schoolgirl hair had become thick. Our skin glowed salmon pink and we knew that the early morning mirror had dazzled us with teeth whiter than usual; all down to the contrast with our emergent tan. We were becoming 'interesting' in a *'failing novice nun'* kind of way and we could not believe our change in fortune.

The attention that we began to receive from the local Lotharios had been, in equal parts, as thrilling as it had been unexpected. Back in England, we had never had so much as a wolf whistle, yet here the wolves had been hunting in packs; packs loaded into cars that cruised the coast road constantly during the late afternoon and throughout the evening.

This unexpected turn of events caused Mum and Dad considerable unease.

"Youths grow up very quickly here in the heat, Darlings. Ha-huh-ha," was Mum's way of explaining the new social dynamics that played out every time we walked the coastal path between Bugibba and St. Paul's Bay.

*

"We were so brave, weren't we?" I said to Janine as we made irritatingly good progress on our journey.

"Lucky, as much as anything. When you think of what might have happened. When those two lads offered *to show us the island* and Mum and Dad felt they had to let us go, believing we would be going round Malta on the buses. But how were any of us meant to know they really meant the tiny island in the bay accessible only by boat?"

"Yeah, like Bali Hi on the horizon - but completely uninhabited- the only human form on it was St Paul - and he was a statue! It was the biggest misunderstanding since the day we thought we were going to see the monkeys at Mount St. Bernard's Abbey." I laughed.

"We were so naïve and amazingly those young men turned out to be worthy of our trust," Janine replied wryly. "Good Maltese boys; their mothers would have been proud."

"I think they must have wondered what on earth they had on their hands. What a liability we must have presented. We were no fun for them at all. With a single Grade One swimming certificate between us we were hopeless. On that boat, I was as nautical as a cow with a musket and just as dangerous – I nearly capsized us all!" I remembered with shame.

"No wonder they did not keep up any penfriend correspondence after we flew home. And they must have been so shocked when we returned the following year! There we were at the *festa* fireworks and we spotted them and gave them our best smouldering look from across the square – and they had the gall to look the other way and scarper!"

"Anyhow when we went back to school, we stood a lot taller than our five feet nothing. We had holiday romances to whisper about," Janine smiled.

"Poor Mum and Dad though, they must have been at their wits' end. I do remember that on the plane home, Dad actually had two fingers of whisky, bless him," I said trying to swallow an equally large measure of guilt.

"Yes, dear Dad and Mum. I wonder how Dad is today. We must visit him soon, once we've seen how Mum is," Janine replied.

"Yes, we must. How much further? And I want you to say *at least a hundred miles,*" I whined.

"Sorry. You'll have to be content with just five."

The five miles went by in a flash and it was once again 'face up to reality' time.

We turned into the hospital grounds and took the circular route that led us eventually to the appropriate carpark for Gibson Eliot ward. With our whimsical Thelma and Louise sunglasses flung once again upon the dashboard – it was December after all- we reverted to becoming two middle aged housewives, losing all our confidence in the process. We were not sure of what we were about to find.

Mum was in a ward on the second floor, in an airy room overlooking a landscaped area of shrubs, trees, paths and benches. Hospital buildings surrounded this green oasis but did not overpower it. However, Mum's bed was facing away from the window and at first sight it was clear that she was not happy. Her lovely face that could so readily transform into a beautiful smile, was wearing a decidedly determined expression: her mouth was downturned and in the shape of an x like Miffy the rabbit's. Not a good sign. We approached with caution and a certain amount of trepidation.

"Hello Mum," we chorused. Mum looked at us both and smiled her dazzling smile. "Darlings, how wonderful to see you."

Our sighs of relief were audible. Mum had recognised us. Whilst Janine went off to get a chair for herself, I sat in the armchair beside the bed and took in the surroundings. Above the bed was a sign that read *Nil by mouth* and another inscribed *Anice Ellis.* Mum was wearing a cotton nightdress that may have been her own but I certainly did not recognise it. I surmised that Tom had provided some essential items for the stay in hospital. Janine and I had brought some more clothing and toiletries with us so that Mum should be well stocked, especially as we were unsure as to how long her stay in hospital might be. There was a drip stand on one side of the bed and a bedside cabinet on the other, with Mum's handbag sitting smugly upon it. These observations took seconds before I launched into my usual 'visitor to someone in hospital' speech. I was about to ask about hospital food when I realised that of course Mum was not being served meals –*nil by mouth*. I guessed that she was being nourished by the drip feed. The drip feed with a line that, as I further investigated, did not appear to be attached to Mum's body.

"Tell me about yourselves," said Mum as Janine joined me at the bedside. It was clear that Mum would rather not talk about her own situation. Knowing her, she would be feeling vanquished, made to submit to treatment that she did not feel she needed. There was still a great deal of Nordic Woman still present in the elderly patient holding court here. While Janine delivered her news snippets including the latest tale of the Duke of Edinburgh Awards orienteering adventure with her pupils on Dartmoor, I took the opportunity to seek out the nursing staff. This proved to be enlightening. Apparently, Mrs Anice Ellis had been a tricky patient to deal with.

"One thing that may help to tell you is that although her first name is Anice, she has been called Joan - her middle name - all her life," I told the young and cheery nurse at her station in the foyer.

"Well that will indeed help, and does explain a lot. Your mam docs not look up when you call her name and when she gets out of bed and tries to escape from the ward, she does not look back when you call her."

"Oh dear. Has she been trying to escape?"

"It's not a problem. She can't go far. Although she did go next door into the male ward yesterday. We found her sat down drinking another patient's cup of tea and chatting to some visitors."

"I am sorry. I think she does get confused. Can she have tea and meals now that she's not on a drip any longer?"

"Well, she has started to have light meals but she is still on a drip," said the nurse looking puzzled. She came out from behind her counter and set off to Mum's bed space with me hot on her heels. What we found was Mum smiling away at something Janine had said, her hands folded on the bedsheets in front of her.

"Mrs Ellis? Joan?" inquired the nurse, "have you pulled your drip line out again?"

"My whatty?" smiled Mum to the nurse. "These little girls are so sweet to me, you know," she reported to Janine and me. "Could you pass me my handbag, Darlings?" As the nurse went about resetting the equipment stand, Janine passed Mum the mothership with brown handles. Mum rootled round the vast cavity and produced a bundle of bandages in the same way a magician might pull a bouquet of flowers from a top hat. "All this knitting was wrapped around my arm and when I wanted to get out of bed, it kept pulling me back. Would you care for it?" she offered the blood stained bundle to the nurse as if she were offering her a selection of chocolates.

"Now Mrs Ellis, Joan, I think we had better put your line back in. You will feel all the benefit of it. But you must leave it alone," said the long suffering and patient nurse. Whilst she went off to get the medical pack, Janine and I tried to persuade Mum that the drip was best for her and would make her feel better.

"Ha-huh-ha. Is that so? Now tell me about yourselves. Such lovely teeth. Both of you. Do you work here?"

I saw the whites of Janine's eyes as they went into a -we've lost her again- roll.

"Mum," I entreated. "We're Janine and Julie, your daughters."

"Daughters? Have I got children? Oh how lovely. Where are they? Have they gone out to play?"

The nurse returned and deftly reattached the line to Mum's shrinking limb. *How did she get so very thin?* When she had finished adjusting the bedclothes to ensure that Mum was comfortable and securely positioned, I asked her if I could have another word. She took me off to the nurses' station, leaving Janine to battle on in *Anice's Wonderland.*

"Could you give me any idea of what the doctor thinks might be wrong with our Mum, please?"

"Well," said the nurse, opening up a buff file, "it's thought that your mam had a minor gastric problem which has now settled down. But she also showed signs of a urine infection and got herself a bit dehydrated. The elderly, they get a bit disorientated by a water problem and so the main purpose here has been to treat the infection and rehydrate her. She'll be ready to be discharged in the next few days. Don't worry. She'll soon be home."

Chapter 20
Double or drop

Julie and Janine

When we were growing up in the nineteen sixties, there used to be a children's television programme that we all loved, called *'Crackerjack!'* In the show, a game was played where child contestants had to answer quiz questions whilst standing on a pedestal. Their correct answers were rewarded with prize items like cricket bats, skipping ropes, books, boxed games, and soft toys – all of which they could take home if, and only if, they could keep them held in their arms for the length of the game. If they gave an incorrect answer, they were given something far less interesting to hold: a vegetable. A lady presenter would continue to add toys and boxed games to the child's pile and the child's aim was to avoid dropping anything. If something did fall from their arms, a loud buzzer sounded and the game ended abruptly with the child giving back all the toys in return for a consolation prize of a *Crackerjack!* pencil.

The excitement and suspense gradually built for all watching when the stack of things got heavier and more unwieldy, threatening to submit to the forces of gravity. In the small child's arms the tennis racket would begin to teeter, the soft stuffed bunny would slip, the skipping rope would unravel from its loosely wound coil, the pile of annuals would slide, the Etch-a sketch pad would slither over the Meccano set, the boxed chess set would wobble and then, then...to this mini avalanche in motion, would be added....a cabbage.

*

"What are we going to do? If they discharge Mum in the next few days, where is she going to go? She can't be left on her own in the bungalow all day can she? She has definitely deteriorated mentally since the gastric problem and the urine infection and I reckon that she

153

will need more extensive care than she's been having at home up until now. Don't you think so, Janine?" I panicked.

"God yes, the carers- as lovely as they are- just calling in at regular times to help her with meals and meds won't be enough after the round-the-clock care she has been receiving in hospital. I think she needs more time in a supportive setting in order to recuperate," replied Janine, equally panicked.

"But you heard what the doctor said, as far as the hospital is concerned, case closed. They have treated Mum and she needs to move out and free up a bed. I know he did not say that in so many words, but his meaning was clear."

"Ok then. Let's look at the options," said Janine struggling to adopt a calm, problem solving mode. "Could one of the three of us move in with Mum for a few weeks? Until she is better? Well, until she is better able to cope on her own again?" She looked at the expression on my face; it was an almost perfect copy of Edvard Munch's portrait '*The Scream*'. She drew a deep breath before continuing, "I think you'll agree that the answer to that has got to be a 'No'."

"Yes. I mean No. I mean I agree with you," I stammered. It was coming home to me just how much Janine and I had relied on our brother to run the *Mum and Dad Show;* a business which was now running out of control. Behind the bravado, our Thelma and Louise headscarves were slipping over our eyes as we tried to hide from the reality before us. Our mother was no longer presenting as our mother. She did not know us most of the time and instead of being the warm parent full of wisdom and love that we had spent our whole lives taking for granted, she had become this other person who did weird things and who distrusted us and was suspicious of everyone around her. Time spent with her was becoming more and more distressing and painful as we witnessed her decline. Whatever we tried to say or do did not seem to be halting that process. Selfishly, we wanted our Mum back; *but what must it be like for her? What could be going through her head when she finds herself away from all that is familiar?* The truth was we had to face up to making a monumental decision and we were struggling. "We need to help her return home where at least she knows where she is - and familiar surroundings would help her memory and help her feel secure. But I think we'll all agree that at the moment she's too vulnerable to take that step. Even if we all took it in turns to stay with her, we don't know how long it might be before she can cope on her own, well with the support of visiting carers again. The prospect is too open-ended," I feared.

Whilst nodding in agreement, Janine valiantly continued to talk us through the problem logically and practically. "Yes, I know that but we still need to look at possibilities. Now, Tom might be the closest to Mum geographically but he's got the demands of a full time job and could not possibly put that on hold for an indefinite amount of time."

"And anyway, he will have only just returned from Oz at the time when Mum is most likely to be discharged," I stated, feeling light-headed. "What would his employer think of him coming back from holiday and then asking for a month off to look after his mum?"

"True," said Janine, her hands together with fingers steepled in the pose of a magistrate. "Then if we take the case of you, Julie, you live over a hundred miles from Mum; you also have a full time job and a family to run. So it's a no brainer; you wouldn't be able to leave your home, family and job for an unspecified amount of time in order to provide the care Mum needs at the moment."

"And you, Janine," I said, taking up her virtual gavel, "you live fifty miles away and also have a full time live-in job teaching at the boarding school – along with all the extra-curricular duties that take up your evenings and weekends. Even if you moved in with Mum during the school holidays, that would only be a band aid solution, we would not be tackling the real problem.

And the same applies to the idea of having Mum come to stay with one of us," I continued. "None of us could supply the care she really needs right now. After all, she has reached a stage where she ought to be more closely monitored – look at what happened when she wandered out of the bungalow the other day. That was the start of this latest episode that led to her being admitted to hospital. We must find a way to keep her safe."

"And then there's Dad to consider," Janine replied, "we must keep up our visits to him. At least he is in a safe place. Will he ever be fit enough to come home I wonder? He's been in the psychiatric unit a long time now."

"We're going to have to share all our thoughts with Tom. It's time we rang Big Bro in Dandenong," I hyperventilated.

*

155

A week of frenzied telephone based activity went by with much *weeping and gnashing of teeth,* as Charlton Heston would say in his dramatic delivery of Bible excerpts on Dad's treasured gramophone record. Eventually, the hospital staff agreed that whilst Mrs Ellis had completed her treatment in their care and should be discharged from hospital, she was in too frail a state to return to independent living. Advice was sought from Social Services and this led to a temporary solution: it had been agreed that Mum should be transferred to a local nursing home for a limited period.

All three of us were vastly relieved as this would mean Mum would be kept safe and have the specialist care she needed whilst she convalesced. It also bought us some time, a chance to plan what we were going to do next. It felt more than uncomfortable to realise that the fate of Mum and Dad was truly in our hands. There was no going back now; whether we liked it or not, we were taking control and responsibility for our parents' lives. *How had it come so swiftly to this? It seemed only a few weeks ago when I shared frequent three-way phone conversations with Mum and Dad. They listened patiently and lovingly to every tiny insignificant detail of our lives. They loved to hear about how the kids were doing at school, what was being planned for birthdays and holidays. They were always ready to come to the rescue, to soothe the children in the event of little fisticuffs in the playground, tummy aches and colds. I would turn to them in happy times and sad times, when the dinner got spoilt or the washing caught in the rain, when the picture fell off the wall and smashed and when someone drove into the back of our car. When we were ill and when we were well. When we were flushed and when we were hard up. They had been two of the pillars that held me up, from whom I sought and received praise, reassurance, comfort and unconditional love. Somehow these pillars had tumbled as surely as if they had been smote by the mighty Samson of Charlton's Bible reading.*

*

Bramwell turned out to be a very pleasant convalescent home in the depths of the undulating Leicestershire countryside. Janine and I took to the road once again to visit Mum in her new surroundings. As guilt ridden as prodigal daughters, we had set off to the nursing home whose management had kindly agreed to admit Mum straight from the hospital. Tom, returning from his trip of a lifetime, had lost no time in

156

visiting Mum in the home a few days before us. He had reported that Mum seemed to be settling into the new surroundings *Bramwell* provided – an establishment that appeared to be well run. He shared our worries about Mum, noting that she had got a lot thinner and was more confused and forgetful than before he went away. He had taken his Australian holiday snaps to show her, hoping that photographs of the antipodean branch of the family would prompt her memory. She shocked him by her entirely blank response to the picture showing her cousin receiving the gift of the '*Hands across the Sea*' embroidery that Mum had taken years to create. Even though Mum had rushed to finish it, had wrapped it in a cardboard tube and only weeks ago charged Tom with the important duty of delivering it, the piece now seemed to mean absolutely nothing to her.

It was eleven o'clock on a bitterly cold and windy morning when Janine drove her car into the grounds. There were no other cars present in the visitors' carpark causing us to pause and question whether we had followed correctly the instructions given to us by Tom in a recent phone call.

"No, this is right," said Janine, referring to her notes. "We can visit at any point on any day, but if possible we must try to avoid meal times." It was not meal time but time to get out of the warm cocoon of the car and face the cold, the wind and the music.

Before us was the imposing main entrance with reception area. Here, we were greeted by a huge talking floral display. Or so it seemed. Suddenly a young woman, the real owner of the voice we had heard emanating from the agapanthus, popped up from behind the high wooden parapet attached to the top of her desk and smiled.

"I'm sorry," she said, "I didn't mean to startle you." Like someone in a fantasy movie, she seemed to know who we were and whom we were visiting. She even seemed to know the latest on Mum, telling us that she was "a sweet lady who was settling in just fine." She then left her fragrant floral bower and came away from her heavy desk with its Victorian privacy panelling and on the ethereal feet of a fairy, guided us out of the reception hall and into a wide corridor. This walkway branched off to left and right at regular intervals; each branch led to separate single storey wards painted different shades of green, *like leaves,* I thought to myself.

"There's a big dining room at the end of this corridor," she enlightened us, "I shall take you there first to have a look and then I'll take you to your mum."

The dining room smelt as we had come to expect, of boiled cabbage and cauliflower. However, its large windows looked out onto tidily kept gardens and hedges clipped to within an inch of their lives.

With our fairy guide, we returned to the corridor and following her directions, approached a set of wooden double doors. "Mrs Ellis is in *Bluebell*, her bed-space is at the end of the room by the window," she told us before she returned to her fragrant reception desk. Taking a deep breath, we pressed the key pad of the secure door as instructed, and entered.

Standing there at the far end of the room, swathed in a pale blue nightdress and trailing dressing gown was a tiny person that I did not recognise as our mother. She seemed to have become very short suddenly, although my brain told me that this was not possible. Recently, we had only seen her in a bed; she must have been gradually diminishing over the weeks and months and I had not properly observed the change. In sympathy with her body, her horizons had shrunk to what she could see from the window. But what could she see from her window?

"Over the hills and far away...Tom he was a piper's son... he learnt to play when he was young, but the only tune that he could play was over the hills and far away. Over the hills and a great way off the wind shall blow my topknot off." Mum was singing in her reedy voice I had only heard in church.

"Hello Mum," we both said in unison, like Tweedledum and Tweedledee. She looked at us balefully at first before apparent recognition dawned and rearranged her features into her smile.

"Darlings, how lovely to see you. Have you come to take me home?"

"Not today, Mum," I ventured, "you have a bit more healing to do after your nasty bout. Are you being well looked after here? It seems very posh. And you have a nice view from the window."

"Yes. I know my house is just over that hill and through some fields so when the wind stops blowing, I shall walk home. Only a couple of stiles to cross and I shall be there," she replied, as she shifted from one bare foot to another, pointing excitedly to the route she had planned to take. *"Over the hills and far away..."* she resumed her song.

Janine and I exchanged worried glances. *Mum may know who we are but not where she is and we will have to warn the fairy and her fellow sprites that an escape plan may be in development.* I knew

Janine had received my telepathic message when she quickly changed the subject.

"We saw a very pleasant dining room down the corridor. Have you been enjoying the food served here?" Janine asked. This led to a rambling commentary about the meals Mum had enjoyed or endured. It transpired that she did not have a keen appetite at the moment, fuelling our concern that she may be at risk of diminishing in size even further.

"I have brought you some of your sewing to do as I know how you might be missing it." Casually, I passed Mum a tablecloth marked out with floral sprigs in navy blue ink along with a wallet of needles, her embroidery thread and scissors. She looked at the cloth as if she had never seen it before in her life, yet three of the motifs had already been worked by her several months before. She then took up the tiny pair of scissors, placing them in her palm as if she held a precious jewel. Then it was the turn of the threads to gain her attention and she stroked each skein as if it was a precious lock of baby hair.

"What do I have to do?" she asked in a little girl voice.

"You don't *have* to do anything with these things," I answered, "I just thought you might like to do some more of your sewing."

Looking at me as if I was her teacher, she said, "I will try to do my best." Then with great reverence, she placed the items into the plastic bag I had brought and tied the handles tightly into her habitual 'bunny ears' style and put it on her bed without saying another word.

More worried glances were reflected in the faces of Janine and I. *Has Mum forgotten how to sew? Such a prospect would be unthinkable; as unimaginable as her forgetting how to walk.*

"Can I try your shoes on?" Mum asked suddenly, looking at me. I took off my black court shoes and offered them to her Cinderella feet. Ever since the 'manly shoe style confusion' episode, I had made a point of wearing obviously female footwear whenever I came to see Mum. She popped on the shoes and went straight into her tap routine, bringing a smile of relief to our faces. *Some things have stayed the same.*

There was one other lady staying in the room but she appeared to be asleep. A large hoist was parked next to a bed containing a person even tinier than Mum. All you could see was her small head peeping above the white coverlet, looking like a lost raisin. *What must it be like for this lady's family?* In comparison, Mum looked vital, shuffle-hop-stepping her way across the parquet.

Finishing on a theatrical flourish with a final stamp in my shoes, Mum looked up to her small audience to take her bow. "Who *are* you two nice young ladies that have come to watch the show?"

"We've lost her again," I whispered to Janine as Mum sat on her bed and began removing my shoes, "I can't bear it. It's as if she has the memory of an Etch-a-sketch, turn it upside down and shake it and you lose the picture entirely."

For the rest of our stay we were treated politely as if we were strangers and then just as politely dismissed. We both gave Mum a hug and said we would visit her again soon and as we turned to go, she sprang into action, following us to the double doors and trying to accompany us as we negotiated our exit from the room. It took much careful manoeuvring to extricate ourselves from her persistent efforts to escape. Ensuring that her little bare foot was kept out of the gap between the two heavy doors was a tricky task that we finally engineered whilst all the time feeling that we must be completely heartless. With her little face framed in the door's small pane of glass, looking like a Dickensian waif pressed up against a cake shop window, we continued to look back to wave and smile in spite of the tears of guilt coursing down our faces. Until, with a final sigh of self-reproach, we turned the corner into the main corridor to gain the emotional safety of the floral Reception and sign ourselves out.

Back in the car, we sat inactive in the front seats feeling as stunned as if we had just committed a crime. I do not know how long we sat there but I know that we shared Tic Tac mints, poor substitutes for strong drink.

The short hours of winter daylight were beginning to dwindle as Janine started her car with renewed determination and we set off in the direction of her home near Oxford. From there, I was to take leave of my sister and would catch the train back to my home in Winchester.

Unusually for us, we were quiet on the return journey, silently processing our own thoughts so before we knew it, we had crossed the border into Oxfordshire. Suddenly we were shocked out of our reverie by the loud blast of an electric guitar.

"Sorry Janine, I think that must be my new mobile," I told her, eyebrows raised, as I scrabbled in my voluminous handbag for my phone. *Perhaps it had not been wise to let my son Simon personalise the settings for me. Or does he think his ancient mother is a rock chick? Hardly. Not with these shoes.*

The call was from Tom.

"Julie where are you at the moment?"

"Janine and I have just got back to Oxford after seeing Mum at Bramwell." Before I could give him one of my rambling updates, he stopped me with:

"Listen. I've just been contacted by the hospital where Dad is. The Ward Manager said that they can't find him and that none of the Staff have seen him since breakfast. They think he may have wandered out of the hospital."

Chapter 21
The Wanderer

George

"*A wandering minstrel I, a thing of shreds and patches, of ballads songs and snatches, of dreamy lullaby,*" George sung quietly to himself as he swung his arms in time to the music playing in his head. He needed to keep moving to conserve the meagre warmth provided by the beige polyester light weight slacks, flannelette shirt and the knitted acrylic cardigan with its mock leather buttons. He pushed his hands firmly into his cardigan pockets in an attempt to stop his fingers getting stiffer with the cold, discovering a black plastic comb and a folded linen handkerchief in the process.

He had not felt such fresh air for such a long time; fresh air that had reached the bottom of his lungs and begun a chilling process. But just at this moment, he did not care; he was enjoying every breath free of that cloying antiseptic disinfectant smell that he had been inhaling for as long as he could remember. Seeing that hangar door standing open was a welcome sight. He had to take off before anyone stopped him.

That air base served up reasonable grub but he and the rest of the chaps had been sitting around in the mess for too long without being issued a kite to fly or a sortie to go on. Yet that doc had given him some of those yellow devils to take with a tumbler of grog so he could stay awake all night but he still hadn't been given a mission. What a first class clot.

He checked his trouser pockets for anything that might be incriminating or that might leak information into the wrong hands. On Special Ops flights when air lifting agents from enemy territory, there were strict precautions to follow. Important information had to be committed to memory, no paper trails were allowed. If he was shot down, God forbid, he must not risk being picked up by the enemy with a pocket of crumpled bus tickets or a rough paper stub from the flicks - forgotten souvenirs of his date with a popsie. Neither should they find one of his cartoon pictures illustrating the weather forecast transmissions he had received through his headset. All the chaps liked them, especially those in the gunner's blister or in the cockpit, always as noisy as a bag of hammers. In his quickly drawn sketches, the crew could see instantly an image of the weather system ahead without having to hear a wordy description. But it would be bad form to have anything like that on him now. After all, he did not know who or what he might meet. A trawl of his deep pockets revealed a small piece of foil with '*Anchor Butter*' written on it and a boiled sweet. The butter wrapper was quickly deposited in a nearby bin after a quick, subtle glance around to check that no one was following him, and the sweet was placed in his mouth.

The apron tarmac was coming to an end but there seemed to be an extension of an old runway leading off it to the west which seemed worth following. A few chaps and their popsies passed him on the road but he did not know them, so he did not draw attention to himself but just kept on walking. After all, the enemy came in different forms and different guises.

*

"I intend to drive up to the hospital," said Tom, "but on the way, I'll drive around the locality to see if I can spot him."

"Oh my God! This is dreadful, Tom. Where can he be? It's so cold today. He could get hypothermia. I wonder what he's wearing. Have they got a search party out?" I piped. Janine, who had parked the car in a layby, sat as close as possible to me with her ear to the handset between us so that she could hear what Tom was saying. I had not yet worked out how to use speakerphone mode.

"Yes, the hospital has sent people to search their grounds and the police have been alerted so I guess their patrol cars will be looking out for him. When I rang the hospital just now, they said that the police are likely to get a helicopter to join the search. Dad's wearing trousers, shirt and thick cardigan – no coat – but at least he's not in his pyjamas," Tom said trying to keep the panic from his voice.

"What should we do?"

"Well as you are almost at Janine's, I think you should both continue on home. The hospital staff are clearly taking it seriously and there are people out looking so the best you can do is get home and wait for news. I promise I will call you if and when I hear anything. I feel one of us needs to be there to keep on top of things. Dad may still be holed up in one of the toilets in the hospital- you know how he likes to be left alone. He could be warm and safe while we are panicking."

"I do so hope you're right, Tom. Promise you'll keep us informed."

"Of course, Julie. Tell Janine too. I'll ring you both every hour."

"Thanks Tom, and let's hope he's found very soon."

*

George knew that he must have covered a considerable distance; the tarmac airstrip had given way to an old concrete road which he had followed until his legs ached. Many vehicles had passed him and he had crossed two bridges, one over a river and one over a railway line. In spite of this progress, it was clear that all his navigation skills had failed him. He did not know where he was. All he was sure of was that the light was fast beginning to fade and the fresh air that he had enjoyed at the start of his sortie was beginning to affect his breathing in a negative way. Each breath was becoming laboured and his former brisk pace had slowed to more of an amble, and an unsteady one at that. He was starting to shiver with the cold and his hands and feet were growing numb.

The road had taken him to a street of terraced houses. He considered knocking on a door, but he was not sure of the welcome he might receive, after all this was enemy territory. Instead, he turned down an alleyway, passing a series of long narrow gardens criss-crossed with pale gravel footpaths that stood out starkly in the dusk. In the distance he saw a light and he homed in on this beacon as if it were a landing flare. As he got closer to its source, the path suddenly widened, opening out into a large square area enclosed on two opposite sides by parallel rows of scruffy looking lock-up garages. One of the bent metal doors was partially open; its 'up and over' mechanism had failed miserably, giving the resulting aperture the appearance of a crooked grin. Within its lop-sided maw was a car being worked on by two men who spoke to each other in a language George had last heard on the streets of Baghdad. Sure enough, as he got closer to the light - a single electric bulb in a metal cage hung by a cable from the garage door handle - the faces it illuminated confirmed his theory. He was in Iraq.

Always drawn to the workings of the motorcar, he watched the mechanics in fascination. He came to the conclusion that they were trying to help each other out. They appeared to be trying to join the front part of one car to the back end of another car to make a whole new vehicle. The clue was in the detail: the front was white and the back was silver. He had heard about this practice but he had never seen it done before and so he moved closer until he was looking over the shoulder of one of the men leaning over the engine.

The mechanic felt an uninvited presence puffing warm air down the neck of his grey pullover and with a sudden jolt lifted his head, banging it with skull-cracking force on the underside of the hood. Rubbing his sore crown, he turned angrily to discover who or what had caused the unwelcome interruption. His companion, who by this time was also alerted to the appearance of a stranger in the camp, said something short and sharp in his native language.

More from their facial expressions than any words they directed at him, George got the message. Quickly, he uttered an apology; quite loudly and in a well enunciated fashion that he had learnt was required when one spoke in English to foreigners.

"I'm so sorry old chap. Didn't mean to startle you. Just interested in motors. That's all. Can I help? Know a thing or two about motor cars. Are you having a spot of bother with your distributor?" George pointed into the oily guts of the motor. "Looks like you've had a prang - or a couple of prangs for that matter. She'll be quite a beast when you've finished with her."

The men looked at each other sheepishly and then, stepping away from their mechanical version of Doctor Frankenstein's creation, gave George their full attention. They seemed to be assessing him and trying to discover whether he was alone or if any other person might be hiding in the shadows. After looking him up and down, they left the vehicle and investigated the shabby garage mews, eventually returning satisfied that no one else lurked in the penumbra of their tiny light. Then they attempted to communicate directly with their uninvited visitor once again. Meanwhile for his part, George was doing his own summing up of the situation. *Something dodgy was going on.*

He put up his hands, palms facing forward in a defensive gesture, just like a cowboy giving himself up in an old western. But then, overcome by the continued drop in temperature, he could not stop himself from rubbing his hands together and hugging his body and slapping his arms to fend off the cold.

Without an English word being spoken, the mechanics' body language began to relax. One of them pointed to the interior of the garage where a small primus stove was set up. They moved an upturned crate into position near the stove and motioned for George to sit on it while they brewed a hot drink. Suspicious as he might be, here were two men who shared his love of the workings of motorcars– *chaps like that can't be all bad, and you never know I might be able to lend them a hand…anyway, I'm on home ground if I'm with chaps that mend motors.* He thought to himself. *After all is said and done, we aren't at war with Iraq, are we?*

The mechanics talked together as the tiny kettle struggled to boil in the confined space of the draughty garage. George was able to identify a few of their words especially those that applied to motor car parts. One of the men, the shorter of the two, took a mobile phone from the pocket of his overalls and made a call in a staccato of words unintelligible to George apart from 'bye bye'.

George peered through the gloom of the garage as it was now fully dark outside. It was good to feel some warmth returning to his hands and even his feet were beginning to thaw now that they rested on a fragment of soiled and frayed Persian carpet that was trying hard to cover the concrete floor. This was the most comfortable he had felt in several hours. In spite of a bad start, he was beginning to feel accepted by the mechanic chaps especially when one of them presented him with a cup of hot black coffee.

The men returned to their project and their conversation began to lose its interest for George, retreating to background noise as his eyelids became heavy. Then cutting through the soft babble of voices he heard a high pitched and tuneful whistle, accompanied by the squeak and grind of a set of small wheels. The wheels had brought another person to the lock up garages. The scene before George's tired eyes, distorted by cataracts and lit by the limited beams of the suspended light bulb, resembled an oil painting of an old master. From the shadows, a boy about ten years old emerged into the corona of light holding a battered skateboard in his hands, his face upturned to talk to the mechanics. *Like the painting of the Christ child talking to the elders in the temple,* George thought fancifully, in his limbo state between sleep and wakefulness. After a brief exchange with the men, the boy peered into the garage interior and approached the huddled elderly figure sitting on the upturned crate.

"Hello. You are lost? My uncle, he has found you. Where do you live?"

"I'm not lost exactly and I cannot tell you where I live," said George, remembering the protocol. *Just my name, rank and number are all you will get from me,* he thought to himself.

The boy, acting as interpreter, relayed George's answer to the men who in turn, shrugged their shoulders in exasperation. It was their turn to raise their hands, this time in a gesture of dismissal. After a few more heated exchanges, the mechanic reached into his pocket for his mobile phone and barked some more orders to the Christ child who came forward to stand before George once again.

"You want to make a phone call to someone who can help you?" he asked, thrusting the small handset into George's stiff and swollen fingers. George examined the phone closely. After a few studied moments, the Christ child lost patience and leaning over the apparently confused and elderly gentleman showed him how to make a phone call using tiny buttons backlit with a florescent glow.

Telephone numbers, George thought. *What do I know of telephone numbers? Wraysbury two seven double two. How do I put in Wraysbury? I will need the operator. How do I get the operator? No that's not right. My billet? No. Got to be careful. Wait a minute. Joanie. I need our number. Mine and Joanie's. Let me think. If I put in O then one four five five six three five eight one nine? Whose number is that? Joanie's?*

He punched in the number series and to his delight, the phone made a purring sound. He was making a call. He was not sure to whom. But no one answered anyway.

"No go," he said into the expectant face of the Christ child. "No one there." The Christ child continued to look hopeful.

"We ring doctor if you like?" he offered, his small head caught in the light beam, giving it a halo.

George sat silently, feeling the chill ever more keenly. He noted that the mechanics were beginning to clear up, putting oily rags into plastic bags and throwing tools into battered metal boxes with noisy clunking sounds.

"No need. I shall come up with a number, just got to think," replied George. *I don't want to worry the doc. That would be bad form. Go on my record. No, must think this one through. A number is there somewhere on the tip of my tongue.*

*

"Janine, it's Shirley at porter's lodge here, we have a phone call come through from a gentleman, I didn't catch his name but he seemed agitated. I'll patch him through if you wish to accept the call?"

"Oh. Thanks Shirley. That must be my brother. He said he would ring. Do put him through, please. Thanks."

Janine waited impatiently and with some trepidation for Tom's latest report. Recent calls had brought no positive sightings and she was feeling so anxious that she had come to a decision in the past half hour. She would get back in the car and help with the search. At least then she would be doing something. All this inactivity was driving her mad. These thoughts flashed through her mind in quick succession while she waited to be connected. As she twirled the phone cord round her fingers, a question raised itself: *why had Tom used the main school number rather than her mobile number? There must be a problem with the mobile signal again.*

"Hello? Who's there?" she heard the unmistakable voice of her dad. *Thank God! He's found. He's really found.* Her legs could not hold her up any longer and she plumped down onto the arm of the sofa, calling out to her husband Nick – "It's Dad!"

"Oh Dad! Where have you been? Where are you? Are you ok? Are you warm? We have been so worried."

"Well I'm here with a couple of chaps in a garage. They've been good to me, made me a coffee, and the Christ child, he does all the translating. I'm calling you from Iraq. I don't know which part."

"Dad, Dad, stay there. Don't go away. Is there someone there with you? Someone I can talk to?"

"You could speak to the Christ child. I'll get him for you," said Dad sounding as if he had matters fully under control. She heard the line crackle as the handset was passed to another person. Simultaneously, Nick's excited voice reached her from the kitchen. It was clear that he had lost no time in contacting Tom to tell him the good news that Dad was found safe and was promising to relay more detailed information as soon as Janine had come off the phone.

Meanwhile Janine began attempting to piece together what might be happening in a lock up garage far away in 'Iraq'. She tried to

168

decipher some foreign sounding background conversation on Dad's end of the line before a young voice took over.

"Hello. I am Mo."

"Hello Mo. Thank you so much for looking after my dad. I am his daughter Janine and I am speaking to you from Oxford. Can you tell me how he is, please? He has been staying at the hospital in Leicester for many months and we think he must have just wandered out. He does get very confused. People have been out searching for him for hours. My brother has been involved in the search so he should be fairly close to where you are."

"My uncle, he find your father tonight in his garage. He is ok but cold and needs to go home. He won't tell us where he lives. He did not tell us that he had come from the hospital."

"He is very confused, I'm afraid. That's one of the reasons why we are so grateful that he has been found. Thank you. Thank you, Mo - and your uncle for helping our Dad. We have been so worried. Now, could you tell me exactly where you are and I will get my brother to come and collect Dad."

*

"Julie, how Dad remembered the school phone number is beyond me. It's not even a number that he used very often. Janine said Mum and Dad usually contacted her on her own landline. It's a mystery," said Tom many hours later. He had called me several times to keep me abreast of events and now we were fully able to relax, aware that Dad was safely ensconced back in the psychiatric ward, in bed with a mug of hot chocolate.

"Mind you, Dad's memory has always astounded us, hasn't it Tom? He recalls details of things that happened years and years ago, details that most of us would not consider worth remembering," I said, soaking up the good news that Dad had been eventually located in an area on the outskirts of Leicester. Thanks to the care and help given by the mechanics followed by Janine and Tom's prompt action, Dad had been conveyed to the Infirmary by ambulance and after a health check, was found to be none the worse from his ordeal.

"I'm pleased that I could accompany the medical team so I could reassure Dad and persuade him it was safe to go into the ambulance. The guys who'd found him were great. They'd realised that he was confused, noticed that he was cold and had taken care of him, keeping him warm. We are so lucky they were there and took the action that they did," said Tom, his voice breaking with fatigue and relief.

"Aren't we lucky? They did an amazing job. Can we give them something to thank them?" I suggested, tears threatening my voice too.

"Already sorted, Julie. I have plans to go and see them tomorrow evening to thank them properly."

"And you'll know where to find them – four miles from the hospital and just over three and a half thousand miles from Iraq."

Chapter 22
The safe option

Julie and Tom

"And do you know what I found out, Janine?" I could not wait to tell my sister the latest titbit of news amongst the long list of practical items we covered in our regular phone calls. "You'll remember that Mum told us that *Bramwell* is only a few fields away from her bungalow?"

"Yes. She was well and truly confused about that, wasn't she? Bless her, she kept singing that song about *over the hills*," replied my sister, her voice at the end of the line echoing in her cavernous kitchen at *Treetops*.

"Well maybe we both ought to go back to school and put up with old Halitosis breath again," I offered.

"Who do you mean? All the teachers seemed to have bad breath if they got close enough," she replied. Although I could not see her, I knew that she was pulling that face: the one where the corners of her mouth were pulled downwards and her top lip curled with disgust.

"I mean him with the dingy checked shirt of the typical Geography teacher – made of flannelette and coloured with the horizontal axis stripe of contour line brown and vertical axis stripe of deciduous forest green. You must know who I mean. What was his name now? Mr Beecholm?" I persisted.

"Something like that. *Old Beecham Powders*, we called him," Janine remembered.

"Well he always did seem to have a cold anyway - on top of his acrid breath that could strip paint at three yards. Anyhow I digress. Tom, the only one of us born with the bit of lodestone in his head, has told me that Mum was spot on and that Burnage is actually only a few miles away from *Bramwell*, as the crow flies."

"Blimey," Janine chuckled, "So Mum really could have skipped over the hills and home, after all. And there we were thinking she was well confused about that. Just shows you what *we* know. Never underestimate an OAP."

"True. We should have realised when we saw that sign to the Fosse Way."

"Not the Fosse Way. No Way. That's Dad's favourite route to everywhere," Janine reminded me, although I did not need reminding.

It was time to be serious again. "Now, Janine, there's something Tom and I were discussing and would like your take on it."

"Ok. Go for it," said Janine, "I'm all ears."

"Well, Mum is due to be discharged from *Bramwell* in the next couple of weeks and so we shall have to make some preparations for her return to the bungalow. As you and I have discussed before, she will need a more comprehensive care package than she had before she went into hospital - to keep her safe and prevent another incident. Tom has been looking into the options and it does seem that whatever care plan we choose, it is bound to be quite expensive."

"Ok I can see that. Put simply, there has been a decrease in the level of Mum's ability to look after herself, coupled with an increase in the level of risk for her if she's left alone. But this means effectively round the clock care and that's got to be expensive. How are we going to pay for it all?"

"Well as none of us has power of attorney, Tom has sought advice from the Court of Protection and apparently they can gain access to some of Mum and Dad's funds to pay for the care that is considered appropriate and necessary. Of course, the Court is very stringent and we will have to fill in loads of forms. But once the applications have been made and a detailed record of accounts has been examined by the Court, it should be possible to secure funds to pay for the help that Mum needs at this moment."

"And in the future," Janine finished for me.

"Yes sure," I continued, "Obviously we have to accept that Mum's needs may change over time. And we might even be able to get Dad back home too if we have a system of care set up in the bungalow. We were looking at the possibility of getting some carers who might be prepared to live in with Mum or even both Mum and Dad. There are teams of people that will work either day or night shifts. Tom has been looking into it all."

"That sounds a good plan, Julie. Keeping Mum in a place where everything is familiar to her must help her memory and prevent her getting so confused. And if we could reunite Dad with Mum under the same roof that would be really a good thing to aim for."

Much later that day, Tom and I were at a crucial stage of our continuing mission to boldly go where no man (or at least only one man) has gone before. We were naughty children once again, invading our parents' inner sanctum, crossing the frontier into further guilt. This monumental act of trespass and violation was taking place in the spare bedroom at the bungalow in Caldron close.

In front of us squatted the sumo wrestler of a security safe. It was sizing us up from its dusty corner; through its facial features of knobs and dials it was giving us a smug grin. It was not giving anything else away.

"The thing is," said Tom, "The Court of Protection needs details of Mum and Dad's assets and I've looked through all the boxes and files around the place and have come up with some bits and bobs that might prove useful but the main details have got to be in that safe." He pointed to our squatting implacable friend.

"Shall we try a few numbers that might be likely? You know like dates of birth, phone numbers and that kind of thing?" I asked him.

"Julie, I've tried everything I could think of, but it's got me nowhere. It's not as if it's a particularly sophisticated model – just a bog standard safe that Dad got from that DIY store up the road."

"Have you tried hitting it with a hammer?" I smiled sheepishly at him.

"Don't tempt me. It's as heavy as lead anyway so I don't think I'd get very far. No there's nothing for it but to ask Dad himself. His memory for numbers is amazing – as was proved all too recently with Janine's school phone number."

"Ok then, no good lemoning about here, as my son would say, let's go and ask Dad."

*

Dad was pleased to see us when Tom and I encountered him on the holodeck. Like a member of the crew of *Star Ship 'Enterprise'*, he seemed fully immersed in his own world of recreational escape. It was soon made apparent to us that he had been transported to *World War Two World*. Here there were secrets to be kept and no one to be

173

trusted. Clearly this was not a day conducive to extracting information, however subtly we had intended to try. When a fellow patient walked past, Dad gave him the, "Hello old boy," treatment before turning to us and in a conspiratorial whisper said, "Don't say anything to him. He's one of *Them* and not to be trusted - ever."

Tom and I sat weakly on the squeaky plastic chairs in the usual ward bay where Dad spent much of his daylight hours. We looked on as Dad spoke to us about his war time experiences as if they were current, with all the energy and animation that must have been present in his youth. We had not witnessed such vitality in him for a very long time. He even laughed. While we watched, he began to put on what I can only describe as a kind of performance.

"I was so hungry this morning that my backbone was scraping my belly button and so my pal said we should go and get breakfast at the mess. Well, all they had was bread with marge and a scrape of marmite. 'But it can't be all that bad because you never know,' I said to him, 'Mar-mite change her mind about me' and we did laugh. So he said to me, 'Well George, what's it all about?' and I said to him, 'What? The hokey cokey? That's what it's all about.'"

As audience to this impromptu mini concert, our feelings became ambivalent. On the one hand, it was tragic to witness someone we love in such a confused and delusional state. On the other hand, Dad seemed to be cheerful, reliving some happy experiences of his past. For my money, Dad's holodeck reality was infinitely superior to the reality of the drab hospital ward surrounding Tom and I.

Other patients came and went on their meander round the ward's circular route but most paid Dad no attention. Dad must do this re-enactment often. I looked at Tom meaningfully and then began to think of some subtle questions I could ask Dad that might help us discover the code to the safe. I could not help comparing our quest with the scene from the old black and white spy film starring Robert Donat where the *Mr Memory* character on the music hall stage is asked, "What are the thirty nine steps?"

Our own *Mr Memory* was holding forth about the tall tales he had heard that he maintained must be true. *"Like the man that had a baby. He did, he really did. The doctor cut him open and there was a baby inside him. They say it was his twin that somehow got inside him before he was born. It's a true story, stranger than fiction. And then there was the man who swallowed a seed and a small tree grew inside him. It's true, I tell you. You can laugh. Others have, and regretted it."*

We both tried not to smile. We had indeed heard these tales before. As children, sitting around the family table at meal times, Dad's 'fantastical tales' as we had called them, were dismissed as nonsense. Shame on us; we had scoffed.

Searching about for a subject to distract him, I fell back unimaginatively to my default topic. "We came up today on the Fosse Way," I announced. However, this statement did not have quite the effect I anticipated.

"Well Newark is on the Fosse Way and my house in Newark is very different to this," Dad amazed us both by saying. Dad did not have, and to our knowledge, never did have, a house in Newark. Tom could not resist following this up. After all, out of the mouths of babes and (in our recent experience) OAP's...how does the saying go?

"Dad, did you say that you had a house in Newark? Where is that then, how do you get there?" he asked. Dad proceeded to give Tom a detailed description of the journey to Newark; a route that my brother, aka Mr Lodestone, was later to confirm was accurate. When I asked Dad what the house looked like, he gave a description of the bungalow at Burnage. Even so, both Tom and I were left with several questions left unanswered. This was the most fantastical tale we had heard in a very long time and we still did not have the answer we came for. So as a last resort, I decided on a direct approach.

"Dad, can you remember the code for the safe at home?"

"Yes of course I can. Now let me see now. One nine three nine four five. Just the job. They're getting the machines out on the tarmac. Got to go now. Over and out." We were dismissed.

Settling back into Tom's car, I looked at the numbers that I had scribbled hurriedly into my diary. "Tom, it's the war years."

"Got it! Of course. Why didn't we think of that?" he replied.

*

Back in the spare bedroom at the bungalow, the sumo wrestler was poised for another bout. This time we were confident. This time we came at him from his blind side and tweaked his dials with deft movements. But it was all to no avail. As we tried to push down the sturdy handle, it would not budge a centimetre. *No joy, old boy,* as Dad would say.

"Well Julie, what do we do now?" said Tom, wrinkling up the pale green candlewick bedspread on the lumpy spare mattress, his shoulders slumped and arms loosely resting on his knees. I knew that gesture but it was rarely seen in my optimistic brother.

"Have you tried the DIY store, to see if they have any tips on how to crack their safes?" I realised as I said this just how stupid it sounded. "Forget I said that Tom. They are hardly likely to point out weaknesses to their product. After all we could be thieves, mugging up on how to commit a burglary." Tom continued to slouch on the bed to think while I, feeling powerless and bereft of ideas, went off to the kitchen to make instant coffee from the blackened granules stuck to the base of a brown clouded jar.

"Here you go, coffee. No milk, I'm afraid, and not much in the way of coffee either, but it's wet and warm, as they say." Tom took the proffered mug and turned to me with a thoughtful expression.

"I've been thinking," he said, chewing his lower lip, "perhaps the best person to ask would be the locksmith in town. We could show him the Court of Protection paperwork and explain our dilemma and if he came to the house he would see that it was a bona fide situation and that we were not thieves."

"Worth a try, let's give them a call," I said, relieved that we had a plan.

After successfully arranging an appointment for the following afternoon with the local locksmith, Tom took me to the railway station. We parted with our usual well-worn sibling exchange, "Remember vice is nice," he said.

"But incest's best," I returned sotto voce; there were people within earshot who might not know this as an alternative version of "Bye."

*

Larry, the manager of the local lock smithy, parked his gaudily decorated van on the drive outside the bungalow. Its signage proudly displayed the firm's name, *Lock, Stock and Apparel* and proclaimed the many services that the establishment offered and got nosey neighbour Vera on day watch, very excited. Tom greeted Larry warmly at the door and after showing him the necessary paperwork he proceeded, like a Children's TV presenter, to introduce Larry the locksmith to Sumo the safe. The two were not destined to get along.

Larry, a thick set and jovial sort, who one could tell from his appearance, was no stranger to fish and chip suppers, had brought along a heavy metal tool box. He exuded the confidence of the professional and set about the task of unlocking the safe in the confines of the spare bedroom. Opening the much dented and scratched cantilevered box to its fullest extent, thereby taking up the majority of the available floor space, he revealed his impressive arsenal of implements. He proceeded to apply these tools to the safe's mechanism in sequence before returning them to the box's ample trays. Over the next half hour, there was much grunting from Larry and a reciprocal metal screeching sound from Sumo but as the bedroom clock ticked tirelessly onwards, there was no satisfying, resolving clunk from Sumo. After a succession of failures, the tools ceased to be returned to the box, but became discarded to lie haphazardly across the pink shag pile. Tom witnessed the marked decline in tool organisation along with the spluttering deterioration in Larry's temperament - neither of which could solely have been attributed to the mug of black goo purporting to be coffee that he had provided earlier.

Eventually, with perspiration rising as a mist about his rosy countenance, Larry had to concede defeat. "She ain't budgin,"he said unnecessarily. "There's only one thing for it. It'll haf to be a job for Mr Snudge," he declared, clearly embarrassed that the proud boasts advertised on the side of his van amounted that day to nothing. "I'll give yous a ring when I haf made contact with himself. See if he has the time to help us out, like."

"Who is this Mr Snudge? Is he one of your employees?" asked Tom.

"Oh no indeed Mister Ellis, he ain't . He is what you might call ah *specialist.* What we call in the business, *a cracker.* There ain't no job too big for the likes of Mr Snudge. But he does insist on payment in advance. Cash only, no cheques. But if you don't mind, you will haf to bring this 'ere safe down to our own workshops . Mr Snudge, he don't do house calls. Well leastways not these days," he smiled at his own private joke.

With this fleeting enigmatic comment from someone otherwise open-faced and blunt, Larry took his leave. He climbed into the bright van whose effusive livery would have seemed more at home in a circus enclosure than in a suburban housing estate. Tom waved him off, spotting the tell-tale twitch of starched net curtain in Vera's lounge window, followed by an apparent answering twitch from the curtains in the house across the road. *Twitching... old lady version of tweeting, I suppose,* thought Tom.

The lock smith's workshop was a large and dusty room full of huge metal cabinets stacked with drawers that Tom assumed housed tools. The workbench that was positioned in the centre of the floor space, held a vast array of gadgets with which Tom had become curiously familiar having seen the like casually displayed on the spare bedroom carpet a few days previously during Larry's abortive attempt.

Larry was looking nervous. He was stationed at the back entrance having settled Tom on a plastic chair at the opposite end of the room, on the side of the bench furthest away from the door. Anxiously he paced the area near the entrance and kept checking for the specialist's arrival. Tom, in the meantime, thought about the prospect of meeting this famous Mr Snudge and fantasised that he was really a crook from the criminal underworld, an infamous safe breaker with a nickname like *Fingers Fogoty or Vicious Vimy or Jemmy Jack (quickly discarding the latter as sounding too much like the baddies in Enid Blyton's stories).* He would be bald, curt and have a minder, in his fertile typecasting imagination. He smiled to himself; this was all rather like something from a *Carry On* film. He decided he had better *get real*; he really ought to get out more. *In a minute,* he thought, *a perfectly normal locksmith would arrive looking a bit like Larry but with a smarter cantilever tool box.*

Like a watch dog, Larry's quick movements alerted Tom to the large black vehicle gliding soundlessly past the square of thick reinforced glass in the back door. He could not see who was in the car as the windows were heavily tinted. Larry opened the workshop door and holding its handle, appeared to take up a military bearing, standing to attention. Three men emerged from the vehicle and as if they had taken pains not to disappoint Tom's imagination, they all wore dark suits, were bald and sported sun glasses with mirror lenses.

Thick set and muscled like bouncers, they offered no smiles of greeting, no introductions, no comments, just quiet action. With nods and shrugs and the occasional mildly lethargic eye brow movement, the three entered the workshop and stationed themselves along the opposite side of the workbench to Tom. The man in the middle, who Tom assumed must be Mr Snudge, sat down at the bench; his two vast acolytes remained standing either side of him. Only when he was seated, his face obscured by Sumo, did Mr Snudge remove his reflective pair of shades; passing them to the acolyte on his left. Then

178

at some subtle signal from Mr Snudge , the minder to his right produced a black executive style briefcase and positioned it squarely on the bench beside Sumo. With the briefcase lid lifted, a shield was formed, covering Mr Snudge's movements. Tom did not realise that he had been staring.

Larry whose spinal column, in the previous minutes, had dissolved and become refashioned into a backbone worthy of the obsequious Uriah Heep, came up to Tom and whispered in stilted tones, " Mr S insists that you remain in your seat until the device has been opened. He does not wish you to observe precisely what he does. It is very technical and private work he does, you understand. You are allowed to remain in the room purely so you witness nothing is removed at the moment of successful opening of the device, like."

Tom had no trouble taking Larry's words seriously. After all, he had already taken in the broken nose of Acolyte Number One and the cauliflower ear of Acolyte Number Two. He was just thinking that his sisters would never believe him when he told them about this scene from 'The Sweeney', when he noticed Acolyte Number One passing his boss a stethoscope. All Tom could see was Mr Snudge's capacious forehead and he watched with fascination as it pleated in concentration. Tiny noises broke the otherwise hushed silence until finally there was a resounding click and the frown lines on the dry forehead relaxed. Tom knew it was over when Mr Snudge clicked his fingers and the dark glasses were produced by Acolyte Number Two from the deep recesses of his dark jacket.

Swiftly and almost silently, tools were replaced in the briefcase which Tom guessed would be filled with dense grey sponge specially carved and tailored to fit snugly around every implement. Mr Snudge left the workshop with a ghost of a nod to Larry whilst simultaneously the two acolytes rotated the safe on the workbench as if it was a magician's cabinet that had once held a lady in a sequined swim suit. Instead of a disappeared show girl, Tom viewed the gaping exposed innards of the violated Sumo. As Tom studied the dark interior, the Specialist's two side-kicks left abruptly to follow their boss to the waiting vehicle.

Revealed were no slim boxes of jewellery as in a Regency novel's fictional accounts of a strong box's contents... 'I would like you to wear the blue diamonds; bought by my grandfather before the revolution...on your tiny neck they would look divine...made for such as you.' Neither were there canvas bags or leather pouches filled with gold nuggets or coins as in a spaghetti western. Nothing like that. Just a couple of Building Society passbooks and a pack of cards. Bankcards. All out of date and held loosely together with a perished rubber band. And envelopes, all unsealed and empty.

Chapter 23
The Whip Hand

Julie and James

"It's good of you to come with me. I know it's not going to be much of a fun filled weekend," I told my husband James as we took the motorway heading north to Gibbet Roundabout, raising my voice against the rhythmic background noise of the windscreen wipers working at double stroke speed to cope with the recent cloud burst. As our kids would have reminded us in times gone by, we were certainly entering the *Land without Aslan*, where it seemed forever winter.

"Well aside from having to put up with all these lorries chucking up oceans of spray, I'm happy to drive you. It's not the time of year for you to be standing about on cold railway stations- and anyhow I'd like to see your dad, see how he's getting on."

"Well, you'll see a few changes in him, I'm afraid, since the last time you saw him. I wonder if he'll recognise you. He doesn't always know me," I said weakly.

These days I was having trouble swallowing. There seemed to be a hard lump in my throat. Permanently. What with that and the feeling that I was constantly on the verge of tears, I could well have been suffering from a hormonal imbalance. Like pregnancy. But not like pregnancy. Like grieving. I knew all too well what was prompting this pre-bereavement grief. Mentally, I shook myself. I had to come to terms with the fact that my parents were not my parents anymore. Their bodies were holding the same shape that had been occupied by my Mum and Dad for the past seventy plus years, but what inhabited the shells now were not the people I knew and loved. But of course I continue to love them. I was not ready to let them go and there was a part of me that continued to be convinced that I could get them back; that they might somehow indicate that they were still there. I was constantly vigilant, looking for a sign.

Sitting there in the car beside James, each motorway road sign ticking off the miles to our destination, I came to the realisation that however hard it was to achieve, I must take control, whip myself into the shape of a capable caring daughter. If I did not maintain the demeanour of a professional during this challenging time, then I would be completely lost and become a big blob of jelly like that ectoplasm the *Ghost Busters* collect in their weird vacuum cleaners. I would be utterly useless to everyone; especially Mum and Dad. There was no doubt about it, my personal emotion settings had been polarised to either *'professional rigid'* or *'useless goo'*.

Since his original walkabout, my father in the manner of Steve McQueen in *'The Great Escape'* had not hesitated in roving away from the hospital ward again. In spite of his presence being regularly monitored by staff, he had managed to slip off the radar screen and go for another wander. This time, he had been found relatively quickly, holed up hugging a radiator in a waiting room in one of the numerous buildings on the vast hospital site. This most recent sortie prompted staff to arrange for him to be relocated to another hospital unit in the city, one that provided a greater level of security: *The Everdene Centre*. This was where James and I were going that day and it was with relief that we navigated the final furlong, having turned on Gibbet Roundabout and negotiated heavy city rush- hour traffic on slick rain-washed roads.

As for the visit, it had all begun so well. If I was looking for signs, then there were many that day shining brightly like neon arrows, letting me know that Dad was still in residence within the shell that I had been maudlin about all the way to *Everdene*. *'What a lot of unnecessary angst I put myself through. Here he is, sitting in his beige knitted cardigan with the mock leather buttons (one missing, I notice) with a cosy flannelette shirt and his falling down Charlie Chaplin trousers (with a little hem of pyjama trouser leg peeping out from beneath his turn-ups)'*, I thought to myself as we entered the Day Room.

This open and airy lounge, decorated in pale shades of purple, had been accessed via two sets of secure doors using the ubiquitous key pads. We were becoming expert with these devices and ever vigilant to the wily meet and greeters that lurked at the inner border control points, ever poised to escape. The large social area had a range of plastic covered lilac and blue standard couch style chairs and high backed fireside armchairs. Most of the furniture was set in rows but in the four corners of the room, groups of chairs were circled around coffee tables. We had spotted Dad in one of these furniture corrals. He was seated next to an elderly lady with her feet on display; they were both enjoying sticky buns and cups of tea. Dad was looking about the room watching the activity around the tea trolley and when he saw us approach, his face became animated and he gestured for us to join him. We entered the enclosure and prepared to take seats opposite him, checking that the plump upholstered cushions were dry before we sat down – another skill that we had learnt to perfect in recent times.

"Well how nice to see you both. I was telling Joanie here," pointing to Mrs Feet-On-Display, "that there are three things that get news sent about the place."

"Really?" I answered, looking across at Dad's companion and smiling the humouring smile that signalled *You aren't really Joanie. You aren't really my mum. But it's nice of you to keep Dad company.*

"Well there's the Telegraph," he paused for dramatic effect. "Telephone." Another pause followed while we smiled our most benign and patronising smiles. " And... wait for it... Tell-a-woman!" He announce with a flourish. I found myself clapping but stopped immediately when I realised where I was and that Mrs Feet-On-Display had nodded off and was beginning to snore quietly. Undeterred, Dad continued his stand up, sitting down in his high backed armchair. "Do you know what a dyslexic melon is? It's a lemon!" Dad laughed. He actually laughed again; this was becoming a new habit. And we laughed too. The relief was so great that I felt as if I had imbibed champagne on an empty stomach; it went straight to my head and I began to gush.

"We had a good journey up here; we came on the motorway, Dad. It only took us a couple of hours."

"Ah, so you didn't come on the Fosse Way then?" he replied.

"W-ell no," I stuttered. I looked across at James, realising my mistake. He did not say anything, but I could read much from his expression. As a head teacher of primary school children, he has mastered the art of being able to *quell them with a look.* Usually I require a more sophisticated gurning from him in order to get the message. Mind you, that day his particular message was being transmitted loud and clear through a certain combination of frown lines and eyebrow movement -a kind of facial line dancing that only I can decipher, it said *change the subject quick!*

I looked away from the virtual Aran cable jumper that James' brows were now knitting effectively and, casting about for ideas for conversation, I picked up my new handbag. "Do you like my bag, Dad? James bought it for me."

"Very nice. But I dunno, James," Dad rolled his eyes and slapped his thigh, "what will they think of next? It's covered in magnets all over. And so are you," he said, lifting his eyes to my face. This was all starting to get a little weird. I wondered what he could see on my face, was he hallucinating? At least he had recognised James which was a good sign and I had been wishing for good signs.

Meanwhile, Dad seemed to have lost interest in the magnets and was continuing his animated presentation. "I scream, you scream, we all scream for ice cream." Dad sang with the energy of a school boy on his first day of the summer holidays. " Get your hokey pokey ices from the Hokey Pokey man," he said patting his leg in time with each syllable.

"Well, we don't have ice cream Dad but we have got a box of chocolates," I said, revealing the carton of his favourite wrapped sweets that I had stored in the depths of my new mothership handbag – the one I imagined I could now see magnets studded all over its surface.

"Ooh, lovely," he said. "Make sure Joanie has some." Obediently, we placed a couple by the side of 'Joanie's' half eaten bun. Dad took one of the chocolates, covered in shiny foil like an emerald, and began to unwrap it. After he put the sweet into his mouth, he took its wrapping, smoothed the foil and, just as he had done when I was a child, he folded and twisted the paper until it resembled a tiny goblet that he placed on the coffee table. The little model stood up unsupported. I found myself clapping again like an excited toddler.

Sitting on my hands, my new handbag placed out of sight under my seat, I tried to think of what to say next. James had been keeping the show going by talking to Dad about the meals and the routines in the hospital. He was so good at this; at maintaining the pretence that everything was normal. It was having a calming effect on Dad who talked about lumpy mashed potato and cold soup and moaned that he was told to go to bed when he was not tired but that he was made to get up when he was fast asleep. "I just wish they'd make up their minds," he finished, slapping his thigh again in a gesture of irritation.

Making a quick summary of events in my mind, apart from the hallucinatory moment, Dad was showing clear signs that he was getting back to his old self. He recognised us, maintained a sensible conversation and - *gave us a bit of a cabaret floor show*. Granted that part was a bit bizarre, but he was always a wonderful story-teller and *then he continues to mistake a series of other ladies in the hospital for Mum... Mrs Feet-On-Display does not bear the slightest resemblance to Mum.* But could this just be normal for a lonely old man who has always been used to having his wife beside him? In the court of law still sitting in my mind, Dad was totally forgiven; his little aberrations could all be explained away. *It's all absolutely normal Darlings,* Mum was saying, from her place in the witness box in my mental judiciary.

I shook my head to clear my mind and behold, there was my Dad, chatting away to my husband about the merits of treacle pudding and custard.

"That's James' favourite," I interrupted. "I buy those little individual packs that you can microwave." I realised that my contribution was lame and tried desperately to think of a topic that would engage Dad's interest whilst we were on a winning streak of normality.

It was then that Dad stood up with an air of thinly veiled excitement and began to tap his thigh with barely concealed impatience. "Sorry folks. Got to go. Can't stop. Saved myself some time by keeping my jockey silks on under my trousers. Must dash. I'm riding in the 2.30 race at Haydock Park."

Chapter 24
Home on the Grange

Julie

James and I needed our bottle of medicine that night; the natural remedy that is suspended in a red liquid, stoppered with a cork and complete with a label that contains no dosage instructions.

After a couple of glasses, we exchanged meaningful looks- this time without any woven frown lines or forehead line dance strutting; in each was mirrored starkly the facial expression that means *hope vanquished*.

"We are going to have to accept that things are as they are. There's little we can do about it. Dad has moved into the twilight zone," I announced, my heart struggling to accept this new reality: that Dad now existed in a state of unreality. But I believed that if I kept saying it out loud, I might eventually become convinced.

"What will Tom say when you ring him?" said James.

Hysteria may have crept into the room at that point as I found myself starting to giggle. Now that the wine had leached into my system, I began to see the funny side of the events that had played out earlier that day. There had been my diminutive elderly father, actually of the reduced height and stature of a champion jockey, dressed in his homely homespun cardigan and with his saggy trousers slipping down over silky pyjama bottoms worn underneath, an imaginary whip in his hand, getting ready to take part in a horse race. Dad, who to my knowledge had never even ridden a horse in his entire life; it was all so bizarre.

"I'm not sure what Tom will make of it all." I paused before being taken over by another rip curl of giggles. "All the time we were there, he kept s-slapping his thigh," I said ashamedly with tears of mirth forming in my eyes. "All the time we were there, he kept wh-whipping his leg. Just like a p-pantomime p-principal boy." I was starting to dissolve.

James picked up the image and ran with it, "And he fair cantered out of the Day Room. Did you see him taking the whip to his rump as he passed by the tea trolley along the inside fence?" Now James was giving in to it too as I noticed he was wiping his eyes with the heel of his hands.

"Wah, stop it! No really, what should we do?" I said, trying to get sensible - to get us both sensible. "Who could help, do you think?"

"A horse-whisperer?" he replied.

*

"This next one, called *'The Grange'*, might be just the place we need," said Tom. "It looks really pleasant, if the brochure is to be believed, and it's the closest to Burnage." He and I had been driving around the Midlands, visiting different care homes with a view to finding somewhere Dad could settle once he left hospital.

"Well I hope you're right, the last three all fell short of what we are looking for," I replied, wishing that I could stay within the confines of his well-appointed car. The soft leather of the reclining car seat had moulded itself to my frame, cradling me like a new born and warming me with its heated seat cushion. I was more ready to go to sleep than I was to explore the finer points of yet another care home. But this lethargy was fuelled by a desire to avoid and deny; *Shame on me.*

"Yes I agree. Although the first place we saw, that one called *'The Gables'* –did seem to fit the bill. It even had a paddock out the back," he winked at me.

"Don't let's start on the old horse riding semantic field, please, I beg of you. I'll get the giggles again," I said, beginning to rise out of my torpor.

"I know Julie, me too. When you told me about it, I could just imagine the scene. Dad in his silks, bless him, getting ready for the big race."

We both found ourselves grinning widely and sheepishly. Then in an effort to return to the purpose of our mission, I continued, "Anyhow, *'The Gables'* smelt very odd and whilst I don't want to be over- particular, I just couldn't envision Dad there."

"Most probably because there weren't any other men there," said Tom. During our visits that day, we were unwittingly attending a virtual Sociology lecture on Demographics. We were learning the sad fact that most men did not live as long as most women. The homes that we had viewed were full to bursting with elderly ladies; men were as rare as hen's teeth. "Dad definitely needs some other blokes around." Tom continued. "Did you notice that man in that place called *'The Beeches'*? He had a chess set, all laid out on the coffee table next to him. It just looked like he was waiting for someone to play. Now that would be just the job, the right kind of atmosphere that Dad could fit into."

"Yes, I agree but that place was so small, there were only ten residents and they all seemed to have mobility problems. I don't know how they would cope if Dad had one of his more *active* moments."

Tom nodded in agreement, "Well that's true. I keep forgetting that Dad has changed so much. Maybe he's no longer up to playing board games or even reading a book."

"It's so sad. He used to love those sorts of things so much. He used to spend hours with his books and his crosswords."

"And his computer," Tom added. "That old Amstrad was a real source of enjoyment and entertainment for him; gave him a new interest in life, something to do after he retired. Do you remember he used it to catalogue all his music and make lists of all his video tapes?"

"Yes, especially all his video tapes. He's got loads. He has got three just devoted to Princess Diana's funeral."

We drove on in silence. I gazed wistfully through the windscreen reflecting on the past. *Depression was always just below the surface however hard Dad tried to overcome it and distract himself. Should we have stepped in when we noticed Dad was low? Though precisely at what point would that have been? Depression always seemed a facet of his personality for as long as I could remember. Did we neglect him, too busy with our own lives? Did we neglect Mum? Could the mental crumbling of our parents have been avoided if we had intervened in some way?*

Shaking off these troubling questions that I could not even begin to answer, I stuck my head in the proverbial sand once again. It was safe and warm there. It was also safe and warm remembering scenes of my kids enjoying playing with Dad. "Dad loved his computer and my kids used to love sitting by his side at the keyboard. Lizzy and Simon and their *Grandpa George,* they used to play that never-ending video game where they had to solve all those complex clues in order to move about the magic kingdom of mystery, collecting tools and weapons to fight goblins and save princesses from dragons. I

188

remember a time when they got stuck for hours in a virtual bar with some lumberjack characters and had to keep obeying the barman – *want some rye?"* I quoted, attempting an American drawl.

"Sure yer do!" completed Tom in insistent bar tender mode.

For a few seconds, I was back there again; in the spare bedroom of the bungalow- the same aforementioned room wherein Sumo lived. In the dusky late afternoon light that filtered through the open weave curtains, there would be outlined the profiles of grandfather, granddaughter and grandson. In my memory's tableau, they were all earnestly scrutinising the small screen of a humming computer monitor which in itself represented *state of the art technology* for its time. Noisily clicking arrow buttons on the chunky keyboard, they negotiated their way through virtual tunnels, their pixelated hero bouncing off rock platforms and creeping behind waterfalls leaving them enough time between scene changes and puzzle challenges to refresh their glasses of squash or steal a chocolate éclair toffee from the kitchen.

Tom brought me back on track with a reminder of the task in hand. "It's good that Dad is being discharged from hospital and allowed to transfer to a care home for the time being. For a short while back there, I was worried that he would have to stay in psychiatric hospital and become institutionalised, never to come out."

Tom is someone who can usually be relied upon to look on the bright side; without the bolstering of his tireless optimism, I was in danger of transforming to *Ghost Buster* goo again. He carried on, chirpy as ever, "Now that we have been able to transfer Mum back to the bungalow with a more comprehensive package than before, we can concentrate on Dad's needs. When Mr Chundra gave us the all clear to find a placement in a home for Dad, I did think we should have an eye to the future – I thought that if the right place can be found, then maybe it could be the right place for Mum too – eventually."

"You're right, I guess. Equally, if we see how Mum goes with the extra carer visits, it might be OK for Dad to come back to the bungalow. That's what Janine and I were chatting about the other day." Tom's optimism was always infectious; he was a tonic better than a feel-good movie. He should be bottled.

"True, Julie. Although I think that could only happen if they had twenty-four hour care at Caldron Close; and we're not there yet," he replied. We left the motorway and set off towards the small market town of Shelton. Our selection of care homes had included all those within a small radius of the Burnage bungalow. We had started our inspection at *'The Gables'*, twenty miles away from Base Camp Burnage and we had then traced a return route, visiting care homes along the way, until we came to our final stop: *'The Grange'*.

"I must admit, I did like *'The Ivy'*, it seemed very friendly," I said.

"Yes the staff members were very pleasant weren't they? And I liked the en suite rooms and that lovely big lounge with the chintz covered lampshades and cosy sofas - all a very homely feel," Tom agreed. "But, there was that major problem wasn't there?"

"The bus stop!" we both said together, emphatically. *'The Ivy'* was situated on the main road of a large village with a bus shelter at the end of the drive that led through landscaped grounds to a pleasant and rambling manor house converted for elderly residents. If Dad had been issued with one of his imaginary missions, he could have easily stolen by the watch towers in his carpet slippers, snuck onto a bus and been ten miles away before morning Tenko.

Tom parked in the large carpark outside *'The Grange'* next to a smart BMW with a personalised number plate Z 123. Tom, who notices such things, was very impressed and took several minutes to examine what he could view of the leather and walnut trimmed interior and appreciate the flowing lines of the metal body work. Annoyed that I had had to leave the embryonic warmth of his car, I threatened that if he did not get a move on, I would consider reclining on the bonnet with my Marks and Spencer duffle coat untoggled (a valiantly heroic threat, considering the temperature.) However Tom had no intention of taking me seriously, he had been to enough Motor Shows to know that I was unlikely to carry out my stunt notwithstanding the fact that I sadly lacked the assets of a super model. It was then that I realised that I was in cognitive overload; I was care-homed-out and starting to get a little silly.

The modern purpose-built care home was constructed of warm rose coloured brick. There appeared to be a main central section flanked by two elegant wings; the whole set in extensive grounds laid to lawn and bordered by flowering shrubs. We walked up the wide and imposing path to the entrance, noting the large flower arrangements placed tastefully in every window, their foliage serving to obliterate any little wan face that might be looking out.

The radio door entry system passed our first security test as, having pressed the buzzer, we were required to announce our names and the nature of our business into the small microphone set into the keypad. Unseen hands triggered the door release mechanism and we gained entry to the air lock, also known as the reception foyer. Here we were greeted by a neat and tidy receptionist who, after signing us in, told us that the owner of *The Grange* was expecting us and would be giving us a tour of the premises. Whilst we waited for Mr Papadopoulos, the olfactory reception part of our test procedure commenced. *So far so good.* Emanating from three pyramids of a gel like substance, set along the reception desk at intervals like air strip landing lights, came the smell of apple blossom with undertones of cherry. These combined to provide a veritable orchard of fragrance under which we sheltered as we breathed in and considered the many pictures and notices on the hessian covered walls. The largest of these was a notice printed in red block capitals, underlined, strongly reminding visitors to ensure that they secure the door on leaving, warning not to allow any of the residents to follow them out. This ticked another box on our mental list of requirements. *They are alert to potential escapees.* Next to the notice was a series of framed texts that on closer inspection, appeared to be poems with the dignity of old age as their subject. Each text was illustrated with water coloured skies, its margins framed with leaning willows or stout upright oaks.

Lost in a picture of a brave old soldier walking into the sunset and hooked on a line about the frailty of the human condition and the selfishness of youth, I was duly chastened and then abruptly sprung from my reverie by the appearance of the owner entering to the fanfare of another buzzer, this time of a musically higher register than that of the front portal. Tom and I approached him and he introduced himself. Immediately, I was charmed by his Greek accent as thick and creamy as honey yoghurt. We followed in his broad wake as he took us through the double doors into the main corridor where the atmosphere was quiet and calm and the carpets were as verdant and thick as forest floor moss. He indicated the dining room, pointing to the left with his plump arm, the shoulder seams of his dog tooth jacket straining. Thence he led us by the nose and I was pleased and surprised to detect not even a slight whiff of cabbage. Instead, the fruity warm smell of something sugary and treacly began its sensual assault and my stomach began to rumble in response.

Presented with a dining room looking like a stylish but homely restaurant, its tables covered with raspberry coloured drapery topped with practical and disposable white paper cloths, my mouth fell open.

My nose was now receiving the homely satisfying fragrance of eggy sponge and a song my father used to sing came echoing into my mind. *There is a happy land, far, far away, where the kids eat bread and jam nine times a day. You should hear them laugh and sing when the bread and jam comes in. There is a happy land far, far away.* "Can you jam... I mean seat, all your residents in this room, Zeus?" I asked; we were on first name terms by the time we had reached the serving hatch.

"Yes, indeed we like everyone to eat together. Some of our residents have special dietary requirements of course and some have special feeding regimens. All are accommodated here and there are plenty of staff members ready on hand to help. The food is very good. You know some of our visitors- they join their relative for a meal. There's one old gentleman that bakes bread at home and brings it in - for him and his wife to share during his visits. He comes every day. We welcome all that sort of thing, whatever makes our residents feel comfortable and make them feel at home."

My mental tick list continued to keep a good score as Zeus led us from the dining room, into a corridor where he drew our attention to two special rooms: one a dedicated hair salon and another, a shop. "We have a visiting hairdresser who keeps our residents tidy and smart. It makes everyone feel good if they can keep up their appearance," he said stroking his own thick black locks that framed his face and curled over his collar in a style that would tick boxes on Beau Brummell's 'a la Brutus' check list. It took but a few seconds to visualise Dad seated in the cushioned barber's chair in this mini salon, enjoying having his wild grey-black hair being snipped off cleanly into an RAF style short back and sides. *I wonder if they use Brylcreem?*

"Then there's the little shop," continued Zeus proudly pointing to a large window that faced into the corridor displaying a selection of essential items in a seasonally decorated setting. For those elderly residents who rarely left the care home, and who could not see above the floral displays in the windowsill parapets, spring was being brought to them. Through the window they could see little birds formed from woollen pom-poms placed on twigs covered in pink tissue paper blossom. Also dangling from the tree were tooth brushes, tablets of soap on ropes and shower gel packs. "It stocks all sorts of items our residents might need like toiletries and some little extras like biscuits and chocolates, and greetings cards. We also have a limited range of clothing, pyjamas, nightdresses and that type of thing. The shop is only open a couple of hours each day and is run by staff members. And it is very popular." I was sold and I knew by the impressed look on Tom's face, that he felt the same. This had the feel of a cosy community and was light years away from the atmosphere of a hospital.

The next part of the tour served to confirm these initial positive impressions, as we viewed the comfortable reception rooms. Indeed there was not just one lounge but several linked areas, all furnished with high backed armchairs and footstools left ready and waiting for tired legs. The largest area was designated for television watching and therefore the chairs were grouped around the edge of the room so that every resident had an unimpeded view of the enormous screen. Tom and I smiled at the female and male (*Yes there was even a sprinkling of men here*) residents and apologised to the few that were actually awake for interrupting their TV programme; but they mainly ignored us, continuing to stare vacantly at the screen. It was that dead time, the quiet twilight time after the satisfaction of lunch and before the excitement of dinner. Along with Demographics, Tom and I had also learnt about Biorhythms during our traverse of the steep learning curve.

I spotted an upright piano in the corner of the lounge and Zeus told us that often staff organised old time singalong sessions, keep fit classes, and quiz games with the residents in that particular room. Linked to the large room were other spaces with chairs set out in small clusters around coffee tables and beyond these main social areas, there were two smaller rooms. The latter were dedicated as places for quiet reflection or they could be used by residents as a base in which to entertain family visitors. He showed us that one such room had been occupied earlier that day by a resident holding an impromptu coffee morning with their visiting relatives. The furniture here consisted of sofas and footstools arranged around a fire place of traditional homely design complete with a coal-effect gas fire. On the mantelpiece were dainty pseudo-porcelain pastoral figures suggesting Little Boy Blue and Little Bo-Peep, whilst upon the hearth quarry tiles stood a massive ceramic carthorse hitched by intricately detailed harnessing to a brightly coloured gypsy caravan.

It was time to view the first floor and this was accessed via a cosy lift. The air in this confined space was understandably stale but the most noticeable feature was the extremely sticky surface to the floor. I did not feel I could ask what might have caused this viscosity; our shoes made squeaks and belches as we shifted from one foot to another adjusting our positions to avoid intersecting our personal space bubbles. It was to no avail, by the time we arrived at dormitory level, the confines of the elevator had forced the three of us to merge into a Venn diagram of monumental Mathematical importance. It was little wonder that our exit from the lift was to be signalled by a ripping sound usually only heard in a Swiss Velcro factory.

Leaving the lift and its destructive force behind us, we were led down a long, wide passageway with doors set at regular intervals on either side, just like a hotel corridor. A member of staff was in the process of cleaning one of the rooms and with Zeus' permission, we were allowed to enter and view the apartment's facilities. This met with our approval one hundred per cent. The bedroom and adjoining personal bathroom was of high quality and tastefully decorated. The secure windows made the room bright and gave a view of the grounds and the housing estate beyond.

"We like the residents to bring their own things in to make it like their own home. Pictures and ornaments and such like, as you see here," said Zeus, proudly. He had to raise his voice above the constant sound of the hissing aerosol can wielded by the cleaning staff. The spray bouquet of lavender and bergamot was energetically being deployed like a latter day Agent Orange to counteract the unmistakable base note of urine.

Zeus guided us as we retraced our steps, descending via the sticky lift and through the main lounge where pre-dinner sherry was being served. *Yes, Sherry considered the ambrosia of the gods, by anyone over seventy.* He led us to his office and invited us to sit down. By this time, Tom and I were eating out of Zeus' large and finely sculpted hand and so, thoroughly impressed, we gave our positive feedback. Zeus, for his part asked details of our father's presentation and stated that he had limited places available for residents with needs associated with dementia but that an assessment of his suitability would be made by *The Grange's* manager, Rosina, as part of the application process.

Zeus passed us a folder containing details of fees and methods of payment. We tried not to show our shock but he must have been used to witnessing a certain blanching about the gills in potential clients as he said, "To provide the care for the elderly that is needed, it does not come without a big price tag. But you can be assured that here at *The Grange*, we do our very best."

It was what he said next that removed any doubts I may have had, left me bereft of speech and on the point of morphing into Ghost buster goo.

"You know when you visit your elderly relative in their own home, you don't *see* the person. You just see all the things that need doing. Like that light bulb that needs replacing, that rug that needs straightening so they don't trip, or that carpet that wants cleaning. You empty the bins, you clear out the fridge of all the out of date food and you collect the washing. But when they are with us in a home we provide, they are looked after, kept clean and fed and so when you visit, you can spend the whole time actually in their company, talking to them. It is much nicer for the old person. They are actually visited, they are actually *seen*."

Coming out of the care home into the late afternoon light found me confused; as if I had visited another world. I was reminded of the feeling experienced as a child when coming out of a cinema at the end of a matinee show. Everything in the darkness of the cinema had been intensely real and yet reality was the bright sunshine world going on in the street outside, far beyond the tiers of plush crimson seating. Just as the enduring afterglow of the family movie experience meant anything was possible, so too was the knowledge that whatever had occurred in that rose brick building behind me meant hope was still alive.

Chapter 25
Back at the Hotel Phoenicia

George

George left his room and padded soundlessly along the smoothly carpeted runway of a corridor, in search of the bar. He thought he might have walked through it earlier when the maid took him up to his room, although it had looked very different from how he had remembered it. He had not had any change in his pocket to give that little girl a tip but he guessed that if he saw her again he could put that right. It felt good to be back in a decent hotel, one that provided a blend of creature comforts with a hint of luxury. The old place had certainly been refurbished and he began to wonder if the colonial style bar still had the photographs of all the chaps that had visited Malta during the war. It had been quite a rogues' gallery. There had even been colour pictures taken at Luqa airport of the arrival of the very first civilian air flight to land in Malta after the war. A real landmark moment - and he had been part of it as radio officer of the crew. *Good old times,* he mused, *we put on a good show.*

He saw the shiny steel doors of the elevator ahead and pressed the large illuminated arrow button and waited. His short ride took him to the ground floor where, as the sliding doors opened, he immediately looked to his left and then right like a child operating his Green Cross Code on a main road. *Some clumsy chump has spilt his drink on the deck in there,* he thought as he left the steel cabinet of the elevator behind and struck out in the direction of the bar. He found it soon enough, a large room with soft deep carpets and plenty of armchairs. *Lots of old folk here; must be one of those parties on a package holiday. I've not seen a bunch like this for a while on our service. I suppose Malta is getting pretty popular - and old folk, well they do like the warmth and the sunshine. And they do seem to love jet travel. I wonder where the rest of the crew is.*

He sat down in a chair near the piano with a good view of the television. Some programme about antiques was showing; made him think of home. There was an old gent sitting nearby with his flat cap still on. *Bad form old chap.* He looked up at George and said, "'Afternoon."

George smiled and quipped, "Get ahead - wear a hat." The old gent responded with a nod.

They know how to look after you here. The food is always good. That's why they make up all the in-flight meals in their kitchens. Nothing but the best for our passengers that fly BEA. Mind you, this lot look like they could prove to be pretty fussy.

George heard glasses clinking and looked up to see the little girl he had met earlier offering small glasses of liquor to everyone in the club. He sighed with relief. *Now this is more like it.*

*

"So how is it all going to be paid for? Mum's new care package and Dad's care home place I mean?" I asked Tom, catching up on the latest news in one of our regular phone calls. After the Sumo safe opening fiasco, I had taken my eye off the financial ball and did not know the state of play.

"Well Julie," he replied, "it's all really complicated."

"Are we going to have to borrow from Peter to pay Paul - and all the disciples in between?" I ventured.

"No, at least, I hope not. I have been in touch with the Court of Protection and I think if we are careful, we should be able to cover the cost of both. There are the proceeds from the sale of Mum's car which will help to begin with and Mum's and Dad's income from their pensions and some Attendance Allowance Benefit - all that combined should cover bills for the time being."

"That's a relief then, because I remember those figures in the file at *The Grange*. An image of them got burnt into my retinas," I pulled my Edvard Munch *Scream* face again; it was becoming my default setting.

"It should be OK but we have to take this one step at a time. But I hope you agree it's the right action to take at this moment," said Tom.

"Absolutely, Tom. And I know Janine agrees, she said she felt the same way when I told her about *The Grange*. She is going to see it herself this weekend. She's taking Mum to see Dad on Saturday."

"That's great, Julie. I have seen Dad a couple of times since he moved in there and he seemed to be settling in OK, making himself quite at home. And Rosina, the manager, she seems a very nice person and she described Dad as a 'proper gentleman'. So that's good isn't it?"

*

"How did it go?" I asked Janine. It was my turn to phone my sister after the completion of her mission; I could not wait to hear how she had managed linking Mum with Dad and what she thought of *The Grange.*

"Well I don't know where to start really, Julie. How do you begin to describe a nightmare?"

"Oh dear, I'm so sorry to hear that. I'd hoped that Dad would be happy at *The Grange.* It seemed so lovely; I thought he would find it so much better than hospital. Tom said he was really getting on well. What happened?" I asked weakly.

"No, you misunderstand, Julie. Dad was fine. He wasn't the problem. It was Mum!"

"Mum?"

"Yes, Mum. I went to the bungalow at Burnage and it took ages to get her ready. She was in the middle of cutting up all the packets of cake in the cupboard into slices like she was holding a high tea for twenty. She made plates and plates of Jamaican ginger and Madeira cake and spread them all out on the dining room table. She got really annoyed when I told her it would get stale. I put as much as I could in cake tins and the rest I covered in cling film. She thought I was stopping her tea party. She clearly did not know me and I think she thought I was the care worker- a care worker that was bossing her around."

"You weren't wearing navy blue were you?"

"Well, yes I was. It couldn't be helped, Julie. I'd dashed out of school and I had my school teacher gear on, you know my navy blazer," moaned Janine. Although I could not see her, I knew what she would also be wearing today - her own version of an Edvard Munch *Scream* face.

"Anyhow," she continued, "once she knew we were going for a ride in the car, she got all excited, got herself ready by putting on a cardigan."

"A cardigan!" I exclaimed, shocked to the core.

"Well that is, a cardigan that is not a cardigan as you know Mum will never admit to wearing one - *but a little knitted coat with buttons Darlings!* Then she leaped into the car, buckled up her seat belt and off we went."

"Phew! Well done. So what happened then?" I asked, beginning to doodle on the spiral note pad kept by the phone, as a way of de-stressing. Within seconds, zig zag patterns were marching satisfyingly across the page.

"We set off to Shelton and on the way there she started asking me questions showing that she had no idea who I was and no idea who *she* was – again. She asked me where I worked and I told her the name of my school but that didn't trigger her memory. It was worse than how she was at *Bramwell*. I suppose we can't expect that her memory will have improved. But I kept trying to get through to her as she was obviously anti the carer who she thought I was. So I kept saying that I was her daughter but she just looked surprised and mystified. I told her about you and Tom and she proceeded to ask, *so you have a sister do you? Is she married? Oh, I have a son, do I? What's his wife called?* - all those sorts of questions all the way to *The Grange*."

"No change there then," I said in jaundiced tones. On my notepad, the zig zags were becoming shark teeth and saw blades.

"When we got to *The Grange* she got out of the car and began looking round the grounds as if we had arrived at a garden centre. By the time I'd locked the car, she had wandered off into the shrubbery and it took a while before I managed to lasso and wrangle her then coax her up the path to the front door. The receptionist must have watched our antics on CCTV as she came to the door and let us in, no problem. She took us straight in to Dad in one of the little lounges. It's a lovely place isn't it? I met Rosina and she arranged for cups of tea to be brought in. It was good because we had the lounge to ourselves."

"I am so pleased about that. How were they together, did they know each other?" I asked, holding my breath. Meanwhile in doodle world a great white shark had made an entrance and begun a stand-off with my saw blade that had by then, morphed into the slashing appendage of a sword fish.

"Well they did greet each other by name which was a good sign but after that they did not really connect. I found myself trying to get them to chat to each other but most of the time they could not seem to engage. Mum did not appear to be able to focus on anything and just kept repeating her loop of phrases like a little doll. Dad was a bit more talkative and kept telling me about chamber maids and meals like he was in a hotel. It reminded me -you know how he used to say – *let's get a Me and You* when he looked at the Menu card in a restaurant?"

I smiled at the recollection. "Yes, happy days. Do you remember when he used to take us to Lyon's Corner House in London and we would choose from the 'Me and You' the mixed grill with those delicious baked mushrooms and the lemon meringue pie with that gorgeous thick sugary topping? Heaven for us little girls and Tom, he loved it too. It was all so posh. It made us feel grown up. Do you remember once he asked you what you would like to order and you said, 'the usual'? It made him and Mum laugh so much. I suppose it would have sounded like you were a seasoned diner."

"Some seasoned diner I would have looked – seven years old, with a blonde pony- tail and white ankle socks! But yes, it was all wonderful. Anyhow, I digress," said Janine, picking up her thread. "Things started to go downhill after the tea and biscuits, I got the box of sweets out and that took up another quarter of an hour. Dad took a couple and seemed to enjoy them whilst Mum sat looking at the wrapped bonbon in her hand as if she didn't know what to do with it."

"I know she does that. It's like with her tablets, she sits gazing at them for ages with them in the palm of her hand," I added.

"Anyhow, Dad told her to put them in her mouth and chew and she immediately obeyed – but the wrapper was still on! So I had to get her to open up and I had to pull the half chewed and mashed up toffee from her teeth!"

"*Ooh, Darlings!*" I said in Mum's tone of voice, all the while over-working the shark teeth on my notepad with pressure sufficient to carve wood.

"Exactly, even though she was stuck up with toffee and bits of silver paper and clearing her throat like my cat with a fur ball, she still managed to slip into the groove of automatic responses -one of her *ha-huh- ha* laughs and an *absolutely gorgeous Darlings* for good measure," mimicked Janine.

"So how long did you both stay with Dad?"

"About an hour, I guess. Mum started to get twitchy and started *visiting* other residents and so I thought it was time to go. It was then that all the trouble kicked off."

"Why? What happened then?" I asked.

"Well, I was getting ready to leave and went to round up Mum who had been interviewing some residents in the big lounge – but when I got in there, she had disappeared!"

"Oh no!" I exclaimed, as a giant angler fish materialised on my doodle pad. "What did you do?"

"I searched the ground floor and spoke to one of the carers who said that the old lady visitor I had arrived with had made her way to the exit. I shot along to the reception area and sure enough, she had signed herself out."

"She does move mighty fast doesn't she? And I assume, as she is a visitor and they don't know her needs, there would be no official cause to raise the alarm."

"That's right, Julie. When the staff realised my concern they were ever so good. Two of them came with me and we set off on foot trying to find her. Then after about ten minutes we spotted her in one of those little streets off the main drag."

"Gosh! That's a relief!" My angler fish pounced on a Nemo.

"Well it was, until she turned tail and scurried off when she saw us coming after her! We had a Dickens of a job luring her back to the car park."

"Oh, Janine!" I could imagine her exasperation, let alone her fear that Mum had put herself at serious risk.

"Anyhow, with the help of the carers who were *so* nice and knew just what to say to her, we got Mum belted into the car and we set off. But she was not happy, not one bit. When we stopped at the traffic lights on the way back, she tried to get out of the car! I had to lock all the doors to prevent her making a sudden dash for it. She even lashed out at me and hit me on the arm – which is not pleasant when you're trying to drive."

"Oh my God! You poor thing!"

"She ranted for most of the journey and then went very quiet – which was even more worrying."

"I'll bet," I sympathised, "there would be no telling what she might do next."

"That's how it was, well until we got to the railway bridge in Burnage when she put on her best royal voice and said, *would you be so kind as to let me out and I shall walk the rest of the way from here.*"

"You didn't though, did you?"

"No way! I took her all the way home and made sure all was *well and wisely put* back at the bungalow before I left. We got back just as the home help arrived."

"Wearing navy blue?" I asked unnecessarily.

"Wearing navy blue," Janine conceded. "And do you know what? Mum greeted her with her best smile and said *How lovely to see you again!*"

*

Meanwhile back at the Hotel Phoenicia, George was waiting for all the doors in the corridor to close and for the place to shut down for the night. There had been quite some shenanigans with one of the guests who seemed to be very demanding with his room service requests. That poor little girl had been up and down the corridor with bits and pieces all evening. But now it seemed that things were settling down and becoming quiet. George stood like a sentinel in his doorway, a white plastic bathroom stool in his hand and a look of grim determination on his face. As soon as he was sure the coast was clear, he would put his plan into action. Looking down the hallway which was dimly illuminated by tiny cats-eyes set into the ceiling, just one bright light was shining through the glass pane of the door to *old cap man's* room. Finally, this was extinguished showing that he had turned in for the night at last. *I bet he sleeps in that cap,* George mused. The soft carpet allowed him to move towards his target, *with cat-like tread,* he thought with a smile. He began to hum the rest of the tune from his beloved Gilbert and Sullivan, *upon our prey we steal* as he traversed the route he had been planning over the past few hours. *In silence dread...our cautious way we feel...no sound at all...we never speak a word...a fly's foot-fall...would be distinctly heard.*

When he arrived at the end of the corridor farthest from the lift, he placed the stool by a tall cupboard. Then by carefully putting first his right foot then his left on the seat of the stool, he stood– and then began to wobble. Gaining his balance by grabbing the edge of the cupboard, he breathed out slowly and reviewed the situation from his newly elevated position. He was satisfied to see that by stretching out his right arm, he was able to reach the phone. Giddy with success and with the effort of maintaining balance on his precarious perch, he transferred the cream plastic base unit and handset into his arms to cradle gingerly as if it was a baby. Then taking the receiver in his right hand, he punched those special buttons he had never used in that particular sequence ever before.

Chapter 26
It's on the cards

Julie

"So he called the police!" I said, shocked and embarrassed at this new turn of events. Tom and I were on the road once again, breathing in the air of executive luxury emanating from leather and pine – the former from the soft recliner car seats, the latter from a cardboard miniature spruce tree hanging from the windscreen mirror.

"Yes, Julie. He dialled 999 and called for the police to attend. He must have sounded convincing as they took him seriously and came to *The Grange*."

"But, didn't they realise he was ringing from a care home and that it was a nutty old gentleman who was raising the alarm?" I asked my brother.

"Well, yes they did. According to Rosina, it's not the first time this kind of thing has happened. But the police are obliged to attend, to check in case there is a real cause. Apparently though, at *The Grange* they have not had any residents do this since they moved the phone out of normal reach. It is now kept in a concealed location on top of a tall cabinet in the dormitory corridor, purely meant for staff emergency use. But somehow Dad must have spied the phone and got to it during the night. I'm not sure how as he's only a short chap, isn't he? Rosina thinks he must have stood on a chair. "

"It sounds like one of Dad's undercover operations. We know what he's like when he has a mission, don't we, Tom?" I began humming the theme to *Mission Impossible.*

"Too right, Julie," he smiled, humming along with me until the coda when we both upped the volume for the crescendo of *did-dah* augmented with percussive beats on the leather covered steering wheel. *How would we cope without some light diversion?* I thought.

"Seriously though, do we know what he said to the police?" I asked, picking up my nervous thread of anxiety once again; it was never far away. I began to consider all the risks involved in Dad's actions, as well as the inconvenience caused to the staff at *The Grange* and to the police. However, part of me could not help feeling proud, admiring my Dad's determined spirit. *There are no flies on me,* I could hear him say.

"Well, according to Rosina, Dad said he was being held against his will in a hotel."

"A hotel? Oh wait a minute; Janine said that when she visited Dad the other day, he had talked about *The Grange* as if it was a hotel. And of course, if he thought he was a guest, he would expect to be able to leave whenever he felt like it."

"Exactly, Julie. Anyhow, Rosina said that she will keep an eye on things and keep us informed. Everyone wants Dad to feel happy and settled there. I don't want Dad to feel like a prisoner but at the same time we must try and eliminate the risk. If he wasn't living in a secure environment he might end up like that poor old chap we heard about in the news recently."

"On that was so sad. He went wandering in his pyjamas didn't he? And he died of hyperthermia? Yes, you're right, that could easily happen to Dad – well it very nearly did last winter – he's already got form."

"Yes, Julie. That was an experience I shall never forget!"

"Me neither! Anyhow," I continued, as we neared our destination, "what do you think Doctor Challis will have to say?"

"I don't know, Julie. I hope that he will be satisfied with the actions that we have taken in keeping Mum at home with the care package in place and Dad at *The Grange*."

*

Doctor Challis headed the Adult Community Mental Health Team based at *Highway Lodge* just five miles from the ever familiar Gibbet Roundabout. The latter landmark was fast becoming the central pivot of our world. Sometimes I thought this barren roundel of concrete and scrub grass was like the portal to a parallel universe. Reality and fantasy were beginning to merge – an experience I had only previously endured during a whole afternoon session playing one of Simon's ridiculously complicated board games. The challenge of this gaming foray into fantasy world required the player to change character from doughty elf into unspeakably ugly orc or, if you drew a lucky magic card, a venerable wizard through whom you could gain entry to other worlds through whirlpools or magic black portals after throwing a double six.

Through the Gibbet Roundabout portal we travelled that day undeterred, and I am pleased to record that neither Tom nor I changed our appearance. Indeed, I was also relieved to note that Dr Challis did not have a face like a mouldy potato nor was he sporting a pointy hat. However, some transition had clearly occurred: the estimable doctor, although still a young man wore the premature lines of experience etched sharply into his once smooth skin –testament to the long days working on psychiatric wards and the numerous late nights listening to suicidal outpatients' outpourings over the phone. He may not have been a wizard, but this was a man who had insight.

He greeted us warmly and invited us to join him around the small coffee table placed in the centre of his shabby office. There were more than three of us in the room. Our parents' presence took up the space afforded by the chair beside Dr Challis where thick buff coloured folders bore the names George Ellis and Joan Ellis respectively on white sticky labels. Pointing to these, Dr Challis began by asking for an update on our parents' state of health and their current living arrangements.

Like the reverse of a Parent-Teacher meeting, we the children, gave a report of our parents' current presentation and our thoughts on how they were doing. Dr Challis listened attentively throughout our summary without interruption, yet encouraged and empathised all the while through subtle changes to his facial expression and eye contact that indicated a true understanding. He knew what we were suffering. He could see beneath our bluff and bluster to the chinks in our confidence. He knew our struggle as we made feeble attempts to manage a situation that he could foresee was only going to get worse.

When we had finished, he studied the top sheet of each folder and nodded, confirming that the community records were indeed up to date and that they contained feed-back from the various bodies involved in Mum and Dad's care. He then did his own summing up, loosening his tie as he did so and rolling up his shirt sleeves. It was clear that he was not finding this meeting easy and it crossed my mind that we must be missing something.

"It is clear to all of us in this room that your parents, George and Joan, have significant problems with their mental health. The issues we must consider now is how best to maintain their safety and improve their quality of life. I hear from what you say that you are saddened that your parents are living apart. What future plans do you have for arranging for them to live together again?" he asked.

Tom answered for us both when he stated that our ultimate aim was to return Dad to live with Mum in the bungalow and for them jointly to be looked after by visiting carers.

"From what you have said and from what we can deduce from the course of recent events, there seems to be an indication that your father has not fully bonded with *The Grange*. Equally, your mother has been very restless over the past few months whether in hospital or at home. We would all agree that their mental health has declined but we do not know precisely how this has happened. Neither have we a true and detailed clinical picture of their presentation which makes the prescription of medication difficult. Therefore I would like to suggest that both your parents are taken into *The Torran*, a specialist psychiatric assessment centre, where they can be fully observed for a sustained period."

Tom and I looked at each other. I could tell he felt the same wave of shock and disappointment that I did. I realised that in our naivety, we had been basking in the afterglow of achievement gained from setting up *The Grange* for Dad and the tailored care package for Mum. The thought of moving them yet again seemed an extreme step.

Clearly Dr Challis read our thoughts and continued, bringing his point home, "If we could get them both to *The Torran*, and they were assessed as suitable for the new raft of drugs that are being developed for people suffering dementia related diseases, then they could undergo supervised medication trials which could in turn lead to slowing down the progression of their illnesses."

I studied his earnest expression and the sincerity in his wise eyes as I began to realise that he had played his trump card; any hope for the future lay before us through yet another portal.

Chapter 27
The important thing to remember

Joan and Julie

Joan sat in an armchair across the room from Georgie, just like old times. She was still trying to get used to the layout of this new place. In the past few days she had circumnavigated the two large rooms linked by a corridor, travelling back and forth, over and over again like a champion swimmer clocking up her lengths. She thought that she would pause here in the shallows for a bit while she got her breath back and rest her swollen, itchy limbs. She lifted the leg of her cropped woollen trousers and scratched the skin on her shins and around her ankles until it bled. She looked down dispassionately at the damage she had inflicted then pushed herself out of the chair to commence another length. Through the lounge she swam, along the narrow lane formed by the corridor into the next room. She tapped the far wall as she turned then leaned her back briefly against the tiled surface before taking a deep breath and pushing off again. On her way back to the shallows, her progress along the lane was arrested by a little girl who invited her to sit down on a bench beside her.

"Hello Mum," said the little girl.

"How absolutely gorgeous to see you, Darling. How's your mother?"

"Well she's looking fine from where I am sitting," said the little girl whose smile revealed a full set of white teeth.

"Teeth, Hah-Huh-Ha," Joan trilled as she reached across to touch the little girl's cheek. She became fascinated by the girl's teeth, ignoring all else but the flash of dental ivory.

"Where did you get those trousers from, Mum? They're *plus fours*, they're men's trousers – the sort they wear when they go hunting and shooting."

"Whatty? Hunting? Ha-Huh-Ha. Yes very good Darlings."

"And look, you're bleeding. That tweed must be irritating your skin. I'll have a word with the nurse."

"Nurse," echoed Joan in a low voice.

On impulse Joan stood up and continued with her length, leaving behind the little girl person in her wake.

After a few moments, she noticed she was being followed so she stopped her progress up the lounge and turned around. It was a little girl.

"Mum, I'm going to see Dad in the armchair over there now," she appeared to say with white teeth flashing.

"Gorgeous Darlings...who are you?"

Joan watched the little girl overtake her and sit down by the old gentleman who did look vaguely familiar, then turned around again to resume her swim back to the deep end.

*

"It's very good of you to see me, Doctor Benyon. I was just talking to the nurse about the skin irritation on my mother's leg, when she informed me that you wished to see me?" *Complete with an upward inflection, I had neatly turned my statement into a question. I do not think the doctor was impressed. He had more important things to think about; so did I, for that matter. However by distracting myself with the little details, I could avoid facing the bigger picture. Banality over gravity- works for me.*

"Yes Mrs Wood," he answered wearily, from his creaking swivel chair in the cramped office; I sat on a standard plastic moulded chair that squeaked back at him whenever I moved. Throughout this meaningless discourse between items of phonic furniture, we were able to follow Mum's progress through the office's two-way mirror window as she continued her perpetual course slicing through imaginary waves whilst Dad sat, lifeguard alert, in an arm chair in the distance.

"Please, feel free to call me Julie." It was time that the humans in the room spoke and I needed to be distracted from the swimming gala.

"Thank you Julie and you can call me Brian. Now, when I was made aware of your visit, I thought I would take the opportunity to ask you a few questions about your mother and father. If that's ok?" (*So he is not above using an upward inflection either.*) "We are in the process of gathering observational data which will form the main substance of our assessments, but there are a few details as regards your parents'

209

history, habits, diet -that sort of thing that we hope you could help us with - to enhance our research, you understand? If you wouldn't mind?"

"Of course," I replied, "whatever I can do to help, Brian." It felt good to be able to talk to an expert. Dr Benyon had an appearance that embodied most people's idea of a scientific professor; especially if they had grown up reading *Tin Tin* stories. He had greying temples, with a bald crown and a curtain of thick hair that curled naturally under and around the base of his skull. *What Lizzy would call a 'bald bob';* all very reminiscent of *Professor Calculus.* He wore a red paisley bow tie and a blue striped shirt with grey flannel trousers; the whole ensemble yearning to be enclosed in a white coat complete with a breast pocket full of pens.

"Excellent. Thank you. I understand that your parents retired several years ago and lived together in their own home prior to the marked decline in their mental health. Could you describe their lifestyle to me, as it was before they became, shall we say, *confused?*" he asked.

"*Confused* is a kind and gentle way of putting it," I smiled, grateful to talk in euphemisms with this man who would know all the bald scientific facts about what would be happening to the brains of my parents; facts that my cowardly weakness of spirit could not bear to think about, never mind accept.

"Well," I began, trying to adopt a controlled tone, "in the past few years they seem to have drifted into a quiet, subdued way of life. Dad has always been rather diffident and has a history of being depressed – it was normal for him to be of low mood, especially in the mornings. In recent years he became reclusive and spent most of his leisure time indoors, watching television or working at his computer. He did not enjoy entertaining visitors in his own home, apart from family members of course.

Mum was more at ease in company; in fact she was very gregarious and used to go out to meet friends and ex work colleagues occasionally, to attend coffee mornings and other social events. She always loved chatting on the phone to family and friends. She also enjoyed television and did a great deal of dressmaking and fine needlework."

"What about how they looked after themselves - cooking, cleaning, shopping? Did they do any activities together?"

"Mum was a good cook and kept the freezer full of meals although the variety was somewhat limited. They both shared cleaning chores and kept their home tidy. They used to do the supermarket shopping together. Mum usually drove the car owing to Dad's poor sight – he had cataracts. They belonged to the local Church and before all this happened, they had held posts on Church committees – for example, Dad was the treasurer. Mum used to make tea cosies and bags et cetera to sell at Church fund raisers and bazaars, that sort of thing."

"So a fairly stable and steady life style, then. How independent were they?"

"Well," I replied, "they were fairly independent, able to run their own household finances – in fact they were very private about such matters. However, during the past three years, they became increasingly reliant on us children -especially my brother who lives near them- for advice on many aspects of the modern world as they became increasingly challenged by change. It became clear that they were beginning to lose confidence for trying new things. They had stopped taking little breaks and holidays away or even trips out other than in their locality."

"I see. Well I guess as we get older, and our health becomes more fragile, we are disinclined to take risks."

"That's true. But there is something about Mum and Dad's apparent independence that you should be made aware of. They did rely on each other very heavily and we used to say that they made two halves of a whole. Mum was the 'eyes' and Dad was the 'cars' – owing to Dad's weak sight and Mum's poor hearing. As a team, they were able to cope with most things that day to day life threw at them. My brother, sister and I had not realised just how reliant they were on each other's faculties until relatively recently. We began to anticipate that should one of them pass away, the one left behind would find it extremely challenging. Though I guess that is a common tragedy for any couple that have been married as long as Mum and Dad. "

"Yes, indeed. It follows that when your father became ill, that would have a very significant impact on your mother – particularly as they were so inter-reliant. This might go towards explaining why two people who are not genetically linked, should show symptoms of dementia at practically the same time – well within weeks of each other," the doctor suggested.

"We have been wondering that ourselves," I agreed. *We have been looking for reasons and causes ever since this nightmare started.*

"Well at this moment, this is merely speculation," he paused looking at my troubled expression. "You said that your parents used to do their own shopping; did they cook for themselves, have ready meals? What was their diet like?"

In my mind's eye I was back in Mum and Dad's kitchen in the bungalow before the whole mental health game had kicked off, before they had 'lost the time'. I conjured up the vision of the interior of their refrigerator. Pots of church bazaar jam, packs of new potatoes and plastic trays of chicken breasts were stored on the laminated wire shelves. The mini freezer section boasted a bag of garden peas. On the worktop there would be two pears in ying – yang position in the fruit bowl, beside two sharp green apples and bracketed by two over ripe bananas. Then poked into one side of the arrangement would be the obligatory stash of Mars bars. This assortment of foods comprised their diet.

When my husband James and I, along with our two small children, visited my parents, we were always served a meal of chicken, potatoes and peas and we thought little of it, imagining that it was a Menu chosen to suit all tastes, as indeed it did. The meal would be supplemented with items I would bring with me and we would all sit around the big table, and enjoy each other's company. Full of the cares and joys of my own little family's life, I was unaware that this meal was being served almost every day at my parents' table. How long had that been going on?

In the early 1970's, when my brother, sister and I were going off to college and absorbing ourselves in very important things like (in reverse order) how to change the world, find a partner and how to sustain a flicked back fringe, our parents' eating habits were not our concern. As we brutally flew the nest, trying not to trample on those who had raised and nurtured us, we were blissfully unaware that our parents were about to embark on a path of self- denial.

Dr Benyon listened attentively as I described the main elements of the crude and monotonous diet on which Mum and Dad had survived for many years. He nodded sagely as I explained how they had adopted a pattern of eating that was designed to help them lose weight and maintain healthy hearts. Unfortunately, they made modifications to the original diet sheet given to them by their GP, eliminating some foods that they did not enjoy, making the variety and nutritional range extremely limited.

"They both lost weight, which was good," I said making a big tick shape in the air between us. "But now here is the worst part, they kept on this diet not for weeks or months, but for years. In so doing they were cutting out nutritional elements that I believe are at the very least desirable for a healthy lifestyle." I drew a big cross in the air. "Clearly, I am no medical expert, but I think I am beginning to join up the dots, these very large significant dots." *I sat on my hands, fighting the urge to draw the dots and lines in the air. The stress of mentally opening up my parents' fridge cum Pandora's Box was making me light headed again.*

"There are many elements to consider in your parents' profiles and it may be too soon to draw any conclusions but there is no doubt that it is possible that poor diet contributed to your parents' decline in mental health. Their avoidance of key elements in their diet like fats and oils and leafy green vegetables is likely to have impacted significantly on their brain function."

"Apart from the fat in the odd Mars bar," I said, offering this rare ingredient to the mix.

"Apart from the odd Mars bar," he agreed tolerantly. Then, looking at me with a wry smile, he stated a universal truth.

"The important thing we must all remember about essential fatty acids… *is that they are essential.*"

Chapter 28
Black Mass

Julie

>   *In a dark, dark inn, down some Bible black stairs, in a caldron black basement, in a coal dark corner, around a black ash table – was a ghost!*

Well, three actually, looking like some re-enactment of a children's scary story; we made a ghostly tableau, all of us sitting at the pub table in our own twilight world. Tom looked as pale as *Banquo* in Act 3, Janine was doing her best unconscious impression of an ethereal *will-o'-the-wisp*, and me a too, too solid fleshly member of the supernatural brethren: the *Grey Lady* – before she lost her head – although I do not wish to split hairs on a prophecy that might have already come to pass.

All of us looked as though we had been on the run from a spectre, we had picked up the ancient bone whistle in the graveyard bearing the inscription, *whistle and I'll come to you*, and blown it.

Ironically, despite our haggard appearance, we had been given some respite from the 'Mum and Dad situation' owing to the fact that their assessment at *The Torran* had taken all of *four months*. Mum and Dad had been in a secure, safe place for *four months*. This posed a break for us of *four months*, a break that prevented adrenalin running at its usual high level to meet our habitual panic mode. As a consequence, we had achieved a state of imminent collapse.

We had all made countless hollow journeys to see Mum and Dad; unfulfilling visits when they did not recognise us and rarely engaged, for *four months*. We may not have had the day-to-day anxiety associated with their care but during the *four months*, there had been other more poignant challenges. We had witnessed scenes redolent of '*Witchfinder General*' at Dad's Care Review meeting when he appeared to be interrogated with questions way beyond his understanding. Meek and mild he sat, at pains to plead his innocence of a crime he knew nothing about and of which he had not been accused, begging for more time in which to finish 'The Guyana Project'.

Mum's Care Review 'inquisition' left her looking baffled but still did not stem her flow of her idiomatic phrases. She was praised for her eloquence and articulation; praise sadly misplaced.

Four months of this and we were wearing away, becoming transparent and if Tom's cough was anything to go by, fit to expectorate ectoplasm.

"At least we now know the verdict," said Tom.

"Yeah, like we didn't know before," responded Janine with jaundice.

"The diagnoses do make sense though," I offered as the piggy-in-the-middle sibling and possessor of the Libra zodiac birth sign, in my attempt to maintain balance in this topsy-turvy underworld. "Right, so we all know that Mum and Dad have entered the twilight zone technically called 'Dementia'. But they do not behave in exactly the same way; they each have their own form of dementia."

"That's right," said Tom. "According to Dr Benyon, Dad has got vascular dementia and Mum has Alzheimer's but with some idiosyncratic complications."

"But does knowing that make any difference to the outcome? We know that there's no going back. They aren't going to get well," stated Janine.

"That's sadly true. But what do you think we should do now?" asked Tom, "Do we put them both in *The Grange*?"

"Hang on a minute - they went into *The Torran* to get a diagnosis but also to assess their suitability for the new Alzheimer's type drugs. What was the conclusion that they came to on that?" asked Janine.

"Well," said Tom, "when Julie and I saw Doctor Benyon at the feed-back meeting last week he just asked us which care home we had chosen for Mum and Dad. When I said that our intention was for them to go back to living in their bungalow together, he appeared surprised and advised against it."

"And," I continued with a certain feeling of indignation combined with disappointment, "during the four months that they've been at *The Torran*, they were not even put onto a medication programme to trial the Alzheimer's type drugs as the presumption held by the assessors was that Mum and Dad would be transferring to a care home and not going home."

"That's so unjust as that was not what we were led to understand before the assessment," said Janine.

I drew breath to add more fuel to the fire but we were interrupted in our rant by a waitress bringing some wafer thin sandwiches served on pieces of slate tile, looking like they had fallen off the back of a church roof. The appearance of food galvanised us into sitting up more formally at the table, adjusting the upcycled pew chairs designed to provide a level of discomfort conducive for staying awake during the sermon. Menus now sprouted from the chair back boxes that once held hymnals and missals.

I took a bite of the wafer, swallowed and then took another breath, "They told me that the policy is to only use the Alzheimer's drug –as it is so expensive – on patients who will be living in the community. It is not usually given to those who are supported in a care home."

"That's what I've been told," confirmed Tom. "They must have believed early on in their assessment that Mum and Dad were unsuitable for returning to the community so the drugs weren't offered or tried."

"I can't believe they let us think there was a chance Mum and Dad could get onto meds that might slow things down. It's as if they have written them off," said Janine.

"I don't think it was deliberate. I think Dr Challis at Community Mental Health believed there might be a chance to help them. I guess when they got to *The Torran*, Mum and Dad presented as cases that were deemed to be of the kind that could not be supported effectively outside a secure care home," replied Tom.

"And I do respect and trust Doctor Benyon's judgement. I think he knows what he's talking about," I had to concede.

"But we've been told all along that familiar surroundings help trigger memory, and keep the person suffering dementia, calm. That's why we've focused our plans around putting Mum and Dad back together at home," protested Janine.

"I love the two meanings of that statement, Janine – putting them back together – if only it were that simple," I mused over my wine glass, half full of full bodied red.

"Yes, if only," agreed Janine. "I know they don't seem to engage much in the hospital, there is a chance that once they are back in the bungalow, some memories may start to re-awaken or at the very

216

least, some stability may come about. They may be less restless, especially Mum."

We ordered another round of drinks from the bar upstairs. The pub was in Reading, a town that provided a central meeting place for us all and was rich with family associations and memories. We were sitting in a place not far from the house where Mum and Dad had made their first home together and where Tom had been born. We were keenly aware that like the fedora hatted characters in the film 'The Adjustment Bureau', we were plotting the lifelines of George and Joan Ellis. We felt their presence ghosting our table, listening in to the three of us as we aired our thoughts on how best their lives could be organised, and their futures planned.

"Tom, some time ago you did some research on how we could get Mum and Dad looked after in the bungalow with round the clock care rather than daily home helps. Can we revisit that idea, do you think?" I asked.

"That's what I've been thinking about seriously, Julie. In fact it's what I've been working on for a long time and been building up a file of possible options and information on contacts. It's a big project but it could still be the right one to follow in spite of the response we got from the doctors at *The Torran*," he replied, the sparkle of enthusiasm back in his eye.

"We know that the alternative would be for them both to become residents at *The Grange* and maybe that is something we may have to think about in the future. Just now it seems to me that the familiar setting of their own home might be just what they need to re-connect and settle," said Janine.

"I'm incline to agree," I threw in, "I feel very positive about *The Grange* and maybe it would be the right place for Mum and Dad ultimately, but it's worth giving a 'return to the bungalow plan' a shot. After all it's going to be expensive, but so is *The Grange*."

"It's a radical step," said Janine, "Does anyone else do it?"

"Apparently so, from what I've found out, there are people who are prepared to live with an elderly person, to be their main carer. It's not common but it does happen," said Tom with some authority.

"My nursy friend Christine lived for a month with an old lady, she used to say it was like being the lady's companion in a story book. She enjoyed it; the old gal taught her to play Bridge and Canasta, for goodness sake. But with Mum and Dad, the situation would hardly be like the plot of a Daphne Du Maurier novel – there would be no free

217

trips for the carer accompanying them to Monte Carlo or San Moritz," I said.

"More likely Morrison's or Sainsbury's!" quipped Janine. "Mind you, even shopping trips could be dicey as Mum and Dad may not be safe in the outside world. Effectively, the carer-companion would be locked in with them."

"I know, Janine," Tom affirmed, "but apparently there are people prepared to do it – at a price, of course. I shall need to talk to the Court of Protection people and Mum and Dad's Bank and Building Society again if we are considering this as a prospect. "

"But who would take that kind of job on? Living full time with someone, or in our case two people, who are losing their marbles?" said Janine.

"I know I couldn't do it, Janine. But then it is worse for all of us because they are our parents and emotions and memories of how they once were - get in the way, making it painful all round," said Tom.

"I can see that. I suppose if being a carer for those with dementia is your profession, then you have a professional approach." I replied. "I still can't see how they can do it though as they would be practically imprisoned in the bungalow with them. I mean they won't be able to leave them for one second for fear that they might come to harm."

"Well I guess we will have to make the bungalow as safe and as secure as possible and minimise the risks; put locks on things et cetera. Also we will have to convert the spare bedroom into a living base for the carer. We ought to provide them with their own set of furniture, TV and radio so that they can gain some respite. And we must fit locks on the internal doors as well as the outside doors. There will be lots to do to prepare the bungalow. "

"Of course," I agreed. It was clear Tom had been giving this project a lot of thought. "Will they change shifts daily, like one doing days and one doing nights?"

"From what I can gather, it's more likely that one person will stay for several weeks, up to a month," reported Tom.

"Gosh, they're brave. I really couldn't do that," said Janine. I found myself shaking my head in agreement. Such a concept was beyond my comprehension.

"I could visit them every day; in fact I am considering parking my car in their drive and then walking to the railway station and taking the train to work from there. That would mean I would have daily contact with Mum and Dad and the carer so as to monitor the situation," volunteered Tom.

"You really have thought this through, Tom, haven't you?" said Janine. "I could try and visit on a regular basis as I did before but it can't be every week owing to school commitments and the distance involved."

"Of course, Janine," said Tom.

"Obviously, with me living over a hundred miles away that's my difficulty too. I think I could come up and relieve the carer for a weekend, maybe? Every so often?" I offered without thinking it through.

"Well if we all pull together, we could just make this work," said Tom.

*

As we came out of the cellar of the dark pub into the bright sunlight, that feeling came over me again; the sense of disorientation as we moved from darkness into light, mirroring a transition from unreality to reality. Perhaps when we were young children making all those journeys through the tunnel under the runway at London Airport had left a deep and lasting impression. Through the dimly lit tube we used to accompany our mother, the angry roar of car engines augmented within the enclosed space, frightening us. But it was terror of the fairground sort, laced with excited anticipation. We knew that at the end of the tunnel, would be the prize: our father full of stories of his adventures flying passengers abroad, his kit bag bursting with presents. The prospect made us silly with delight. All those early experiences of emerging from darkness into stark sunlight had been wired into my soul so that always afterwards whenever such an experience was repeated, I would feel a sense of hope.

I think a similar sensation was affecting the others as we parted on a high note quoting Shakespeare's three witches and hoping that we would meet again, *when the hurlyburly's done*, referring to the preparation for Dad's forthcoming birthday party. Hugging and air kissing we separated and I set off to the busy railway concourse to await my train.

It was only when I had gained an elusive double seat facing south that I realised there had been no chorus from '*Salad Days*' nor a single mention of '*The Plank story*' at our meeting. We must be growing up.

Chapter 29
The Letter

Julie

My Dear George,

It has been so long since I have heard from you that I am beginning to worry that something may have happened to you or to Joan. Please get in touch, my phone number is the same as it has always been.

We are all going on fine apart from the odd cold. Cameron and his wife have a new house just outside Aberdeen. He's doing very well for himself, he has just got a new job with a computer firm. My granddaughter Briony is nineteen now – where does the time go? She's getting on well at St Andrew's – she's studying Law. Then my youngest grandchild, Sophie, she's twelve now and at big school. She's a bundle of fun- mad about horses. She has been learning to ride and hopes to do show jumping someday.

I do hope that you and your family are all OK. Please drop me a line or give me a phone call.

Lots of love,

Moira

The letter was nearly missed. Written neatly on narrow lines on a single sheet of pale blue paper and folded up into a tiny square, it had dropped out of the birthday card onto the grass. There was a breeze that day and it lifted the paper into the air, opening its folds, causing it to take flight like some delicate blue butterfly. It was this that drew our attention as we sat around the picnic table in Tom's back garden.

Tom and his wife Barbara had kindly, and very bravely, organised the birthday celebrations for Dad. They had collected Mum and Dad from *The Torran* and had brought them to their house in Sheepy Hollow for the afternoon. This would be the first time Mum and Dad would have left *The Torran* in over four months and we were all anxious as to how they would cope in the world outside the hospital. Tom had already whispered to me that when he collected them, Mum had wanted to take control of the steering wheel and the challenge to get her settled in the car's rear seat was not to be easily forgotten.

However, now everyone was seated safely at the picnic table and Tom, Barbara and I were taking the supervisory roles just as if we were in charge of a school party; *and we had organised a fair few of those in our teaching careers.* The important rule was to keep our charges in their places; we could not let either of them roam freely.

So far so good, I thought as I passed around the sandwiches. Mum was highly excited by the change of environment and was looking around with interest and fascination. Something must have jogged her memory and she pointed to the pansies tumbling gaily out of the flower pots adorning the patio. "Lovely Darlings, gorgeous, yellow." I knew these were her favourite flowers and told her that I always tried to make sure I had some pansies planted in my plant pots at home. "Pants Darlings, ha-huh-ha." I gave up on the attempt at floral conversation and offered her A SALMON SANDWICH yelling at the top of my voice, enough to make the local cats salivate. "Gorgeous Darlings," she said as she by-passed the proffered plate to take a handful of crisps. Meanwhile Dad was on his second sandwich and was looking fondly at the plate of scotch eggs. Barbara, ever the observant hostess, made sure his plate became loaded with a selection of delicacies.

One thing was becoming abundantly clear, Mum and Dad had expanded their diet to include a wider range of foods whilst they had been at *The Torran.* They looked healthier too, physically more rounded and rosy, having lost that grey pallor.

Dad said very little during the first part of the party but when the birthday cake was brought out, he became quite animated, blowing out his candles with efficiency helped no doubt by the prevailing breeze. During the *Happy Birthday to you,* he smiled and nodded. Mum sprang into action when she spotted the gourmet cake server beside the china plate and began cutting slices in time-honoured style. "Ha- huh-ha. A baker's daughter I shall always be." Tom and I exchanged glances; this was going better than we had dared to hope.

Tom had a stack of birthday cards from family members and friends ready for Dad to open. These included some that had arrived in the mail and been delivered to the bungalow in Burnage. Dad was encouraged to work his way through the pile of envelopes and we all took an interest in the messages the cards contained and passed them round the table. It was when he opened a card from a person signing themselves as *Moira* that he paused. I read over his shoulder and asked, "Who's Moira?" to which he gave no answer neither did he relinquish the card but held on to it tightly.

Tom and I looked at each other, raising our eyebrows in a melodramatic way. Meanwhile Mum, who had been utterly absorbed in the engineering process of zipping and unzipping her seat cushion repeatedly, suddenly remarked, "Oh that's his old girlfriend, ha-huh-ha!" It was then that the butterfly took flight to be captured by a pouncing salivating cat, disappointed to have not yet received A SALMON SANDWICH.

Capitalising on the cat's disappointment, I ran to its aid, smoothly swapping the now soggy blue paper for a tasty fishy treat. With my back to the party, I cast my eyes over the letter surreptitiously and then passed it to Tom with a theatrically whispered instruction to photocopy it. *Quick!* Within a few minutes, he had taken his leave from the small gathering on the pretext of needing the bathroom and I was to hear the whir of his printer-copier through an open window shortly afterwards. Then back into the garden he came with the original fragile missive in his hand which he presented to Dad.

"This must've fallen out of your card, Dad." Dad seemed to take note of the author of the letter before folding the paper and placing it beside his plate along with the card that he had stubbornly refused to part with. A sense of inquisitive expectation hung in the air, but it was clear Dad had no intention of satisfying our curiosity with an explanation. The hiatus was beginning to embarrass some of us round the table and on such occasions, one casts around for a topic that will cause a distraction, like the weather or the host's pet. The salivating cat popped into the frame obligingly by first pouncing on some dry leaves caught up by the breeze and then having completed a feline cirque du soleil act, proceeded to stretch out in a patch of sun in an attempt to look cute. We all watched the entertainment; even Mum and Dad who, unlike the rest of us, were not ill at ease in the slightest. Eventually, Dad opened the rest of his cards and unwrapped his gifts, the latter causing him to smile or look baffled in equal measure. Then it was time to return Mum and Dad to *The Torran*. Tom manfully agreed to do this duty alone to give Barbara and I chance to clear up the wreckage of the birthday tea; debris that included all the cards, all the gifts, but neither sight nor sound of the blue paper butterfly.

*

"But did you see the address?" I said to Tom later that evening over the phone. I held one of the copies of Moira's letter in my hand.

"Yes Julie, Newark. But not the Newark we know, but one in Scotland!"

"I didn't even know there was one in Scotland, did you?" I asked.

"Well I had heard of it but I've never been there. I wonder if this is what Dad means when he mentions Newark. Although when he last told me about *the house in Newark* he went on to give me directions of how to get there and the route would have taken you to the Newark we know in the Midlands."

"I guess it's all part of his confusion; he gets one Newark mixed up with another. Easy to do, I guess. But what do you make of Mum's reaction? There must be something to it. Then I remembered something – do you recall when we went camping in Scotland in the early seventies? We camped by a loch and got bitten to bits by midges."

"Yes, Julie, I do remember. It was a good holiday, apart from the insects. Me and insects, we don't get on do we?" he admitted ruefully.

"So this would not be the time to remind you of the Maltese mozzies then?" I could not resist mentioning the mosquito bites that turned his hand into the size of a bunch of ripe bananas.

"Ooof, no thanks. Anyway, meanwhile back to Scotland, what were you going to say?"

"Well you know me and my memory, you always said *'elephants never forget'* and I do remember that we went on a visit to some ruins of an abbey and Dad asked one of the local guides if they knew the whereabouts of someone he had met during the war. The guide seemed to know of the person and was able to tell Dad that they lived nearby."

"I do vaguely remember Dad leaving us and going off on his own which was very unusual as we almost always went everywhere as a family, didn't we? We were at the abbey in the border country but I can't remember its name. It wasn't Newark. Do you think that's connected to this Moira then?" asked Tom.

"I think it might be. You see Mum told me once that Dad had a penfriend in Scotland when he was a schoolboy. The penfriend might be this Moira and he might have gone to look her up."

"Yes, Julie, but surely he hasn't still got a penfriend. He's a bit old for that, don't you think? I don't know anything about this Moira lady but I think we should get in touch with her and let her know what is going on. She sounds as if she's very worried."

"I'll have a chat with Janine and ask her if she knows anything about it and what she remembers of that holiday. I'll either write to Moira, or if I can get hold of her telephone number, I'll make contact that way. Leave it with me. I love a good mystery."

*

George felt his trousers were slipping down and he hitched them up with his elbow, a habitual movement he had honed to perfection. He must track down those braces. He was back in the billet where the food was good. Sensing gravity winning its battle again with the weight of his pocket contents, he gave up the struggle of adjusting his trousers and sat down in the nearest vacant armchair. Annoyingly, now that he was seated, an item in his right pocket began digging into his leg. He decided to investigate and started to empty the contents into his lap. He took a bemused inventory of the random objects that lay on the grey cloth of his baggy trousers: a pair of broken spectacles, a ball of perished rubber bands, a set of bent safety-pins and three plastic combs with blunt or missing teeth. Aware that there was still something lodged in the copious pocket, he took a final trawl and fished out a piece of blue paper.

He sighed her name, so quietly that he could not even hear it, *Moira.*

Chapter 30
Monosyllables

Julie

"How is your head today?" I asked James.

"Sore."

This could mean only one thing: he was in pain. One of the things I had learnt over the many years we had been married was that a monosyllabic answer meant he was *really* suffering. If the response had been couched in a few words, with a risk of poetry, or even sarcasm, I would have been reassured. But monosyllabic answers had me reaching for the kettle and paracetamol, never mind what medicine *he* might require.

So in this snappy mood, he was hardly likely to want to listen to my prattle; but prattle I must. "Do you remember when we first started going out?" I began.

"Yes." I detected a certain whitening of the gills, an eye twitch and a tight lip accompanying this response. Relentlessly, I ploughed on; it was too late for regrets. *Mine for pestering him or his for marrying a prattling wife?*

"It was in the summer of 1973. You stayed at home during the long college break because you were doing that drayman job on the beer lorry and I went off on that holiday with my parents. We went camping in Scotland."

"Lucky you." *Three syllables; things are looking slightly better and he must be listening. I must strike while the husband is hot.*

"Do you remember I had just been given a camera for my twenty first and I took loads of photos on black and white film? Most of the pictures I took were of mountains and streams but I also took a few photos of some ruins of an old abbey. Did I tell you that when we were visiting the ruins, Dad left us for a while to look up an old friend? We think it was an old flame, probably someone he met during the war. Do you remember me telling you about it?" I gabbled.

"No."

"I am beginning to think I might have imagined it. I must speak to Janine. Would you like a cup of tea? Paracetamol?"

*

To contact Moira was a plan I kept putting off. After James' monosyllabic interlude, I had spoken to Janine at length. She and I had chatted for well over an hour recounting our own versions of the Scottish holiday all those years ago. Our memories were recalled but somewhat distorted through our own individual filters. I had taken 'the high road' to Scotland all the while missing my new boyfriend. Everything we did or saw I considered either important if it could be linked in some way to James or unimportant if not. *James would like to fish in this loch so I'll take a picture of it, James told me he had a bad experience with Edinburgh rock so I won't have any, thank you very much.*

For Janine, her perception of events was affected by her own boyfriend filter. She had been preoccupied with the complex machinations involved in her plan to leave the family group for a couple of hours to meet a man. This was no mean feat given our sheltered upbringing. It turned out that a fellow student from her university just happened to be holidaying in Scotland around the same time that we were. My sister and Glynn had a rendezvous arranged, but the time they had chosen coincided with the family outing to the Highland Games. It looked as though their carefully laid plans were going to be scuppered.

"But you did get to meet him in the end, didn't you? How did we manage in those days before mobile phones?" I said.

"I just don't know. I remember this guy saying he would meet me in the town square of Inverness at midday on a particular Saturday in July. Dad and Mum gave up on the Highland Games, as you know, and finally agreed to take me into Inverness. And the guy was actually there, where he said he'd be. We went to a pub together," she recalled with a smile.

"Yes. He looked a nice bloke. I think Mum and Dad found it all difficult dropping you off in a strange town to meet with a stranger. Now talking of strangers, do you remember Dad going off to look someone up when we were going round that old abbey?"

"Yes I sure do. I was annoyed cos at the time I was planning my big meet with Glynn and I wished I had the same freedom to just

227

go off and follow any whim. Teenage angst I guess. Why? What's important about that?"

I told her about the circumstances surrounding the letter and even read the whole missive out to her, word for word.

"Well I never. I wonder if this Moira is the person he went off to visit?"

"That's what Tom and I were wondering. I thought I would try and get in touch with her," I ventured, relieved that Janine was on the same page.

*

"Hello. Is that Moira?" my heart was in my mouth as I pressed the receiver closer to my ear.

"It is. Who is speaking please?" She had a soft, lilting accent as sweet as heather honey. *I imagined her talking to me from a kitchen, cosy with tartan rugs and warmed by an Aga. There would be willow patterned plates on the wall and a jug of wild flowers on the window sill.* All this seemed to be conveyed in a voice as Scottish as shortbread.

"You don't know me but I think you are acquainted with my father. His name is George. George Ellis." I heard a sharp intake of breath and then Moira replied.

"George, yes he is an auld friend, a very auld friend. And you must be his wee daughter, now let me see, he has Tom and two daughters, now are you Julie or are you Janine?"

"Julie. I'm Julie."

"Is your dad OK?" I could not miss the anxious note of concern in her inquiry.

"Well, physically he is doing fine, but I'm afraid to tell you that mentally he is struggling. At this moment he is in a psychiatric hospital."

"Oh my goodness, I am so very sorry to hear this. This is such sad news, sad for all of you bairns. How is your mum coping?"

"Well, Moira it's a long story I almost don't know where to begin. But let's just say Mum is in the same psychiatric ward as Dad."

"What both of them? That would explain why I have not heard from them. Oh my dear, what awful news. You poor wee things. Tell me all about it."

Whether it was because we had not been able to talk to our parents for so long or whether it was because Moira had such warmth and empathy about her, I do not know, but I found myself opening up to her. Maybe it is just easier telling a stranger, a stranger whose facial expression you cannot read. Whatever the reason, I found myself unburdening, telling her all the challenges that had beset us in the past months and describing the tragic deterioration we had witnessed in our mother and father. She listened with patience and skill; I learnt that she had been a nurse before she retired. She seemed to know all about our family in even minute detail and she understood our pain. Indeed it became clear that she took a share in it too.

I told her how we had discovered her letter in the birthday card, and how we had decided that we should make contact with her ourselves. I asked her if I could talk to her about how she knew Dad but at this point she paused and told me that she was glad I had rung but that she was a little overwhelmed with all that I had told her. She said she needed to rest and that we would have to save the remainder of the story, the '*history*' she called it, for another phone call.

"Is it a long story?" I asked.

"Yes," she replied.

Chapter 31
Open the box!

Julie

When we were growing up in the nineteen sixties, there used to be a television game show called '*Take Your Pick!*' In the show, contestants won money for questions answered correctly. At the end of the game, they would be shown a display of small boxes stacked like baked bean tins in a supermarket. (*Or, as Mum had recently reminded us, very like the arrangement of tiny containers in her drug dosette box.*) Contestants could choose to walk away with all the money they had earned in the show, or they could take a risk by accepting instead a key which fitted the lock of only one of the boxes. The excitement of the game revolved around this gamble; the box could contain treasure in the form of prize money, a holiday package or a major luxury item. Alternatively, it could contain a worthless booby prize such as a used bus ticket. The audience would shout to the contestants to encourage them to *Take the money!* or squeal in excitement *Open the box!*

The box I was about to open was much larger than those in '*Take Your Pick!*' But just like the game show contestants, I knew not what I might find inside. This box was in reality a bungalow, a red bricked three bedroomed bungalow built in the nineteen seventies - Mum and Dad's home in Burnage. As I walked up the paved drive towards the front door, my thoughts ran as follows: *this box could contain two people sitting calmly enjoying a cup of tea, holding a conversation with their new live-in carer, the aptly named Patience. In which case, this would be a prize indeed: 'emotional treasure'.*

As I inserted the key, to *open the box!* I knew with a weary heart that such optimism might be unfounded.

The first thing I noticed was a pair of pink mules, their toe posts adorned with large artificial daisies. They were placed on the hall runner with the right shoe in front of the left shoe in a formation similar to starting blocks on a race track. Bursting through the lounge door, her cotton knit top askew as it stretched over her matronly bosom and her abundant curly black hair held back by a bright pink silk scarf, was Patience. She gave me a smile that would melt an ice berg and we bonded immediately.

Patience had impressed Tom; he told me how pleasant and efficient he had found her during the crucial settling in period. I had had the chance to speak at length with her over on the phone during the previous week and she had similarly impressed me. I believed that beneath her friendly chatter lay the experience and wisdom of a kind and thoughtful woman. Her responses to my questions revealed insight, empathy and a clear understanding of Mum and Dad's health difficulties. Moreover, so far she seemed able to tolerate their behaviour. Maybe there was treasure in this box; perhaps in finding Patience we had struck gold.

I had learnt that Patience came from Zimbabwe and had left her family behind to gain employment in the UK. She returned to Zimbabwe regularly after she had completed 'a tour of duty'. I had to smile at her phrase, recognising that she may well consider herself living in a war zone. A handover of sorts had occurred as part of our mobile phone conversation during my train journey. In this way, there was no time taken from Patience's precious weekend of freedom. All that was left to be said was confirmation of Patience's time of return: four o'clock the following day. Therefore as I stood in the small hall of the bungalow, my assortment of luggage and shopping bags standing to mute attention on the carpet runner, I watched as she breathlessly made her escape, gathering her voluminous pink handbag and stepping into her daisy starting blocks before sprinting off through the door at a record speed.

I watched her get into her tiny car that closely resembled a large training shoe, and waved her off ineffectually as she drove out of the close without a backward glance. As I closed and secured the front door, I thought of the *Tupperware burp*; from now on Mum, Dad and I were hermetically sealed in a cuboid.

I turned my back on the front door to find Mum examining my bags. Dressed in a lacy nightdress, her hair a mass of grey floss, she was clearly intrigued by the contents of the food shopping bags which she had already begun to empty out onto the hall carpet. I greeted her and embraced her bony frame. "Gorgeous Darlings," she said. Inwardly beginning to relax, I suggested that we should take the groceries into the kitchen. At this point, she turned and seemed to see me for the first time.

"Ha-huh-ha. Who are you and what are you doing in my house?" she said.

I told her I was her daughter Julie and she looked distinctly baffled and not a little suspicious. I was used to this kind of exchange and apart from experiencing the usual sinking and dispirited feeling I took the hit on the chin. *I cannot wilt at the first hurdle, there will be many more to negotiate this weekend.* Squaring my shoulders, I turned left out of the central hallway, and took one of the food bags into the kitchen expecting Mum to follow me with the second bag. However, Mum had other ideas; she had decided to turn right and walk off in the opposite direction, pulling my trolley suitcase behind her with the confidence and urgency of a commuter at Waterloo station. Seeing the view of her ramrod straight back disappear into the double bedroom, I decided to allow her to accomplish her mission, whatever that might be, and went into the lounge where I found Dad. Dressed in a shirt and trousers, he appeared to be resting in an arm chair while a children's programme involving a brown dog piloting a biplane was being shown on the large screened television set. He opened his eyes at my approach but showed no sign of recognising me. I knelt down and gave him a hug telling him who I was and that I had come to stay for a couple of days. "The orphans will be grateful for the dog oil," he said mysteriously.

I left the lounge in search of Mum. I had a bad feeling; *a long time ago I had learnt to hide my luggage when visiting the bungalow. Why had I relaxed my guard?* Sure enough whilst I had been in the lounge with Dad, Mum had unpacked for me, arranging all my belongings on her bed; her efforts unconsciously demonstrating a nightmarish parody of the origami towel folding that is done in some high class hotels. Laid out on the duvet cover, as if awaiting sacrifice was an abomination: a half swan, half hamster creature fashioned from a hand towel, and decorated grotesquely with an underwired bra and two pairs of knickers. This display amused rather than bothered me until I noticed that several items I was sure I had packed, seemed to be missing. These included my hair brush, which I considered essential, my make-up bag which I considered absolutely vital and even the trolley suitcase itself. But it was when I discovered that my handbag, which contained my purse with my train ticket home, had also disappeared, that I started to hyperventilate. Between rapid breaths, I asked Mum where she had put these items, a request that drew a baffled response. I set about searching the room, my irritation and anxiety escalating. Eventually, I tracked down the missing items: the case was under Dad's bed, the hairbrush was under Mum's pillow and the make-up bag was on the window sill behind a curtain. Only the handbag continued to elude me until I discovered it upon frantically lifting the domed lid of the laundry basket. I sighed heavily in an effort to resume a normal pattern of breathing before reaching for my cherished bag then quickly gathering my belongings and replacing them in the retrieved trolley case. Then I dragged the latter into the dining room at the speed of Patience, storing it well out of sight behind the bed settee and under a tartan blanket.

I had a sudden flashback of happier times when I loved nothing better than to show Mum my treasured purchases after a shopping trip. When Janine and I were in our teens, we would spend hours in Lewis's department store browsing every floor, starting at the basement where gardening equipment and saucepans were artfully displayed, before traipsing longingly round the cosmetics counters and testing fragrances on the ground floor. We would then invade the ladies' fashion department and try on as many garments as we dared before entering the holy of holies: the haberdashery and dress fabrics department. This was where the serious business of shopping began for us and we would spend our money with great care and a huge amount of excitement. But what completed the whole experience and made it meaningful, happened on the sofa when we got home. Here Mum would sit, with her cup balanced elegantly on its saucer, enjoying tea whilst we showed her our prized purchases. She would ooh and ah at the ribbons and sequins, feel the texture of the fabric and sagely review the dress patterns. Her approval meant everything to us and the interest she showed gave us confidence to create and accomplish.

When was the switch made; the switch from wanting to show Mum all that sparkles in my life to the point where I hide my things from her?

Back in the kitchen, I approached Mum and dressed her in a quilted house coat that I had found in the bedroom. By now, she had re-focused her attention on unpacking the groceries. These were clearly of great interest to her and she was examining every item before putting it away – just at that moment she was absorbed in the task of placing milk and cheese in the cupboard under the sink. I opened the fridge to find two tins of beans and a bottle of shampoo. Then in the open bread bin squatted the roasted chicken, grinning at me through its plastic film, its plump legs crossed in the sad caricature of a boxer's muscled arms preparing to pull a punch. *"Now that's not where you go"*, I found myself saying out loud to the poultry, before placing it in the fridge.

"I was only going into the garden," said hard-of-hearing Mum who, against all odds, must have actually heard me this time as she stood at the back door rattling the handle. As if bargaining with a small child, I told her that I would finish putting the food away and then we could take a stroll in the garden as long as she kept the dressing gown on. She continued to agitate the door handle whilst I rearranged the groceries until I noticed that the washing machine had finished its wash cycle.

"Would you help me put the washing on the line?" I asked, planning to kill two birds with one stone. It took a few repeats of the question and some pantomime actions before Mum received the message and advanced towards the Zanussi automatic. With enthusiastic zeal she proceeded to draw (*and quarter*) the washing machine – pulling out its entrails with the practised skill of a Tudor executioner. There on the spongey and marred stain-resistant kitchen carpet now lay bed sheets twisted with several pairs of tights into intestine-like ropes. Together, she and I separated the laundry and were rewarded with the treat of going outside. *Round One to me; eat your heart out Tupperware!*

To one side of the garden plot stood a rotary clothes dryer, its frame listing drunkenly towards the fence and its overstretched line sagging and covered sporadically in weathered pegs. Mum approached this sorry excuse for a dryer undeterred; in her newly confident mode she made short work of hanging the unwieldy laundry with minimal help from me. Knowing that the garden boundaries were secure, I felt it safe for us to wander the plot for a while, looking at the plants and shrubs that Mum had once lovingly cultivated and nurtured. All that seemed a hundred years ago.

"Let's go inside and get you dressed," I suggested. I do not know whether Mum heard me but she proceeded to follow me into the bungalow and thence into the bedroom. I opened the wardrobe to find a complete jumble of Mum and Dad's clothing in a pile at the bottom; the only item lucky enough to grace a coat hanger was a single leather belt. From the pile I extracted a few garments that I hoped might be suitable for Mum, dislodging a couple of tea spoons and a wooden ruler in the process.

Taking Mum's wiry arm, I escorted her to the bathroom where, with a combination of gesturing and exaggerated mouthing to help her lip read, I prompted her to wash herself. She was unwilling at first, saying, "I'm not doing this in front of a man." I looked around the small bathroom, to see if Dad had slipped in unnoticed but finding the room empty, I replied, "There is no man here, Mum, just me." Her suspicious expression was one that I had seen before; then it dawned on me, she believed me to be male – again!

"I'm not a man, Mum; I'm your daughter Julie. Look, as I have told you before, I may have had my hair cut short and I am wearing trousers and flat shoes but that does not make me a man!" She continued to look at me with the mistrust of a maid at *Goblin Market* so I began lathering up the face flannel with soap, in a least manly way as possible, until she became distracted by the bubbles in the sink. Getting Mum to wash herself and put on her clothing took considerable coaxing and I attempted to jolly her along, tempting her with the prospect of breakfast. When I asked her what she would like to eat, she said, "I'll have some of that *Credit Crunch*, please."

Once dressed, she joined me in the kitchen while I began to fix breakfast. I had to leave the room at intervals to lay the table in the dining room; a task that proved challenging as the cutlery drawer had been raided by our very own Sheffield Steel pirate. Patience had reported that Mum was continuing to hide knives and forks around the house and of course I had discovered a small cache of tea spoons in the wardrobe earlier. Eventually, after some scavenging, I found three plastic dessert spoons and a metal knife; the latter immediately drew Mum's excited attention so I slipped it into my pocket with my improving 'sleight of hand' skills. I took three cereal bowls from a kitchen cupboard and placed them on the counter. While I was in the dining room, Mum started to fill the bowls with corn flakes (unsurprisingly, the kitchen cupboard failed to supply the elusive *Credit Crunch* she had requested). I returned just in time to stop her adding custard powder to the cereal. Confiscating the old blue and yellow Bird's carton and shoving it to the darkest depths of the larder cupboard, I began making a pot of tea. Mum stood rooted to the spot like a toddler watching the kettle boil and I found myself warning her not to touch it. After what became another one of our lengthy tea making ceremonies without the kimonos, we loaded the tray and set off for the dining room. On the way, we collected Dad, having persuaded him to abandon the adventures of the brown dog pilot of the *Sopwith Camel*.

The three of us sat silently around the dining room table like Victorians. I was reminded of the tale Dad used to tell us when we were children. The story featured a strict Victorian father who admonished his small son for trying to speak during dinner. Then at the end of the meal, the father asked his son what it was that he had been so very impatient to say, to which the boy replied, "Father, I wanted you to know that there was a huge hairy caterpillar in your salad."

Fortunately, there were no such horrors at our meal table but even so, Mum started to gag on something and coughed profusely. Dad looked alarmed and I got up to tap Mum smartly between her shoulder blades in an effort to dislodge whatever it was that was obstructing her airways. She smiled, tears streaming down her face. "Gorgeous Darlings, cough, cough, I'm fine. Ha-huh-ha." But she proceeded to cough for a good five minutes once she was out of danger and understandably did not seem to find her breakfast cereal particularly edible after that. She toyed with her plastic spoon, taking tiny mouthfuls. Dad consumed his cereal passively and then appeared to enjoy his cup of tea. I offered to make some toast, a gesture that gained a blank response from the pair of them but undeterred, I set off for the kitchen. I achieved the task, applying sunflower spread with my newly acquired and already-proving-to-be-invaluable 'pocket' knife. This tool was fast gaining the valued status akin to the trusty blade of *Robinson Crusoe*.

After the toast course which seemed to have been consumed with some appreciation, I cleared away the dirty dishes and placed them on the kitchen counter, planning to load the dishwasher later. I returned to the dining room to encourage Dad and Mum to leave the table and move into the lounge. They both followed me willingly and settled into their favourite chairs whilst I located the remote control, which had been stuffed under a seat cushion, and then selected a television programme that I hoped they might enjoy. When I turned from the screen, having tuned in to a documentary about seaside resorts in the nineteen fifties, Mum's armchair was empty.

Following the unmistakable sound of crockery in motion, I tracked Mum to the kitchen. Here I found her in the process of putting the dirty dishes back into the kitchen cabinets. It took all my teaching skills to convey a more suitable destination for the soiled bowls and mugs; as fast as I placed the items in the dish washer, Mum would remove them and place them in the cupboard. I was beginning to give up and think that I would need to add 'plate spinning' to my 'sleight of hand' compendium of circus skills, when Mum finally placed the last bowl on the rack and shut the dish washer door with a decisive snap.

Medication; this was the next item on my agenda and I retrieved the two white plastic dosette boxes from the top shelf of the cupboard, in readiness. Transferring the tablets to a small plastic dispensing pot and filling a tumbler with water, I proceeded to offer Mum her morning dose of drugs. At the sight of the medication, Mum tossed her head like a young colt and charged out of the kitchen. I gave chase albeit at a slower pace further impeded by items of furniture that seemed to be lying in wait to trip me up. In the corridor lurked the tall Victorian cabinet of vibrant stuffed birds, the monolith of Doctor Agnew's chest and the cupboard of Melancholy (so named by us children as it contained the last rasping recording of Poetry readings made by Robert Donat before he died, episodes of the Tony Hancock Show before he committed suicide, and of course those numerous video-taped documentaries about Princess Diana's death and funeral). Then, when I had gained the hallway, there sat Granny B's low sewing chair waiting to arrest my progress before meeting at grazing knee height, the authentic Arabian camel saddle. Meanwhile Mum negotiated these obstacles with the sure footedness of a mountain pony, dodging away from me, leading me a merry dressage dance in and out of all the rooms in the bungalow. It was only when she came to the spare bedroom, now the newly converted private room for Patience that she was brought to a standstill in finding the door locked. I had her cornered but it still took several attempts to coax her into accepting the tablets into her hand. She then sat on the afore-mentioned low sewing chair, considering the tiny capsules in her palm for at least five minutes while I tried to encourage her to swallow them. In the end, she did put them in her mouth and then drank a glass of water, by which time I was weak with relief.

After having prepared Dad's medication, I entered the lounge expecting a similar struggle, only to be delighted by his passive acceptance of the proffered tablets of which there were many. Toasting our success with another round of tea, I collapsed into the sofa, grateful for its firm back. Together, we watched Blackpool tower being built and strings of coloured lightbulbs being fitted to trams for the winter illuminations. When the programme came to its literal highlight and the trams were revealed in glorious technicolour, re-modelled as Mississippi paddle steamers and Saturn V rockets, I looked across at Dad to see his reaction, but he had dozed off. Mum, on the other hand, was as lively as a filly and equally fidgety. She had started to unzip one of the scatter cushions and then, removing the foam pad, began placing ornaments into the resulting 'bag' that she had made. Thinking that this was a relatively low risk activity, I felt it safe to leave her for a few minutes whilst I continued to savour my drink.

Such peace was short lived; we were soon to be interrupted by the sound of the doorbell. Dad awoke and looked around bewildered, his cheeks rosy from his nap. Then with surprising alacrity, he stood up.

"I am not 'in' to any visitors," he said before disappearing from the lounge at Patience-miles-an-hour. I heard the toilet door being slammed and bolted as I left the room to discover who had the audacity to disturb our fragile calm.

Standing on the doorstep, in the act of deadheading the potted geraniums, was Vera.

"Ooh, our Julie, guilty as charged, here I goes with me hands hup!" she declared as she crossed the threshold. "Just couldn't resist pinchin off them there 'eads. It'll mek 'em grow better with a bit of hexecution like, won't it Duck?"

I did not have chance to reply to this horticultural question as at that moment Mum came into the hall hugging the overflowing cushion bag from which peered the head of a stuffed kangaroo.

"Ooh our Joanie, Duck. Yous look like one of them ventricles off the telly. Does he speak, your little furry friend?" commented Vera. I could not help but laugh as despite her malapropism, her description was accurate. Mum was Rod Hull to a tee. Mum, however, did not appear to hear or understand the joke. Instead of joining us in our hilarity, she tucked Kanger and his cushion pouch further under her arm and stretched out her hands in front of her. She fixed Vera with a steely stare; one that I did not know Mum possessed in her wide armoury of facial expressions.

"What's up Duck?" said the innocent Vera, beginning to sense a change in the atmosphere.

"Look at my hands. No rings. What have you done with them?" accused Mum.

"I think you are a little confused, Mum. Vera has not taken your rings - they will be somewhere safe in the house. We'll look for them, don't worry," I tried to reassure her. However, she would not be placated.

"You are a thief. You have taken my rings and look you have lots of your own already," she continued getting more and more agitated while the squashed neck of Kanger was getting more and more crushed under the vice of her arm. Vera, for once, was speechless with astonishment. She put her left hand up to her face in a gesture of shock, her many rings flashing in the sunlight beaming through the hall window. Clearly she had taken offence, and who could blame her? I took her arm gently and steered her to the front door where we could whisper.

"I'm afraid Mum gets even more confused these days, Vera, and she has become suspicious of everyone. She does not even know who I am consistently, never mind trust me."

"Ooh, Duck, it's a tragedy, that's what it is. Yer poor Mam, what's 'appened to 'er? Is yer Dad alright? I've not seen him since they both got back from the 'orse-pital."

"Dad is doing as well as can be expected, Vera. Mum and Dad-well their mental health is very fragile and it is not likely to improve. The best we can do is keep them safe from harm and as calm as we can. Patience, the new carer seems to be doing a good job of looking after them." I said.

"That girlie, Patience yous calls her? Well she seems nice enough but when I came to see yer Mam this week she wouldn't let me in. Oh no, she said, it weren't possible to hentertain me."

"Well I think that she felt the need for a quiet settling in period for Mum and Dad. I guess there's some shaking down to do but I hope that eventually, you will be able to visit them. Thank you for caring and please don't take offence. Mum is very mixed up."

Hearing the sound of Mum's staccato sobbing coming from the lounge accompanied by the rhythmic bass created by Dad who was knocking on the toilet wall, I persuaded Vera out of the bungalow and turned to face the music.

*

"Well done for getting through so far," said Tom.

"Thank you," I replied with feeling. Never mind all the challenges of childbirth or trying to teach Grammar to Form 3M on a Friday afternoon at *The Warren School* or even taking that plane flight to Malta all on my own - nothing could compare with what had challenged and tested me in that bungalow that week end. Proudly, I gave Tom a blow by blow account of events from my arrival to the incident of the rings. And it was not even lunch time yet.

"Where are Mum and Dad now?" he asked.

"They're in the lounge –at least that's where I left them. Mum is searching for her rings and Dad is watching television from his position standing to attention by the settee – like when he was a sides-man at church. He told me very firmly that he was *on duty* when I suggested he sat down. That was what they were doing up till when you rang, but I'd better get back to them and check just in case."

"OK Julie, I'll leave you to it. Just to say that Mum and Dad's bank has been in touch and they want to set up a meeting."

"Anything we should be worried about? I mean there will be enough funds to cover the carer long term won't there?"

"Oh yes, Julie, certainly for the foreseeable future. I guess the bank want to meet to discuss the current situation and the role of the Court of Protection. Anyway, I'll call you again this evening."

We said our goodbyes and I tucked my mobile phone away in its secure hiding place where Mum and Dad couldn't find it; they had been known to try to use it to change the channels on the TV in the past. Back in the lounge Dad was still *on duty* and Mum had cut a swathe through the room, displacing every object in her path in search of her jewellery. Her cushion bag lay at her feet as she worked her way through the chest of drawers packed with photographs. Her face, that had been wet with tears, now wore a determined expression; Nordic woman had made her reappearance.

"Are you still searching for your rings?" I mouthed and mimed unnecessarily. *Of course she was looking for her rings. And I knew the place where they might be.* At first she resisted when I took her by the arm but eventually she allowed me to lead her gently to the double bedroom. Once inside the room, I approached the dressing table that was built neatly into the space between two wardrobes. The mirror at the back of this vanity unit was in fact a door which when opened, revealed a set of secret shelving. Mum's face was a picture of delight.

"Goody Goody," she said as she started to open the many little cardboard and leatherette jewellers' boxes stacked on the narrow shelves. My joy was two-fold. Firstly I was glad that we would find her rings at last as I knew that this would be the very place where she would have stored them to keep them safe. Secondly, I was gaining satisfaction from solving this mystery, basking in the glory of feeling a bit of a star in bringing Mum's rings back to her.

I watched happily as, with barely concealed excitement, Mum took down a small domed box of the type a young man might hold forth in his right hand whilst bending his left knee in supplication to his lady. Empty. Discarding it on the dressing table, she chose a small white cardboard box with the name of a jeweller embossed in silver on its lid. Empty. Then a larger box that might hold a bangle was opened. Empty. Systematically, Mum went through every box as she worked her way across the rows of tiny shelves. Empty,empty,empty. Every box was empty.

It felt as if I had played a cruel joke by raising her expectation, only to dash her hopes. I felt sick. I did not want to play this game anymore. Life was becoming a painful parody of a game show, where there was not even a booby prize to be won.

Chapter 32
Lost on the Fens

Julie

"Where do you think Mum's rings are, Julie?" asked Janine during her phone call later that day.

"I don't know. I *do* know that they are definitely not in the safe. She always used to keep her jewellery in those little boxes, didn't she? She has that big jewellery casket that Tom made for her when he was at college, you know, the one with the copper engraved lid – she keeps her costume jewellery in that. But she kept her more valuable pieces out of sight behind the mirror. I think Dad told her that if she kept her treasures in an obvious *jewellery box*, it would just be a gift to a thief. But when I slid back the mirrored glass and revealed the hidden shelves, it was as if she hadn't realised they were there. Shows you how much her memory has failed. Maybe she put the rings in some other kind of receptacle. She seems to put things that she thinks are valuable, in the most odd places. Look where she puts the cutlery. I shall keep searching whilst I'm here," I replied.

"Do you think the carer may have taken her jewellery?"

"That did occur to me, but I really don't think so. It's the classic situation isn't it when the carer has the run of a place and a vulnerable elderly person loses things and immediately suspects the carer? These carers come highly recommended and with brilliant references, it's more than their job's worth to do such a thing. I don't believe that Mum has been robbed. It's far more likely that she has put the rings and her other treasures somewhere safe and then forgotten where she put them."

"How is Mum now, has she got over the upset?" Janine asked.

"Yes, surprisingly, she has. She's doing better than me – I'm really upset about it all. She had a cry but then she got distracted by her dressmaker's dummy in the corner of the bedroom and began draping it with ropes of beads she found on her dressing table. Then I was able to get her back to the lounge where she carried on cushion-bag filling whilst I was able to get the lunch prepared."

"How did lunch go? Did they eat much?"

"Well I gave them cold roast chicken, thought I couldn't go wrong with that and they ate reasonably well."

"Not with the obligatory boiled potatoes?" asked Janine.

"No, with chips! And they both looked as if they had arrived in heaven, poor things. They tucked in, even ate all the salad. Goodness only knows why they put themselves on that silly diet for all those years. At least they have been having more normal foods whilst they were in hospital and since we started on the frozen meal deliveries."

"What are you doing this evening?"

"I guess we could try and watch some TV together. Hang on. I can hear a commotion coming from the lounge, I should sign off."

"Ok, I guess you'd better. I hope everything's alright," said my sister. After a few parting words, I shoved my phone into my jeans pocket and raced into the lounge.

The scene before me looked innocuous enough. Dad was clearly *off duty* and was seated in his armchair appearing to have a conversation with Mum who had started another cushion 'bag', having filled the first to the point of overflowing. She held the new 'bag' tucked under her arm and, with one of Janine's old plastic school recorders sticking out of the top, it looked for all the world as if she was playing the bagpipes.

Then I heard what Dad was saying in vehement tones, stressing every syllable. "It's no good you telling me the money was yours. It was not meant for you. It was meant for the poor orphans. What is going to happen to them now?"

Mum stood opposite him looking bewildered. She started biting her thumb and then began her loop of placating phrases peppered with her multi- purpose laugh, followed by a random quote from a sixties puppet show : "Gorgeous darling. Ha-huh-ha. Lovely. Ha-huh-ha. Priceless. Don't worry, friend Zarrin. "

"Well, Mum," I interjected, "Fancy you remembering *'Supercar'!"* I could not help but smile and I hoped to lighten the mood that was fast descending on my parents like a black cloud.

"Whatty?" she replied. I started to mouth and mime but quickly realised that even the great Marcel Marceau would have a problem conveying the term *'supermarionation'*. I stopped mid mime, my right leg raised and bent at the knee while my left arm was pulled up as if by

243

an invisible string with my wrist limp and my hand hanging down uselessly.

"It's all very well for you to laugh, and fool around," said Dad looking angrily at me. "Who's going to put the money back?" Suddenly, his wrath turned to tears and he began to sob. I approached him to offer comfort but he batted away my arms aggressively.

"Leave me alone!" he shouted. "You are both thieves!"

I drew Mum away to the sanctuary of the homely kitchen and began making a cup of tea. Mum began to cry and I wiped her tears with the Buckfast Abbey tea towel. I found that I was shaking; I had not seen Dad this angry since the chapter of my life entitled, *Julie becomes a teenager.* Just like then, I did not know what to do to make it better.

Under the cover of the noisily boiling kettle Mum must have walked out as when I turned round to take the milk out of the fridge, the room was empty. I left the safety of the kitchen and looked through the slit between the lounge door where it hinged with the door jamb and checked that she had not returned to the lion's den. The lion himself, my usually loving, kind and generous father, was looking extremely ruffled and irate. I thought it best to err on the side of caution and *let sleeping lions lie.* I continued down the corridor of obstacles in search of Mum. I found her easily, homing in on her location by listening to her voice.

"Ha-huh-ha. Yes you're very nice. How nice of you to call by. Yes, I'll wave to you. How nice of you to wave back. So nice to meet you. Do you come here often?"

As I entered the double bedroom, I saw that Mum was sitting at her dressing table. She turned and saw me and then with an excitable expression, began telling me that she had just met an old lady. The old lady had seemed quite friendly and she had been waving at Mum. Mum said that she waved back.

She seemed so delighted with her new friend that I did not have the heart to tell her that she had been talking to her own reflection in the mirror.

*

The events of late afternoon and evening continued in similar vein. Storm clouds persisted in threatening to overwhelm the atmosphere in the lounge and Dad was not to be placated, regularly returning to harp on about the plight of the poor orphans. Supper was a miserable affair and neither Mum nor Dad seemed interested in their favourite tinned salmon and salad cream sandwiches that I had prepared. I had served Mum and Dad in the lounge hoping to distract them with the television but the mealtime became even more oppressive than the silent Victorian breakfast we had endured earlier that day.

The evening wore on and I found myself looking regularly at the enormous digital clock on the wall and counting down the hours until an early bedtime. I welcomed each loud click that signalled a change to the black figures, sounding as if the pages of The Book of Time were being turned by a giant and powerful hand. Mum and Dad seemed oblivious and insensible to this device; *not only had they appeared to have lost the time but they had now lost the plot as well,* I thought wryly.

When it was time for their medication, I approached Dad with equal measures of fear and trepidation but it was quickly apparent that he had calmed down over the preceding hours and he took his tablets passively. It was a different story with Mum. I prepared her doses, which amongst other drugs included a sleeping pill, but she flatly refused to take any of the tablets in the little pot I proffered. The cat and mouse scenario was played out yet again but past experience had made me wily and I managed to ambush her in the dining room. Having taken her tablets eventually under sufferance, with a 'games up' expression of defeat on her face, she continued to rove up and down the bungalow for the rest of the evening and then resisted any suggestion that she should get ready for bed. I gave up the fight realising that I could never win this particular battle of wills and joined Dad in the lounge. His dear old head, no longer covered with the dark curls he used to keep tidy and smooth with Brylcreem, now had wayward tufts of grey hair, some strands long enough to reach right across his crown. His eyes were hooded and his cheeks were flushed; it was clear that he was having trouble staying awake. The next half hour was devoted to getting him ready for bed whilst Mum continued her ward round like an adrenalin charged Florence Nightingale.

Wishing Dad a good night's sleep; having tucked him into his twin bed, I went to find Mum. I saw her slight figure at the end of the corridor disappearing into the kitchen and gave chase. However, before I reached her, she had exited the kitchen and was en route to the lounge. Something about her appearance was different though; she was moving more slowly, her gait was awkward and it looked as though her knees were beginning to buckle. Evidently, the sleeping pill had started to work – and it seemed to be working from the ground up. As if I was viewing a film in slow motion, I watched Mum sink down towards the welcome of the soft woollen carpet, her legs still moving relentlessly forward as her whole body contracted into a crouch position. She was literally crumpling, her knees now level with her shoulders, but still she persisted in forging ahead. It was at this point that I saw my chance to intervene and I caught her up, checked her progress and helped her to stand. I led her into the bathroom, taking advantage of this induced passive state. Like a drunken person in the movies who has to be frogmarched up and down a room and forced into chain-drinking cups of black coffee to sober up, so appeared Mum. With a slurred but elegant acceptance speech she co-operated, allowing me to help her get undressed and then finally and thankfully, tuck her into her bed alongside the now slumbering Dad.

With the absence of any alcohol in the bungalow, I made do with a quiet sit down in the cosy lounge. At last I could relax. I made a few whispered phone calls to James, Tom and Janine to keep them abreast of events before deciding to turn in for the night. It was only nine o'clock.

It was as I was making up the sofa bed for myself in the dining room, that I heard the muffled cry for help. It sounded like Dad's voice but from much further away than the double bedroom across the corridor. Nevertheless, I decided to check out my parents' room first. On entering the bedroom, I found Mum bending over Dad's bed, pulling his sheets and blankets tightly across his body, apparently swaddling him like a baby. Naturally, Dad was not making this task easy and was writhing about in protest, his legs kicking violently. A low moaning sound, coming from amidst the bundle of sheets, whilst indecipherable, was clearly a cry for help in any language. Alarmingly, I could not see Dad's face at all; indeed his whole head seemed to be covered by his pillows. With mounting panic, I firmly pushed Mum out of the way and removed the pillows and sheets from Dad's airways so he could breathe more easily. I sat him up and made him take a drink. He told me he had been potholing and had got stuck in a tunnel and could not find daylight. Once he was breathing steadily again, I began re-adjusting the bedclothes to ensure his comfort but this caused an avalanche of cutlery and other household objects to fall out of the covers and crash noisily onto the floor.

"That's my equipment hitting the deck," he cried.

A quick inventory revealed four knives, six forks, three dessert spoons, an alarm clock, an umbrella, a hairbrush, a plate and several books; all had been hidden between the layers of bedding. I recognised several of these items as those collected by Mum in her cushion bags during her day's trawl. What had made Mum wrap Dad as if he was a package in a *Pass the Parcel* party game, I could not even begin to hazard a guess.

Meanwhile beachcomber Mum had given in to the effects of the sleeping pill and was snoring loudly. I was relieved to find that Dad seemed to have succumbed once again to the arms of Morpheus to continue his dream of potholing but this time without his caving paraphernalia. I considered sleeping on the floor between the twin beds, but thought that might frighten and confuse Mum and Dad if either of them woke in the night. I was aware that I would have difficulty sleeping anyway so I retreated to the dining room to keep watch, leaving the door open a crack to allow the glow of the plug-in night lights in the hallway to enter the room.

*

I thought of our happy childhood: one that our parents had created to ensure that we had a better start in life than they had experienced themselves. They sheltered us from harm and through their combination of generosity and careful economy they taught us the value of money, providing insulation from the austerity that they had endured as they were growing up. Sometimes they were guilty of doing their job too well, of providing a shelter too dense and a comfort blanket too thick. But then it must be acknowledged that they were cutting a new path, without a map to guide them.

And so history repeats itself; here we are cutting a new path of our own, without a pattern to follow, trying to provide comfort and security for our parents' final stage of their lives.

In spite of my good intentions, I must have drifted off to sleep as during the early hours of the morning, I was suddenly and rudely awakened by a knocking on my door. It was so dramatic and heavy fisted; it reminded me of the alarming rapping of the French Resistance as they pounded on *Albert Foiret's* back door in the series '*Secret Army'*. My heart began to beat wildly. *Where was I? What was happening? What's the panic about?*

"Just a minute," I said blearily to whomsoever was about to demand me to hide the British Airmen. I fumbled with the small lamp on the side table, tracing its lead to the rocker switch near the skirting board. The bulb flickered into life and with it, reality returned. I was at Mum and Dad's. I got up from my make-shift bed and opened the dining room door fully.

The sight that greeted me made me shut my eyes again.

Before very recent times, I had never seen my mother without her clothes. Yet here she was totally naked, apart from a large box of Maltesers barely covering her modesty. As modesty goes, this was as effectively shielded as that of Botticelli's Venus rising from the waves. I did not know where to look, so I stared at the Maltesers.

"Who are you?" she said, apparently shocked by my presence. "What are you doing in my house?"

"It's the middle of the night, Mum," was all I could come up with. "Aren't you getting cold?"

"Nice lady. Would you like one of these, Ha-huh-Ha," Mum said, all the while rattling the box so the tiny chocolate spheres rolled around and crashed noisily into each other.

"Mum it's time to get back into bed. Look, let me get you something to cover you up." I found her dressing gown on the floor of the bedroom and made her put it on, removing the box of chocolates as I did so. I persuaded her to lie down again and pulled up the bedclothes, tucking her in as neatly as possible.

"Now go to sleep and dream of the fairies at the bottom of the garden," I found myself telling her impulsively, my throat suddenly thick with emotion.

Within ten minutes, a regular pattern of snoring indicated a return to a state of peace and an end to the short-lived Malteser party. I returned to my bed in the dining room with the intention of resting, yet continuing to keep watch. Someone once told me that once you have children of your own, you lose the ability to sleep that deep sleep of abandonment to the point of oblivion; your sleep patterns become relatively shallow so you remain alert to every tiny sound that might signal danger. I do not know if this is true and I was certainly not in a position to test the theory that night as within half an hour, the knocking began again. This time I was ready.

"Who are you?" a shocked Mum asked me as she stood at the door. Fortunately, this time she was draped in the dressing gown but she had managed to retrieve the box of Maltesers from the bedside chair where I had so carelessly left it and was playing it like a tambourine.

With the ease of recently acquired practice, I persuaded Mum back to bed, hid the Maltesers and retreated to my bed once again. This pattern of behaviour was to be repeated three more times, thankfully now without the playgroup style percussion. After the last visit from the *Mum Resistance*, I decided to give up trying to rest. Instead I planned to sit up and wait for the morning.

It was then that I heard Dad's voice. "Help me. I'm lost on the Fens." I got up again to discover Dad and Mum wandering up and down the dimly lit hallway trying all the doors. Dad seemed to have his eyes closed and was walking with arms outstretched in front of him, like a sleepwalker. Mum was muttering to herself and following Dad wherever he went. When they both came to the kitchen door that I had locked before coming to bed, they collided. Using the keys I kept on a lanyard round my neck, I unlocked the door to prevent Mum and Dad hurting themselves and switched on one of the cosy wall lights.

I asked Dad if he needed the toilet and opened the relevant door for him and switched on the bathroom light; he shuffled into the tiled room. I asked Mum if she needed the toilet or a drink but she then became distracted by Dad's re-emergence from the toilet and began to follow him back to the bedroom.

*

Then followed a blissful time when I believed I was half awake and yet my mind conjured up the most amazing and vibrant dreams. In my final dream of this pleasurable sequence, everything in the bungalow had returned to its original place, order had been restored and Mum and Dad were normal again. In fact, everything was back to how it should be to the point where Mum was making us all one of her delicious full English breakfasts. I could even smell it.

Smell it. I woke with a start and hurried into the kitchen that I had foolishly unlocked during the night. There was Mum, queen of all she surveyed, wooden spatula in hand and cremated bacon in a pan. On the counter was a large mixing bowl full of some kind of liquid, possibly milk, afloat with samples of several different breakfast cereals, pieces of cucumber and a streak of yellow, possibly mustard *or was it raw egg?* The cardboard egg carton filled with shells provided the answer to that question. Beside the bowl were boxes of gravy browning and sugar along with the packet of custard powder. *I had not even hidden that well enough, had I?*

Mum must have read my forlorn expression of failure.

"Don't worry friend Zarrin," she said.

Chapter 33
A chair is just a chair

Julie

The train journey home allowed me to unwind to the point of unravelling. I had the luxury of a double seat to myself and was able to sit back and lose myself, loosen all those tight threads. The guard's announcements were muffled as if he was talking into a jug full of wool. I did not care what he said anyway; my ears filtered out all sounds apart from one: the word *Winchester*. I travelled south seeing nothing through the blinds of night except occasional lights flashing like the retinal light show released when you rub your eyes too hard.

At last, after three hours of day dreaming trying not to relive every poignant moment of the weekend, I heard the sound I had been longing for - my signal to leave the confines of the carriage and step into the fresh, chilly air of my destination. With a subtle smile of tenderness and understanding, my husband approached me on the station forecourt, where he had been getting cold waiting in his shirt sleeves. Shrugging off my concern when I nagged him for not wearing a coat, he took hold of my bags and led me to the car. After the short drive, he welcomed me into our warm house that he proclaimed proudly he had cleaned *from top to bottom* to his own *exacting standards*. I thanked him from the *top to bottom* of my heart as he continued his saintly ministrations, pulling on the manly padded gauntlets to lift the red casserole dish from the oven and inviting me to take a shower while he carried out the final touches to our supper. I staggered up the stairs, at every step feeling intensely grateful for my very own support team.

*

It was the following evening before I had chance to report back to my brother on the events of the weekend.

"So he thought he was lost on the Fens," said Tom, "I wonder where that idea came from."

"Didn't he spend some time there during the war?" I asked.

"Well yes of course, he was stationed in Lincolnshire for a time - the Fens stretch that far I believe."

"I suppose they do. Dad has a real problem navigating his way round the bungalow, doesn't he? Not just at night time. While I was staying with them, I noticed him trying all the doors before he found the room he wanted lots of times during the daytime. I guess his cataracts don't help his situation either."

"No Julie, they don't. We are waiting to hear about his next op - but you know, his ability to orientate himself has been getting worse and worse over the last few years. And talking of Lincolnshire reminds me - do you remember when Barbara and I took Mum and Dad away for the weekend to that holiday cottage in Grantham some years back?"

"Yes, and I remember them telling me how much they enjoyed it. They loved the fact that from the cottage, they could walk into town – an easy distance and all on the flat."

"Indeed. Well on one of the days, I think it was the Sunday - we were all sitting down in the lounge at the back of the cottage having a cuppa, when Dad got up and left the room saying he was off to the bathroom. We carried on chatting but he didn't return. Then Mum saw him pass by the lounge window, and she suggested that he must have gone outside to look at the garden. Then *blow me down* if ten minutes later he didn't walk past the window again in the opposite direction. Then another few minutes went by and he went past again, but still didn't come back to the lounge!"

I could feel a bubble of guilty laughter trying to escape as, in my mind's eye, I could see the small figure of my Dad walking backwards and forwards past the tiny cottage, like in a scene from a French farce. I could also hear the suppressed mirth in Tom's voice as he continued, "And then, and then," he stuttered, "he went past the window again! We realised he must have been circling the cottage and couldn't find a way back in."

"Wh-what did you do then?" I asked, the bubble of laughter bursting.

"Well I went out and ambushed him on his next lap and guided him in. Poor chap. And do you know what? He told me he had not even found the toilet yet. He had come out of the lounge and turned

252

right instead of left and found himself in the garden. From there he just literally went round and round. He had forgotten that the toilet was upstairs!"

"Aw, bless him!"

"Even *he* had a laugh about it at the time," said Tom.

"I know he used to get lost looking for the toilets at *The Harvester* when he and Mum took us all out for a meal there when my kids were young. I put it down to the fact that as the restaurant was regularly upgraded and refurbished it threw him. One time there were barn doors here and a paddock fence there and when you went again that had all been removed and replaced with a corrugated iron and chicken wire. So I assumed that had been the cause of his confusion – and I guess it might well have been partly so. But given what we know now..."

"Yes, Julie, hindsight is a wonderful thing. If only we could have read all the signs at the time."

"I agree – if only," I bleated.

"Anyhow, thanks again for doing your bit at the weekend. I bet you were pleased to see Patience come back to take over from you."

"I've never been so relieved to see her little shoe- type car drive into the close – I could have kissed her!"

"I really don't know how Patience does it - well, without going potty. I know it would drive us mad if we lived with Mum and Dad like she does," confessed Tom.

"I have the deepest of respect for her. Like you say, we could not do it - well not for longer than a weekend. That's my limit. But - by what I'm about to say I don't wish to take anything away from our praise of Patience - but I have been thinking a lot about this - to Patience, a chair in the bungalow is just a chair."

"What do you mean, Julie?" asked Tom.

"Well, I mean that when she looks at, for example, the chair in the hall - you know the one I mean, the low chair with the golden coloured embroidered cushion on it - she just sees an old chair."

"O...K," said Tom, thoughtfully. I could tell he was struggling to understand what I meant.

"Well, when we see the same chair, we see layer upon and layer of memories, associations and meanings. Like, we think, *this is a low chair because Granny sawed the legs off, the cushion was one that Aunty Violet embroidered when she was a young woman,* and so on.

Then we remember how much Mum loves that chair and we recall her sitting on it at various times when we were growing up."

"I do see what you mean. I guess everything in the bungalow has its own special place in our lives."

"Yes it does, everything we see there triggers memories of our childhood and reminds us of how things used to be and how Mum and Dad used to be. Everything underscores how much they have altered," I replied.

"I do find that I get very emotional in there, more so even than when I used to visit Mum and Dad in hospital or the care home," Tom admitted.

"Me too. It's all painful for us, as every item is instilled with memories. Every bit helps to highlight just how far Mum and Dad have deteriorated. Now, for Patience who is a professional and is that one step away from all that emotion that we are dealing with - she only knows Mum and Dad as the fragile human beings that they are now and has no knowledge of how they once were. She works with them brilliantly, caring for their needs as they present. She does provide an excellent service. Granted, it must be extremely challenging at times," I said.

"Well most of the time, I would think," said Tom.

"Absolutely," I agreed. "But," I continued, "Patience is not prey to the emotional triggers that waylay us at every turn. To Patience that chair is just a chair."

"Yeah I've got it. I do see what you mean. I still think she's great."

"Great? I think she's a saint."

*

Saint Patience had arrived full of smiles at the end of my first weekend, her pink head scarf waving a greeting in the breeze as she came bouncing up the drive on Sunday afternoon. She was precisely on time although I did notice that her pink daisy mules were not moving as quickly as they were the last time I had seen them. *And who could blame them?*

Following her pattern, I had my bags packed ready and waiting on the hallway runner but I had surpassed her in one key element of my preparation: my shoes were already on my feet.

In through the door she came, full of questions as to how Mr and Mrs Ellis had fared during her absence. Speaking at top speed, I told her of events and showed her the notes I had made in the care log book. As she listened to my rapid summary she took her bags into her private room and locked the door. *Wise woman*, I thought.

I had already gone through the motions of saying farewell to Mum and Dad, although their lack of reaction spoke volumes. So there was nothing left to do but give thanks to all the saints (Saint Patience in particular) and set off for the railway station, giving a nod to the low chair in the hall on my way out.

Chapter 34
Puzzle pieces

George and Julie

Life was becoming so very confusing. George felt that he was in the middle of some kind of puzzle – a black and white chequered square that made no sense. Where were the words? He could not find the words.

Then there were the women. Different ones kept coming in and out and would not leave him alone, bringing food and drinks he did not always want. Joanie was there but she never sat still. No one sat still. Except him.

But somehow the place felt like home. But why did all these strangers keep coming in? Joanie knows that I don't like strangers.

George closed his eyes. He would try and work things out. He was good at puzzles.

*

It was the middle of the week, following my trial weekend of taking over Patience's duties, when Tom phoned me at my home.

"Julie, I have been to Mum and Dad's bank today and been through a load of paperwork with them. It was quite useful as it gave me an overview of what Mum and Dad have in their joint account although I do not know yet what is in their other accounts."

"Other accounts? I thought that they only had a current account and that they put their savings in their building society account," I said, grateful that Tom had taken on the complicated role of looking after Mum and Dad's finances in co-ordination with the Court of Protection.

"Well Julie, if only it were that simple. Sure, Mum and Dad have a current account at the bank but there are other accounts as well. Apparently, some have small amounts of money in them and some are empty."

"Well I never," I said, surprised. "I guess the Court of Protection will need a complete breakdown of them."

"Yes, that seems to be the plan, but the bloke at the bank said that there were some anomalies that they need to investigate before releasing a cohesive set of statements."

"I expect they are little pockets where they put dividends from their shares. I remember going through all the share certificates with Mum that day a while back. They have, or at least they *had* quite a few shares – not that any of them did particularly well on the stock market. I think Dad only dabbled."

"You're right, Julie. I know they had some shares in British Airways, BAE and British Telecom - all chosen, I guess to reflect Dad's interest in his past careers. Maybe that's what he used the accounts for. Well, no doubt we'll find out in due course."

*

"Helloo," said a small, uncertain voice, echoing shrilly down the phone lines.

"Hello Moira, it's me here again: Julie, George's daughter."

"Oh Julie, my dear, how lovely," said Moira, her voice gaining strength, "I was hoping that you would call again. I have been thinking so much about what you told me the last time we talked."

"You have been in my thoughts a lot too, Moira. How are you keeping?"

"Och, not soo bad, thank you very much for asking. Not helped by the dreadful cauld weather we are getting up here. I hope that it's much warmer in your sunny south."

"It is quite pleasant here, although not warm enough to leave the house without my coat – or my umbrella!"

It had taken me a couple of weeks to re-connect with Moira. In the interim I had found myself avoiding emotional encounters wherever possible, as I processed the experiences of my weekend 'Mum and Dad sitting'. Gradually becoming aware that time was marching on and conscious that I had so many questions left unanswered, I took the phone by the horns one evening and dialled Moira's number. Once we had exchanged pleasantries and health updates, I hoped that we would continue our communication on a deeper level; a *historic* level.

I was not to be disappointed.

However, before she began telling me anything of what she called the '*history*', she thanked me graciously for making initial contact saying, "With George, I had a strong feeling that something was wrong health wise but didna' ken exactly what. You see, we always kept in touch at Christmas and birthdays, but last year I heard nothing from your Dad. All mail just stopped. Then one day I did get through to your Mum on the phone and she told me your Dad was in hospital but she gave me no indication as to what was wrong with him. It did seem strange. Yet again I felt there was just a wee something wrong with your Mum. She kept calling me *Una* and asked me many times, over and over, how I was keeping. She also mentioned that the car had been taken away and she was not allowed to drive. I didna' like to ask her too many questions. I can be forgetful too soo I tried not to think the worst. It is soo very, very sad to see such lovely people become like this."

"I can only wonder what Mum and Dad are going through. They are so very confused now. We just don't know what to do for the best. No one can prepare you for this kind of experience. It has been extremely traumatic to see Mum and Dad tumble into a kind of twilight world where they do not know where they are half the time, neither do they recognise each other consistently or remember their nearest and dearest. It makes us feel helpless as we know we can't stop what has clearly started to happen to them. "

"Och yes. It must be very tough indeed, Julie. Dementia is soo very cruel."

Taking a deep breath, I said, "It is very cruel and this is all very sad to talk about. Let's focus on happier times. I was hoping that you would feel ready to tell me how you and Dad became friends."

Moira started from the beginning. Her friendship with George had formed at school, in classrooms three hundred miles apart. It had been the result of a joint project of two old friends, one who became George's schoolmaster in England and one who was Moira's schoolmaster in Scotland. The two teachers had thought it would be a good idea for their pupils to have practice writing letters to others of their own age in another country, so they paired up their pupils based on their class positions. George and Moira were at the top of their respective classes and so they were considered compatible as penfriends. So on grey lined paper torn from exercise books, using sharp nib pens dipped in the ceramic ink wells of their wooden desks, they began their correspondence. They were both twelve years old.

"Your father has the most beautiful handwriting and he always had something amusing and interesting to write about. I used to look forward to receiving his letters soo much. We wrote to each other all through our school days, not that we were at school soo very long as by the time we were fourteen we had left and gone out into the world to find work. But we carried on our letter writing, not so frequently now that the schoolmaster was no longer breathing down our necks, it's true, but we did still write several times a year.

Anyhow, then war broke out and we were both around sixteen, but we still continued to write to each other. Everyone thought that war would all be over in about six months but it ended up lasting six years! Well it carried on and on and by now George was working for a company that made webbing and suchlike in the Midlands – I expect you know about all that- and I had a wee job in an accountant's office up here in Scotland. Well, still the war dragged on and George wrote to say that he thought he would soon be called up to fight as that year he would be eighteen - it must have been 1941. As of course you know, he wanted to join the RAF so he decided he would volunteer. I think he was still only seventeen when he enlisted, but he fibbed about his age, saying that his birthday was in April when as you well know it's June. Lots of laddies did that kind of thing, they were all desperate to get involved.

Now, as you know, once he had completed his induction, he had to do lots and lots more training. There was all the drill and the weapon training and all that business. George must have been put forward to train as air crew and he had to learn all about wireless and radio, Morse code and the like. Airmen like George got sent all over the country to complete their courses. One day I got a letter from him to say that he had been posted to a new airbase.

It turned out that as luck would have it, he was stationed just a few miles from my home town and so when he had some time on leave, he came to look me up. Well it was lovely to actually meet him after all the years of being penfriends and we got on like a house on fire. In fact we both said we felt that we knew each other really well already because of our letters so you see, meeting him just confirmed that he was really the nice man that had shown through his beautifully written letters.

He bowled me over – as they used to say then- he was soo very dashing in his service uniform, so very smart. I felt proud walking down the road with him. He had the most beautiful brown eyes, so warm and kind. He was so very generous. No one had much in those days during the war, but he was very free with what money he had, nonetheless."

I found myself so drawn in by Moira's story of wartime friendship, forgetting for 'a wee while' that the man of whom we spoke was in fact my own dear father. I could not stop myself from asking, "So was there a budding romance between the two of you?"

"Och well, yes, we did become very fond of each other. We met many times while he was in Scotland and in the end, well he even asked me to marry him. I said 'No' but he kept asking and asking – and I will admit that I was very tempted but you see we were soo very young and it was wartime and I felt that I had to turn him down. We would only have been eighteen or nineteen then and everything was so uncertain and I wasn't ready to get engaged – and my parents, although they liked him, thought we were far too young to be thinking of marriage."

"Oh dear, it must have been so difficult for you, knowing that he would have been broken hearted," I said gently.

"It was all a very upsetting time for both of us which is why I have trouble talking about it even now, after all these years."

"Moira, thank you for being prepared to tell me your story. Forgive me – I had no idea that the two of you had been so close. I gathered that you were friends from way back but I had not realised that feelings had run so deep."

"Och, well that all happened a very long time ago."

"I assume you both stopped writing to each other after that?" I asked.

"Well the war made communication with forces personnel difficult because they were on the move so very much. Although I did write to him, I cannot be sure that he received my letters. In the final months of the war, he wrote to tell me he was engaged to be married to Joan and after that, our communication sort of fizzled out. I did not hear from George again - well not until about thirty years later."

"That must have been when we were on a family holiday in Scotland in the seventies. I remember going round the abbey ruins and Dad left us saying that he was going to look up an old friend. Was that when he came to see you again?" I asked, feeling the seismic sensation of giant metaphorical Jenga puzzle pieces slide smoothly into place with a clunk.

"Yes, Julie. That was when he came to see me. Just like that. Out of the blue. It was such a shock. After that he started to write to me again," she said wistfully.

"You clearly meant a lot to him, Moira."

"Och well, we were great friends for a long, long time. And of course, eventually, I got to know Joan too. Your Dad would write and sometimes, like at Christmas, your Mum and I would have a wee chat on the phone."

I was beginning to realise that much had been going on in the world of Mum and Dad to which my siblings and I were not privy. But then the seventies marked that chapter when we were all away at college with our minds on other things; our interests certainly did not run to creating and monitoring an inventory of all our parents' friends.

"Now Julie, I want to tell you that I am so delighted that you have made contact. I'm just so very sad about the circumstances -that it has been as a result of you own dear parents' ill health."

"Yes, it's a great pity that I have not known about you before but I'm so pleased that we have had this chance to talk. In a way, it helps to put another piece in the puzzle. You have given me an insight as to what my father was like when he was a very young man. Dad has always played his cards quite close to his chest and there is so much about his early life that he kept secret. I think the war had that effect on him – there are so many things that I would like to ask him – but the opportunity for getting a sensible and truthful answer from him has become very slight."

"He was certainly very deep, Julie, very deep and thoughtful even when I knew him as a laddie," Moira observed.

"Anyway," I said, trying to break the tension that I sensed was being held tightly between us, "tell me more about yourself – and about your husband and your family."

"Och well, I met Stefan during the war, he was a Polish airman you know, and he became my husband. He was a good man and we had many happy years together. In December, it will be five years since he passed away."

"Oh, Moira, I'm so very sorry to hear that."

"Life can be very sad and we both know that. But I do have my four children and now six grandchildren and they are all a great comfort to me. They keep me busy and out of mischief," she finished on a lighter note.

"Gosh, I didn't realise your family was so large. Tell me all about them," I asked.

"Julie I shall, when we have more time. This call will be costing you a pretty penny. I was thinking I would send you some photos. I have some lovely ones. Anita, that's my eldest daughter, she took some wonderful pictures of her wee children. I was telling Anita all about you contacting me and I asked her to carry on the contact even after I've gone."

"Why, where are you going?" I teased her, although I knew exactly what she meant. It had not taken us long to build a warm rapport; I knew my flippant comment would not offend her.

"Well we all must go upstairs one of these days, you know Julie. When you get to my age, you realise that life is soo very precious and it does not last for ever. Anyhow," she continued, getting back into her stride, "I will sort out some pictures and send them to you. Maybe you could show them to your Dad? It might spark something in his memory."

"That is a lovely thought," I replied.

Chapter 35
Danger Money

Julie

"Hey Julie, we can always tell when you've got a weekend with your Mum and Dad coming up," said Caroline as she blew on the surface of the plain hot water in her mug.

"Yep we sure do," agreed Annie and Suze, in joyful chorus. The three of them sat in a row on battered staff room chairs, high fiving their coffee mugs together with a resounding clink.

My shoulders slumped further.

"We knew it," added Mandy and Mo who were adding to the atmosphere of omniscience with their lively double handed stirring-the-pot movements.

"Am I that obvious?" I asked them in defeat, walking the shredded carpet as I shovelled a dose of paracetamol into my mouth along with a side order of Vitamin B12 and a chaser of Cod Liver oil, too nervous to do anything other than pace the staff room.

"Yes,'fraid so," said Annie. "You've got *that look*. You know, girls, the one where she stops smiling. And you know, Julie, you don't usually stop smiling. Not for anything."

"I'm a grinning idiot - it's my big mouth, it kind of falls open all the time - it just looks like I'm smiling," I said in my defence.

"Not when you start *dreading*," said Caroline sagely and with emphasis, "*dreading the respite cover weekend*. We know we're right."

"Yes, OK I give in. You are all absolutely right, it's another Gibbet Roundabout weekend coming up," I conceded with a proper smile. I could not help myself; my work mates had lightened my mood with their teasing and helped me to put *the dread feeling* on hold.

"Well then, sit yourself down and get this down your neck," ordered Sissy, passing me a cup of coffee made just the way I like it.

My work colleagues had been an important part of my support network for such a long time. I do not know how I could have coped without them. Tease me and taunt me they may have done, but it was all good natured banter and behind it lay genuine concern and interest. They would not let me go under, of that I was sure.

Meanwhile there were other more important topics to discuss.

"I got a new dress on Saturday ready for that wedding I was telling you all about," said Caroline; with her introduction of a popular subject, she was guaranteed our full attention. "It's floaty midnight blue tulle with spaghetti shoulder straps."

"Well, out of all of us, you are probably *the only one* who could get away with wearing *spaghetti shoulder straps*," said Mo, with authority. This ignited a raucous peal of laughter from the group.

"Spaghetti straps?" I said warming to the theme, "I'd require tagliatelle at the very least and then only *steel reinforced tagliatelle*."

Caroline took the teasing in good part, knowing that no offence was meant and that all present admired her neat figure, kept trim through regular exercise and the consumption of plain boiled water. We were all envious.

"What are you doing in the way of accessories, hat, bag, shoes and suchlike? Are you going nude or blue?" asked Mandy.

"Both, I expect," guffawed Mo, "the one leads to the other, especially in cold weather."

"Now girls, let's be sensible," laughed Annie in a vain effort to keep the conversation on track. As usual, it was in danger of heading down the lines of innuendo like a runaway train.

Caroline, flapping her arms to quieten us in a gesture of mock authority, answered Mandy's question. "I cannot find shoes of the right shade of blue so I may go pale beige for both shoes and bag," she said, painstakingly avoiding using the word 'nude'. "After all, you can't go wrong with accessories of that skin colour as they can go with anything and be used again and again. I might have another look in town on Saturday."

"I have a nude clutch in my attic I could loan you," said Sissy.

"Ooh! Hark at her, she should be so lucky!" proclaimed Mandy and Mo with the slick delivery of a comic double act.

As the laughter in the room was beginning to subside, Terry walked in. She had barely reached the kettle before she was pounced upon and fired at with questions from all sides.

"Well Terry's *All Gold*, our sweet little box of chockies, how did you get on with your latest date?" asked Annie, the first to get her question to reach its target. Terry was the youngest person on the staff and, unlike the rest of us, was single. She had begun internet dating recently and either out of naiveté or bravery had agreed to give regular updates to the staff room coven. "You know you want to tell us all about it, Terry," continued Annie, "you have to feel sorry for all of us - we are the poor females in our wilderness years with nothing juicy to enjoy."

"Oh, I get it," said Terry, "you lot are living your lives vicariously through me!"

"That's about it," agreed Mo, "think of it like this- it is a noble thing you do, you are our *avatar*."

"God, we're back to being blue again," said Sissy.

Terry gave us a brief account of her latest romantic encounter which turned out to have been a complete disaster owing to the young man's bad breath and obsessive vanity. Apparently, he arrived smelling heavily of garlic and tobacco and looked at his reflection in every shop window that they passed. His conversation revolved around his comprehensive knife collection and his 'guns' – this was the name he gave to his biceps that were covered with many intertwining snake tattoos. It was when he said '*here comes the sun, out comes my guns*' that she found herself having to fight back waves of giggles by biting on her fist. She had already decided she would want to be paid danger money for going out on a second date with him when he had delivered the final lethal bullet of information that was to kill the relationship stone dead: he worked at an abattoir.

There was a moment's silence before the room erupted again and cutting through the sound of whooping was Mo's steady voice, "So our avatar had a date with the boy from the abattoir!"

When the noise of cackling eventually died down, it was time to rescue Terry from the spotlight by changing the subject.

"Did you see that diet break-through programme on telly last night?" Annie asked of the assembled company. Dieting was one of our favourite topics; we were all on a diet, or had just been on a diet, or about to go on a diet. We were all experts. And we all sat up straighter, pulled in our tummies and lifted up our chins as the mini Diet Conference opened. It was amazing how much information could be exchanged during morning break. This time the data related to measuring calories without the use of scales.

"You see, you don't have to weigh anything, you just use your hand," explained Annie. "Your fist, now that's the size of your vegetable portion." She made a fist and so did everyone else in the staff room. Caroline being sporty put up both her fists and began to air punch like a boxer. "Now, now girls," Annie continued like a proper school mistress, "we want no fisticuffs in here. They then said on the programme that your palm, that's your protein measurement."

"Ooh I say," said Suze, "so how do you measure your carbs then?"

"Carbs are measured by your cupped hand," said Mandy who had also watched the programme.

"Yes, that's right," said Annie, holding up her thumb. "Now, your thumb – that apparently is how you measure your fat portion."

The next few moments saw us all communicating with hand gestures until Madeleine walked into the room, "What's all this? Some kind of Makaton practice?"

"That's right," quipped Caroline, "Diet Makaton!" This caused another wave of hilarity and more elaborate hand gestures with varying degrees of accuracy.

"I'm trying to give up carbs like bread and I'm not drinking any wine at the moment," I said, simultaneously testing out my sign language skills.

"No bread and wine? That actually sounds a bit irreligious," said Mo, "that can't be right!"

Under cover of the tidal wave of happy screeching, Suze took me to one side and asked about the details behind my bland statements that I had issued over recent weeks when asked for updates on Mum and Dad. Ever supportive, she empathised with the situation in which I found myself and was a good sounding board for new ideas and problem solving. However, our discussion was soon to be interrupted:

"Break's over. Show time ladies," announced Caroline as she washed her mug in the tiny sink.

*

Later that day, I wheeled my overnight bag through the city streets to the railway station, hurrying to catch the late afternoon train to Coventry. I was now a frequent traveller on the Friday afternoon service, becoming well acquainted with the best and safest seat to secure if the train was empty and precisely the best place to stand if it was full – and it was almost always full. Many a journey was spent standing all the way to the Midlands; a journey that usually lasted two hours. I did not mind, I could not relax anyway and learning to balance on one and a half feet (the other half of a foot acting as a brake to my bag's wheels) was good for my core muscles - or so I told myself. On this particular occasion I was in luck as I found a single empty seat and once my overnight bag was stowed in the overhead rack, I could breathe more easily.

It was a warm day and so without a book to read but surrounded by fellow passengers in summer attire, I was able to amuse myself by decoding the tattoos on the exposed flesh around me. There were lots of both. I found I was smiling to myself remembering Terry's date, *'here comes the sun, out comes my guns'*. On display around me in the packed train carriage, many a skimpy vest top, turned down collar, rolled up shirt sleeve and Bermuda shorts cut off revealed an inky record of personal history. Indeed, my brief observation led me to realise that these days there seemed even more to read on the tattoo front (and back and sides) than ever before. The trend for ink embellishments on arms, legs and chests had developed in a sophisticated direction, increasingly taking the form of inscriptions, affirmations, testimonies and memorials. Then there were the pictures of pop stars and pets, though not usually co-existing on the same body. There were tiny designs, worked in the kind of script the Queen might use on her palace invitations, incongruously adorning a muscled male décolletage, whilst bold letters from ancient oriental calligraphy emblazoned a hairless forearm bearing a message which only an ancient Oriental could decipher. Primeval Celtic patterns decorated the back of a youthful neck that would never be seen by its owner, while Maori patterns swirled around a limb like a living sleeve constantly in the owner's eye line.

Then there were the tattoos formed simply of single words *Mum and Dad*...

Mum and Dad. Too deep for a tattoo, they were way down under my skin.

I reflected on how their needs had become as important for me to consider as those of my own children. How the dynamics had shifted from the limited responsibility of being one of their offspring to the massive responsibility involved in being one of their care givers.

Then there was the thorny question of the impact Mum and Dad's health was having on their grandchildren. I wanted to give Lizzy and Simon the choice of taking their own path; to witness or not to witness the gradual decline of their beloved Grandpa George and Grandma Joan. I had told them that we were now at a virtual crossroads where one road would take them with me as I attempted to take on the challenges associated with visiting and caring for their grandparents, whilst another road would allow them shelter from the exposure, to let them simply cherish the memories of Grandma and Grandpa as they had presented before Dementia had taken a hold. Truly, I respected whichever decision they made.

But love does not follow neat paths. Decisions like this are not simple. My wonderful children were not only suffering themselves, they were hurting for me too. They both wished to treasure their memories but both wanted to help meet the challenge of the road ahead in their own individual ways. James and I were indeed blessed, I reflected.

Such thoughts led me to take out from the recesses of my mothership handbag, the photographs of another family. Moira had sent the pictures to me along with a brief note saying that she hoped they would jog Dad's memory and that she would be sending more when she had ' *finished the wee film reel in the camera'*. The first photograph was of a strikingly handsome lady, with silver hair styled in a long bob. She was elegantly dressed in a lilac cowl necked sweater and was posed sitting relaxed and smiling upon a floral patterned sofa. Her smooth skin and attractively even features created an appearance that belied her age. On the back was inscribed *Moira 2003*.

The second photograph featured a little girl in full riding gear, show jumping. On the back were the words, *My granddaughter Sophie (age12) riding Pixie*.

The third photograph's inscription listed family members joining Moira on the sofa : *from left to right, Anita(my eldest daughter), Sophie(12), Me, Daniel (17). Standing behind the sofa is Derek (Anita's husband) and Joey (20).* Moira had told me that Anita was close to me in age and it would seem that we began our families within a few years of each other – both factors meant that we would have at least a few experiences in common if we did find ourselves following Moira's wishes in the event of her 'going upstairs'. It did seem a shame if the pen-friendship between two families that had lasted for well over half a century should come to an end.

In the train carriage, the shutters on The Body Art Show were coming down as the train's progress took us into the cooler part of the day. Cardigans and jackets were liberated from bags and draped over any exposed designs. "Getting a bit parky," somebody muttered. It was then that I realised we were close to my destination and as the train began its deceleration, I gathered my belongings together.

268

My connecting train was subject to delays and so I took the opportunity of contacting Mum and Dad's current live-in carer on my mobile. Patience had completed her tour of duty and had been replaced by Priscilla with whom I had previously chatted on the phone but had not yet met.

"Hello, it's Julie here. Is that Priscilla?"

"It is, Julie. Are you still coming?" I could hear the hope in her voice and a halt to her breathing as she awaited my answer. Then the tension on the line evaporated as I confirmed that indeed I would be taking over from her for the weekend and was now only an hour away. I asked her for a brief report on Mum and Dad's health to which she gave a positive summary, relating that meals had been consumed and medication had been taken and minor ailments were showing improvements. *Good so far.* However, it was when I asked Priscilla how *she* was and how she was settling in, that the flood gates opened. It transpired that the previous day she had been chased about the bungalow by Mum brandishing a broom and telling her in no uncertain terms that she did not want her in her house. Priscilla, the poor woman, had taken refuge in the kitchen and locked herself in. Meanwhile, Mum had entered Priscilla's room and gathering up all her possessions, had thrown them out of the window into the front garden.

"Oh my God, I'm so sorry, what can I say?" I told her in shock, shame and embarrassment. Then the second wave of reaction hit me; it was one of fear. *What if Priscilla didn't come back after her weekend off?*

It was my turn to convey hope in a voice that begged for reassurance from her. She told me in soothing tones that although Mum's behaviour had taken her by surprise, she guessed it was Mum's way of reacting to change. Somehow or other, Priscilla had effected a state of peace in the bungalow during the ensuing hours, managing to retrieve her property and locking it in her private room. According to Priscilla, Mum seemed to have forgotten her actions after a relatively short time and had become distracted by other things. Priscilla's tolerance, understanding and capacity for forgiveness took my breath away. Zimbabwe had produced yet another living saint to be sculpted in marble and positioned next to Saint Patience on the roof of St Peter's.

When our conversation ended, I made a few more calls so that when I met Priscilla at the entrance to the bungalow, I had an envelope of cash in my hand. When I handed this little well- earned bonus to her, she refused to accept it. Eventually, I took her hand in both of mine and forced the envelope into her palm, closing her fingers over it.

"Call it *danger money*," I said.

Chapter 36
Absurdity over gravity equals the square root of guilt.

Julie

So, hermetically sealed once more in the bungalow at Burnage, another weekend began. I was becoming more used to the experience, becoming skilled in predicting the unpredictable, becoming prepared to rescue anyone from imagined emergencies even more dangerous than being *lost on the Fens*. I was also becoming strangely detached from the concept that these two fascinating human beings were in fact my parents. It seemed that all of the connections that bound us were working loose on both a functioning level and an emotional level.

That weekend they were both so very silent so much of the time that when I recall that period, I think of it as a silent movie playing out...

*

'The Lost Weekend'
A movie for the silver screen
Starring
Charlie Chaplin as *George*
Harpo Marx as *Joan*
Stan Laurel as *Julie*

Scene 1 *The dining room*

Action: *It is Friday evening. Julie (Stan) serves a fish and chip dinner to her two parents before joining them to eat at the table. Then all three actors put their hands to their cheeks in horror.*

Intertitle card: What no knives and forks?

Action: *George(Charlie) looks under his tie, then under his plate and then under the table, Joan (Harpo) looks inside the poacher's pockets in her coat, discovering a clock, two books and a candlestick, all of which she places on top of the table - but no knives and forks. Julie (Stan) runs from the room with her hands raised in panic. She returns with her handbag from which she produces four plastic forks. The three start to eat their dinner. George(Charlie) sticks the tines of two forks into two bread rolls to make pretend feet and makes them dance on the table. Everyone at the table claps. Julie(Stan) clears the table and carries the plates out of the dining room.*

Scene 2 *The Kitchen*

Action: *Julie (Stan) begins to scrape all the left- over food from the plates into the waste bin. She stops, looks directly in the camera with a puzzled expression and scratches her head with one hand until her hair sticks up in the air.*

Intertitle Card: No wonder they were playing with the dinner she gave them! They had already eaten dinner before she arrived!

Action: *Close up of the inside of the bin showing empty meal packages.*

Scene 3 *The dining room*

Action : *George (Charlie) and Joan (Harpo) are seen rubbing their stomachs with apparent tummy ache.*

Intertitle Card: Full up now, but we are still thirsty!

Action: *Joan (Harpo) picks up the vase of flowers on the dining table and drinks the water from it. Julie (Stan) enters the room and snatches the vase from Joan (Harpo) and runs out of the room with her hands raised in the air in panic.*

Intertitle Card: The End.

*

Why had Mum and Dad been silent when I presented them with a second dinner? I had asked myself; although sadly I knew the answer: they had forgotten that Priscilla had already fed them. I told Tom when he called to see us all on Saturday afternoon. Having shared a cup of tea in the lounge with Mum and Dad, Tom and I went to the kitchen to discuss the implication of the repeated meal consumption, seeing it as a signal of further deterioration to our parents' memory skills. Rubbing his eyes in tiredness, it was then that he realised he had mislaid his spectacles.

"God, I must be losing it too," he said, "I know I had them when I arrived, I must have put them down somewhere." He and I began an extensive but stealthy search of the bungalow, anxious not to disturb the old folk. Eventually however, we had to enter the lounge where we were met with wide staring eyes and faces bemused and puzzled. Then weirdly and totally unpredictably, Mum and Dad seemed to understand that Tom had lost his glasses and they joined the search with alacrity and enthusiasm.

"This is a good sign," I muttered to Tom under my breath, "they seem to know what's happening."

Meanwhile cushion 'bags' were emptied, light shades were lifted and rugs rolled back, chair seat cushions were removed, shelves were rearranged and drawers dragged open. The atmosphere became tense as the feverish search continued unabated into areas where Tom had not even strayed that day.

"This is like one of Dad's Sunday searches," said Tom. "Do you remember when he used to spend hours trying to find an essential item until instead he found lots of other things that he did not know he had lost and then forgot what he was looking for in the first place?"

"Aw, those good old days," I said, with heavy irony. "Let's give up for now and have a tea break."

As the lounge had been turned over (as if by a burglar with attendant dyspraxia), we gathered once more around the table in the dining room. I was just pouring the tea into Mum's cup when I realised that she had something foreign balanced on her nose – Tom's spectacles.

When Tom and I rejoiced in the discovery of the lost item, Mum with the deadpan expression of Buster Keaton, did not seem to be aware of the fact she was wearing spectacles at all. Furthermore, we realised later that she may have had them on her nose throughout the time we had been turning the house upside down in search of them.

273

When Tom could at last see to drive himself home and some order had been restored to the bungalow, I prepared the main meal of the day. After the previous day's double whammy, I had kept the meals light, but for dinner I had chosen to serve an authentic Cornish pasty with salad as a departure from the normal frozen meals. The pasties sat on plates like small brooding hens, confusing Dad who poked and prodded them suspiciously at first before daring to taste. It was clear that Mum was not sure what to do with hers and sat and stroked it for a while as if it might at any moment start clucking and lay her an egg.

Another lowlight of the weekend was the discovery of the embroidery kit that I had brought to Mum to finish when she was in *Bramwell*. The linen told a story for anyone to see; it mapped a decline. In the centre of the cloth was an exquisite silk rose that Mum had worked in satin and stem stitch with skill and proficiency many months before. But around it were her more recent efforts: the long, ugly, random stitches of a small child.

As for Moira's hope that Dad's memory would be jolted by a set of photographs; that also proved to be in vain. He barely seemed to register the fact that he was looking at someone he knew. Even when I named Moira, he seemed to retreat into himself, close his eyes and appear to doze.

As usual, I have Vera to thank for her welcome intrusion on Sunday morning – her consequential floor show kept the silence at bay for a while. Although her visit did not begin well, her arrival causing an immediate negative effect: Dad instantly expressed the wish to leave the room. I helped him to get up from the cosy armchair, supporting him gently until he gained an upright position. He was of short stature and had lost so much weight that for me it felt like standing up a pint of milk on the doorstep. Once mobile, he muttered, "Doctor Collis Browne to the rescue," as a Parthian shot on leaving the room. Maybe the hen style pasties were wreaking their revenge or perhaps this was all subterfuge; he just needed to retreat from the invader.

Meanwhile, left in the lounge with Mum and me, our friendly intruder went into her routine like a seasoned performer. Surprisingly, this was matched by a new bright and shiny Mum who seemed to spring into life in Vera's company. Mum was on top form, incorporating her usual loop of phrases into the conversation but this time adding odd nuggets of language drawn from her love of Nevil

Shute novels and television commercials of the twentieth century. *Excellent specialist subjects for a Mastermind challenge*, I thought to myself.

Mum had 'helped' me get the tea and this prompted her broadcast with splash of Shute and embedded jingle, "I had a prang with the tray but you know *tea revives you!*" before adding as her own signature full stop: "Darlings."

"Ooh m' duckie, you don't half talk posh," said Vera. "I love a good cuppa. Does yous like me new wedgies? I saw 'em in the shop winder and I thought to meself I'll have them. Me – I like to be as trendy as a gonk!"

"They are very smart shoes, aren't they Mum? Would you like a biscuit, Vera?" I asked, offering her a chocolate digestive.

"*A Mars a day helps you work, rest and play,*" announced Mum as eloquently as Judith Chalmers.

"Thanks duck, I'll have one of them there disgustives. Ooh me," Vera continued, "I like to look stylish, me. What me old Ma used to say, *Smart - up to Dick and down to Bob.*"

With sensitive ears honed from weekends of practice, I heard the bolt being drawn back on the bathroom door before the sound of soft footfalls on the thick carpet indicated that Dad was retreating further from society by seeking out the darkness of the bedroom. *High Noon in the dark.* An image flashed into my mind which made me smile, a remembered scene from childhood: Dad watching the classic gunfighter film '*High Noon*' on the tiny screened television set, in the dim lounge with curtains drawn against the high summer afternoon.

My attention reverted to the cabaret in the lounge where Vera was observing her own tea ceremony which would make a geisha blush. With biscuit poised over her cup she confessed boldly "I don't skinny dip, I chunky dunk", all for our amusement as huge chunks of crumb fell Kamikaze-like into her brew.

"*A drink's too wet without one,*" jingled Mum with admirable advertising slogan accuracy.

"Ooh what we want now is a bit o' sun," said Vera, looking like the conductor of an orchestra as she waved her arms at the dismal weather scene visible through the window. "A nice bit o' the old currant bun, as me Ma used to say."

"Ha-huh-ha," said Mum looking wistfully at the plate of biscuits in search of a currant bun.

"No m'duck, not a bun, *the sun!* it's rhyming like. Like apples and pears means *stairs,* and tea leaf means *thief!"*

I felt we were straying into dangerous waters where the memory of thief accusations could bob to the surface at any moment but Mum seemed to have become far more interested in searching for apples and pears. The cushion 'bag' came back in evidence and its inside was invaded by a rootling hand. Reaching for a stiff drink and realising that tea would have to suffice; I hooked my cup only to discover it empty. *The tea thief has been at it again,* I muttered to myself in exasperation. Mum often drank your tea when you were not looking.

Meanwhile Vera, oblivious to these undercurrents, continued to mine her rich seam of memory; cockney rhyming slang would definitely be her specialist subject on *Mastermind.*

"Now what do yer think *'have a butcher's'* comes from? Well *'butcher's hook'* rhymes with *'look'* so it means *'have a look.'* Then there's *'let's scarper'* now that comes from *'Scapa Flow'* what rhymes with *'go'* so *'let's scarper'* means *'let's go.'* Where's our George gone then?" she finished with a flourish.

"Beyond the black stump," said Mum enigmatically.

"He's scarpered then has he? He'll be missing his Rosie Lee - that's tea," Vera explained from behind her hand in theatrical gesture.

"Tea leaf!" said Mum suddenly sitting up and taking notice. "Tea leaf, what did you say it meant? Thief?"

Before I could intervene and distract Mum from her imagined quarry, she had started her *'jewel thief'* accusations. Clearly Mum's memory for facts had been impaired yet her memory of imagined crimes was in this instance shiny and new. Vera, surprised and shocked by Mum's sudden change in mood, allowed herself to be shepherded off the 'stage' and out of the lounge to the chorus of my profuse apologies. Once again, she accepted the rebuff gracefully and with admirable tolerance, made her elegant exit via the front door to achieve the sanctuary of her neat bungalow where all was predictable and ordered down to the colour co-ordinated toilet rolls.

So it was with the feeling of intense relief a few hours later, that I heard Priscilla's car drive into the close. As I opened the door to fall on her neck with profound gratitude for her return, I saw the welcome figure of James standing behind her. An embarrassed Priscilla extricated herself gently from my bear hug allowing me to transfer my fevered embrace to my husband – a much more tolerant recipient. The latter beneficiary of my sweaty affection had surprised me by driving over one hundred miles just to pick me up and take me home. *Let me add his name to the list of worthies that deserve to be canonised.*

I turned to thank Saint Priscilla profusely again for not deserting us after her weekend of freedom and updated her on the events of the previous few hours. We all entered the lounge together to find Mum and Dad had returned to their default settings of looking puzzled and bemused in their armchairs. To give Priscilla chance to settle in, I went off to make yet another pot of ubiquitous tea, leaving James with Mum and Dad. I could hear from the kitchen the sounds of conversation and smiled to myself at the marvel that was occurring; James had managed to engage them and furthermore what was being said sounded quite sensible. Just as I was collecting the tray and trying not to *have a prang,* I heard voices raised in apparent delight.

I rushed into the lounge to find out what was happening and there sat Mum with a faded blue velvet cosmetic bag from which tumbled a tangle of necklaces, bracelets and rings. She was holding the gems up to the light to enjoy the sparkle of her long lost jewellery. It made a wonderful scene, both Mum and Dad smiling and James looking modest and shy with a dash of smugness. It transpires that in the short time that I had been making the tea, James' sharp eyes had noticed the tiny fabric edge poking out of the tidy stack of video tapes. His hunter-fisherman's instincts had demonstrated superiority over us lesser pot-stirring mortals; we who had spent many hours in the vain search for the hidden bounty that was now bringing such pleasure to my mother.

As we drove out of the close in the pale light of late afternoon, I felt a sense of euphoria that arose from the recovery of the jewellery and the temporary freedom from responsibility, almost sufficient to overcome fatigue and guilt. Almost. I talked non- stop to James as hungrily, I soaked up every mile that took me closer to our home. He listened patiently, and it was not until we reached Brackley, the half way point on our journey, before I let him get a word in edgeways.

"Something came in the post for you," he said as his long arm reached across me to extract the mail from the confines of his neat glove box. Amongst the drab manila envelopes, the pale blue rectangle was luminescent.

"It's from Moira," I said unnecessarily.

"Yes, I thought so. I imagined you'd like to see it. Looks as if it contains a few more prints. More little girls on ponies winning rosettes, I expect."

I slid my finger under the flap and gently tore the envelope open. I drew out the familiar pale blue lined paper covered in neat rows of looping script and unfolded it.

"What's up?" said James when I stared silently at the photograph that had fallen from the folds of the letter into my lap.

"How come Moira has sent me a picture of Tom?" I uttered, bewildered.

Chapter 37
The Bonnie Banks

Julie

Of course it could not be a picture of Tom. On closer inspection, the person in the photograph did not have Tom's hair with its severe side parting, neither was he wearing spectacles. Even so, the resemblance was so close that the hairs on the back of my neck began to stand up. I sat stunned in the contour hugging car seat for several minutes before my mind seemed to break free of its moorings and begin to whirl like the components of the decoding machines at Bletchley Park. Equally fascinated by the brief glimpses of the photograph that had dangerously distracted his attention away from the traffic, James pulled the car into a lay-by. The two of us pored over the tiny rectangle of shiny card, our minds in denial of what it might mean.

"Well that could explain a lot," I found myself saying eventually. "This is Moira's eldest. He not only looks like Tom but also looks to be about Tom's age or maybe a tad older."

"He's so like Tom, it's uncanny," said James.

"Moira told me that she felt, or at least her parents felt, that she was too young to get married when Dad had proposed. However she got married to her Polish chappie during the war so it must have been quite soon after she turned Dad down – and when she would not have been that much older. This son of hers, now what's his name?" I turned over the photograph to find the answer in Moira's neat script. "Cameron. That's his name. I wonder if he was the one to make her change her mind as regards getting married."

"So let's think about what we're saying here. Do you think that Moira *had to get married* and that the father was your dad?" said James, helping me put our suspicions into words; words spoken aloud.

"I think that is what I am saying. Obviously, it could be true that Moira had a whirlwind romance with Stefan, got married to him and Cameron was the offspring of that union. But then the

279

photographic evidence is quite compelling. I think it is more than likely that Moira was already pregnant when she met Stefan and that he married her to help her get 'out of trouble'. Poor dear lady, if that had been the case, it must have been so awful for her. People were so harsh and judgemental in those days. The shame would have been intolerable for her."

"If Cameron is the true son of your dad," continued James, "that might explain why Moira wants our two families to remain connected even if something happens to her. Didn't she say she had asked her eldest daughter to continue the correspondence with our family in the event of her passing? What did you say her name was?"

"Anita, her name's Anita," I stuttered, feeling shivers course down my spine which had nothing to do with the temperature in the car. "Moira has got four children and they all have names that sound like popular Polish names: Anita, Gertie and Irena. All except her first born called Cameron- now that's definitely more of a Scottish name." I thought back to the different conversations that I had had with the enigmatic Moira. I now believed that she had been trying to tell me something and the clues and hints that she had dropped, as clear and bright as Hansel and Gretel's breadcrumbs, were beginning to form a trail that was leading to answers to questions I had not even known I was asking.

"All this might also have been a contributory cause of your dad's increasing confusion. When you consider how mixed up he has appeared, talking about *the house in Newark* and all that stuff. With that kind of knowledge on his conscience, it would be bound to trouble someone as sensitive as him. He would have been wracked with guilt."

"I wonder if Mum knows," I thought out loud. *But of course she would know. I bet she's known since that Scottish holiday when Dad went off to look up his old school penfriend, Moira- when I suspect he learnt the truth for the first time.*

I thought about the little hints that Mum had let slip, the references to 'Daddy's girlfriend' and other little comments she had made between parentheses of her two tone laughs of embarrassment. Yet she would never have talked openly about it to anyone. That sort of thing was considered a taboo subject in Mum's book.

"Oh, I think she knows," I answered my own question.

It was ironic that just as things were unravelling in the minds of Mum and Dad, so much was beginning to fit together to make some kind of sense to me.

"Julie, Barbara said that you had something important to tell me. I'm sorry I wasn't in earlier but I've been to a meeting and I've got some information for you and Janine. Nothing is wrong is it? Is everything alright?" said Tom on Monday evening. I was still processing the implications of the photograph I had seen the previous day and so I asked him to divulge his news first.

"Ok, well the chap at Mum and Dad's bank, he was very thorough and has printed off statements for us with copies for the Court of Protection."

"That's good," I said trying to damp down my excitement; I felt heavy with the weight of a suppressed secret that could rival the Greek myth of the barber who could not tell a living soul that King Midas had the ears of an ass. Tom, a natural accountant was on his own spree of financial fervour, reporting facts and figures that left me cold and wishing he would be brief so that I could deliver the secret of all secrets: *we have a half-brother!*

"So you see - that was why it has taken the bank so long," he finished. His words fell on the ears of an ass. I had zoned out.

"Sorry, Tom, *why* had *what* taken so long?" I asked, wishing he would get to the point. Patiently, he did. Again. Just for my benefit, he spelt it out.

"Finding out about Dad's accounts – it took the bank ages as bizarrely they were all in banks in Scotland -that's where Dad's extra accounts were, all twenty-two of them."

Chapter 38
The shifting of the tectonic plates

Julie

"I can't understand it," said Tom, "why would Dad have all these accounts based in Scotland?"

Feeling calm now, I was ready to share my secret theory. I amazed myself since I had been ready to erupt like a long dormant volcano just moments before. I even managed to adopt the mantle of Daphne Oxenford and in '*Listen with Mother*' soft tones I asked, "Are you sitting comfortably? Good, then I'll begin."

*

Janine was sitting comfortably when I shared the secret with her; in fact she was sitting very comfortably side by side with a glass of wine on a picnic rug laid out at the bottom of her long garden. She had gone there to relax after a stressful day in the classroom. Via her mobile phone, in my benign Daphne Oxenford style voice I managed to inadvertently rock her world.

Now the news had erupted, the three of us were on shifting ground that felt so unstable it could open up and swallow us at any moment. But the lava from the Scottish volcano barely had chance to cool before we suffered another earth shattering shock with the news that Mum had collapsed at home and had been rushed into hospital.

Ideas of a half sibling, real or imagined, had to be shelved as we rallied our resources to meet the demands of this new emergency. We consigned our theories to the bottom drawer, a very deep drawer with a stout lock; it was no longer a time to dwell on possibilities evoked from the past - the *here and now* were what mattered.

So *here and now* we were all sitting together in the quiet family room off the busy hospital ward, staring at the cheerful posters decorated with coloured balloons promoting the fund raising events for local charities alongside the less comforting displays comprising graphic illustrations that warn of the dire consequences of ignoring a mole. For a set of siblings that have been known to use language as a

282

first line of defence or attack or to fill any unsuspecting passing silence – even during sleep, we were strangely quiet. I had resumed my old habit of biting my nails and having found myself painfully down to the quick, my mind cast about for something to do. Momentarily, the thought of taking up smoking seemed an attractive occupation. Fortunately, this idea was quickly quashed by the sight of that poster of the diseased lungs blasting me from across the room. Janine equally challenged, had resorted to going through her handbag, weeding out shop receipts, tissues and old cosmetic items. I watched her with interest, wistfully envying her nails that were presently being smoothed with an emery board she had retrieved from the bottomless pit that was her bowling style handbag. I had not got the stomach to plumb the depths of my battered mothership reticule; I feared getting the bends. In desperation, I started to flick through a well-thumbed and torn magazine that was as seriously distressed as its recent waiting room readers must have been. As I turned its tattered pages that spoke of high style country living, I buried my worries in landscaped gardens approached by long drives lined with ubiquitous topiaries of peacocks and cockerels. I roved the featured houses, patting a stray Labrador, poking a fire in an elegant inglenook fireplace, fluffing up a sheepskin rug, punching and repositioning a silk cushion until I was completely absorbed in the country lifestyle of Little Chipsodbury or some such place where Major and Mrs Farquhar had their pied de sod. I had just mentally purchased a huge welsh dresser and a chest to store riding boots and riding crops (me having never ridden a horse in my life) both items crafted in Cotswold veneercd MDF, when the doctor came into the room.

We were informed that the initial medical test results indicated that Mum had suffered a minor stroke. We were advised that we could visit but that we should be prepared to expect Mum to be confused. We looked at each other and then Tom, as spokesperson, informed the doctor in many eloquent words that for us that was 'no change there then.'

The three of us took turns to visit Mum, finding her sleepy and uncommunicative during those first few days on the ward. In spite of this vulnerable presentation, we thought it sensible to ensure that hospital staff members were aware of what had occurred the last time Mum had been hospitalised – events that might be repeated when Mum regained her strength. We advised them to be prepared for her unpredictable behaviour; how she might rip out her drip line and go walkabout at any moment; how she would appear to acquiesce to any demand from them but in reality she may not have actually heard or understood their request.

We also divided our time by visiting Dad to keep a regular check on his well-being. By now, there were five new statues of saints gracing the roof of St Peter's and the current carer, soon to be canonised Saint Debbie of Burnage, was endeavouring to provide a stable environment for Dad. Although Mum was temporarily off the scene, her influence held sway and was signalled by empty cutlery drawers and overstuffed cushions that were lumpy and misshapen with a filling of random foreign objects. It was clear that Dad deeply missed Mum and during this period, he appeared to retreat further, lacking interest in his surroundings, eating little and interacting even less.

Meanwhile, contrary to anyone's prediction, Mum's condition improved to the point where she seemed to be flourishing, appearing to suffer few enduring ill effects as a result of her ordeal. From her white hospital bed, she held court to any passing nurse or visitor, blissfully unaware of what she had experienced and where precisely she was. The ward environment had the effect of stimulating her into communicating and she blossomed into a superficial version of the socially adept woman she once was. It was heart- breaking to see the 'not quite Mum' smiling and chatting to us, complimenting us on our teeth, treating us politely as benign strangers with whom she had no association.

I was reminded of an old fashioned barometer formed of a miniature house adorned with two tiny figures. One was of a woman in a summer dress who would appear in the doorway of the house when the weather was predicted to be fine. The gentleman figure carried a black umbrella and would only appear in the doorway when rain was anticipated. In the microcosm of our family, Mum was at her best amongst the sunshine of other people whilst Dad sheltered from the rain of social contact under his black umbrella.

Sadly unlike the diminutive figure in her pretty summer dress, Mum was not going back into her own little house. In preparation for her discharge from hospital, we were strongly advised by both the Health Team and Social Services that Mum now required the more intense level of attention that a residential care home could provide. Furthermore, since it was clear that Dad was not thriving in Mum's absence, it was sensible to apply for him to transfer to a care home also.

Game over, then. For us all, it was quite a shock. All our efforts had been in vain. All the 'saints' that had marched in through the front door of the bungalow to provide care for our parents over the best part of a year would have to receive their marching orders. All the daily checks, regular visits and weekend stays we made– all of it was to come to an end.

It was with a sense of déjà vu that we applied for Mum and Dad to take up residence at *The Grange*. Along with the feeling of déjà vu, came the real sense of failure that we carried with us as we sat across the desk from the magnificently burnished and statuesque Zeus once again. Whilst we were undoubtedly impressed by *The Grange* and recognised this was the appropriate course of action to take, we also knew that we had failed in our attempt to provide a safe future for our parents in the familiar surroundings of their own home.

With this realisation came the knowledge that they would never again live in their own home. The bungalow they had lovingly furnished together and enjoyed for so many happy years would no longer be their shelter. There would be no room in their future home for the majority of their possessions. All the photographs, paintings, books and treasured belongings would remain behind; each item loaded with memories to which they no longer held the key, each one once prompted a tale worthy of telling, all now long forgotten.

Their new living space would be compact, stylish and functional, comprising smartly furnished adjacent en-suite rooms off an impersonal carpeted corridor.

Chapter 39
Let's press on

Julie

"It was so sad saying goodbye to Debbie and all the carers. They've done an amazing job haven't they? But I expect there must have been a huge sense of relief for them too, knowing that they won't be living for spells with Mum and Dad in La La Land any more. God what a challenge!" said Janine over the phone.

"Too right," I replied, "they are all saints in my book. It was a shame that we didn't get to see Patience again. Poor dear lady - fancy surviving a tour of duty in somewhere equivalent to a bungalow sized theatre of war and returning to your home in Zimbabwe to recuperate - but then to find when you are ready to get back to your job to earn money vital to your family, you are not allowed back into the UK again. She'll be a real loss to the caring team; they'll be missing her loads, I'll bet."

"Yes, life's so unfair. I hope she will be able to get her visa sorted eventually... I was thinking, Julie, that even though it's such a relief for us all to know that Mum and Dad are safely tucked up in *The Grange*, there is still just as much for us to do and worry about," said Janine.

"I know, I was thinking the same thing. Tom said that if we have to accept Mum and Dad won't be living at home again, then we should put the bungalow in the hands of a letting agency to help offset the cost of the care home fees."

"It's all so sad, Julie, but I think that would be a sound plan. By the way, what's that dreadful noise I can hear in the background?"

"That's my washing machine just coming in to land in my kitchen," said I, as calmly as a self-styled domestic goddess. "I think the bearings are going."

"So you're not talking to me from Heathrow Airport then?"

"No, nowhere so romantic as that. Can you hear that hissing sound now, like a large angry snake? That's my steam iron, did you know you're helping me get through a gigantic pile of James' shirts and tea towels and God knows what else. Where does it all come from?" I wondered, while the landing lights of the Hotpoint flashed as it ceased its deafening gyrations.

"Well don't get *steamed* up!" Janine jested. Pathetically.

"Stop, I can't cope - that is so ultra-lame, I'm already feeling *flattened* by the *pressure*," was my equally limping reply. "The last time we started one of your pun challenges, it went on for days. It's not funny I can tell you when you find yourself snorting and eye rolling during a staff meeting when one of your sister's text equivalents of a cracker joke comes through. Not a good look."

"I'm sorry Julie, I did not mean you to *crease up* in the staff room. Look, let's get back to the *ironing board* I mean drawing board. If we are going to let the house, we will have to clear it out and get it ready won't we?"

"Yes, Tom and I were thinking we would organise a series of weekends when we could all work on the project together. There will be loads of stuff to sort and furniture to store in order to empty the place completely. I can't imagine what's in the loft. Tom had a quick look and said that there were boxes that have remained unopened since Mum and Dad moved into the bungalow over thirty years ago."

"You mean that they moved in but haven't finished unpacking yet? That's going to be a massive task and we'll have to work *flat out.*"

"Stop it! You just can't resist can you? Yes we will have to work *flat out* as you say and then there will be some cleaning and redecorating needed to get it up to standard ready to let," I moaned.

"Yes all the wrinkles will need to be *smoothed out.* Ok I can hear the *steam* coming out of your ears so I'll leave you to *press on* and *dash* off - get it? *Dashing away with the smoothing iron....* I'll talk to Nick, have a look at the calendar and then I'll get back to you as regards the next free weekend we have."

*

In the end it took several weekends. Several weekends composed of discovering strange items in even stranger places. The bungalow was a lonely beach strewn with objects deposited by some giant hand of random tide. On carpet covered floors, behind curtains and on every wooden or tiled surface were thrown sewing machine

287

parts, silk ties and war medal ribbons, plastic hair combs, purses, items of cutlery and a myriad of keys that defied logic since they did not fit any of the existing locks on the property. Each find took us on a journey down memory motorway where there were no comfort stations. Here memories reigned supreme, loading every inanimate object, reaching out with powerful sinuous neurons to stimulate the conscience of the innocent interloper, making them walk that emotionally painful path.

How ironic to realise that the former guardians of this memory trove could no longer remember.

The main hub of memories seemed to be formed by the wall of book shelves in the dining room. Here some shelves contained volumes that had not been touched for thirty years. That is unless they had been disturbed by a gentle hand that held a photograph to be slipped between pages to keep it flat or ten pound notes to be hidden in bindings and dust jackets to keep them safe and then forgotten. Within this mini library, where titles ranged from the benign and fluffy '*Cats in Camera*' to the malignant and steely '*Adolf Hitler*', a thin spine declared '*You are a Top Girl*' in 1960's type face. I smiled at its discovery; it proclaimed an achievement never to be attained by me, either during the sixties or subsequently. I remembered Mum giving the book to me at Christmas at the height of my —what she termed: 'awkward phase, Darlings'. Apparently she read it and it helped her to understand my awkward and contrary behaviour better. I was too awkward and contrary to ever read it, of course. Maybe my life would have been very different if I had. Maybe I would be a super confident captain of industry now. Or maybe not.

Gradually and systematically the memory hub was dismantled and books, divested of their jackets and their pages fanned, were packed in boxes to be stored in Mum and Dad's garage. With huffing and puffing and the popping of bubble wrap, we added all the furniture, pictures and other movable chattels to the secure and dry storage space that once accommodated the family car. The rest of Mum and Dad's belongings that could not join them in the care home were sorted and packed and stacked in rows so that the space was crammed.

This may have been an emotional task but it failed to rival the previous challenge we had undertaken, one of selecting the belongings and keepsakes that were to decorate and feather Mum and Dad's new en-suite nests in the care home. Montages of photographs, carefully labelled by the experienced teachers that we were, had been prepared for each of them. Along with these, their favourite pictures and ornaments (the unbreakable ones) were carefully chosen to engender a sense of familiarity and to prompt failing memory.

We were optimistic by nature and we knew we had to begin moving forward, begin to *press* on.

Chapter 40
Wantacupoftea!

George, Julie

The tent flaps allowed a triangle of weak light to enter George's tired eyes. He had been roused several minutes earlier by the screeching of the parrot and had lain awake, allowing his eyes to adjust to the daylight. He had not slept well in these unfamiliar surroundings during a night full of the thumps and bangs of large animals disturbing the ground and releasing the foetid smell of the jungle's rotting vegetation. It reminded him of the poor air in a London underground station where a warm draught brings no breezy freshness. He knew he could not find fresh air while he was stationed here in this Godforsaken place.

He shifted in the bed to try to get more comfortable but in this humidity, where clothing became moist and stuck to the skin, it was a vain hope. Condensation was a real issue for these remote telecommunication relay stations. He would have to get onto the blower and talk to Jaffa about it. All this moisture was playing havoc with the equipment.

The parrot began its mantra again. To George it even sounded as if it was talking and as he focused on the squawking cadence, he became convinced he heard the bird saying something about a cup of tea. He decided his mind, robbed of a decent night's kip, was playing tricks on him. *For God's sake!* A parrot in the middle of a rain forest, in an *almost* inaccessible part of a rain forest in darkest Guyana would not be asking for a cup of tea! He must be losing the plot.

But then as if to prove him wrong, there it was again *'wantacupoftea!'*

Someone opened the tent flaps wide, forcing him to cover his eyes against the brighter, more intense light of the advancing morning.

"Good morning George. I hope you slept well. I have brought you a nice cup of tea to drink before you go down to breakfast. I think it's going to be a lovely day. The weather forecaster on the radio said so anyway, but you never know who to believe, do you? It's very warm in here, and oh dear, I think your bed clothes need a bit of a change. I'll get Nancy to come and give me a hand."

George continued to lie on the damp bed with his arm flung across his eyes while his mind continued in its attempt to make sense of the situation. Clearly there were chamber maids in the camp and at least one had the wondrous ability to supply tea in this jungle. *Wizard!*

After a short time, George's eyes were fully accustomed to the sunlight and he was able to enjoy the contents of his tea cup perched on its saucer. *How very civilised.* Then the chamber maid returned with a colleague, presumably the Nancy person mentioned earlier, who was pushing a squeaking trolley full of folded bed linen.

"Those wheels could do with a drop of WD40. I think I might have some in my kit bag," said George helpfully.

"Don't you worry about that George, we'll get it seen to. Meanwhile let's make you comfortable. Nancy, help me get Mr Ellis into the shower, will you?" said Ethel –she of the tea pot and the tent flap opening ceremony.

'Wantacupoftea!'

"Hark at that noise," remarked her companion, Nancy, sotto voce and with the air of a conspirator. "*Beryl the peril* is at it again. I swear she's had three cups already this morning and if we give her any more she'll definitely be needing those new super- duper extra leakage proof incontinence pants."

" Did you know that with the new regs and them pants being so expensive that we're going to be asked to weigh 'em after we change 'em?" whispered Ethel dropping into deadpan bedpan vernacular.

"What, the residents?"

"No Nancy, you dafty. The pants! We gotta show that they really really needed a change, like," laughed Ethel.

'Wantacupoftea!'

"Excuse me ladies but could you direct me to the bathroom?" asked George. All this whispered talk of incontinence was having an effect on his bladder control.

"Aw, bless!" murmured Ethel in an aside to Nancy, then straightening up, she directed her speech at George. "Well Mr Ellis, the bathroom is just behind that wall and we are taking you there so that you can have a shower." This was said in her brisk, loud professional voice, modelled on a BBC presenter. Ethel's dial of verbal delivery could be adjusted to suit a wide range of receivers. She could move seamlessly between *cosy comforting nurse natter* through *standard English medical speak* right up to her *highest level* where her enunciation of every syllable with exaggerated mouth movements produced a communication worthy of satisfying the demands of the most challenged lip reader.

"I am receiving you on all frequencies," said George, with the practised aplomb of a radio ham.

*

So here we were, Janine and I, parked in front of *The Grange* alongside the Zeus Mobile that was as bright shiningly incongruous in this sheltered grove as a *Mr Whippy* ice cream van would be. We were studying the flashy appendages of the vehicle whose bodywork must have been sprayed by the same artist who had been better known for his more important work: Waltzer ride pods in fairgrounds throughout the world.

We were finding reasons to delay going into the building that was the new home of both our parents. We had visited it many times before when Dad had been in residence and we knew how homely and welcoming it was. However, this was a new situation; the care home was now the *forever home* for Dad and Mum. From here there would be no going home. We were so anxious that it would work for them and could not face a prospect of it all going wrong.

In our cowardice, we were not in any hurry to find out. We had arrived before lunchtime and so we felt justified in hanging back to give Mum and Dad a chance to eat in peace. Then, we considered, what if they had an after lunch nap, should we disturb them? Should we leave it a bit longer?

We did leave it quite a bit longer, enjoying the comfort of the car and being able to talk to each other unrestricted by phone call charges, and other sorts of charges - like children. Eventually, even our fertile imaginations could not come up with a reason to put the visit off any longer and we began the countdown. It was like how we finished our phone calls to each other, starting to say 'good bye' ten minutes before we actually meant it with lots of 'one more thing's' and 'just before you go's.'

Ten: "Look I've got the new pants that Rosina the lovely manager asked us to bring. They are all pastel shades and flowery for

Mum and for Dad the ones I got are all dark and proper men's underpants." I told Janine, proudly.

"Oh well done, that man. Medal's in the post. Fancy poor Dad being made to put on those size 14 ladies black cotton briefs that you'd got for Mum!"

"Oh, I know. Thank goodness Rosina found out what had happened. At first she could not understand what was wrong with him and why he was walking with a sort of waddle. She even worried that he might actually have a hernia this time. Then it transpires that Mum had made him wear them – you know how she believes that *ladies only wear pastels and it's gentlemen that wear black*!"

Nine: We stripped ourselves of our possessions, hiding them under car seats. It would not do to take in coats or handbags – that is, if we did not want them to disappear. Mum had a fascination for such things and a habit of secreting them in places where they would never see the light of day again.

Eight: On second thoughts, as an extra measure of security, we took the handbags from under the seats and locked them in the car boot.

Seven: "Sweets! Better get them out of the glove compartment and make sure that we unwrap each one before we offer them to Mum or Dad. You know what happened last time we gave Mum that *Roses* chocolate, she just put it in her mouth whole – with the silver paper still attached!" I reminded Janine, although by the look on her face, she did not need reminding.

Six: "Nearly forgot the pants. Should we take the poly bag off them? You know how Mum hoards them," I fussed, reaching back into the car for the packets of substantial smalls.

Five: "Right; time to go, have we got everything?" Janine asked.

Four: "Should we have a code word?" I suggested.

"A code word. How do you mean?"

"Well you know if one of us feels that it's time we went, we say something – um – I don't know – um – *Fish!*" I exclaimed with sudden inspiration. I was as excited as if I had just found out how a body displaces water in a bath. I had found a way of bringing an end to the task I had been dreading. I may be a coward but I knew that the next hour would take us through a whole gambit of emotions; not a single one of which I was prepared for.

293

Three: "I see, you mean if I say the word '*Fish*' you will know that I think it's time we left," said Janine, thoughtfully.

Two: "Yes that's the code word. But it might not be easy to work it into the conversation, so we might have to be more subtle…"

One: "Ok got it. Show time. Deep breath and off-we-go," said Janine as we linked arms and began a falsely confident march up the path to the main entrance. Our approach resembled that doggedly self-kidding determination of *Fraulein Maria* as she first arrives at the Von Trapp's mansion in '*The Sound of Music*'.

By the time we were allowed entrance to the foyer which acted like an air lock in a space station, we had used up all our oxygen confidence. Fortunately, the omniscient Rosina was there to greet us and encourage us. I could not help but wonder that here was a lady whose role is to manage the care of our enfeebled confused parents and yet here she is steering two enfeebled confused women through the wooden double doors to the inner sanctum. For her, the circle of care is complete.

We were led down the familiar corridor and into one of the smaller reception lounges empty of people but full of overstuffed, plastic covered furniture and pottery ornaments. She told us to make ourselves comfortable and wait while she arranged for Mum and Dad to join us. It was quiet here with only distance sounds of chinking crockery and the burbling hum from a television set, punctuated by the regular wail from a resident '*Wantacupoftea!*', a phrase that was repeated over and over again and was reminiscent of the signal from an Asian transmitter that overtook the air waves when as teenagers we turned the dial too far on our transistor radio.

Janine and I sat wondering in this lounge that was not a lounge. I had been fooled into thinking it was homely and cosy when Zeus had first given us the tour. But now I felt differently. It called to mind a stage set where all the elements of an elderly person's home were arranged in a generic way, but absent of any real personal item or memento. In here, no one would have cause to remark, "I got this when we went to Weymouth" or "that was given to me by my grandson."

The enormous ceramic carthorse with its trailing gypsy caravan was still there however. Evidently its sheer size and cumbersome attributes prevented it being moved. Maybe it held some association for someone in the home but I thought not. I believed its purpose was to be a talking point, a focus for visitors or residents who do not know what to say to each other.

"Wantacupoftea!" I mimicked the lonely wailer.

"Me too," said Janine, "and some *fish* and chips!" her eyes sparkled with spirit.

"No you don't. Too soon! Nice try though!"

A squeaking tea trolley was the vanguard of the little procession that slowly entered the room. Then followed Rosina, guiding a shuffling Dad whose weighted pockets were causing his trousers to slide over his polyester shirt. When he reached his chair, he had the complex engineering job of lifting the loose fabric around his knees to allow him enough slack to sit down. Janine and I smiled indulgently, taking it in turns to bend down to give him a hug and kiss his dear dry forehead. He said nothing and looked bemused as he began to study the coal effect gas fire until his eyes became inevitably hooked on the ceramic monstrosity in its frozen trot across the hearth.

Mum followed shortly afterwards, entering the room without support and looking to left and right, smiling like the queen on a state visit. We pulled up a fireside chair for her and she ensconced herself on the plastic covered throne as if to the manner born. Janine and I paid equal homage to her with our hugs and she graciously announced: "Lovely Darlings. Isn't it wonderful George?"

Encouraged by this positive comment, Rosina and her colleague with the tea trolley clearly felt their presence was superfluous. They had settled us into our places in the tableau so they left us to act out the scenario of a normal family visit; which, of course, it was not.

I cleared my throat. "Well hello you two, how are you doing?" No response was the response to this. Mum, still holding her face in a contorted smile looked at us both and then asked, "How is your mother?"

"She's fine, from where I'm sitting," replied Janine.

[Off stage] *'Wantacupoftea!'*

"There's that parrot again. It's bloomin' annoying. A chap can't get any rest in this jungle," said Dad.

Janine looked at me and whispered, "All this *whaling* about tea; I'm *floundering* already!"

"Still too soon," I countered with a conspiratorial smile.

In order to do something with hands that wanted to hold my head in Edward Munch '*Scream*' pose, I clinked the crockery about and poured the tea.

"Wantacupoftea!" mimicked Dad and we all found ourselves relaxing for the first time since the show started. We all concentrated on balancing our cups and saucers on our laps and began slowly sipping. Janine offered round a handful of the unwrapped sweets and following our directions, Dad and then Mum placed their chosen bon bons on their respective saucers.

"Try one," suggested Janine, demonstrating by putting her sweet into her mouth. Her action was not copied by either Mum or Dad. However, Mum did study Janine and proclaimed, "Teeth. You have good teeth. Such teeth."

"It's time to close the tent flaps," said Dad, "the sun is in my eyes." A shaft of late afternoon sun was indeed piercing the dim corners of the room and picking out the horse brasses on the ceramic caravan.

"So nice of you to come. Would you like a cup of tea?" said Mum as she got up and closed the curtains as if it really was her lounge in the bungalow.

"We're fine, thank you. We have our tea here already," I replied. Mum sat down again and then fixing her attention of the ceramic display, bent down and – to the amazement of all of us - managed to pick up the whole carthorse and caravan. With its wild eye thrust under Janine's nose, the horse looked equally alarmed.

"I'd like you to have this," announced Mum.

"That's very kind of you," said Janine, "but I think it belongs here."

"Belongs here," echoed Mum as reluctantly, she allowed Janine and me to wrestle the magnificent Shire horse and wagon from her embrace and return it to its place on the hearth. "Who's that strange gentleman over there? He wanted the curtains drawn."

"That's your husband, George," I replied.

"Is it? I don't think so," Mum answered. She got up from her chair and began pacing the room, stopping occasionally to straighten a seat cushion or adjust the pleats of the curtains and their swag embellishment, fingering the fabric with a rapt expression. It was the first time she seemed almost content since entering the room. The muted tones of a piano found its way into the lounge and somehow managed to register with hard-of-hearing Mum. Without a backward glance, she left the room. We heard her soft footsteps in the corridor; clearly she was off on a mission to find the source of the sound.

"I think the piano needs a *tuna*!" said Janine.

"Yes, I agree, the piano definitely needs a *tuna*!" I replied in defeat.

We took Dad with us in our search for Mum. Our unspoken plan was to reunite them in the main lounge before taking our leave. We gently escorted Dad to a chair by the huge television and continued to look for Mum. We found her in a small bay where she sat with a gentleman, both listening to a fellow resident plonking out a tune on the upright piano. He was playing in the pub style, his left hand doing all the travelling up and down the key board in a regular and heavy march whilst his right hand tapped the high notes of a medley of half- forgotten melodies.

Mum was entranced. "I was just saying to George," pointing at the unknown gentleman who sat next to her, "it's so lovely hearing my Daddy playing again."

We made our hollow farewells to Mum, with whom they did not register, and then to Dad, who by now had fallen asleep, before progressing swiftly to the air lock to sign out.

Chapter 41
The elephant in the room

Julie

"Helloo is that Julie?"

"It is. That must be Moira, Hello how are you?" I had to sit down; I had been dreading this moment.

"I'm fine thank you, apart from the odd ache and pain. But I'm an auld lady now, so what can I expect? A creaking gate as they say, I mustn't complain. I had not heard from you for a wee while and I've been thinking so much about your Mum and Dad and I thought I'd just give you a wee call and you could tell me how things are with them."

"Oh dear, so much has happened. I don't really know where to begin." I had sensed an air of expectancy in Moira's voice. *She wants me to say something about the photograph but I can't. I'm not ready for this yet.*

In my mind's eye a large elephant began to materialise in the space between us.

I decided to adopt the 'Mum' way of coping; a strategy that has two paths. Firstly, if I do not acknowledge something, it does not exist. Failing this, the unpleasant subject should be defused or disabled thereby limiting its power to deliver a shock to the senses. Like when as children, we reported the stark lack of lavatory paper in the toilet to which Mum would reply: *"Lovely Darlings, I think we have some bathroom stationery in the cupboard."*

I would not mention the photograph or anything connected with it. I ploughed on with an update on Mum and Dad's health: a relatively safe subject and one that had enough of a powerful impact to detract from the behemoth waving its trunk at me.

"Well I'll start from now and work backwards. Let me say that at this moment Mum and Dad are both safe and are settling into a care home. It's the same one that Dad stayed in for a little while and it's very nice. Janine and I visited them there last week."

"Och that's good to know that they are settling somewhere that you approve of, Julie." I could tell that Moira was beginning to process

298

this ostensibly comforting information but I could sense her doubt and her unspoken questions.

"Well, yes Moira. *The Grange* is very pleasant and Mum and Dad have adjacent rooms with their own bathrooms. The manager is lovely and the care staff seem to take good care of them."

"That's good, Julie- but such a shame that they had to move out of their own home. I know how much they loved their bungalow and they had those live-in carers for quite some time didn't they?" There it was - the doubt had come to the surface.

"Yes indeed that was a system that worked for a while. However, lots went wrong when Mum and Dad's mental health started to deteriorate further and the risks for their safety became greater. The carers were excellent but the task of looking after Mum and Dad gradually became unworkable. Dad became quite reclusive but Mum did not sleep at night and only napped lightly during the day so the carer got no proper rest. Mum roamed about the bungalow at all hours getting up to all sorts of mischief."

"Oh dear, it's such a shame. It must have been such a worry to you all."

"Yes Moira and it became very risky too. The carer found Mum trying to burn paper on the coal-effect gas fire – the sort with the gas jets. And although the kitchen was locked at night, Mum sometimes managed to get in there during the day when the carer was busy with Dad and start cooking on the stove. We were all worried that she might cause a fire. The poor carer became exhausted trying to manage Mum and Dad and keep them safe out of harm's way."

"Och, it's such a shame. Your Mum and Dad are such lovely people. Life is so unfair, Julie. How can it have happened so quickly? It doesn't seem long ago when George, Joan and I, well, we used to talk on the phone and they seemed so happy."

"It's tragic to think that they have gone downhill so rapidly, Moira. But sadly I have more to tell you. You see the situation with the live-in care was already reaching a crisis point when Mum was admitted to hospital suffering from a suspected stroke."

"Oh no! That's dreadful, on top of everything else."

"Indeed," I took a deep breath before continuing, "well anyway she was in hospital for several days and actually, she seems to have recovered quite well from the ordeal. She appears not to have been affected physically but she is definitely more confused than she was. The doctors think it was a minor stroke but they did advise us that

299

Mum could have more of these and that we should reconsider the care arrangements. Social Services also recommended that a care home would be more appropriate to meet her needs and those of Dad."

"Och you poor wee things. You have had so much to deal with. I feel very sorry for you and your brother and sister."

Moira's comforting voice soothed my spirit; once again I allowed myself to pretend she was my surrogate mother. I had been robbed of the chance of meaningful communication with my own mother and yet here was a person whose empathy I appreciated and who really seemed to understand the pain I was experiencing. She allowed me to churn out my worries and my fears, listening attentively and reassuring me at every turn of our conversation. How can this be? I had not even met Moira face to face? Perhaps I was unconsciously accepting that we had ties beyond the ones I felt safe to acknowledge.

As we said our goodbyes, I opened my mind's eye to reveal the elephant had remained stubbornly in the room. And it was wearing tartan.

Chapter 42
A testing time

George, Joan

George awoke to much squeaking of wheels and gnashing of metal parts. *Lubricant is needed,* he surmised; *decent oil would do the trick or some WD 40. I must look in my kit bag, or is it in the shed? I've got some somewhere, I'm sure.* He loved a good project, enjoyed getting his hands dirty. He got himself out of bed and dressed in his work clothes although he could not find his tie. *He always wore a tie didn't he? Even when he worked under the car.*

He opened his door and went to look for the machine that required his attention. Judging from the sound that woke him, it must be something large, most likely a steam engine. There were women everywhere, walking up and down the line chattering as women do. One was moving quite fast, hanging onto the handrail at the side of the tunnel. She looked like Joanie but when he called her name, she did not turn her head and soon she disappeared through a side door. He was getting anxious as the noise seemed to be getting louder and he was afraid that at any moment the train would appear and there was no room for him to take refuge in this narrow tunnel.

"Hello George, what are you doing?" One of those women had stopped his progress up the tunnel by holding his elbow; he did not like being detracted from his purpose and snatched his arm away.

"If you must know I'm needed in the engine room. That machine sounds like a bag of hammers and it needs some lubricant," he replied testily. The woman was relentless and taking his arm again, redirected his course by drawing him firmly back the way he had come, out of the tunnel and into a metal shaft where doors closed on them both and he found himself back at the Phoenicia Hotel. "This is a bit more like it," he had to concede. "It's quieter here without that steam engine roaring up and down the tunnel."

"It sure is," said the woman who seemed familiar now that he had the chance to study her in better light. "Here we go, George. Let's see if we can find Joan and you can both enjoy breakfast together."

"That'll be nice," agreed George as the woman escorted him to the deep pink dining room and seated him at a window table where between the flowery drapes and the dried grass arrangement, he could see a triangular slice of garden. He watched the gentle movement of the leaves in the breeze; it was as if the branches were waving to him. The moment of peace was destroyed by a roaring of tyres in friction with the ribbed polyester carpet. *Those damned turbo charged vehicles racing up and down the place, for Pete's sake!* He complained to himself, or he may have said some of it aloud judging by the stern look of the old boy wheeling his power chair to a table near him.

"Here we are George, here's your Joanie," said the woman reappearing with an old lady on her arm who she then cajoled into sitting opposite him. The old woman, who had needed considerable persuasion to join him, did have a familiar look about her. *Could it be Joanie? Why is her hair grey and cut into that severe style? And she is so thin. And she's got gent's trousers on, they look like plus fours.*

"Gorgeous, Darlings. Such a nice table," said the old woman eventually. She smiled at him before giving a little ha-huh-ha chuckle.

"That's my Joanie," George said.

*

"Now Mr Ellis, we have just got a few questions to ask of you, a kind of quiz. I understand that you enjoy quizzes; Rosina told me that you enjoyed the quiz game that was held the other evening in the residents' lounge."

George considered the earnest young man with the large black framed spectacles. To George the appendages balanced on the man's nose were so oversized they looked like clown spectacles that were missing a vital fun attachment - a plastic Kitchener moustache. "I am sorry could you repeat that?" said George.

"I was just saying that I hear you like quizzes?" said Lord Kitchener of the clown spectacles, lifting his voice at the end of his statement, converting it to a question.

"Well, yes, I suppose I do," George replied. "Is there a prize?"

"Not a prize exactly, Mr Ellis, or may I call you George?"

"Well that's my name," said George, shrugging his narrow shoulders dismissively.

"Well George, my name is Peter and this young lady here is my colleague, Emma. She is here to write down your answers. OK?"

"O...K that means *ORL KORRECT,*" answered George, "there was this man who could not spell, that's who started it.*"*

"Oh dear me, we haven't started the quiz yet," said Peter as he shared a knowing look with his assistant who sat modestly with her clipboard on her lap and her gel pen poised over the test paper.

"Now George, I understand that you are married to Joan and she is also a resident here. How long have you been married?"

George thought for a moment, pursing his lips and closing his eyes for several seconds. Eventually the answer came to him, "One hundred years."

The young man and his assistant seemed to have a problem with this answer. They smiled that smile that seemed to show that they were trying to hold in a bubble of laughter. *Had someone said something funny?*

"By the way you are looking I think I may have to rethink my answer. I don't think it can be correct," said George.

"I don't want to get off on the wrong foot," said Peter. That was not part of the quiz either; it was just to break the ice. I thought you might be cracking a joke!"

"A joke, I see. Well a hundred years seems about right to me," replied George with apparent honesty.

"OK, now let's begin. Now George what was the surname of the famous aviator whose son was kidnapped in the 1930's."

"Lindberg."

"Good. Now can you tell me the name of our present monarch?"

"Queen Elizabeth." The young girl wrote George's answers down in spiky handwriting, holding her pen in a grip that required all the fingers of her right hand as if she was holding a potato. George was distracted by the girl's long finger nails, each one had a union jack painted on it. "Rule Britannia," he found himself chanting.

"Rule Britannia indeed," echoed the young man. "Now could you tell me the year the First World War started?"

"First World War, now that was nineteen hundred and one." Scratch went the gel pen in Miss Potato's hand as it recorded George's response.

"And the year the Second World War started?" asked the young man.

"That would be nineteen hundred and two," said George with his own brand of 'knowing look'. After all, he had been there.

*

"Now Mrs Ellis, we have asked you to come and sit with us for a little while as we have just got a few questions to ask of you, a kind of quiz. I understand that you quite like quizzes?"

"Pizza? No not really," replied Joan, "all cheese and a little one, a tomato I think."

The young man pulled himself up short, recalling suddenly that he had been advised to speak clearly and over emphasise his mouth movements when communicating with Mrs Ellis. "I'm sorry, Let me start again. Rosina told me that you were in the residents' lounge when they held a quiz last week. Do you like quizzes?"

The young man with the flashing white teeth sat across from Joan and she smiled her engaging smile and gave her ha-huh-ha laugh. A little girl sat next to him and appeared to have a pen and paper on her lap.

"Gorgeous, Darlings. This is so nice. Aren't we lucky?" Joan said.

"Yes indeed we are. Now Mrs Ellis, or may I call you Joan?" He was gratified that now he seemed to be getting through to the pleasant elderly lady who was graciously smiling up and him.

"Gorgeous. Ha-huh-ha."

The young man took this as an affirmative and began the test. "OK, now let's begin. Can you tell me the name of our present monarch?"

"Monarch. The Queen. That's right I'm sure…. or is it Charles now? Oh dear it's getting away from me, ha-huh-ha."

"Who was the leader of Germany during the Second World War?"

"It was a bad man. A nasty man," answered Joan.

"He certainly was. But can you give me his name?" persisted the young man, pushing his giant spectacles up his nose to the bridge.

"No. Gone. Sorry, ha-huh-ha," apologised Joan.

More questions followed that were answered in a similarly blank way and Joan began to flag, her smile becoming tired and her

304

shoulders that had been so erect when she arrived, were going into a demoralised slump. It was time to introduce the next section of the test. This required the subject to spell the word WORLD backwards. Joan valiantly supplied a few of the letters but the concept of 'backwards' defeated her. Taking a deep breath and giving her an encouraging smile, the young man tried a different tack.

"My assistant Emma has been doing all the writing today. Now I would like you to do a little drawing and writing for me," he said, hoping to revive the spirit of the old lady in front of him who was clearly anxious to please.

"Ah. Gorgeous. This is such fun. Ha-huh-ha," said Joan almost convincingly, as she took the proffered clip board complete with paper. The page before her had some diamond shapes marked upon it and she was asked to copy the pattern underneath. Joan, who had demonstrated her excellent skills and abilities in pattern cutting, dressmaking and tailoring throughout her life found that she could not make marks on the paper that looked anything like the pattern she had been given. "Sorry. Gone," she said, looking at her attempt in defeat.

There was a final task to do; she was asked to write a sentence below her design. Here she seemed to have a sudden burst of energy and inspiration, writing with confidence in her loopy cursive style: *I love George.*

Chapter 43
If you've got the moves, I've got the motion!

Julie

My brother Tom sat across the dining table from me after we had finished clearing away the breakfast pots. His face was looking as weary as I felt yet still I noticed with admiration that he was able to remain buoyant and cheerful. Whatever he was taking, I'd like the same prescription, please, plus maybe a double dose of Vitamin B12.

I had travelled up to the Midlands the previous evening and had stayed the night in his home ready to fulfil my next assignment. He was in the process of giving me the final instructions necessary for executing my mission; ones that I may not have to destroy afterwards. But just in case, I began humming the theme to *Mission Impossible*.

"Lick stamp," he said with a grin when he heard me hum. I knew exactly what he meant. He was referring to the detailed instructions given to us by Dad whenever a new set of commemorative postage stamps was released. As semi-bored teenagers, the three of us were often tasked with procuring and sticking the precise sequence of stamps onto a set of First Day Covers. It always took up half a day queuing at the city's central post office and following Dad's list of instructions that seemed a yard long, exacerbated by the pressure of getting the envelopes in the designated post box to meet the deadline for commemorative franking.

"Lick stamp!" I replied.

"Right, are you OK with everything? Dad's operation should take a couple of hours so make sure you have a book with you. The removal of the cataract on his other eye went very smoothly but obviously, that was some time ago and things are a bit different now," said Tom.

"They sure are!" I agreed, "I hope he knows what's happening and that he won't be frightened."

Tom dropped me off at *The Grange* on his way to work and I was let into the familiar air lock where Rosina awaited me at the welcome desk.

"Your dad is all ready. I think he *might* know what's happening today, it's difficult to tell. I have explained it all to him. Your Mam is having one of her big sleeps so she's not down at the moment. But your dad, he's in the main lounge, if you'd like to collect him from there. I'll ring for your taxi but if you're not back here in five minutes, I'll come and give you a hand. It may be difficult extricating him from the activity going on in there. We've got Mr Motion in today," said Rosina with a twinkle in her eyes that I had not seen before.

As soon as I opened the double wooden doors, I heard disco music and it was set at *need-ear-defenders* volume. As I entered the lounge it was as if I had walked onto the set of *'Saturday Night Fever'*. Well almost. In a bizarre twist of reality, I saw at the end of the large room where the tea trolley was usually parked, a mini stage on top of which stood a tall black man flanked on either side by tall black speakers. The man had magnificent dreadlocks kept in check by his Alice band headphones with attached microphone; he also sported a bright red vest and fluorescent green track suit bottoms. Dancing energetically, which was causing him to sweat profusely, he shouted instructions simultaneously over the loud music. His audience sat in their habitual chairs around the edges of the room, watching him with apparent fascination as he put himself through his energetic paces. I spotted my father in the middle of the row on the right side of the room. He seemed to be moving his head from one side to the other but not, it would seem, in time with the music. Then I realised that he was staring at the LED moving message sign picked out in flashing red bulbs. The sign, which extended across the stage between the speakers, issued a constant loop of *HI EVERYBODY AT THE GRANGE! MR MOTION IS HERE TODAY! IF YOU'VE GOT THE MOVES I'VE GOT THE MOTION!* Dad seemed to be mesmerised. It was time to intervene and I looked for a way to walk across the room without interrupting the action. I need not have worried. The whole room was transfixed by Mr Motion as he kept up his act that seemed as perpetual as his LED light show. No one would have noticed if I had walked forward and committed murder in the middle of the stain resistant carpet.

"Burn Baby Burn! Now everybody put both your hands in the air, as far as you can reach, that's it, now clap, clap, clap, that's it!

Burn Baby Burn! Now lift your right leg as far as you can, straighten that knee, easy does it, now shake your foot and give those toes a wiggle, that's right, count , one, two, now put your foot down. That's it! Now with the left leg, lift it up as far as you can, it's like we're doing the Hokey Cokey, that's it, same again, straighten that knee, shake that foot and give those toes a wiggle, count one and a two, that's right! That's cool! Now we're really pumping."

I looked around at the pale audience while the increasingly purpling complexion of Mr Motion was making me fear for his health. I realised with considerable shock that no one was actually following any of his instructions. The audience appeared frozen; there were no elderly feet moving or toes wriggling, no arms were reaching into the air. Not even a shadow of a Hokey Cokey was in sight.

One had to admire the man's extraordinary optimism and good humour as he relentlessly kept to his spirited script. At last he registered some responding movement across the room. Rosina had entered the lounge and began jig-walking, like I have been known to do at weddings once I have imbibed sufficient wine to persuade me to take to the dance floor. For me it is not a good look but for Rosina, it looked *perfectly normal Darlings.* A graceful shimmy brought her to a spot in front of my father. Dad looked up at her and smiled as she helped him from his chair and guided him, still keeping up with the beat, out of the room. Ever the professional, it must have been hard to resist the powerful urge to execute a parting move - *an upper body twist, head thrown back and leg back-kick as she exited through the double doors* would have made a wondrous spectacle. We were to be denied such however as Rosina quickly reverted to Manager mode. I followed clumsily in her wake, meeting up with her in the entrance hall where she was in the process of helping Dad into his overcoat.

*

"Hi Tom, Yes, Dad's still in theatre; I don't know how much longer he will be, no one seems to be able to tell me and it's beginning to get dark now. We had a bit of a nightmare when we arrived."

"Really Julie? What happened?"

"Well the surgeon came to see Dad before the op and it turns out he's the same man who did Dad's other eye. Anyhow he was very pleasant and told Dad that he would be treating the right eye today. *Oh no you're not,* said Dad, *that's the one you operated on the last time."*

"Oh God," said Tom, "it's the left eye he had done last time!"

"Yes indeed. We all know that now, but the poor surgeon had to go down to his car, open his boot, find his notes to make absolutely sure he was not making a mistake. Dad had us all confused. He'd convinced me. So you see it delayed the whole procedure, so I'm not surprised that they're running late."

After I finished talking to Tom, I sat in the waiting room reduced to fiddling with my phone and sifting through the dog eared magazines on offer as I had finished reading the novel I had brought with me. I was beginning to get anxious again when the kind member of staff, who had dealt with my previous inquiries, approached me.

"Your dad is coming out of Recovery and is on his way back to the Day Ward. It appears he needed a longer than usual time there but they said he's OK. Doctor says that your dad should be able to go home after he has had something to eat and drink."

I thanked her and returned to my seat where I texted Tom and Janine to reassure them that things were going to plan, albeit rather later than anticipated. It was as I was replacing my mobile into my copious bag that I heard the singing.

"Show me the way to go home, I'm tired and I wantta go to bed. I hadda little drinky about an hour ago and it's gone straight to my head..."

I looked around the waiting room and people were looking up from their magazines, books and phones and craning their necks to see who was causing the row. I could imagine them thinking: *someone must have let a drunk in, what is the world coming to?* Then I watched them return their attention to their magazines, books and phones on pretence that they did not hear the noise or that whatever it was- was not really happening.

But I recognised the voice.

I left the waiting area, pretended I was going to the Ladies toilets before changing direction and doubling back along a corridor, following the sound that was increasing in volume and that continued to draw me with the power of a mythical Siren to its source in the Day Ward. By now, Dad had changed his tune to embark on a rendition of Hymns, Ancient and Modern.

After making myself known to the nurse at her station, I was taken hastily into Dad's room. Dad was sitting up in bed with a large bandage over his right eye; his left eye was closed. His arms were outstretched, making shapes in the air and moving in time to the music he was making. I learnt from the staff in attendance that Dad had reacted atypically to the anaesthetic and that it had taken him longer than expected to come round after surgery. They anticipated that gradually, Dad would calm and that food and drink would definitely help the process. I came forward and touched Dad's arm but he did not pause for a second in his conducting of *O God our help in ages past.*

Fortunately, a cup of tea arrived at that opportune moment and Dad opened his good eye and allowed me to help him drink. If I had not been told otherwise, I would have believed that Dad was drunk. This was truly bizarre to witness; I had never seen Dad fully inebriated in my life. Yet here he was doing a great impersonation of Freddie Frinton in his glory days of doing his drunken-man-in-evening-dress act.

The light meal arrived promptly after the tea and I showed it to Dad, hoping to engage his interest. He examined it with his good eye and then pulled a face as if he had been served up a dead hedgehog instead of fish pie and peas. I tempted him with a forkful of tender morsels but he closed his mouth firmly and turned his head away like a recalcitrant toddler. Desperate to get him to eat, aware that the Day Unit would be closing shortly, I turned my attention to the pudding course. It was jelly, red jelly with cream; Dad's favourite.

"Look Dad, it's red jelly…yum…yum, your favourite."

"Dad gave me the Freddie Frinton look, his uncovered eyebrow arching and one side of his mouth lifting before saying, "Hic I don't mind if I do." This phrase prefaced every mouthful I fed him as unsteadily he worked his way through the dessert. I never knew a dish to take so long to eat or be so thoroughly enjoyed. By the last spoonful, Dad was calm.

"That's magic jelly," I told him.

"Magic Jelly," he agreed.

Chapter 44
Just like that!

Julie and Janine

"So Julie, how have you been keeping?" asked Janine, as we drove the lanes of rural Oxfordshire on our way to visit Mum and Dad at *The Grange*. We knew the route off by heart, having made the journey together many times in the past year.

"Still suffering terminal football of the televisual kind," was my cryptic reply.

"Oh dear," sympathised my sister. "At least you don't have to stand on the touchline on a real pitch in the cold, watching the boys from Form Remove play!"

"Touché! Ok you darn got me beat there; I'll stop complaining in a minute. It's just that I don't get why football has to be on TV almost every night and all over the weekend – well that's what's on my telly anyway. I wonder if they ever show matches on *The Grange's* TV? Dad used to enjoy watching footie and cricket."

"They might, I guess, although whenever I've visited, the TV seems to be showing old black and white films or kiddies' programmes," replied Janine.

"I think some of the best programmes are the ones intended for kids. '*In the Night Garden*' makes me so calm, have you ever seen it? I only have to hear the theme music and I find myself settling on the sofa and reaching for a blanky."

"No I haven't but is that the one with a guy in a blue furry suit, I've seen pictures."

"Yes that's the one, that's *Igglepiggle*. Mum and Dad used to watch kids' programmes before they wandered into twilight world. I think because they found them pleasant to watch during the daytime – and definitely less stressful and upsetting than the News channel – that used to get them well wound up with its constant repeats and horrific clips of emergencies and wars."

"Yes that channel wouldn't be appropriate for the residents at *The Grange*. I cannot believe how the time has flown - do you know Mum and Dad have been in the Home for over a year now?"

"It is amazing," I replied. "I still feel the responsibility for our parents very keenly but there is no doubt that my life has been easier since they've been living there. The staff's great –after all, with them taking over control of Mum and Dad's care, they are allowing us to live our lives. I no longer feel as if I am on constant red alert."

"That's right, Julie. I can concentrate on work better these days and I think Tom feels the same - although as he lives the closest, he is still the first line of defence should anything go wrong at the Home."

"Indeed. I did feel sorry for him when he got the call from Rosina about Dad's Tommy Cooper act!"

"I must have missed hearing about that, what happened?" asked Janine.

"Apparently, Dad had been singing in the main lounge again and one of the residents complained. A member of staff persuaded Dad to go with them into the dining room and then left him sitting at a table while she went off to get them both a cup of tea. The tables were all laid up with paper table cloths draped over cloth ones – this is relevant, by the way – anyhow, she came back with cups and saucers and placed them on the table. It was after she had poured the tea that Dad stood up and gripping the paper table cloth with both hands, pulled it smartly off the table with a flourish!"

"Wah – just like Tommy Cooper used to do! *Just like that!*" said Janine, slipping into an impersonation of the beloved comic magician that had entertained us on TV all our lives.

"It seems though that Dad was not quite as proficient as Tommy Cooper and the tea got splattered up the wall, the crockery got smashed and the cutlery flew everywhere! Rosina's colleague was not amused."

"Oh dear, I don't expect she was," chuckled Janine, guiltily.

*

Eventually, we arrived at *The Grange*. Leaving the car parked in our usual bay, there was no prevarication in our progress to the air lock today. Maybe we were becoming desensitised; no longer hopeful of being recognised or being able to hold a meaningful conversation with our parents. We were well along in the numbing process of *coming to terms.*

Rosina was there to greet us and give us a brief update on Mum and Dad's week. "Your Mam is awake today and quite lively with it. She and your Dad are in the main lounge."

"No magic tricks this week then?" I asked as I mimed the whipping off of a table cloth, an apology embedded in my inquiry and in my cringing facial expression.

"No more magic tricks, I'm pleased to report," said Rosina with a tolerant smile.

Janine and I left Rosina and made our way to the lounge. In the corridor, we caught sight of a display of photographs under the title, *'Art and Craft'* in bubble writing. One picture showed Mum apparently icing fairy cakes and another included Dad gluing small pompoms on paper.

"Aw, that's so sweet," said Janine.

Below these was another set of photographs featured under the spikey lettered heading *'Halloween at The Grange.'* Clearly the staff had made a huge effort to dress up and apply ghoulish make up. Alongside them the pale residents posed without the apparent need for make up or costume…Janine and I looked at each other. We did not need to say anything, telepathy was working spookily well.

Entering the lounge, we found a warm and sleepy atmosphere had settled on the residents in post prandial contentment. Dad was dozing in a corner and so, not wishing to disturb him, we went on a hunt for Mum. After not finding her sitting in any of the armchairs placed around the room, Janine finally spotted a glimpse of our quarry disappearing down a distant corridor. We gave chase, catching up with her in one of the smaller reception lounges. She was not alone.

"Now take a letter," said a tall man, brusquely directing his demand to our slender Mum who was following him three paces behind. He paid no attention to us even though we interrupted his progress by greeting our mother. Mum smiled at us both, turning her head and saying, "Lovely Darlings ha-huh-ha."

"Dear Sirs, the subject of your letter dated the sixth of whatever et cetera etcetera – make sure you insert the date, was a revelation, full stop," spouted the man as he paced the lounge. He turned to Mum periodically to ask in an over-bearing manner, "Did you get that last bit or *must* I repeat it?"

Mum continued to walk behind the man, holding an imaginary notebook and pen in her hands, miming the act of keeping notes as he dictated. Janine and I watched dumbfounded for several minutes until the increasingly intimidating behaviour of the man prompted us to take action. He seemed rather a bully to us and we did not like to see our mother being thus controlled.

"Mum, we have come to visit you, let's go into the other room," I said making demands of my own and taking her by the arm.

"But this is my husband and he's the boss," she said as she pulled her arm free from my grasp and turned to resume her steps behind the tall man, all the while executing the same mime that my husband makes to a waiter when he is asking for the bill.

At a loss as to what we could do about the office bully and his mild mannered secretary, we made our way to Dad's cosy corner. Dad was still dozing and we were on the point of retreating again when one of the care staff approached.

"You'll have come a long way and he'll want to see you. Besides he was very late getting up this morning, it's only the jam pud that has made him go sleepy again." She introduced herself as Kath before she reached across to Dad and gently walked her fingers up his arm in the time honoured nursing manner of Incey Wincey spider. Dad opened his eyes slowly and looked at Kath with some recognition, in fact it was more than recognition, it was affection that was shining from his face, lined and rosy from slumber.

"There, there now George, it's your daughters here to see you," said Kath, patting his arm. Dad's face gained a bewildered look as he turned from her to examine Janine and me. However, before we could engage with him, the 'boss' passed by trailing the ever conscientious Mum. The pair of them seemed to have picked up speed not only in their pace but in the number of words per minute that were being dictated. We turned to Kath with an unspoken plea for help.

"Oh, Mr Turner and your Mam, they do that often. As you know your Mam always likes to be on the move and Mr Turner he's the same. Did your Mam ever work in an office?"

Suddenly, Dad spoke up, "County Hall. Treasury. Works too hard," he continued as if Mum still worked there. "Don't appreciate her. Absolute shower!"

"I'll go and fetch your Mam," said Kath, winking kindly at Janine and me while we began moving chairs to accommodate our little family pow wow. Dad flicked one thumb nail against the other – his classic sign of anxiety. "Absolute shower," he muttered again.

"It's alright now Dad," Janine comforted, "Mum has retired. She does not have to go there anymore."

"That's what you think," he said.

I do not know how she managed to achieve her aim but within a few moments, Kath returned with a bemused looking Mum on her arm.

"Here we are Joan, here's your daughters come to see you. Sit yourself down next to George."

Mum did sit and went through her opening three tone laugh gambit followed by a 'Gorgeous, Darlings' for good measure. Then she asked us how our mother was to which we gave our wearing-thin reply. Then she asked who the strange gentleman was. We thought she meant the over-bearing boss man that she had semi-introduced us to earlier, but before we could give our answer, she became excited saying, "There's my husband," and getting up, she promptly followed the tall brusque man who, it would seem, had another letter to dictate.

"Gone. *Just like that!*" said Dad.

Chapter 45
The Present of Time Past

Julie

"Tom, I've found something in that box of paperwork of Mum and Dad's that you and Janine must see."

"What have you found Julie?"

"Well it's a video tape. At first I thought it was one of the Princess Diana funeral tapes, you know how many copies they had of that. But it is labelled simply 'George and Joan'. I was on my own at home when I found it underneath all the buff folders, so I slung it in the machine and Oh My God – you'll never believe what it shows."

*

The first scene shows the kitchen of the bungalow at Burnage. Joan is standing at the kitchen counter, a rolling pin in her hand. Although she is working with pastry, she is immaculately dressed and groomed and wears no apron.

"Joanie, what are you making today?" says George who is holding the video camera.

"I am making an apple pie for the freezer," says Joan in her best Queen Elizabeth accent.

"Lucky freezer," says George.

Back at the Grange, Joan is dressed in a brushed nylon nightdress over a pair of saggy trousers. She is standing at the large sink in the vast kitchen. She picks up the bottle of washing-up liquid and takes a swig.

"Cheers," says Joan to the camera as she sips her coffee in her pristine kitchen.

"Where's mine?" asks George, cheerfully.

Back at the Grange, George is being interviewed by the doctor who perceives that his patient is depressed. George concedes that he feels low and that sometimes he wants to open the door of his cockpit and let the wind take him.

The second scene shows Joan standing by the fire place in the lounge. She points to ornaments displayed on the mantelpiece. Picking up each object with reverence she describes the story behind its existence as a part of her and George's treasured possessions. With every ornament she draws a virtual circle from origin to eventual destination.

"These brass candlesticks were given to me by my mother. They're a little battered and hard to keep shiny but I always loved them when I was growing up. I would like Julie to have one pair and Janine to have the other pair," announces Joan.

"Sheer dust collectors," comments George, the sardonic cameraman.

Back at the Grange, Joan is being comforted by a carer. She has been looking for her mother but she cannot find her anywhere. Joan is weeping and her throat is sore. The carer leaves briefly to get her a drink. When she is alone, Joan drinks the water from the flower vase on the table.

Joan continues touring the living room, pointing to pictures and articles of furniture that all hold sentimental value for both her and George.

"Ah, yes, the camel saddle- Georgie you got this in Egypt a very long time ago. I think it should go to Tom, he will remember the day you brought it back from your travels. And the pink Persian rug – this I bought when I retired from County Hall with the money they collected for me. I would love Julie to have it."

"All bases covered then, if you want a ride – on a camel or on a carpet," George suggests playfully.

Back at the Grange, George sits on his high backed armchair in his room. There is a wardrobe, a bed and a small cabinet beside it. On top of the cabinet sits a biscuit tin and a Roberts' radio. There are pictures and photographs on the wall and some of the women who come into his room look at them. If they ask questions about them he does not answer. He knows he must keep his silence and the radio safe from intruders.

The next scene is set in the large double bedroom. Here everything is spick and span, the beds are neatly made and the surfaces tidy and free from dust. There is a dressmaker's dummy in the corner of the room, wearing a large brimmed hat on its headless neck, draped with many silk scarves and strings of beads.

"Ha-huh-ha, that's Joanie Number Two," chuckles Joan patting the dummy on the shoulder.

"She's quite a lot quieter that Number One," quips George.

"Oh Georgie, you are awful. Now here are the wardrobes."

Back at the Grange, Joan is in the empty bedroom of a fellow resident. She opens the wardrobe and begins searching though the clothing neatly hung on wooden hangers. She removes a garment and after holding it up against her, decides to try it on. Dissatisfied by the result, she pulls it over her head and drops it on the floor. She continues trying on clothing until the wardrobe is empty and clothes litter the carpet. The rightful owner of the wardrobe returns to her room and seeing the disorder that Joan has caused proceeds to attack her with her walking stick. Joan leaves the room quickly to escape the blows.

The final scene includes both Joan and George talking to the camera. They are holding hands and give loving glances to each other throughout their closing speech.

"Darlings, we hope you have enjoyed our little film. We have had a wonderful life together. We are so proud of you and we love you all very much."

*

It is now three years since I found the video; that wonderful gift from the past. The past: that hallowed time of existence before Mum and Dad's lives telescoped into the limitations of the twilight world into which they shambled. The video kept our memories alive, reminding us of the vibrant people our parents had been. Inevitably, along with this gift came the stark realisation of what we had lost; of what they had lost. Sadly, the time was not the only thing they lost.

It is now eight years since I first wrote to Mum and Dad's doctor with my concerns regarding their mental health. I guess we knew then that it was not going to end well. Eight years that have witnessed our parents gradually fade away and disappear, bit by bit, stroke by stroke, kiss by kiss, smile by smile, look by look, loving glance by loving glance, *Darling by Darling.*

We have grieved for them every day of those eight years. Eight years of having to stand by powerlessly, while their minds embarked on a process of degeneration. Their thoughts, that at first were muddled and confused, became irrevocably disconnected. As their memories failed so their personalities began wearing away to become pale and brittle shadows of their former selves until the sole motivation of their lives was reduced to simply a response to basic urge and need.

Then their bodies, those fragile shells, began to fail so that first Dad and then Mum were lost to us completely.

Except in our memories.

Epilogue
No time to lose

The orphans are going on a trip. Outside, the day is bright and sunny but within the airport tunnel, the artificial light is dull and dusty yellow. The tunnel seems just as long as it was when we were children. The amplified noise of the traffic inside the enclosed space made dramatic by the thunder of the massive fans brings memories flooding back. Then that special moment when we emerge into the daylight still holds an air of expectation replicating those childhood journeys of long ago. In those days, we were meeting our father from his latest flight, desperate to find out what treats and presents would be awaiting us in his bountiful kit bag. But today, the anticipation we share is of quite a different kind. This time, it is the three of us that are making a journey of our own.

"It's changed a bit since the old days of London Airport when there was not much more than the Queen's building and the control tower," Tom reminisces. He has travelled through Heathrow many times before but today is all about lighting up our personal memory lane.

"And one ess-le-clator," I add, mimicking my own childish patter of circa 1955. "Never could say that word right. Do you remember Mum used to let us go for rides on it over and over again while we were waiting for Dad?"

"Yes," says Janine, "and the waving bay – we used to love going up there to watch his plane come in. We would watch the staircase being wheeled up to the plane's door and locked into position and then we'd wait and wait – it seemed ages. Until, after all the passengers had come out, the flight crew would follow and then we saw him come down the steps."

"I can see him now, walking across the tarmac and looking up to see if we were there waving. It was so exciting!" I remember.

"It's a very different world now," says Tom as we cross the threshold into the vast entrance hall.

*

A short time later sees us at the departure gate ready for our flight to Glasgow. We are on our way to meet our half-brother at last, hitherto our 'tartan elephant'. Moira has gently and graciously allowed us into her secret and into her family.

We have spent the past eight years saying 'Goodbye' to the dearest people in our lives. We have no time to lose; after all, we are much better at saying 'Hello'.

"Do you think Moira would like to hear *The Plank story*?" says Tom.

Somewhere in the airport, the flight from Amsterdam has just arrived.

Acknowledgements

The writing of this book would not have been possible without the enduring and loving support of the very special people I am fortunate to have in my life: my husband, our daughter and her husband, our son and his wife and their daughter. My brother and my sister helped me remember so much of our wonderful childhood and enabled me to commit to paper the experiences we shared then and those we encountered during the period when our parents '*appeared to have lost the time.*'
I deeply appreciate the encouragement for this project that I have received from my relatives and friends. Thank you all.

JW

Lightning Source UK Ltd.
Milton Keynes UK
UKHW010257200819
348225UK00004B/1538/P

9 781788 768290